~ THE HARBINGER CHRONICLES ~

RETRIBUTION

WRITTEN BY
CHRISTOPHER HUNTINGFORD

COPYRIGHT © 2014
BY CHRISTOPHER HUNTINGFORD

The intent of this book is to offer information of a general nature to help the reader attain insight on the concepts and systems developed by the author. All stories, accounts and otherwise are based on the author's personal experience and recollection of events. This includes acknowledgements of various people, companies and otherwise who are mentioned within the content for the sole purpose of sharing the author's personal accounts and interpretations.

Published by Christopher Huntingford

www.HarbingerChronicles

Printed in the United States of America

Book Cover Design Gordon Napier

Library of Congress
Cataloging-in-Publication Data
Huntingford, Christopher.

Harbinger Chronicles: Retribution
April 2014
August 2014 Re-Release

Christopher Huntingford – 2nd Edition
ISBN-13: 978-0-615-98177-2
(The Harbinger)
ISBN-10: 0615981771

DEDICATION

DEDICATION PAGES ARE EASY AT TIMES. I COULD GRANDSTAND WHILE STANDING ON MY SOAPBOX THANKING EVERYONE FOR THE PIECES OF LIFE THEY SHARED WITH ME. I COULD ALSO GET EXCITED ABOUT PEOPLE I KNEW IN SEVENTH GRADE AND DEDICATE MY BOOK TO THE PRETTY GIRL THAT SAT NEXT TO ME IN HISTORY CLASS. HER IMPACT TO MY BOOK WOULD BE NORMAL, AS WOULD ANYONE ELSE THAT I WOULD SEEK TO RECOGNIZE AS A RECURRING REFRAIN FROM MY BOOK.

THIS ISN'T A HAPPY BOOK, I FEEL AWKWARD DEDICATING THIS STORY TO A PARTICULAR INDIVIDUAL AS THAT WOULD BE AN UNDERHANDED COMPLIMENT. DEAR PERSON, THANK YOU SO MUCH GOT INSPIRING ME TO WRITE THIS STORY ABOUT REVENGE. IT WAS AN AWESOME EXPERIENCE BEING TORN APART BY YOU.

AND THEREIN LIES THE STRUGGLE. WE ALL HAVE ENDURED A STRUGGLE IN SIDE OF US THAT MADE US GREATER THAN WE WERE. THEY COULD HAVE BEEN THE BULLY IN GRAD SCHOOL, OR THE SIGNIFICANT OTHER THAT STOLE OUR HEARTS AND CRUSHED IT BY CHOOSING ANOTHER, OR A DIVORCE THAT SENDS YOU SPIRALING TO THE DEPTHS OF DESPAIR.
SO THIS IS TO THE PAIN OF LIFE AND THE EXPERIENCES THAT MAKE US GREATER.

AS WE ARE SLOW TO LEARN, RETRIBUTION IS A DOUBLE EDGED SWORD. WE CAN SEEK TO PAY BACK FOR CRIMES AGAINST US, TO PROPEL VICIOUS ATTACKS, UNTIL WE FEEL VINDICATED BY THE BLOOD ON OUR HANDS. OR WE CAN GROW, AND IMPROVE OURSELVES SO THAT WE MAY BE MASTERS TO THOSE WHO CANNOT BE BETTER.

HERE'S TO THE RESILIENT. THIS BOOK IS DEDICATED TO YOU.

PROLOGUE

The old man hadn't left his seat in hours. He had been content to sit there, directing his gaze into the fire that danced before him. Every now and again, he shifted his thin frame for the slightest hint of comfort. The chair, made from the bones and antlers of deer, offered little-prolonged rest. The long fur bear skin coat that covered the chair offered warmth, and a chance to wrap his legs, but the bones aggravated him and he could not find a spot to sit for long. Between shifting spots, he would lift his hand and, with his finger, mimicked drawing a form. The flames followed his finger's movement and danced lightly in the air as if they were his puppet. The fire was the lone source of light in his room and captured the man's full attention.

The door to the massive room opened slowly and sent a cold draft into his room. He shivered a bit and pulled the bear skin closer.

A few shadows appeared on the wall next to him. They interested him for a moment, but when he realized they were of no consequence he returned his attention to the fire.

He followed the same motion with his fingers in an attempt to bend the flames to his will. At first, the fire responded to him and grew but then quickly lost its luster and returned to its nominal size. He sighed in frustration and turned his irritation to the intruders.

"Why have you disturbed my meditation?"

His growl echoed through the chamber and upset a nearby nest of ravens. The ravens protested the noise with a din of their own. They flapped their wings and clawed back at the intruders below their nest. The constant sounds and growing echo in the great room agitated the visitors, but they regained their composure and bowed to the old man in fear.

"Forgive me, My Master, the man bowed." The witches asked to consult with you about what they have seen.

"So," the ancient one mused, waving the three hideous women to approach him.

"Tell me what you know." He wiped a bead of sweat that collected on his brow. The heat hadn't made him sweat, and neither did the room.

An arched roof that stretched eighteen feet into the air as a castle turret rendered it impossible to warm up.

It was the quest for new power that had taken its toll on him and worn him down.

His hand fell from his brow to his cheeks. The old man's face bore many new wrinkles, for he felt himself aging rapidly.

The first witch pressed forward boldly and shoved a darkened ferret liver into his hand.

"There is a force building against us," she said. "The portents are unfavorable."

"He is coming!" The second witch hissed in fear. "We took one so dear, his hatred is unquenchable." She grabbed her unkempt hair and pulled clumps of hair from her already balding head, and shoved it towards him.

The sorcerer examined the liver with his fingers and sneered.

"So you have come to tell me that he is angry? That I should fear a mortal man because his brother died? I am the greatest power who walks the earth, what can a mortal do to me?" He tossed the liver onto the chamber floor, several feet away from his chair.

Two ravens flew down from their nest and fought for the right to consume it.

"Of course he should come after us." He motioned to the older man that had brought the witches in,

"This fool killed his brother in an act of cowardice!"

The old man collected his composure and closed his eyes. He took slow breaths, and his head moved about slowly as he attempted to peer into the future. He whispered a few words to himself and the fire behind him grew.

"I can feel his hatred," the man agreed. So powerful that it is easily found and accessed. I would love to have that energy. It would give me another hundred years, at least."

"He is a threat, Master!" the third witch interrupted. "We must hurry before he destroys us. The portents are here for us to see. Do not ignore them."

The old man scoffed and shook his head.

"You see nothing," he laughed. The old witch was blind, but she was the most powerful of the three.

"And for all the portents you have read, there is no possibility of mistake?"

The blind witch was indignant. Her carved teeth gnashed like an animal while she spoke. "We are descended from the Haruspex Order. Our order has been reading the signs for over two thousand years, and we have never been questioned."

"I do not disagree with your signs witches, but in the manner of which you are reading them. The future is as plain as your ugly faces. He comes for this one." The old man pointed at his servant.

"And when he comes, he will find the rest of us waiting."

He brought himself from his chair, and stiffened himself as his bones cracked. "Tell me Duncan, when you are in danger of wild animals, what do you do?

Duncan's response was terse.

"Set traps, Master Abiyram."

"And lay them we shall," the sorcerer nodded.

"Our enemy is a mortal man who has had some luck, but that will desert him soon enough. I will not be denied this ending." He turned his attention back to the witches. "Go to my brothers, and tell them to make ready, for the harbinger is bringing retribution."

"Are we not worried that he will bring the Alveun warmongers with him? If they were to bring their troops, they will kill everything in their path."

"No!" The sorcerer responded confidently. "Reckless and immature, this is his war, and no one will lift a finger to help. He will be alone in his efforts.

Besides, I welcome an Alveun return to my lands. They weren't so successful thirty years ago." He smiled and rubbed his bony hands together, partly to warm them, partly in glee.

"How shall your brothers lay their traps for him, Master?" The first witch frowned and didn't appear appreciative of her Master's confidence.

"It is up to them. They will bring me his head or bring him as a sacrifice. I know a special girl that is dying to meet him," he chuckled and ignored Duncan's hateful stare.

The witches exchanged glances. The sorcerer knew what was in their minds. They were unhappy with him, but they needed to remember who ruled them. They bowed low, almost touching the floor, and left the men to talk between themselves.

"It was my arrow, but I was not the one who killed the heir to Alveus," Duncan insisted.

"It was that fool Jacob. He should never have gone with me. Between him and Patrick…" He gritted his teeth and shook his head.

"They have their uses," the sorcerer soothed. "They are kingdom men who can travel undetected through their borders."

"I went there to kill Alexander and have my revenge. Edward was a fool to get in our way. Even Alexander should understand that."

Duncan punched the stone wall in frustration. Blood trickled from scrapes on his knuckles and dripped down to the floor. He gritted his teeth and clenched his fists. "I can fix this for us if you allow me to take my men. We will make short work of them."

"And have you fail as miserably as before?" The old man reprimanded Duncan sharply.

"In these walls we are protected. Look around you. We are impregnable. Anyone who comes near this structure will die. I would have them come to us, instead of us going to them."

He stroked his long white beard, pulling spiders out as he went.

"You wanted revenge for your sister's death and you clumsily allowed his brother to die instead of him. That was incredibly incompetent, and now I should give you freedom to make an even bigger mess?"

Duncan straightened himself to the accusations and gave a hint of authority to his voice.

"As I planned, we stole the armor and crept our way in past the guards. Everything unfolded exactly as you said, but that little girl from Greystone who keeps following him around ruined it.
Even with Edward dead, we could have finished Alexander if she had not raised the alarm." Duncan folded his arms and rested himself against the wall.

"I give you orders based upon the information I glean from the spirit realm. When they guide me, I am obliged to follow them to the last detail.

Sometimes, details do not emerge until later. That is where I depend on you, who is supposed to be the greatest assassin in the land, to carry it out. A child prevented you from killing a man. Not only a child but some inconsequential girl from a town that you were supposed to have wiped out to the last person." The sorcerer grabbed his staff and pointed it towards Duncan.

Duncan felt a presence grip around his throat. He stiffened and his hands reached towards his throat as if to stop from being choked.

A moment of clarity flashed in the sorcerer's eyes, and he lowered his staff. Duncan gasped for breath and mentally breathed a sigh of relief.

Abiyram placed his staff upon his chair and glided his fingers over the gnarled wood.

"What is it that I should have such incompetence swirling around me?

This prince is the one detail preventing me from my occupying my rightful place in this world. Duncan, your incompetence has thrown this world out of balance.

The spirits are confused. The portents are inconsistent." He paused enough to focus his thoughts on several strands of ivy creeping down the stone wall nearest Duncan.

"I am the most powerful man in the world," the sorcerer hissed.

"I will no longer be a man once he is dead. I will be a demigod! I will be eternal and I will rule once more over Alveus!"

The ivy quickly wrapped itself around Duncan's neck and squeezed just enough for him to labor through his breathing. Another strand wrapped its coils around his sword hand. Duncan stayed still, praying his submission would delay his end.

"Our order has achieved power over death. I even brought your wretched traitorous sister back from the grave! And you repay me by failing the most important task I have for you."

"I'm sorry master," Duncan whispered hoarsely.

"There is no forgiveness here, Duncan." The old man turned his attention back towards the fire that burned slowly from lack of attention.

He waved his hand at a log and it obeyed his movement and moved quietly into the fire, sending up a shower of sparks.

"The one element I cannot control is fire," he continued. "The person you had orders to kill has the one item that will frustrate me at every turn."

The old man closed his eyes again and slowed his breathing, trying to peer beyond himself and into another realm.

He turned his attention back to Duncan and stood within a whisper of him and frowned.

"I want to kill you," he said matter-of-factly.

"You deserve to die for this, but I still need you. He will come after you and through you, we will set traps for him. You will let him find you, but you will not engage Alexander until I give the order. When you do, whatever happens, get me that sword, or next time it will be your life I take."

Duncan nodded his agreement and the ivy loosened its coils. It retreated back onto the wall as if nothing had happened.

Abiyram lifted his hands into the air and every item in the room that wasn't fastened to the floor or wall lifted with his command. He spoke a word in his sorcerer's tongue and the elements began to fly around him in a circle.

The ravens peered out from the shadows and added to the ruckus with their cawing. They took flight from the arches overhead and began circling above the men's heads in a gesture of obedience to their master.

"Once I have that sword and destroy that armor, I will rule this world. I cannot wait for Alexander to see what is in store for him. I have placed enemies on every side of him."

He studied Duncan's reaction for a moment and motioned to a figure that had stayed hidden to come to them.

"Angelica," Duncan said softly. She was different now in death. The light had gone from her eyes, and she moved with hollow purpose. Her once radiant skin had deteriorated into a scarred mess and her hair hung from her head like coarse strings. He reached out to touch her hand, but a look from Angelica gave him second thoughts.

The dress she wore covered up the grotesque scar she had received when her heart had been cut out. Duncan was all too familiar with that day. Angelica betrayed the Order and switched her allegiance to Prince Alexander. They found her broken body and Abiyram had seen fit to reanimate Duncan's sister into a half-life.

"Go to my General," Abiyram commanded the girl. "Give him my message."
He placed a hand upon her and transferred a small bolt of energy into her head. She bowed stiffly and left without saying a word to her brother.

Duncan tried to subtly conceal a tear from his cheek, but Abiyram noticed it.

The sorcerer's heartlessness demanded he press the point further.

"If you two had kept to the plan, she would still be alive. All along you have had one task.
Bring Prince Alexander to me. This will be your final chance, so go. If you fail, I will chop your sister into bits."

Duncan bowed humbly and hurriedly left Abiyram in the chamber.
The chamber had quieted down now, and the sorcerer approached a raven who had perched on his chair.
The old man picked out a mouse from a bag that hung from his belt.

With a crack, he broke the mouse's neck and placed it in front of the large black bird. The bird snatched it from his fingers and pulled the mouse apart, feasting on its innards.

Abiyram lips broke into a grin and he stroked the bird's black feathers while it ate.

"Alexander Wolfield, the scourge of this world. He is all that stops me." He transferred another small amount of energy into the bird as it finished gobbling down the mouse flesh.

"Find him, follow him. The time is drawing near when I take everything away from him and leave him with nothing. Once he is isolated, I will finish him."

The bird's eyes glowed red, and it nodded to the man. With a screech, it spreads its wings and flapped its way to a nearby window. Within moments, it was out of sight, but Abiyram could see its movements when he closed his eyes.

CHAPTER I

Alexander had suffered the same dream, every night, for two months. His brother, Edward Wolfield, falling lifeless into his arms after being slain by Duncan's arrow. As usual, he was powerless to save him. Alexander would awake upon witnessing his brother's final words, watching the last drops of blood splashing on the stone floor below. He sat alone in the darkness for hours, unable to go back to sleep. The words haunted him, and the strain was unbearable. Adding to his stress, he had yet to find any trace of his brother's killer. He had failed. Duncan still lived. He was out there, somewhere.

Tonight, the stress had drained his body after many sleepless nights. His weakened state allowed him to drift off into unconsciousness.

For the first time in so long, he slept without nightmares.

It was just darkness and muffled voices, until he became cognizant of men having a whispered conversation outside his room. Since Edward's death, he had increased his vigilance against the Thieves Guild and any other forces that Abiyram might send to do him harm. He had stationed a series of rotating guards around both himself and his twin sister Sofia.

His sister had protested vigorously against what she considered an intrusion into her privacy, but Alexander ignored her protests. His concerns over her safety had grown and she would have to become used to his watchful eye.

"Jack?" Alexander called out. Even in his groggy state it was easy to make out the whispers of his most trusted guard.

"Yes, Your Highness?" Jack responded while lighting a torch. The torch quickly brightened up the room, revealing Alexander's disheveled appearance.

"Why are you bringing light into my darkness?" He asked as he rubbed his eyes.

"My Lord, the King's Council is convening." Jack was the first man to sign up for service to Alexander and had quickly proved in the years that followed that he was more than just a blacksmith.

He was incredibly loyal to the prince, and their relationship had developed where Alexander respected his counsel most amongst his guards. Jack was generally regarded as the second in command and made sure the men drilled if Alexander was not around. The King's Council that he referred to were the important decision makers from the surrounding countryside.

"Now? It's not even morning. Does anyone sleep in this kingdom?" Alexander arose from his bed and splashed water on his face from a nearby bowl. The cold water acted as a broom clearing the cobwebs from his mind. He splashed the water on his face once more and ran his wet hands through his hair.

Alexander paused for a brief moment.

"Jack, hand me a mirror, please."

Jack readily produced a mirror and Alexander spent a moment studying his reflection. His once short beautiful blonde hair had grown longer and lost any manageable style. His youthful face was roughened by a beard of several weeks' growth and itched at him.

He studied Jack's face for a moment. Jack embodied the clean cut appearance of a young Alveun. His hair was cut short and there was only stubble found on his chiseled face.

"Maybe you should stand in for me," Alexander commented wryly. "You have more of a princely appearance than I do."   Jack grinned.

"Thank you for the compliment, My Lord, but you have a unique skill set and talents I do not possess."

"By skill set and talents, I assume you mean birthright?"

"Not at all, Sir. You are by far the most skillful swordsman in Alveus and you are also a brilliant strategist."

Alexander took a moment to affix his armor properly. When he finished, he wiped his face with a nearby cloth and heaved a collective sigh.

"I hate politics," he muttered to Jack who nodded his agreement. Alexander frowned and stood lost in his thoughts.

"Jack, bring Chauncey and Fergus with you. Keep the guard outside my sister's door and have them follow her should she leave. Now let me go and see what these Council members have to say."

The nobles had exacerbated Edward's death by demanding the King take immediate action and name a successor. The Crown Prince's sudden passing had scared them for it created a hole in the succession.

If a dynastic war were to break out, everyone would suffer heavily, except for the Alveun military. The army representation, led by General Henri Valmont, lurked in these sessions as vultures circling carrion. It was an opportunity for him to hold great sway.

Alexander made it downstairs and through the Great Hall without any interruption. He headed straight for the room behind the Kings throne. It was there that the King held his private assemblies with the more important members of the nobility. Alexander guessed that this was strictly a meeting of the most important officials in the kingdom, and as he entered the room, and his guard stood outside, his assumptions were proven correct.

General Henri Valmont had already staked his claim to a seat next to the King's chair. After the Battle of Edgebrooke, he had reassumed his role as an active general and Alexander found the General puffed with arrogance and self-importance since then.

Valmont was nearly as old as the king but was in much better shape. His frame hadn't changed much in the latter years, for although he was more of a reserve military general, he kept close ties with the military and acted as a senior trainer for recruits.

Between General Valmont and the now Monsignor Jean-Paul, the King had employed two of the most intimidating generals the kingdom had ever known.

Valmont smirked and nodded at Alexander who just ignored him and went back to greet the others who were in attendance.

Lord Elgin Burrows sat across from the General and looked as if he had fallen asleep. He was the most senior member on the Lords Council and had served the Wolfield house with loyalty and tenacity, having been appointed by Alexander's grandfather. For his loyalty, he had been rewarded with the arrangement of marriage between his daughter Elsie and Crown Prince Edward. Now he found himself struggling to have his voice heard. He made his home in Eastbrooke, and it was his duty to guard the frontier in the east. His diplomatic skills served him well, for while the east held no evil, the Alveun peasants fought over choice pastures with their neighbors.

Alexander's least favorite noble, Baron Brutus Odimir of Edgebrooke, represented the northern borders and was seated next to Lord Burrows.

"Fat bastard," Alexander muttered under his breath as he passed. He hoped the baron heard the comment, but it appeared he did not.

Alexander had born a grudge against Baron Odimir ever since the baron had tried to surrender the city of Edgebrooke to their sworn enemies, the Bete'szek. Alexander was still irritated that in the months that followed, and that no action had been taken by the Crown. It had all been swept aside and forgotten with his brother's passing.

Baron Idren from Brookhaven was there, again wearing the sharpest tunic that money could buy. If there was any contrast to be observed between the old and the new Alveus, one would only need to look at the council to sense the disparity.

The old Alveus philosophy was about building a foundation. The old council members had poured their lives into creating a system of prosperity and setting the foundations of a strong kingdom through their toils. The new Alveuns were built to exploit it.

Across from the Baron sat two of those new Alveuns, Lord Burke and Lord Fitzwilliam. They were newcomers to the King's table, having been appointed recently to their lordships by his late brother. Alexander knew very little of them except by their reputation. They were both reputed to be very smart and considered Midas-touched. They had a knack for making money.

Edward had begun to divide Alveus into counties, with a Lord being established over each county away from the major cities. They were in charge of ensuring the safety and growth of all of the people within them. The Barons continued to be over their cities and the adjoining plots around them. The only exception to this was Lord Burrows, who managed to be both Baron and Lord.

Alexander's other brother Mattias arrived and sat himself at the other end of the king's oval table. He placed himself in Edward's chair and as Alexander thought, assumed the kingship would pass to him. Mattias glared irritatingly at Alexander with his one remaining eye and smirked. Alexander ignored his baiting and made his way to the other side of the table.

Alexander's mentor, Bishop Malachius, greeted him with a firm handshake as did Garrick Whitfield, the head of the merchants' guild, and quite possibly the second richest man in Alveus. He dressed plainly as if not to call attention to his own wealth. He carried himself with humility but was able to put his ideas forth with eloquence. Alexander reached his seat and prepared to sit down as Lady Elsie Burrows glided into the room and stood next to her father.

Alexander remained standing out of respect and he nodded his head towards her. She was tall for an Alveun woman, like his mother, with long straightened auburn hair. Her eyes were puffy, and he remembered Sofia mentioning that Elsie cried herself to sleep each night.

She responded to his nod with a courteous smile. Her long hair had been arranged for this meeting, but it fell well short of the immaculateness that Elsie was known for. In her grief, she had still come to support her father, and with her brothers having taken positions in other kingdoms, was in line to be the first noblewoman on the council. Alexander's twin sister, Sofia, snuck in behind Elsie and waved conspiratorially at Alexander. She was not supposed to be in attendance, but Sofia typically did what she wanted.

After several awkward moments filled with whispers and tension, House Steward Manfred entered the room and announced the arrival of the King. Each person stood respectfully, except for Mattias, who rose last and continued to keep his attention towards some documents in front of him. Manfred assisted King Magnus into his seat, ironic because Manfred was thought to be one of the oldest men in Alveus.

Manfred had served Alexander's grandfather, whose death came at a much earlier age than any other Alveun King. When Alexander's father was crowned, he kept much of the same household, Manfred being one of the most respected stewards in the kingdoms. When King Magnus settled into his chair he waived his hand to instruct the rest of them to do as well. He scanned the table at each of the seated nobles and had a puzzled look on his face.

"Where is Edward?" he asked with genuine concern.

The room was again filled with an equal mix of tension and awkwardness. Alexander and Sofia exchanged confused glances.

"Why has Edward not joined the Council meeting?" He demanded.

The awkwardness grew more prevalent as the nobles were unable to hide their concern over the king's question.

"Edward was murdered father," Alexander reminded him gently.

King Magnus' faced furrowed in confusion. Elsie wiped her face quickly to remove tears that began falling. Sofia gently placed an understanding arm around her waist.

"That's right," King Magnus murmured.

"Edward's dead. We are meeting to decide on a replacement, but there is no replacement for Edward."

"Your Majesty," Lord Burrows interjected.

"Your son's loss was a tremendous one both for your family and the kingdoms. Our nation still mourns for your loss."

"Thank you, my dear friend," the king responded kindly and motioned to Elsie.

"I know my son's loss is felt very deeply by your family as well."

"With that," Lord Burrows continued,

"we know there is no one who could fill Edward's place, for his fairness and devotion to Alveus was unparalleled. Your faithful servants wanted to come forward and ask His Majesty if he had deigned a successor."

"There is no replacement for Edward," the king stated firmly. The attendees exchanged glances with each other. This was obviously not the news that they had hoped for.

"Why is the church here?" Magnus asked, glaring at Bishop Malachius.

Malachius folded his hands in front of him and replied in even measure.

"Because, Your Majesty, the Church has a vested interest in whom our monarch would choose to lead God's people." Until this moment, King Magnus had at least managed to hide his disdain of the church to side conversations and passing remarks.

Alexander rolled his eyes. *It can't get much worse from here*, he thought, but King Magnus had more to say.

"This is a kingdom matter, not a religious matter. I would thank you to stay out of them. Or perhaps I will again be subjected to hear about myself during your sermons again? Do not think the clergy can remain involved in this matter. It is a state issue so stay in your abbey." The King flashed a callous look at Bishop Malachius and dared him to respond.

"Your Majesty," Garrick interjected.

"What the Bishop says has merit. We are all concerned as no successor has yet to be named. If the king would give us an inkling of what he is thinking or allow us into the decision-making process?"

"Allow you into the decision-making process?" King Magnus thundered incredulously.

"I am King of Alveus. I would soon have you remember that.

I am the state and I am the first and final word on every decision. You will not sit there and feign my best interests at heart. You will not influence who will be king. I, and I alone, will make that decision and I will let you know at my convenience, not yours!"

The council grew quiet and no one had a response.

"All these meetings make me tired," the King said softly. "All are vultures circling the throne. What say you, trusted General?"

General Valmont leaned forward with a giddy expression. The King had asked for his input. He puffed out his chest and spoke deliberately.

"Your Majesty, I feel that our country is best served if we follow the line of succession."

Alexander grimaced at his words. Henri had publicly declared the army for Mattias with that one statement.

"Baron?" The king turned to Brutus.

"What do you say?"

That fat bastard, Alexander thought. *There's no telling which side of the fence he's on. He'd sooner surrender to the Bete'szek than defend his own people.*

"I think a man with energy and vigor, with brilliance in actual military tactics, should be king. I place my support with the hero of Edgebrooke. The man who defended my people from death. Alexander."

Alexander's mouth dropped in amazement as the Baron nodded at him. This came as a shocked announcement for him for he felt sure the Baron supported one of his brothers.

"Lord Burrows?"

"Your Majesty, I agree with the Baron that Alexander makes the best candidate for the throne."

Alexander was not surprised. Lord Burrows had nothing kind to say about Mattias. He caught Mattias' hateful glance from the corner of his eyes. He did his best to suppress a rising notion of rubbing in their words.

"Lords Fitzwilliam and Burke?"

"We are uncommitted, Your Majesty, for being appointed by your son we have not yet felt comfortable in entrenching our support behind any candidate," Lord Fitzwilliam said diplomatically and refrained from looking in Mattias' direction.

"Garrick?"

"I would venture to say Calimus, Your Majesty."

"How interesting," the King mocked. "My own council is divided on the matter of opinion of who should be my successor. I should warn you to stay out of this affair. The path that this Council is on will lead to divisiveness and war. I will name a successor, but I will not do it according to your timeline. These meetings are useless. Return to your homes and I will send you my decision."

King Magnus stood up under the assistance of his steward and exited the room with annoyance. The meeting participants breathed a collective sigh and set about to lick their collective wounds from the king's chastisement.

Sofia and Elsie joined Alexander as he attempted to diplomatically assuage the Bishop's embarrassment. It was especially concerning for Alexander because the clergyman had been like a second father to him. It was Malachius who had seen to his education, and given him the special armor that he now wore wherever he went.

"Sir, I apologize for my father's treatment of you," Alexander said honestly.

"He seems to not be himself. It may be from the early hours that this meeting was called."

"The hostility your father feels for the church is unfounded and worrisome.

It is one thing to have personal beliefs, but when he publicly tries to undermine the church's authority." Malachius sighed and placed his hand on Alexander's shoulder.

"Know that the Church is solidly behind you as heir to the throne."

"And so is my family," Elsie chimed in quietly. "Edward would have wanted it that way."

"I'm behind you too," Sofia said, with a supportive smile. "You'll make a good king."

Alexander shook his head no.

"I appreciate your support, but I don't want the throne."

"So you would have Mattias rule? Why do you run from responsibility?" Sofia demanded.

"Run from responsibility? How have I done that? I served my kingdom well. You were with me. Over two years ago I was ready to leave Alveus altogether. I stayed and I fought to protect the people. I challenge anyone to come forward and give an account of what they have done for this kingdom equal to my accomplishments. I have no kingly aspirations; I do not want that responsibility. Give the crown to someone else, please. I would bring forward an overlooked heir. I bring forward Calimus."

"The church will not support Calimus and his indecency!" Malachius exclaimed.

"Can you stand there in all honesty and say that Calimus is a better candidate than you?"

Alexander moved forward to defend his opinion. "Have we not remembered that Calimus is older than me? He should sit upon the throne long before I do. I am not a usurper."

"He is a broken wreck of a man," the Bishop insisted. "He cannot even rule himself!"

"I can fix him," Alexander said firmly.

"I can make him a candidate. Give me time and I will prove it."

"It's madness," Malachius said.

"You risk your kingdom and the people's lives."

"There is more to Calimus than his drunkenness. It wasn't long ago when he was a good brother to me. He lost hope and fell away. He has it within him to be a strong person. I can find it and I can bring it out. You will have your contender and I will support him the entire way."

"Alexander if you can make him a worthy heir then we will support you," Elsie interjected firmly.

"I will trust you."

Bishop Malachius sighed and nodded his head in compliance and left them to join the other Lords in their fervent discussions.

Elsie also took her leave and joined her father's side. Alexander took one last glance at Mattias who stayed behind and spoke quietly with General Valmont in a corner away from the others.

The time was now or never, Alexander sighed. It would eventually come to a conflict between the two brothers unless Calimus was salvageable as a future king.

Sofia and Alexander left the Council and made their way into the Great Hall where his bodyguard waited.

"I appreciate your concern for my safety," Sofia stated, looking in Jack's direction,

"But is it really needed for your men to follow me everywhere."

Her tone irritated Alexander.

"Yes, it is extremely necessary," he responded.

"I would be disinclined to bury you next to Edward. My men will stay with you for they are the most loyal and trustworthy of all the warriors in Alveus. If I trust my life in their hands, I will not hesitate to put your life in their hands as well."

"Fine," Sofia said with mock indignation.

"I will, of course, acquiesce to my brother's instruction. Even though he is not the King."

"Do not mock me, please. These are trying times and any misstep could be fatal."

"That is very morbid, Alex. Mattias would not jeopardize the people for his own ambitions. He must submit to the King, as well. We must believe father will make the best decision."

Sofia brushed the hair out of Alexander's face. "It would be most excellent if my brother would shave before he goes into the presence of the King."

Alexander brushed her hand aside gently.

"You saw what happened in there? He called for Edward. Either he mocks us, knowing full well Edward has passed, or he is still grieving, or there is something wrong that we do not know."

"If there was something wrong, don't you think Mother would tell us?" Sofia uttered hopeful words indeed. "I will go and talk to her if she is awake. Have faith that everything will be all right."

"You expect me to have faith? This is too crucial a time to place in the hands of fate." Alexander heaved a sigh and placed his hands on his hips. He remembered the vision he had in the gryphon's hut.

He had been shown the kingdom at war and being laid waste. There was something else in the vision that he had been shown, but could not remember what it was.

"Did you fail to notice Calimus did not attend?" Sofia asked. "I fear you place your faith in the wrong people. Perhaps if you placed faith in yourself to lead."

"I fail to notice nothing Sofia," he replied.

"I will go and wake Calimus so that I may prepare him for his future. When I am finished with him, he will be the legitimate heir to the Alveun throne."

Within a few minutes of searching, Alexander found his brother Calimus passed out in the kitchen near a flagon of beer. It was hard to have missed him, but few cared to bother with him.

Alexander sighed and picked up a bucket of dirty water that sat nearby. With a jerked motion, he threw the unforgiving water on Calimus' face which startled him awake.

"What! Gods! I've been murdered!" Calimus wailed. He fumbled around to get his bearing and find where the water had come from.

"You have not," Alexander muttered.

"But I might murder you eventually."
Alexander swung his fist at Calimus who had just gotten to his feet.

Alexander's fist connected with Calimus' jaw and the impact sent Calimus flying back across the table he had slept on. He fell to the other side and disappeared from sight with a yelp of pain. To add insult, the flagon rolled along the table and dropped on his head.

"Leave us," Alexander ordered to his guards who readily left the kitchen. He unfastened his armor and laid it on the table in front of him. Calimus stood up and gingerly rubbed his jaw.

"Why did you hit me?" Calimus screamed. His anger mounted as a bruise swelled under his skin.

"Because," Alexander said as he continued to remove his armor. "For the last month I have asked you repeatedly to stop drinking to excess, and yet, today I find my brother passed out in the Royal Kitchen when I offer him up as the heir to the throne." Alexander kept his tone calm but continued to press Calimus.

"So you strike me when I am not looking?" Now Calimus rubbed his head, where the flagon had fallen on him.

"Consider that a lesson, brother. Your enemies will not strike you when you are looking. You must keep your wits about you, and it is impossible to keep your wits when you are drunk!" The ferocity of Alexander's statement took Calimus by surprise and he looked away, ashamed.

"Would you continue this argument?" Alexander asked. "I will be more than happy to continue to beat sense into you."

"Why are you doing this, Alex?" Calimus asked mournfully.

"I am not who you want me to be. You can't force me to be king. I won't do it. I won't!" Calimus stiffened his back and backed away from Alexander.

"They want you, Alex. They don't want me. You would make a better king. You must see that."

Alexander sighed and grabbed some fruit from a nearby basket. He placed the fruit on a plate and tossed an apple at Calimus who mishandled it, but managed to hold on to it before it hit the floor.

"I will tell you what I see," Alexander said quietly.

"I see someone who has hidden himself in his flagon since he figured out their life held no meaning.

Think of it Calimus, ever since you were of age, Edward was the chosen one and we were afterthoughts.
I love my brother and I miss him, but times have changed.
You can continue to be an afterthought or for once you can feel that your life has meaning. I am offering you that opportunity."

"It's too much Alex, I can't do it. You do it. I will support you. Please." Their eyes met for a moment and Calimus' desperation was obvious.

"I know nothing about politics, or leading, or fighting for that matter. All I know is drinking."

"I am sorry Calimus, but I will not usurp your claim. Besides, Father will not hand me the crown and his condition is getting worse. If our kingdom is to have a chance then it has to be you." Alexander picked up a ladle and poked his brother's soft belly. Calimus responded with a snort and swatted at it with annoyance.

I can train you in all things. I will not desert you, so do not fear. The rumor is, I vanquish all who oppose me." He finished his last sentence and grinned with a sense of pride. The victory at Edgebrooke had built confidence within him and he felt invincible.

"Come Calimus. Retire back to your bed. Tomorrow we will start your training."
Alexander offered out his hand to Calimus.
Calimus hesitated briefly.
With great reluctance, he marshaled courage and took Alexander's hand. They shook hands firmly and the brothers smiled.

"You will not regret this brother," Alexander said confidently. "Now come, I will have my men escort you to your room."

"An escort isn't needed," Calimus whined as they left the kitchen.

"I would hate for you to be delayed on your way," Alexander laughed.

"These are perilous times."

Calimus sighed and walked away with Alexander's guards while Jack stayed behind and followed Alexander into the kitchen.

"Did everything go well then, My Lord?" Jack asked. Alexander looked at the table in confusion.

"It did," he said,

"but, my plate of fruit? Has Kiera been in here?"

Jack glanced around for Alexander's dog.

"I have not seen her since last night. I believe she is in the kennels." Alexander looked around the kitchen in a muddled state. The plate was still on the table, but the fruit had disappeared entirely with no evidence of any person or beast beside them in the kitchen.

"How odd," Alexander remarked. He moved his hand shrugged his shoulders at Jack.

"I suppose it is possible that I did not get any fruit," he laughed. Jack gave him a mirthful look and moved towards a sack that hung on a nearby hook.

"Perhaps Your Highness would care for some pears?"

"That is very thoughtful. Thank you, Jack." The guard placed pears on a plate for Alexander, and he pondered the plate for another moment.

"Make sure you never leave Keira in the kennels," the Prince instructed.

"I never want my dog far away from me. If I am not to be murdered in my sleep, I will need her with me."

Jack nodded compliantly.

"Absolutely, My Lord. She has grown quite a bit in the last few months; doubtless her bark is enough to scare assassins away."

Alexander glanced around the kitchen for any sign of his dog. She grew quite large and was almost impossible to be concealed. She was troublesome, though, and her instincts often led her to mischief. The young Prince checked behind every barrel and pan to spot a trace of her. After he circled the kitchen, he shrugged his shoulders.

"It is just like her. Perhaps she snuck in. She's probably outside in the Great Hall. I will go call her." They scanned the room in hopes of spotting Keira. They only found the guards, the brothers Fergus and Chauncey, napping on benches.

"Great pair of guards you are," Jack teased.

"The Prince's breakfast has been stolen as you lay here in slumber?"

"Stolen?" Chauncey questioned. He sat up and rubbed the sleep from his eyes.

"Breakfast?" Fergus moaned. He rubbed his stomach in an attempt to quiet its growling. The red-haired brothers composed themselves and argued if they were looking for the Prince's dog or his breakfast.

"Keira!" Alexander shouted. The Great Hall remained quiet and Alexander whistled loudly in hopes to garner a response. Satisfied that Keira was not in the hall, Alexander shook his head and returned to the kitchen.

Upon entering the kitchen again, Alexander discovered the pears had disappeared from his plate.

"Jack!" He whispered and motioned for Jack to pay strict attention.

"Yes, Sir?"

"Where are my pears?" Jack looked at the plate and his eyes widened.

"There's something not right here, Sir."

"I agree Jack." Alexander turned to the two guards behind him.

"Toss me a sword," he whispered to Chauncey. The guard tossed his own sword to the Prince, and quietly produced a dagger from under his armor.

The four men moved silently through the room and eyed every item two or three times until they were satisfied that it had not been tampered with.

Each one of them eventually stood in a separate corner of the kitchen, and looked back to the center of the room and exchanged eye contact with each other. Jack shook his head in confusion and Chauncey shrugged his shoulders. Alexander's eyes fell upon the large cauldron on the hearth in the center of the room.

Sara, the royal cook, used this cauldron to prepare very large portions of stews, and it was big enough to hide a small person or animal inside. Alexander motioned to his ears. Fergus and Chauncey also halted their movements and listened for a moment. Keira was outside the kitchen door whining to be let inside.

With Keira's whereabouts solved, it was imperative for them to figure out who the breakfast thief could be. Alexander feared the worst.

Between Keira's plaintive whine, Alexander swore he heard a breath that was neither his nor his men's. He swapped the sword to his left hand and picked up a large piece of wood that would be used for firewood.

He moved cautiously to the cauldron. His men followed suit until they were two arms-length apart from it. Alexander raised the thick stick above his head and his men pointed their swords towards the large metal pot, should anything jump out. He swung the log at the cauldron and hit it with such force that the log smashed and a loud thud echoed through the pot.

A small voice yelped and a youthful figure sprang up out of hiding. Every man's sword flew forward and pointed at the uninvited guest. The intruder brought her pear filled hands above her head and glanced sideways at Alexander, who had his sword directed at her neck.

"Prince Alexander?" She asked meekly.

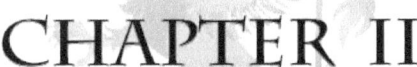

CHAPTER II

"Katrina?" Jack said in amazement.

"We thought you were dead."

Alexander kept his sword pointed at Katrina and said nothing. She turned to face him fully and had tears in her eyes.

"Come out of the cauldron," he ordered cautiously, afraid of what could happen next. His mind flashed through a myriad of possibilities. Assassins and dark magic were the first two that came to mind.

She obeyed him and cautiously climbed out of the cauldron taking great care not to tip it over. Alexander was amazed by her dexterity and when he was satisfied that she held no weapons, he tossed Chauncey's sword back to him.

Once Katrina had managed to climb out of the cauldron, he knelt down on one knee and made eye contact with her.

It had been months since anyone had seen Katrina. Alexander had rescued her when the entire village of Greystone had been slaughtered. Later, her actions at Edward's murder that allowed him the opportunity to save his own life. The young girl still wore the same clothes from that night. She smelled of dirt and mold, and they were quietly ashamed that no one had picked up her scent immediately.

"Where have you been, little one?" Alexander asked softly and he brushed the hair out of her face. Her hair was oily and looked as if it hadn't had a washing or brushing in the two months that she had been missing.

She responded with tears streaming down her face and she threw herself into Alexander's arms. Alexander's legs buckled a bit from the force of her unexpected hug, but he recovered and held her tightly. Katrina cried for a few moments in sweet relief of her circumstances. Relieved, Chauncey and Fergus sheathed their swords while Jack fixed a plate of food for her. Alexander held her and stroked her head gently while they waited for her to calm down.

"Where did you go?" He whispered gently. Katrina realized that she clutched onto a Prince of Alveus and quickly pushed out of her embrace. She nervously shifted from foot to foot.

"Please forgive me, Sir. I didn't mean to take your food. I was very hungry. I haven't had food in two days." Not only was her clothing a thread away from being rags, but her previously well-fed frame had become thin and gaunt. Her hollow eyes begged for nourishment.

"All is well Katrina, there is no need to apologize. Look, Jack is fixing you a plate of food. Eat as much as you want. You are safe here." Alexander smiled reassuringly at Katrina and led her to the plate of food that Jack had made. She sat at a little table and ate greedily and yet, while her stomach was being filled Alexander perceived that Katrina had an empty and lost look about her. Katrina finally broke her silence and chattered nervously.

"Your Highness?" She asked.

"No," Alexander interrupted.

"You don't have to call me that, there's no ceremony here. Why don't you call me Alex. Would you like that?" Katrina's eyes widened and she shook her head no in disagreement.

"It's all right Katrina, I swear it." Katrina studied Alexander's face and he did his best to smile back.

"Prince Alex?" She said slowly. Alexander laughed with his men and shook his head in agreement.

"Tell us Katrina, where did you go? You saved my life in Edgebrooke multiple times, and I need to repay those debts. And if I remember correctly, that included you inflicting a wound upon my shoulder."

Alexander lifted up his sleeve and revealed a scar from an arrow Katrina had inflicted upon him at the Battle for Edgebrooke. She smiled bashfully, but Fergus and Chauncey clapped her back in appreciation.

"I'm very sorry Prince Alex for the wound I gave you."

"One wound, yet how many times did you save my life? Why if you were older I'd wager you would be one of my best guards, and I would certainly not hesitate to make you one." He hoped his words encouraged her, and it seemed to have an effect. Katrina responded to his remarks with a broad grin.

"You're too kind, Prince Alex." She paused and looked about the room at the other men.

"But I fear that you may change your mind when you hear the news that I bring."

"News? What news?"

"After I escaped those men, I hid nearby in hopes that you had also escaped. As they ran off I heard the guards raise the alarm that your brother had been killed. The men that killed your brother ran past my hiding spot."

Alexander stood up and leaned back against the wall with his arms folded. The nightly visions played out in front of his eyes as Katrina revisited the night's events. His eyes grew angry and his brow furrowed in concentration and he did not notice that Katrina had grown silent.

"Your Highness," Jack whispered. Alexander responded with a grunt. His mind had grabbed hold of his brother's death and refused to release the memory.

"Your Highness!" Jack repeated loudly enough to wake Alexander from his trance like state. Jack motioned to Katrina, who had remained silent and sat in fear of Alexander's reaction. Alexander realized his darkened brow seemed to be directed to Katrina.

"I am sorry," Alexander said quickly.

"The death of my brother complicates my thoughts."

"Like my family," Katrina said sadly.

"Yes, like many of our people." Alexander knelt down once again.

"Please forgive me and continue with your story."

"Yes, Sir. As the men ran past me, I followed them to their horses that had been prepared for them. They rode off quickly, but I followed them."

"You followed them!" Alexander said in astonishment.

"You brave little girl! Were you successful?"

"I followed them north, through the forests and beyond the border. They stopped by a cave on a mountain road north and they continued on until they came to rest in a village not far from the border." Katrina took a sniff at a mince pie that Jack set in front of her. She licked her lips and started gobbling it up.

"She puts Brennan to shame with the amount of food she's consumed," Fergus observed to no one in particular. He referenced the largest of the guards' appetite. Brennan was so large that he was continually eating. Or perhaps it was that he was continually eating that he became so large.

Alexander tried to contain his enthusiasm. For two months, he had sent patrols throughout the kingdom and the forests for any trail of the murderers. Now in one conversation, Katrina had delivered all of the information he sought. This was the news he had hoped would come.

"Katrina, can you take me there?" Alexander set a determined gaze upon his newest ally.

Katrina didn't hesitate in her response.

"I will take you there if you can save my family."

"Your family is alive?" Chauncey asked.

"I thought everyone from Greystone had been killed?"

When Alexander and his guard had arrived at Greystone, they found the village ablaze and the townspeople gone. They had assumed that they were butchered by Duncan's men, but they never found the bodies.

"No," she said with tears in her eyes.

"They are being held prisoners at the village. They are being used as slaves for labor by the Bete'szek."

The Bete'szek was the tribe of barbarians whom Alexander had held off at the battle of Edgebrooke. They were an undeveloped people, enslaved by sorcerers in the north.

Alexander placed his hand on her shoulder, and for a moment she put down the mince pie. "Katrina, if you lead me to those men, I'll save everyone. I swear it."

"I'll lead you then, but I won't go near that cave."

"Why? What's in it?"

"Evil. There's evil all around it." Katrina's expression was stone-faced. "I heard things. It was like something was in my head whispering to me."

Alexander sat back and thought for a moment. He ran his fingers over the course stubble that stood out defiantly from his face. The beard had finally ceased irritating him with its length. His thoughts formulated the beginnings of a cunning plan.

"Jack?" He asked after a moment of reflection.

"Yes, My Lord?"

"I need you to ensure the Lords Council is still in attendance. Please delay them from leaving. Fergus, you are to find my sister and ensure the King and Queen are there as well. Make haste!" Jack and Fergus hurried about their charges while Alexander made his way back into the great Hall with Chauncey and Katrina.

"Chauncey, rouse the men before morning. Have them prepare themselves for a long journey.

We will need an additional three horses and a wagon loaded with supplies. I will want to leave this city before noon. We have much to do and little time to do it if we are to catch the men responsible for my brother's death." Chauncey nodded and left Alexander to make his way to the royal barracks.

As he was leaving through the kitchen, Chauncey opened the kitchen door to the courtyard which allowed Alexander's war dog, Keira, to make her way inside. Her tail wagged excitedly as she spotted Katrina.

In the months since the Battle of Edgebrooke, Keira had grown into her large frame and lost any resemblance to the puppy Alexander had raised.

She was still happy and playful, but she was ever vigilant around Alexander and kept a close watch on him. She rested only when Alexander rested and she slept when he slept. Katrina stroked Keira's large head and she responded with a playful bark.

"Katrina?" Alexander asked while she stroked Keira.

"Yes, Sir?"

"How confident are you that you can lead me to them?"

"How confident are you that you can save my family?" Her eyes narrowed and Alexander felt her eyes pierce him as if she looked for the weakness in his answer.

"Very," he said self-assuredly,

"I will save them. Now come with me, and let us make our report to the council."

Jack motioned to Alexander from the door into the Council's room that it was in session. Alexander hastened his pace to rejoin them. The Lords and Barons had stopped discussing the succession and had focused on a new subject which was the topic of expansion.

Alexander had not been involved much with the discussion, but he knew Mattias had focused a great deal of his energies into it for he could hear his excited voice blustering.

"For decades we have been prosperous," Mattias argued. "We have seen our economic might increase faster than any other kingdom. This has translated into a population surplus. Our country is growing quickly. New villages are popping up across the map. We will soon run out of space."

Several of the council members nodded their heads. "It's true," Lord Fitzwilliam agreed. In the northeast alone, there is unrest about wanting to continue on to the Eastern Sea and settle in those lands. My soldiers hold them back, but at their peril."

"The eastern problem is a thorn in our kingdom's side," Mattias challenged.

"Like the Bete'szek they continue to exist, but only at our behest. We should attack them now and assimilate them into our kingdom." He banged the wooden table for effect which startled Lord Burke.

"But my Prince Mattias," Lord Burrows said calmly,
"I have administered the eastern frontier for thirty-five years and besides bands of thieves roaming the

countryside, they have never been a threat to us or our way of life."

"And," Bishop Malachius added,

"They are under the protection of the Holy Church.

They are our brothers. How can you war against those with the same faith? The Church will not support such an endeavor. You have no cause!" Bishop Malachius glared at Mattias angrily and his lips trembled as he spoke.

Mattias dismissed the Bishop's tired refrain. "Brothers? They are foreigners; a rung above the Bete'szek! Their strongest cities are nothing but palisades. Our forges of war would overwhelm them quickly. Why, even Calimus could lead our men to victory."

"But they have done nothing to incur our animosity!" Bishop Malachius stood up and spoke in frustration. He looked around the wooden table for support from the other lords.

"They are under the protection of the Atreides," Lord Burke offered meekly.

"Going to war against the Atriedes is a concerning proposition. Their navy would overwhelm ours easily and we would have their soldiers on our shores."

"They are a protectorate of the Atreides, but the fact remains that we have no reason to war against them."

Lord Burrows tried to reason with Mattias diplomatically while Elsie held her opinion to herself.

Alexander watched in silence from the doorway as the others had not yet noticed him, taking in the dramatic scene.

"Regardless of the Council's restated concerns," Mattias said evenly, "we must seriously consider the prospect of expansion. As the Bishop has agreed, these are a people with our same beliefs. They are nowhere near our equals, so how easy would it be to subjugate them? Do you not see that it is our destiny to rule this entire land? We have just a small slice, but there is more. Why are you such cowards? We have the strongest and best-equipped army in the known world."

He continued his impassioned argument.

"We have more than enough ships to keep the Atreides away from our shores, and conceivably take the war to them if we desired. If we do not have a reason for war let us find one. Let us go into the annals and look for one. In this, maybe, your consciences will allow you to dream instead of being so simple minded."

Mattias rubbed his temples in exasperation. In the month prior, Mattias had shaved his head bald, tossing aside the brown locks he had been known for.

The baldness added to people's perception of him as an aggressive warmonger. The eye patch that covered one blind eye never won him the love of Alveus either.

"And now my son would dream up a way to war against his mother's people?"

The council's focus shifted to the doorway where Queen Caroline now stood. The Council rose out of respect and respected silence as she made her way past them. She walked by Mattias, her glare never leaving him.

King Magnus followed her as he leaned upon Sofia to guide him. Each council member remained standing until he took his seat. Finally, Calimus made his way in quietly and tried to stand unnoticed behind Alexander. He grumbled at the activity in the castle preventing him from sleeping.

"The council will not make war against their family," Queen Caroline warned in Mattias' direction. Mattias smirked as he returned her glare.

"My father may have passed," the queen continued, "but the marriage between your father and I solidified relationships between our nations. As long as your father is King, we are obligated to peace."

"This is true," Lord Burke offered.

"We would suffer much in our relations with other kingdoms.

No matter how mighty our army is, we need to take pause and consider this."

"It will tax the treasury," Garrick added.

"Enough of this," King Magnus said quietly from his chair. "The Saragossans will not be attacked without cause.

As long as there is peace, we will maintain the peace. Now tell me, why has the King been brought into the council once more? Not to bandy your words with your listless complaints of succession I hope?"

"No father," Alexander spoke up quickly.

"I have news that I need to share."

"Edward?" Magnus whispered as he looked at Alexander.

"I thought you were dead."

An awkward silence fell over the room as the occupants shared more uncomfortable glances with each other, except for Alexander. He stood frozen in his spot and stared back into his father's eyes. He saw an empty void while his father stared blankly. Sofia broke the silence.

"Father," she whispered,

"It's Alexander and he brings news." Magnus' blank face changed and his lips curled downward into a frown.

His eyes no longer made contact with Alexander and he turned his focus to the table in front of him. The Prince felt his heart rip as his father's attention shifted.

"What is your news, my son," Queen Caroline asked gently. She smiled sympathetically in support. He gathered his composure and addressed the council with his news.

"For months we have searched for any information on Prince Edward's murderers, and without any luck. But today, fortune smiles upon us. I have received intelligence from this young girl," Alexander motioned at Katrina to enter the room, "of where these cowards hide. She followed them north, past the forests, and into the Bete'szek lands."

"That is good fortune," Lord Fitzwilliam agreed. "Will we send the army after them?"

"Sending the army after a few men is foolhardy," General Valmont interrupted.

"Would we mobilize thousands of men to search for mice in a castle? We all know what happens when we stray too far north of the borders."

"But Edward's death must be avenged," Elsie snapped. Once the words left her mouth she quickly quieted down and blushed behind her father's chair.

"And you forget your place at this council, which is not in it," General Valmont retorted.

"We have now bounced from a full-scale incursion of the east to a full-scale invasion of the Bete'szek in the north to find a handful of men. Let us remember the last time an Alveun army went north. How many men came back alive?"

"There is no doubt that sending an army across the frontier would only provoke the Bete'szek into actions against us, but Edward's death must be avenged." Alexander felt annoyed that he agreed with the general, but it couldn't be helped. He imagined the sorcerer Abiyram eagerly anticipating such a foolish move.

"Father, with your permission I will take Calimus, my guide Katrina, and thirty men to slip across the frontier quietly to find the men that killed your son." Calimus' eyes widened at Alexander's request and he shook his head nervously at the bold claim.

"This is what you want?" The King asked. He mulled the words over as he slumped back in his chair. "When will you leave?" He asked.

"Before noon. I have my men equipping themselves and readying our horses. If our venture is successful we should return in a few weeks."

King Magnus considered Alexander's words carefully. He looked up at his wife and the silver-haired queen shook her head in disagreement.

Alexander was aghast at the lack of support, and his mouth gaped in shock.

"Very well," King Magnus said.

"You have the Crown's blessing in this endeavor."

It was Queen Caroline and Sofia's turn to be astonished. Queen Caroline looked supremely affected but recovered her emotions well. King Magnus rose from his chair and his Lords stood out of respect. They remained silent as the king walked out of the room under his own volition. Once the venerable man left the room, Mattias spoke mockingly.

"Good luck brother," he called out.

"I would hope nothing happens to you and Calimus on your journey for that would leave only me as heir, and I would be lonely."

"Do not become comfortable in that chair," Alexander warned his brother, as he took leave of the council. Several rose up from their seats and followed him into the Great Hall. He turned to face his followers. Queen Caroline, Sofia, Elsie, Bishop Malachius, and Baron Brutus all looked displeased.

"My son," Queen Caroline begged,

"Please do not go on this quest."

"Edward must be avenged," Alexander said mindlessly and shrugged his shoulders.

"After two months of sitting in this castle, I finally have an idea as to where his killer's whereabouts are."

"You heard what Mattias has said," Bishop Malachius stated.

"You would remove yourself and your brother from the succession by leaving now? What if the king were to make a decision based upon your absence?"

"Then," Alexander said firmly,

"It is up to you to stop that from happening."

The group stood there in silence as each knew that the other would not budge from their thoughts.

"My daughter is in Edgebrooke," Baron Brutus finally spoke up, "She will attend to your needs and replenish your supplies."

"You have our support, Prince Alexander," Elsie affirmed.

"I'm going with you," Sofia said determinedly.

"Your horse is being readied," Alexander smiled. "I figured you'd come along."

"I don't like this," Queen Caroline said.

"Your brother machinates to make war. He would spill blood to get to the throne. With you gone, his power and influence will grow."

"Patience my son," Bishop Malachius added.

"I will not have patience," Alexander responded petulantly. "I have been too patient and it has gotten me nowhere. I know where they hide and I can strike at them. I will wage war on them, and then I will bring their heads back so Father will be grateful.

Do you not see? Avenging Edward's death will bring us into favor."

"I think you are motivated by revenge and not the favor you speak of," Bishop Malachius said bluntly.

"Then it is what it is," Alexander argued.

"For too long my personal feelings have been ignored for the best interest of the people. My brother died in my arms and I cannot bring him back. They took him from me! In front of me! They will feel my wrath." The young man approached the holy man respectfully, but determined. "I can't sleep," Alexander admitted, with a touch of sorrow.

"Every time I close my eyes, I see his death replayed. I see shadows where there are none. I am afraid."

The Bishop placed an understanding on Alexander's shoulder and the Queen embraced her son in an attempt to assuage his sorrow.

"You can't help me," Alexander continued,

"But maybe this will."

Calimus slinked across the wall and looked as if he may flee, but Alexander had kept a watchful eye on him.

"Jack, please assist Calimus with making his way to the stables."
Alexander turned his focus back to the others.

"I will not be safe, but I swear that I will come back.
You have my word. I need the Lord and the Baron to continue influencing father from the council's table. He respects Lord Burrows, so let nothing happen to him."

Alexander said his farewells and hugged his mother once more. He clasped hands with the Bishop, the Baron, and received a friendly kiss on the cheek from Elsie.

"While we are all getting ready to travel, maybe I can help Katrina with finding some new clothes," Sofia suggested. She smiled sweetly at Katrina and gave her a big hug while ignoring her stench. "You have been missed little one." Katrina responded with receptiveness to Sofia's embrace. It had been so long since she had felt wanted.

Alexander was not freed of companionship for Bishop Malachius continued to walk with him; although at first his dress robes hindered him from keeping up. He picked up his robes as if it was a dress so that he may chase down the Prince.

"Alexander!" Malachius said breathlessly to the point that the Prince was forced to turn around.

"Sofia," Alexander requested,

"Please take Katrina and Calimus to the stables where I will join you."

Sofia nodded and took Katrina's hand and led her in the direction of the stables. When the females were out of earshot, Alexander turned back to Malachius.

"If you are trying to sway my decision then you are wasting your breath. I cannot be dissuaded from this course of action." Alexander crossed his arms and gave the bishop a hard look.

"Alexander I understand your pain and your need to avenge Edward, but is this in the best interest of the kingdom? Your brother stands ready to claim the throne, he petitions for war, your father's health is deteriorating and you would take yourself and your brother...the last two heirs to challenge Mattias and put Alveus at risk. Why?"

Alexander's face softened at the Bishops words and he relaxed his arms.

"I'm sorry, Father. I know you have the kingdom's best interests at heart, but I have to do this."

Alexander rubbed the temples of his head to relieve the tension that crept on him.

"I can't sleep anymore except out of sheer exhaustion," he reiterated.

"I need to be released from this burden and I will only find that release in my death or in the death of those cowards.

Katrina has given me a chance to be at peace with this memory and I must take it."

"Alexander," Malachius said soothingly,

"Revenge is never the way. There is too much at stake. Why not wait until your brother sits on the throne?"

"It has to be done now. The time fits perfectly."

"How is the time perfect?" The Bishop waved his hands in frustration.

"How do you know this girl does not lead you into a trap? How can you trust her?"

"Because," Alexander smiled,

"We've saved each other's lives. I will put my faith in her and I will put my life in her hands." He folded his arms, signaling the argument was over.

"I will also complete a task for you while I am there. Katrina saw the cave in which they bury their dead. She says that there is a great evil there. I will begin my journey there and find out whatever I can about their rituals."

"Wait. A cave? Really?" The Bishop stroked his chin in thought. His curiosity was piqued.

"I will go with you to this cave. I would like to see for myself the difference between the land's myths, legends, and the truth of it all."

Alexander chuckled at his mentor's words.

"Is there something I said that you find amusing, my son?"

"No, I expected this change of heart, so I asked my men prepare an extra horse for you. Will you meet us at the gate quickly? I wish to preserve as much daylight as possible. Every moment we waste is another moment I spend outside of these walls. Make haste."

"I will take the horse to the abbey and meet you at the gate." Bishop Malachius hurried along as Alexander inspected the progress his men were making.

The Prince's men worked at a furious pace and loaded a wagon for their journey.

Barrels of water and sacks of food had been stacked carefully as well as their weapons.

Swords, shields, quivers of arrows, and axes were laid neatly inside the wagon and Sofia remarked that it looked as if his brother were off to wage his own personal war of retribution with a private army.

Jack ensured Alexander's weapons were already fastened onto Zeus. His two swords laid inside their scabbards and were tied to each side of Zeus' saddle while the Gryphon goblet was tied to the back of his saddle.

The gryphon banner was displayed proudly and mounted to the side of the wagon.

The breeze unfurled it and it fluttered so everyone could make out the golden leafed emblem of their symbol.

When he was satisfied that they had loaded all of their equipment, Alexander led his procession towards the city gates.

Many villagers came out of their hovels and watched in awe as Alexander's finely dressed men galloped by them.

Several children ran by the horses and wagon and played by jumping in and out of the wagon. Alexander smiled dutifully to the people but kept his focus on the path ahead of him. Sofia acted more cordially and reached down to touch the children's hands that were awed by her beauty.

The girls showed their adoration by picking beautiful flowers from a nearby bush and gifting them to the princess. She held them and smiled fondly, remembering everything her mom had taught her about being a princess.

Even Calimus dignified himself with a smile and waved at the villagers outside of their hovels. Calimus handed a few coins to some villagers that appeared destitute which brought him a bigger smile as they showed their appreciation.

Keira played chase with a few children as she bounded about playfully and moved in and out from under the horse's legs.

Alexander's men joked with the children and took a few of them for a short ride through the city as they made their way. The entire procession, except for Alexander, smiled and engaged the villagers with kindness and frivolity until they finally reached the gate.

Bishop Malachius waited for them there. He had removed his ceremonial robes and was dressed as a traveler of no importance. Malachius had a large sack tied to his horse and waited expectantly.

"Listen," Alexander addressed his men from atop Zeus, "the plan is simple. We will head north to Edgebrooke and rest there overnight. From Edgebrooke, we will quietly cross the border into Bete'szek lands. We will look for the men who killed the Crown Prince and Katrina will be our guide. If anyone," he paused,

"If anyone gets in our way, you will not hesitate to kill them. May God bless us in our endeavors and show us favor."

Alexander's men saluted in agreement, and with determination on their faces they followed their Prince out of the gates of Middlebrooke and into the fields of Alveus.

CHAPTER III

The city of Edgebrooke was a brisk days' ride from Middlebrooke, the country's capital. They were ahead of schedule because they left just before sunrise, so Alexander took this opportunity to allow the horses to be watered and the men to stretch their legs.

They stayed a bit later than they wanted, for the wagon wheels looked like they might fall off. Alexander chastised his guards for selecting a poor wagon, and they set about making it sturdier for their trek into Edgebrooke.

Since it was late, they made camp and preparations to bed down for the night. Bishop Malachius made special care with his sack and took shelter in a nearby bed of tall grass. The guards built a separate site for Katrina and Sofia so that they might have some privacy.

Alexander inspected the wagon and ensured its wheels were fastened correctly.

As he inspected the last wheel with his portly guard Brennan, he heard the whispers of a voice that he was unfamiliar with.

"Let me out," it whispered. Alexander batted at his ear as if a fly had landed on him and now whispered evil tidings.

"Please let me out," it whined. Alexander shook his head and blinked his eyes hard. Where was this voice? Brennan responded with a quizzical expression.

"Are you feeling well, my prince?" He asked sympathetically and placed his large hand on Alexander's shoulder.

Alexander closed his eyes and moaned softly. The voice still begged for help and to be let out.

'What is this dark magic?" Alexander insisted. "Which one among us seeks to betray me?"

"Jack!" Brennan called to his captain with alarm. In less than a moment, Jack appeared at their side.

"What is it, Brennan?"

"It's the Prince. He doesn't look well."

Jack knelt on one knee and lowered his voice to Alexander who had crumpled to the ground and had his hands over his ears.

"Sir, is it the headaches?"

"No….," Alexander moaned and he cupped his hands over his ears.

"Make it stop talking to me. Make it stop!"

"Make what stop? Prince, who is speaking to you?"

"It is asking me to let it out and be free. It does not belong here. I need to get it. I need to find it!" The sound was driving him mad, so he grabbed his sword and handled it aggressively.

The group backed away from him in alarm. When he was finally satisfied that none of the men played a trick on him, he clambered amongst the camp and looked around for a sign that pointed to this mystery.

He opened crates of food and tossed blankets about in an increasing state of panic. Sofia heard the ruckus and came by to investigate. She was instantly concerned that Alexander was in a state of madness for his face was contorted with confusion and fear. He continued his mad attempts at placing the final pieces of the puzzle together.

"Alex!" She shouted as she ran towards him. She quickly took his face in her hands and began to rub the sides of his head. "Alex? What is this madness?"

"I am not mad!" He shouted and looked about the camp. "The voice….," he paused and listened about,

"the voice is louder. I am so close to it. Where is it?"

Bishop Malachius appeared next to Sofia and immediately sought to soothe Alexander.

"My son, what troubles you?"

Alexander cocked his head towards the bishop and peered into the site from which his mentor had arrived.

"Let me out! This is not fair! I have done nothing wrong!"

The voice was coming from behind Bishop Malachius. Alexander trembled as he pointed his sword at the bishop.

"You!" Alexander said accusingly.

"Alexander stop it. What? You are accusing the bishop of dark magic? How can you be so absurd?" Sofia tried to make her way between them, but Alexander would not be swayed and lifted his sword up threateningly.

"What do you hide in that sack?" Alexander motioned his sword in the direction of the ragged bag. It thrashed about wildly as if a snake fought to break out of its confinement.

Bishop Malachius' eyes widened with amazement and he gasped. "How did you know there is something in the sack?"

"Because it is telling me that it wants out! Can no one hear this voice but me? Am I mad? You know I'm not mad," he addressed the Bishop with frustration.

"So let's dispose of what is in your sack."

"Very well," the Bishop said calmly,

"Put down your sword and I will show you what is inside."

Alexander followed Malachius through the thicket until they came to his small encampment. There, next to a wooden log, lay the sack that the Bishop had carried and now it struggled against itself. Alexander approached it slowly as did the Bishop.

"What creature is in there?"

"Alexander, surely you remember this creature. You're sworn to protect it." The bishop untied the bag while the rest of the men arrived at the site.

All were interested to see if the prince had gone mad. Even Keira was intrigued by the sack so she came by and investigated it with a suspicious sniff.

Bishop Malachius untied the sack and a baby gryphon rushed out of it with the intent of escaping. It stopped when it realized a large group stood around it. A collective gasp of amazement passed through the crowd for they had never seen a gryphon before.

"I must remind all of you," Malachius said as he tried to pick the gryphon up,

"That this is a secret as important as any for the protection of the kingdom, and of Alexander as well.

You are absolutely forbidden to speak about this to anyone."

The gryphon screeched at the party as if it tried to intimidate them. That had an adverse effect on Sofia and Katrina, as they remarked how adorable it was.

Malachius picked the gryphon up as if he picked up a cat. The unruly beast bit him angrily on the finger and Malchius dropped her on the ground. The gryphon shook her tiny frame, stretched her tiny wings out, and screeched with pride.

That will show you to tie me up. The voice was defiant and Alexander stood unsure of what he should do.

"Who?" he demanded,

"Would have me believe that this creature can speak? Who would do such a thing to their lord?" Alexander whirled angrily and challenged his men.

"This is nothing less than treason!" He spun around so fast that he nearly tripped over the gryphon. It screeched in fear and danced its way out from under Alexander's feet. Alexander tripped over his own clumsiness and fell back onto the soft ground. He rolled onto his side and found himself face to beak with the gryphon. It retreated for a bit but as Alexander remained still it gathered courage, advanced towards him, and sniffed the air between them.

There was a still pause in the air as the gryphon approached within a hair of him.

Keira slowly made her way behind Alexander and stood over him protectively while she watched the young creature. The gryphon ignored the large black dog and continued her examination of Alexander.

Who are you? The voice asked Alexander. Its tone was no longer scared and threatened, but rather soft and assuring.

"I am Alexander, fourth son of Alveus," Alexander whispered. He sat upright and gingerly moved his face away from the creature's beak.

"Alexander?? Can you understand what the gryphon is saying?" Malachius expressed uncontained enthusiasm in his voice.

Alexander nodded his head that he could understand what was being said to him.

"Human? Why do you not answer me?"

Alexander stared directly into the young creatures eyes. Now unfazed, the gryphon refused to break eye contact. The creature was only as large as a young cat yet Alexander felt an indescribable amount of worry.

What does it want from me? He thought.

I have many questions.

Alexander felt the strong rushing of the wind and closed his eyes out of habit.

When he opened them again, he found himself transported back to the Gryphon's temple. He had been here before, years ago, in the presence of Ta'lon, the young Gryphon's father.

All of the traveling companions had disappeared from his presence and he stood alone in the middle of the vast hallway. The last time he had been in this room there had been several statues that designated the amount of gryphons that were gathered together in one place. Some sand crept along the floor and moved to a stand where it started to form a statue. Alexander watched in wonder as the sand formed the statue of the gryphon. Once every speck was in place a pair of yellow eyes flickered open while the rest of the statue remained locked in place.

"What is your name?" The statue asked.

"I am Alexander, Prince of Alveus," Alexander said confidently and walked towards the statue.

"You are a human, why have you enslaved me?"

"I have not enslaved you, I have rescued you."

"If you have rescued me then where are my parents? Why would I be carried like a common beast in a sack?"

"I apologize young gryphon. Your father charged me with your protection so certain precautions had to be taken."

"How am I protected in a smelly sack?" The young gryphon sounded much like a displeased child.

"I am sure the bishop has his reasons," Alexander mused, although he too was not entirely sure of why the bishop had chosen this course of action.

"Where is my father? Why is he not here?" The gryphon's voice rang hollow and was tinged with sadness.

"Do you know this temple?" Alexander asked.

"This is the place of our fathers and mothers. This is where we come together." The creature sighed sadly. "Please tell me where my father is."

"He was forced to leave our country, but he was concerned for your safety. He told me that you could not follow to where they went. That is why he charged me with your security. I am sorry but at this time the world is a dangerous place for a gryphon. You must stay with me for the time being. Perhaps when you are older you can follow them if you know where they went."

The wind blew softly through the chamber and little dust specks began to blow away from the statue.

"Alexander, I sense a great connection with you. Our blood is bonded together as if we were born into the same family.

Your armor is also mixed with our blood. This is why you can be here among us.

We are blood, you and me, a bond not easily broken. It remains to be seen if this is to our benefit or to our demise."

"Why our demise?" Alexander asked with concern.

"You can hear my thoughts and I can hear yours. It's the blood that flows in our veins. Should one of our blood cease to flow…," its voice trailed off. "We should protect each other at all costs until we know for certain." The sand crumpled to the ground until there was nothing left of the statue.

The wind filled the temple and Alexander shut his eyes. When he opened them again he found himself back among his companions. The gryphon broke eye contact with him and sat quietly. *Alexander, it would be in our best interest not to repeat what I've told you.*

Alexander nodded his understanding and stood up relieved that the mystery of the voice had been solved.

"Alexander," Malachius chattered excitedly,

"What did it say to you?"

"Nothing," Alexander lied. "I just explained how she came into my presence."

"Gryphons?" Sofia stomped towards Alexander with indignation.

"My brother gallops around the countryside playing hero and he is not interested in telling his sister about his discovery of gryphons?"

"Everything happened so fast, the battle, Edward's death...it was all too much to take in. At times, I cannot tell what is up and what is down!" Alexander tried to soothe Sofia's hurt feelings.

"There were no gryphons in Edgebrooke. You saw them before the battle," Sofia's tone demanded answers and irritated Alexander. "Your perceptiveness is flawless," Alexander remarked sarcastically.

"I discovered the gryphons in the forest before the battle. You were too busy gushing over Prince Youssef that talking to you regarding mythological creatures would have been pointless. Maybe if you had stopped to ask how I was I might have told you!" Alexander wished he hadn't spoken the last words from his mouth. Sofia looked crestfallen.

"You have my sincerest apologies," she said sarcastically.

"I forgot that you were the last man in Edgebrooke who had feelings. Maybe if you spoke more and hid less I'd have a better understanding of your emotions." Sofia grabbed Katrina's hand and led her back to the encampment. Alexander's men fell in behind her and accompanied the furious princess back to camp.

"Sometimes we must keep secrets to protect those around us," Malachius observed.

"Regardless of their proximity to our hearts."

"I have never lied nor hid anything from my sister," Alexander said sadly.

"I know she is trustworthy…"

His voice trailed off and he sighed deeply. For the first time in his life, he felt isolated. He glanced at Keira who lay on the ground and growled playfully at the gryphon. She playfully rolled over onto her back and kicked her feet in the air. The gryphon approached Keira carefully and sniffed her. Alexander smiled and hoped that his animals developed an immediate rapport. He remembered some familiar nagging thoughts.

"Do you know of Calimus' whereabouts?"

"He sleeps behind the log," Malachius pointed towards the fallen log that he used for his encampment.

Alexander examined the other side and, sure enough, Calimus snored contentedly. Alexander took his sword and gently removed the blanket that Calimus hid under. He flipped it onto the ground beside him and waited. His brother eventually stirred when he missed his blanket to find Alexander and Malachius pouring over him.

"What have I done now?" Calimus asked mournfully.

"You sleep in peace away from the encampment," Alexander said annoyed and shook his head.

"You have no guard in place. I offer you mine for your security, but here you sleep away from your protection."

"I would rather sleep here," Calimus said defiantly as he rose up to face Alexander. Since the young prince had begun to steal his drinks away from him, Calimus had lost considerable girth.

He ran with Alexander and his men most days and had lost the drunken stupor that everyone recognized him with. Even with the work, Calimus still acted indignant like a spoiled child and loathed physical labors.

"It's time for a lesson. Bishop can you equip my brother with a sword, he seems to have misplaced his."

Bishop Malachius drew his sword and handed it hilt first to Calimus who took it with a mocked look of happiness.

"The moon is out Alexander and we have nothing but firelight to guide us. And you wear armor…Surely we can wait until morning?" Calimus emitted a groan mocking the weight of the sword.

"A wonderful idea, brother," Alexander responded, "Perhaps evil will prefer daylight, as well.
Or maybe they will wait until after you eat your breakfast and are properly refreshed?
Oh, what an inconvenience we have made for the great Calimus." Alexander placed his sword down and unfastened his armor. Calimus used his sword to cut through an imaginary opponent and yawned with irritation.

"Really Alexander you're a better mother than I give you credit for. You'll raise some fine children someday." Alexander snorted with derision.

"We'll make a warrior of you yet, regardless of how much wit you choose to carry about." Alexander knelt down and leaned the armor against the log.

Calimus flashed a grin, leapt on top of the log, and with the same motion brought his sword above his head and down towards Alexander.

"Alexander!" Malachius shouted with alarm.

Alexander knew what came. He heard the snap of a twig on the log as Calimus' foot pressed down upon it. He swung his sword above his head and blocked his brother's clumsy swing. Alexander deflected the blow to his left and sprang to his feet and hopped onto the log. He held his arms outstretched to his brother and teased him.

"Come now Calimus and let us see if the lack of stiff drink has improved your balance!" Calimus grunted and jumped on the log and after wavering, steadied himself. They feinted back and forth as both examined the other's position.

Satisfied with his assessment, Calimus rushed forward and swung his sword to the left and then to the right. Alexander ignored them and merely backed away until he sensed he was at the end of the log. When his senses warned him that he had run out of any place to go, he waited until Calimus swung one last time. Alexander crouched down and quickly flipped backward off the log coming to a perfect standing position.

"Very nice Alexander," Malachius applauded.

"You're more a jester," Calimus commented,

"than a fighter tonight. How does waking me up to your jovial nature teach me anything?" Calimus snapped a branch off the log and threw it nonchalantly at his teacher.

"The lesson here, brother, is that you're slow and if you wrote your opponent a letter, the letter would arrive at their place quicker than your sword. You are too predictable!"

"Is that a fact?" Calimus challenged. He threw his sword at Alexander who barely moved out of the way to avoid being hit.

His focus on the sword distracted him from Calimus jumping from the log. Calimus pounced on Alexander and tackled him to the ground. Calimus sprang up quickly and laughed with his arms outstretched.

"I have defeated the mighty hero of Edgebrooke! I am the greatest swordsman in Alveus!"

From the ground, Alexander seized upon his brother's confidence. He swept his legs along the earth and caught Calimus from behind. The force of the kick buckled Calimus' legs and lifted them off the ground. He fell backward with his arms outstretched and found himself next to a chuckling Alexander.

"You disarmed me, but you didn't kill me." He stood up and offered his hand to Calimus who laid in the soft grass. Calimus grinned and took his brother's hand. Together they shared a laugh as they brushed the grass off of their clothes.

Alexander smiled and bantered with Calimus and took note that he had forgotten how alike they truly were.

"Sit with me brother," Calimus said as he dusted himself off and looked off towards the stars.

"Alex, do you really believe I can be King?"

"With all my heart Calimus. Why with the Bishops support, and if we can come home victorious with the heads of those traitors, father will look at you as an equal!"

"I hope you're right Alex. I never thought anything important would ever happen to me." His voice trailed off into an empty hollowness.

"That's all over with Calimus," the bishop said in encouragement. "You have washed away your past flaws and in their place you have strengths. You are a new man, and you have the solid support of the Church behind you."

"I just hope I'm strong enough," Calimus said and he extended his hand to Alexander. Alexander clasped it solidly, keeping eye contact with his brother.

"You're strong enough."

"You two are strong enough for what's to come," Malachius said consolingly.

"With you united, your enemies will certainly fear you. Now come, let us get to sleep for we must be on our guard when we are within the walls of Edgebrooke."

CHAPTER IV

When they arose the next morning, the Bishop called the group together with a very serious look on his face. "The Gryphon," he explained,

"is paramount to our very survival as a kingdom." Seeing the skeptical faces in the group, he felt it wise to explain further.

"None of you have, or should, ever see a gryphon in your lifetime. They are reclusive creatures, preferring to keep to their own and not mix with humans."

"Centuries ago, these creatures were at the vanguard with our ancestors, driving evil from these lands. Our founder, Magnus the first, was able to broker a deal with these creatures. This was important because the sorcerers couldn't kill them."

"So where'd they go?" Linus asked curiously.

"If they're invincible, then why don't we see them?"

"Therein lies the problem, Linus," Malachius continued, as a teacher to young students. "Man can kill them, and they became hunted. Some of them were killed by Bete'szek in revenge, but a lot were killed by Alveuns. Our kingdom hunted them down."

"Are you sure about this?" Calimus asked quizzically. "I may not be up to Alexander's levels of learning, but we were never taught about these creatures."

"Every kingdom has its dark spots," the Bishop reminded them.

"It was sport, and for their wealth. If there is one weakness a gryphon has, it loves its gold. It creates gigantic nests of fabulous wealth to hatch their eggs. It's another example of the greed of man."

The men whispered back and forth to each other, with the word gold on their lips. The wheels were already turning in their minds, Alexander perceived.

Malachius had the same perception.

"You see, your hearts are already corrupted. You talk about fabulous wealth, distracted from your true calling. This gryphon could be the very last one in our kingdom. It's an ancient bloodline. You must never share of disclose that you know of its existence." He paused, choosing his words carefully.

"The moment you reveal its existence, is the moment you kill that creature, and your life will also be forfeit."

Alexander stood next to the Bishop in agreement, and continued the man's charge.

"You are my guards, and sworn to loyalty. That loyalty must carry over to the gryphon. You must protect her as you protect me. Are we understood?"

"What happens if she dies?" Farkas eyed the creature with suspicion. It seemed harmless enough. It was no more than the size of a cat.

"Well Farkas, that's not something the Church wants to find out. By legend, they are symbols of God's fortune. Would you like to see what happens when that last symbol perishes?"

Farkas snorted. He stifled back a chuckle as the rest of the guard looked on disapprovingly.

"According to legend? Come now, you can't expect us to hold onto superstitions like that."

Malachius picked up the gryphon and walked amongst the group. This time, she was more amenable to being held. Kiera followed the priest suspiciously, sniffing in interest, but at the same time holding back.

"Here is your legend," the priest announced, holding out the creature to be petted and stroked.

"If this is now truth, what more could there be? Would you take that chance seeing this in the flesh?"

When the last person had touched the gryphon, proving to themselves this was no illusion, Alexander gave the word to break camp.

Within twenty minutes, they were on their way to Edgebrooke. If the Prince felt that he had a choice and needed to decide between passing by Edgebrooke altogether and staying there overnight, he would have chosen to ignore it completely. For him, it was a mixed bag of confidence and sorrow. It was the site of his greatest triumph and a memorial to severe emotional loss.

As they approached the city, Alexander could not shake the image of Edward dying in his arms. Alexander couldn't suppress the anger and frustration, He truly believed that Edward had unnecessarily saved his life. Alexander would have gladly laid his own life down for his brother. If Edward was here, he would scold Edward for his selfishness. Here Alexander was pursuing his brother's killers into the frontier while behind him the rumbling of civil war was rearing its ugly head.

The horsemen passed by a mass grave that had been hurriedly dug, to toss in the bodies of all of the dead Bete'szek warriors that had been cut down on the day of the battle.

Nearby, other singular graves had been dug for the Alveun soldiers who had fallen during the battle for the city.

Alexander and his guards scanned the graves for a particularly marked tomb.

Once he found the particular tombstone, he slid off of his horse Zeus and bowed his head in silence. His guards did the same and paid their respects to the grave of Jean, their fallen comrade. Alexander felt disappointed because, in the wake of Edward's death, Jean's contributions had gone unnoticed by the Crown.

Jean had been the first to volunteer to follow the Prince, knowing full well the dangers that they were up against. From the moment Alexander had saved Jean from being sacrificed, Jean had served him with complete devotion. His death also lay heavy on Alexander's conscience; for Jean had broken ranks and impulsively charged out of the city, and Alexander had not been quick enough to save him from his fate.

Alexander sighed. Staying in Edgebrooke was unavoidable. They needed to swap their wagon, check their supplies, and hope that Katrina would be quick in picking up the trail in their pursuit of Duncan and Jacob, the men responsible for Edward's death.

Once respects to the fallen were paid, Alexander ignored his companions and kept to himself.

The company respected his silence and kept their joviality to a minimum.

Instead, the party was entertained themselves watching Keira run and play with the gryphon. The dog had seemingly adopted the young gryphon, and sought to mother her.

The gryphon screeched vigorously and tried her very best to fly, but her wings were not strong enough to support her. Each attempt to fly failed, for she would need more strength to be successful.

As they approached the large city, Alexander surmised that the entire company did not need to bed down in Edgebrooke. There were probably spies everywhere, so he just as well wanted to control the information they received. Jack and the brothers Chauncey and Fergus were to accompany Calimus, Sofia, Katrina, and himself into Edgebrooke. The others would stay behind with Bishop Malachius and ensure the safety and non-discovery of the gryphon.

Being in the gryphon's presence for the day had brought an established normalcy to the travelers. The Bishop was right in assuming madness on the part of the other Alveuns. Evil had taken its toll on the gryphons until they had faded from memory. They had become n othing more than children's bedtime stories.

Alexander led his small band through the gate of Edgebrooke. He was relieved to see that Baron had replaced the destroyed wooden entrance with an iron gate for stronger protection and instead of a skeleton garrison, more soldiers manned the ramparts and watched the horizon for adversaries.

Edgebrooke lacked the appeal of the larger cities in the realm. Middlebrooke was the seat of the King with many of Alveus' finest citizens and educated minds gathered there. Edward had often spoken of building a university there to gather all of the scientific minds into one place. Brookehaven, the port city, was very cosmopolitan. It had a great deal of diversity as many traders and merchants settled there from other kingdoms. In contrast, Edgebrooke was where those considered on the fringe settled.

They were there to exploit resources and people, so there was a great amount of money exchanging hands, while the law looked past their vices.

While Brookehaven promoted the very best in what other cultures had to offer, one wouldn't be surprised to run into the less desirable characters making a less honest living on the streets of Edgebrooke.

Alexander made his way through the city until they reached the Baron's palace.

Other than the gate and changes to the garrison, the battle seemed to have left very little impact on the city; people still conducted their dealings as if war had never happened. At least as untrusting as the city had been when he first arrived, people now paused and bowed their heads to him out of respect.

He reached the very steps where, as he saw it, he had finally matured as a leader. The pompous baron had challenged his authority, but he had stood his ground and ignored the threats and barbs that had come.

Now he again stood on the steps but instead of the baron, he needed to deal with the real power of Edgebrooke, the baron's daughter, Isadora. He had not seen her in months but missed her a great deal. Her lasting imprint upon his memory made him long for her presence.

Isadora had first approached Alexander at a ball in the Western Islands. She was truly one of the most beautiful young ladies in the land, and her reputation of using her looks to cast spells over men was widely known. Not that she ever had to take action, receiving a mere smile from her lips commanded even the most stalwart of men.

Lady Isadora approached Alexander's group with an air of regality and grace. She wore a red gown that fluttered behind her as she walked into a breeze.

Two handmaidens followed her and held the train of her dress off of the ground. If this were any other country, Alexander would have bowed to her as a queen, but instead she curtsied low to her visitors.

"Prince Calimus and Princess Sofia," she said delicately,

"You are welcome to my father's house. Our city is your city."

She moved a step closer to Alexander.

"Prince Alexander, the hero and guardian of Edgebrooke. Our city owes you so much. How can we repay you?"

Alexander took her hand and raised her up. Her blue eyes immediately connected with his and he felt an emotional pull towards her.

"Your kindness and your father's support is repayment enough," Alexander said warmly.

"My servants will show you to your chambers." Isadora clapped her hands and her two handmaidens bowed to the party and Calimus, Katrina, and Alexander's men eagerly followed them. Sofia stayed behind and flashed a look of annoyance at Alexander.

"Isadora," she said,

"I have forgotten to thank you for your assistance in nursing my brother back from his wounds."

"It was all I could do," she said as she looked directly at Alexander. "The bravery he displayed in battle was unparalleled, but my father tells me that we will be supporting Prince Calimus as your father's successor?"

"That is a decision we have made," Sofia said, emphasizing the word "we". Isadora ignored Sofia's input and continued to speak directly to Alexander.

"I would not dare question Prince Alexander's wisdom, as one who has proved himself so admirably," she said silkily, "But perhaps Alexander would consider himself a successor. He carries so many kingly qualities about him."

Alexander blushed at her words. He felt uncomfortable at the amount of praise that Isadora had put upon him, but he also felt himself more attracted to her.

"My talents are needed elsewhere Milady, but I appreciate your thoughts. I would never do anything to threaten our kingdom."

"I know My Lord," she bowed again at him. "Perhaps Your Highness and his party would join me for dinner tonight before you make your way north?"

"I- we would be honored and grateful."

When Isadora took her leave and returned to her home, Alexander's eyes did not leave her.

The curly black hair and shapely gown engendered a need within him that he desired to act upon, but knowing his sister was watching him curtailed his thoughts.

"Shall we move off the steps or would you become a statue for her as well?" Alexander was startled by Sofia's bluntness.

"I don't know what you mean by that," Alexander responded.

"I am a woman, I understand them. This one sets a trap for you as if she were the fox and you were a chicken."

"I am no chicken," Alexander said in irritation.

"She has set no traps for me. She is, well, words fail me." Alexander's voice trailed off as he tried to catch one last glimpse of her.

"She nursed you back to health and she wears what is probably her finest gown upon your return. Then she tries to plant thoughts of being King in your head."

"Do you not try to plant those thoughts as well, Sofia?" Alexander glared at her.

"What is the difference between my sister and my father's subjects planting ideas in my head? Why should one idea be any different from the other?"

Sofia's face softened and the irritation left her face.

"You are right Alex. Why should the voice of your sister mean anything more to you than the voice of a shapely girl in a brilliant dress? Maybe you should listen to yourself when you talk to others. It would do you well."

Sofia hurried up the steps to the palace and left Alexander awash with thoughts. He wanted to call after her and set her mind at ease. His mouth opened, but no sound came from his lips, so he remained there with his thoughts.

He walked away from the city palace towards the outer walls of Edgebrooke. He wandered aimlessly through the market, a fact that would have greatly displeased several people. He eschewed the protection for a moment and his eyes flitted from house to house. Alexander entertained silly notions of knocking on doors just to slate his curiosity.

How did others live? He thought. What were they worried about? Did the problems of the kingdom have any impact inside these humble dwellings? No matter, he said to himself. If there were a civil war, it would matter to everyone. He climbed the stairs to the top of the wall and pensively looked over the fields that surrounded the city.

His memories went back to the action and he mindlessly grabbed his sword as his muscles twitched.

His mind replayed every event and he quietly analyzed every decision he had made, from the initial order of the fight to Jean's death. None of the men had spoken of Jean since his death, but Alexander knew Jean's death made them feel a little less invincible just as Edward's death made him feel a little more vulnerable.

A bird drew closer to him, and he watched it make its way directly to him.

A large raven landed next to him on the wall. The prince was taken aback at the bird's boldness and when it cawed loudly, it startled him. He swore the bird stared at him, and wondered if maybe he stood between it and some food.

He made his way to the gate tower, away from the bird, and rounded the steps to the top. He mimicked sequences of the battle in his footsteps and brushed his hand over the blood that had dried against the wall.

The top of the gate afforded him the view over the field and the city when another raven landed next to him. Its sudden appearance startled him.

He heard another sound in the tower, for someone had followed him.

"Jack?" he called out cautiously.

Jack stepped out from the shadows and bowed to Alexander.

"Not bad. How long were you behind me?" Alexander was impressed that he never felt Jack's presence.

"Since you left the protection of your guard," Jack chastised. "Farkas has been giving me some lessons in stealth. No one is better at sneaking around than him."

Alexander nodded his head in agreement and looked around the tower. Disorganized clumps of arrows lay undisturbed on the ground and Alexander recognized several arrows as Sofia's. He felt compelled to organize them so he picked a few up and set them aside.

"Your sister is a skilled archer," Jack said in reference to the arrows.

"She is indeed," Alexander said wistfully.

"May I ask you a presumptuous question? Not that the answer makes a difference."

"Jack, for all intents and purposes you are my chief lieutenant. I even consider you a friend. You can ask me what you would like, but you may never like my answers."

Jack nodded his head in understanding.

"Why are we doing this? I mean, I know why, but the timing? With you and Calimus absent, Mattias will take the throne, if he can, and here we are miles away unable to stop him."

"This isn't about our people Jack. This is about my brother. I am going to avenge my brother's death on the people responsible. If Mattias seizes the throne in our absence, then that is what God wills. I have chosen the path of revenge. I don't care about the Crown, I don't care about Alveus. I need blood to be shed so that I can have peace and that I can finally sleep at night knowing I did what was necessary to avenge my brother."

Jack's face was crestfallen and Alexander read the disappointment on his face.

"I'm sorry Jack," he continued.

"That's not the answer you wanted, but I'm being honest with you. When this is over, and I have my revenge, then we can sort out who wears the Crown."

"If there's a future for us in Alveus." Jack picked up a handful of arrows. With a snap of his hands, he broke them in half and tossed them over the battlement.

"There's always a future for men like us, Jack." Alexander looked back out across the field.

"We are a highly trained band of soldiers who have seen war and won against insurmountable odds. We are far too valuable."

The raven settled next to him again and inched closer to tug at his sleeve. "Hello," Alexander said, "what has you so riled up?" He poked the bird back as if to demand respect for the larger species.

Jack chuckled. "Cheeky bird, isn't it?"

The bird became enraged and cawed loudly. Alexander ignored it until it approached closer and snapped at his arm. The bird's beak cut into his arm enough to produce drops of blood.

"Ouch!" Alexander exclaimed.

"That's not funny at all." He drew his sword out and took a swipe at the malicious bird. The bird flapped its wings and flew back down to the wall. The Prince examined the slight cut on his upper arm, and when he was satisfied it was just a cut, he placed the sword back in his scabbard.

The two men reflected the view for a few moments and continued to study the fields around the castle. The sun prepared to make its way past the trees when Alexander finally spoke. "It's near nightfall; we should probably leave and attend to the dinner that Lady Isadora has prepared for us."

They made their way back through the city town and kept to themselves. Jack's words weighed on Alexander's mind. Doubt crept into his mind and nagged at him as a mother's guilt.

Was this the right course to take?

Was he being selfish? Alexander resolved that this was the course of action he chose, and he would not seek another. The future would have to build itself around this decision.

Isadora had quite the dinner prepared, and Alexander was extremely impressed with her ability to manage a household. Servants ran back and forth with plates and goblets before his companions had been settled into their seats.

The chair at the front of the table had been reserved for Alexander while Isadora sat at the opposite side. Sofia sat next to Alexander and across from Calimus. The rest of his men and Katrina sat in the other spaces eyeing the delicious meal hungrily.

"Prince Alexander," Isadora said sweetly,

"Would you care for some of my father's wine?"

"Yes, I would," Alexander took a goblet from the servant and watched the wine pour into a cup and slosh against the sides. He sniffed the aroma and caught a hint of his favorite fruit, the blackberry.

"Perhaps we would all enjoy some of your father's wine?" Sofia asked.

"Oh yes please, three goblets should be enough," Calimus laughed.

"You are all welcome to our city's stores, but I am sorry, my father's stores are under guard and I could only abscond with enough for Prince Alexander. On our journey to the Western Isles, I became familiar with how much he enjoys it." She referred to the event where she had first met the young prince.

"That I do," Alexander remarked as he lifted the goblet.

"To our hostess and benefactor, Lady Isadora."

All of the men lifted their cups in Isadora's direction and toasted her with enthusiasm. Even Calimus, whose spirits were dampened with the refusal of the special wine, eagerly toasted his hostess.

Throughout the dinner, Alexander ate and drank but kept his eyes firmly fixated on Isadora. She played the role of hostess quite well but found moments to return his gaze and flirt quietly using her demure eyes throughout the dinner.

Calimus and Chauncey exchanged mirthful stories and bantered throughout the meal.

Sofia bonded herself to Katrina, and the two of them made fun of the men at the table. To the prince's chagrin, Sofia shared embarrassing stories from their youth and the adventures that they had before they grew up.

Her favorite story was their first time at the ocean. Edward and Alexander pretended to be warriors while Mattias and Calimus chose to be pirates. They bounced across the galley, ruining each sailor's day by crashing into them and overturning barrels.

They had driven King Magnus mad with their frenzied play and Calimus nearly cut off one of his irate father's fingers. Putting them in the holds did not improve their disposition either.

All four of them broke out of their cells and aligned themselves to a piratical cause. They snuck back up and plotted to ruin Sofia's voyage by dumping a bucket of fish on her head. No one noticed the boys sneaking across the side of the ship. No one, that is, except Sofia. Sofia scrutinized their every move. They had just come to a rope, that when they climbed up on it, would be in a position to dump the fish on her head. With all four of them climbing up the rope, none of them had any hands to hold on to anything else.

Sofia appeared over the side with a grin and an axe. At first, the boys exchanged confused glances as to what she was up to but they all shouted for her to stop once they realized what she was doing. She raised the axe, brought it down, and cut cleanly through the rope.

The four Princes fell back into the ocean, with the bucket of smelly fish raining down on their heads. The King allowed himself a laugh when they were hauled onto the deck, and received even greater pleasure allowing Sofia to boss them around the rest of the day. That was the moment Sofia knew she wanted to be a queen.

Once Alexander finished his wine, he felt absolutely sure he had strong feelings for Isadora. Eventually, the dinner came to an end, and the party excused themselves and retired to their rooms.

Isadora was the last to leave, but she requested Alexander to escort her to her chambers.

He did so willingly and leaped at the opportunity to be alone with her. They walked along the corridors in uncomfortable silence until she finally spoke.

"Will you be leaving early Prince Alexander?"

"Yes, at first light," he said while he tried to breathe evenly.

"Perhaps I could convince you to stay another day," she said as she ran her fingers along his arm. His skin warmed to the touch and he felt a fire raged within him.

"You could convince me to stay forever," he said flatly and then realized what he had said and suddenly hastened to retract his words.

"What I meant to say, Isadora, is…," he thought quickly and continued, "That your hospitality is so overwhelming and gracious that there is no reason to want to leave…and the wine is delicious."

"I seem to have failed in my duties if it's the wine that makes you want to stay Alexander," she said coyly. Her other hand glided along the side of his arm. He backed away a few steps until his back hit the wall.

She followed aggressively and kept her hands on his arms. He brought his hands up and ran his hands along her arms, as well. They were softer than anything he had touched before.

"Not just the wine," he said nervously.

"What then?" Her hands went behind his neck and he pulled her closer to him. There was a pause and they looked at each other.

"Kiss me," she commanded quietly.

It was a command he was more than willing to obey. He leaned down and kissed her lips, softly at first, but the more he kissed her, the more passionate the kiss became. Every thought in his mind demanded more of Isadora. They paused just briefly to breathe.

"My Prince," she said soothingly.

"I should leave you to your thoughts before our actions become inappropriate."

Alexander couldn't breathe. With great difficulty and nodding, he succeeded in tearing himself away from the beautiful girl and stumbled away. His mind was heavy and clouded with her image. He tried to focus on walking but failed miserably and found himself using the walls for support. Once back to the dining area, he straightened his appearance and composed himself to hopefully avert any suspicions that might arise.

When he entered the dining hall, he found only Sofia sitting on a bench picking at a pear. She spotted him and rolled her eyes.

"I was afraid you might have been eaten," she said sarcastically.

"I am fine," Alexander said stoically.

"I escorted Isadora to her chambers and then said good night. It's the least I could do for a wonderful hostess."

"Is that so?" She replied and cocked her eyebrows at him. She stood up from the bench and moved towards him. She pursed her lips and clucked her tongue in disapproval.

"Is everyone off to sleep?" He asked.

"Indeed." When Sofia got closer, she tested out the aroma of his hair with two short sniffs.

"It's amazing how many smart people you lead. It doesn't matter how many sleep and how many eat, your men are quite aware of the demure flirting between the two of you."

"There is no flirting," Alexander objected with an injured air.

"Really Alexander? More lies? I'm your sister and you should treat me as such, and not some common fool for your entertainment."

"What are you talking about?" He asked in sincerity. "That is not how I treat you."

"Do not proceed to tell me how you make me feel. These are my feelings and as such I feel them. I never hide anything from you so why are you hiding things from me?"

"I don't hide anything, I just choose not to talk about my feelings. While others seem to be inconsiderate in not sparing the feelings of others by talking incessantly about how they feel."

"Very well Alexander, I will stop talking to you about my feelings and I am not blind enough to know what you are speaking about." She passed him with tears in her eyes.

"Why are you upset? You have Prince Youssef and I have Isadora.

Are you unhappy that another woman would come into my life and steal away the attention?" Anger built within Alexander. He wanted Isadora and no one would tell him any differently.

"She's not for you and that is my advice as a sister that cares about you greatly. I fear she bewitches you." Her words sounded desperate.

"Bewitches me? That is the best that you have in your defense? You will not mandate my feelings!" he shouted. The hall echoed with his words.

"Okay Alex," Sofia said gently.

"I won't discuss it any further. I will say that you may want to take a bath tonight and rid yourself of her scent. I can't imagine men are following you to hell while you mimic a woman's scent." She left the room without another word and left Alexander alone with his thoughts. He sniffed his shirt and agreed immediately that he smelt too much like Isadora. Once again he found his passion aroused and he desired to go back to her chambers, wake her, and take her in his arms.

Instead, he took his sister's advice and went for a bath. The baron had built a large bathhouse within his chambers and took great pride in it.

The bath was large enough for five people to comfortably swim in, but Alexander wanted solitude. He would not get it this night for Calimus had beaten him to it. Alexander groaned when he spotted his brother, who waved at him to come in

"Come on Alex, this is the best bathhouse I have ever seen. Why look at this," he marveled.

"Marble tile, flowing fountains, and by God this is the sweetest smelling bath I have ever had."

"Best not let the bishop hear the blasphemy," Alexander commented as he slipped into the water.

"I would never hear the end of it."

Calimus laughed.

"Church folk," he scoffed.

"Always so serious. You know, I am shocked that you never took the vows."

"There's still time," Alexander threatened.

"I could take the vows and become a warrior monk who grows potatoes by day and slays demons at night. Or is it the other way around? When do you grow potatoes? Does it matter?"

Alexander chuckled and splashed his face with the warm water. It felt amazing and refreshing.

He picked at the wound the bird had inflicted and washed it as best he could. Some blood washed into the water, and began to dissipate. He pressed down where a new droplet formed, and continued to press until he was comfortable it had stopped bleeding.

"You know what I don't understand," Calimus continued his idea for him.

"How do they have time for farming and fighting? They pray sun up to sun down."

"They have the right idea," Alexander argued.

"If only our family were like that."

Calimus groaned and made a face at Alexander. "You are too serious. For the love of-," he paused and thought about his word choice, "Just say the vows and be done with us then, that is if you can renounce all worldly possessions."

"That is surprisingly easy when you do not put a value on material things. If I give up fine clothing, I will get clothing that suits me well. I give up my sword, I pick up a shovel."

"Yes," Calimus went on, "And you can trade thoughts of Isadora for fifty sweaty men in Mass." He winked at Alexander in a knowing way. "Our Alexander," he grinned. "He has found feelings within himself. You might make it yet as an individual."

"Stop it," Alexander demanded. The old joke was coming, and how he hated it.

"What was it we used to tease you about?" Calimus looked off into the other end of the pool as if his answer bobbed in the water. "Ah yes, if we ever found a wizard we would tell him to make you less serious by giving you humor."

"Think of how great that was for me," Alexander frowned. "For years you and Mattias had nothing but jests and put-ons about how I wasn't a real boy. I was always reading books or in training with Father Malachius. It was always so great coming home to my family to hear the mockery."

"You were always so serious. You never laughed at our jokes. You became aloof, and there were days you didn't speak to any of us."
Calimus pleaded his case for understanding.

"No one ever knew what you were thinking. Whatever burdens or emotions you hid were carried alone, but it was by your choice, not ours."

Alexander refused to comment more. His jaw clenched and he sunk down into the water.

"That." Calimus pointed out. "You are doing that jaw clenching thing.

The ever serious Prince of Alveus. You are leading us on a wild chase to catch a murderer who has never been caught. Why don't you just stay here? Settle down, take Isadora as a wife, and be a good citizen of Alveus."

Alexander listened to what Calimus had to say but ignored the need to elaborate on his feelings.

Nobody understands how I feel, he thought. I must carry on with what I believe is right regardless of what others say. They will never understand why I am doing this. I am alone in my journey, but I must finish it whatever the cost.

CHAPTER V

"Your Highness?" Jack's voice caught Alexander in mid-thought. The prince had awoken early that morning and eagerly anticipated the beginning of the hunt. The trail to Duncan would be a long and difficult one, but he had faith in Katrina and his men.

"We have the horses saddled and ready for our journey. Calimus has joined Bishop Malachius outside of the city to ensure they are ready to leave immediately."

"You've done excellent work, Jack," Alexander said proudly. "You are the most capable of my men and I appreciate your hard work. You are on your way to being a famed warrior."

"Thank you sir!" Jack said enthusiastically.

"But that was never my intention."

Together they walked through the halls towards the entrance of the palace. As they approached the daylight,

Alexander caught sight of his sister sitting on a bench with her head hung low.

Her typical cheery disposition had been replaced with paleness and her eyes were tinged with sadness. One glance at Sofia and Alexander became immediately concerned. He ignored any other preparations and passed by Isadora who had come to wish them a safe journey.

"Sofia?" He asked with genuine concern and took a seat on the bench.

"I'm sorry Alexander," she whispered.

"I am not feeling well today."

"What do you mean? What is the matter?" For a moment, Alexander put the blame on himself. This is obviously because of our argument, he thought. Alexander put his arm around Sofia and she leaned into him.

"I am sorry for last night," he whispered.

"It isn't you," she said.

"I don't know what's wrong with me this morning. I am not able to keep food down. Oh, Alex, I know how important this is to you and I want to be there for you."

"I understand," Alexander said reassuringly,

"We can continue on. I will leave some of my men here to ensure your protection. Isadora, will you ensure that my sister is taken care of?"

"It will be an honor, My Lord," she said as she curtsied and smiled pleasantly at him.

The color in Sofia's cheeks returned and she glared angrily at Alexander. She removed the arm that he had put behind her and stood up.

"There's no need to delay you, Alexander. After all, this is your journey, not mine. I will not impose upon Isadora. I may not be feeling well this morning, but I will not be so easily dissuaded from this journey. I will lay in the wagon for a little while."

"That is not what I meant Sofia," Alexander said in frustration. He shook his head. Why was his sister being so emotional?

"I am merely stating that if you are sick we should have you attended to for your health and nothing more. We must leave so we do not lose whatever trail Edwards killers have left."

"You have your priorities. I will gather my things and meet you outside of Edgebrooke." Sofia walked away from Alexander and he felt an ever growing knot in his stomach. He hated to fight with Sofia and this change between them frustrated him.

Isadora seized the moment and quickly moved to his side and slid her arm around his waist. His thoughts quickly left Sofia and latched onto Isadora.

"Forgive me, My Lord," she said sweetly, "I would watch over your sister if she stayed."

"It is not your fault, she is just acting differently." He gazed into Isadora's eyes and found an invitation in them to pull her closer. He moved his lips closer to her and closed his eyes. Their lips met and Alexander forgot all of his worries and concerns. A cough interrupted them and he broke away from Isadora's embrace.

He looked at Jack, the source of the cough, who glanced at another. Alexander followed his eyes to Sofia who stood there with a disappointed frown. She said nothing but walked past Alexander and Isadora on her way to her horse.

Alexander felt it best to follow Sofia to ensure she refrained from acting foolishly. He quickly said goodbye one last time to Isadora and jogged quickly to Zeus. Jack, Fergus, Chauncey, and Katrina mounted their horses and followed Alexander through the streets of Edgebrooke as he chased down his sister. She refused to heed until she was out of the city. Once she was with them, she tied her horse to the back of the wagon and climbed inside.

There were fifteen more men in camp, wearing standard Alveun armor, and flying Calimus' boar banner. They were separated from Alexander's guards who stood apart with their arms crossed in annoyance.

"What is this, Sean?" Alexander addressed his guard.

The young guard rolled his eyes in an exaggerated fashion. "They are here as Prince Calimus' guard. Your brother sent them."

The captain of the soldiers produced a document that Alexander perused over. They were a detail assigned as Calimus' bodyguard and were to go where he went. The Prince grudgingly agreed to allow them to continue, for if he didn't Mattias would hear about it.

Alexander exchanged glares with Sofia from atop Zeus until, satisfied his men were ready to move, he barked an order for the procession to move forward. Calimus mournfully protested that this journey was the worst idea.

"I wouldn't worry your heads about it," Alexander said, speaking to Sofia, as well.

"Once we are well into the forest certain people's stubbornness will melt."

"What is our strategy?" Bishop Malachius asked.

"A rudimentary one," Alexander responded.

"We will follow our steps back the way that we originally came.
Our party will travel through the forest until we reach the mountains.

Once there we will explore the cave that Katrina mentioned, and from there Katrina will lead us to Duncan."

"You make it sound like a lazy day floating down the Alveus," Calimus groaned.

"You would do well in the political arena. Alexander, the Prince of Everything Will Be All Right if you just shut your eyes and do what he says." He grumbled a bit under his breath and Alexander fought a dual urge to chuckle and chastise his brother's protests.

"What about the thieves and the Bete'szek?" Gerard asked with concern.

"I'm sure they will not be welcoming us with open arms." Gerard slicked his brown hair back and affixed his helmet in perfect fashion. As egos in the group went, Gerard's had grown since the Battle of Edgebrooke. He took personal credit as being the warrior that unleashed the fire that broke the assault and used the story quite frequently to impress the Middlebrooke maidens who were awed with his glossy appearance.

"Since the incursion, the army has been sending large patrols through the forest looking for any signs of the thieves' guild or any signs of Bete'szek movement. Their hideout was demolished and no one has seen them."

"Who has led these patrols?" Bishop Malachius asked.

"General Valmont. He's hated every patrol I've sent him on, but he's gotten the job done."

Alexander felt secure that General Valmont had followed his orders. The General was a military man, and victories mattered to him. Without victories, he could easily fall out of favor with the King and lose his post which was intolerable to the General.

They all felt that singular chill when their horses passed into the forest. The canopy of the trees served to block out much of the sunlight, as the blackened bark of the trees could attest. Each person strained their eyes and ears and kept their senses on heightened alert in case arrows were aimed at their backs.

As they continued on, it certainly seemed that the General had followed Alexander's orders. The procession remained cautious as they rode through the dark forest, but their vigilance revealed no enemies. Alexander felt confident enough that, at one point, they bedded down for the night among the trees. They rotated their guard every few hours to ensure the forest gave them no surprises.

They arose, refreshed and confident, the next morning. The trees eventually ended and gave way to a clearing where Alexander finally saw the mountains.

The men and their horses continued to the clearing and into a mountain pass. It was here that Alexander had been bound and nearly murdered by an enemy he had never known existed.

Devin and Sean, his two youngest guards, had been with him. They too had been taken prisoner, along with Jean, to be sacrificed to whatever demon gods their captives worshipped.

As fate had it, Jack had saved their lives. He had brought along Fergus, Chauncey, and Alexander's great war dog Keira, and together they surprised their enemies and stolen away. It was also there where Angelica, Alexander's first love, met her demise.

"Sir?" Fergus whispered so quietly that Alexander missed it the first time he said it. When Fergus whispered a second time, Keira responded by emitting a low growl in the direction of the forest. The little gryphon, which until this time had laid in the wagon next to Sofia, walked to the back of it and peered behind the riders.

We're being followed, the voice said.

What do you mean? Alexander asked.

Look behind us and into the trees. The gryphon jumped onto Zeus and kept her eyes fixated on the forest behind them.

I don't see anything, he thought.

I have better eyesight, it thought ruefully. *Look, Keira senses it too.*

"What is it, Alexander?" Bishop Malachius asked. They had arrived at the entrance of the cave and the dogs were too well hidden for any of the men to see. Gryphons were rumored to have fantastic eyesight. Alexander also trusted Keira implicitly and if she sensed danger, then he respected her senses.

"We've been followed. I would venture a guess that the dogs have returned."

"Dogs, what dogs?" One of the Alveun soldiers asked. "I haven't seen any dogs."

"Nor would you," Alexander laughed.

"They seem to be interested in my company only. I have seen them a few times, and each time, it does not end well." He dismounted in front of the cave and tied his horse Zeus to a nearby bush.

"What are you doing?" Calimus' question sounded panicked.

"If we're being followed…what are we doing here?"

"He's right," another Alveun soldier said. Up until now, the soldiers had been very accommodating in following orders and staying out of their way.

"If we are being followed then I suggest that we do something about it."

"No one is going anywhere," Alexander ordered. "There are over thirty of us. If we stick together, we have a better chance of survival than if we go backward. Once you are in the forest, they have the advantage."

"All the more reason to charge," said the leader whose name Alexander had guessed to be Robert. He was the largest of the new men, although Brennan had quite a few pounds on him. The leader continued, "Our orders are...-"

"Your orders are to protect the Prince," Alexander interrupted firmly.

"Our orders come directly from Prince Mattias," the Alveun responded smugly.

Alexander leaned back on Zeus' saddle and reached ever so closely to his sword. Each man followed suit, whether part of Alexander's guard or one of Mattias' men.

"So tell me, what orders has my brother given you?"

"Destroy anything related to magic. Burn it all down."

Alexander pondered this for a moment. "Gentlemen, you have put me in an awkward position. I want the same as you, but this needs to be done in a particular order. This cave contains the foulest of evils, and it is into the cavern we must go."

"You are in charge of your own men, Prince Alexander." The head Alveun waved his hand at five men near him. "Go and kill whatever is following us."

The five soldiers nodded and strapped their helmets on. In perfect military fashion, they produced their swords and galloped to the forest. The young gryphon jumped down to the ground and walked several paces forward to get a good view. Keira joined her and sat very still.

In a few moments, the men were out of view, and the party fell silent. The gryphon let out a terrified screech and jumped back into the wagon. It ran towards Sofia and tried to dig its way behind the lady's back.

Everyone became unnerved and the horses pawed the ground until the riders were able to calm them down. From a distance, five horses without riders came galloping back to them. The men let the horses go by but took note of the amount of blood that dripped to the ground as they passed. Sofia quickly grabbed her bow and a quiver of arrows and aimed towards the forest.

"Now we are down five men," Alexander hissed.

"I don't care if you take your orders from my brother, but I will promise you this. You will not see the sunset if you don't do exactly as I tell you to do. Now get off your horses and get ready to go into the cave!"

"They just killed five men!" Calimus howled.

"They will come for us while we are in the cave."

"They won't cross an open field where they would be in plain sight,"
 Fergus said, trying his best to comfort the frightened prince.

"There are only three dogs and we have swords. I'm not particularly worried. If they step out of the trees then we have arrows. You worry too much." Alexander felt irritated at Calimus' lack of courage.

"Now is the time, brother, for you to learn to fight battles and to hold fast."

"What of the horses? We can't all go in the cave? Maybe I should stay behind and watch the horses. If we lose them…." Calimus desperately tried another tactic to not enter the cave.

"Calimus my only concern is that you might be overwhelmed at which point we would lose the horses anyway. I need you by my side and, therefore, we will not be separated. Eight of my men will stay behind with the horses with Keira and the gryphon. Keira is more than a match for those dogs. Sofia and Katrina, it's up to you to make your own choices."

"I'll go in the cave." Sofia's voice was strong and confident and Calimus' hung his head in shame.

Katrina grabbed Sofia's hand and nodded in agreement.

"Alexander, there is a great evil in this cave. I think you might take this too lightly." Bishop Malachius also expressed anxiety.

"The bishop is right Alexander, why don't we listen to him?" Calimus' voice was frantic.

"This is what we have been brought here to do," Alexander shouted irritatingly.

"What did you expect? Were we to enter the cave and find fields and flowers and maidens with skin as soft as silk? Of course there is evil in this cave and we are the men and women who are to meet it!"

"Your highness, your men gladly follow you," Chauncey said.

"No," the main Alveun said.

"We are going in too." The Alveun soldiers dismounted and tied the horses to whatever was nailed down. They frantically looked around to ensure the dogs had kept their distance. Satisfied there was no ambush, they positioned themselves to enter the cave, shields held high and swords out.

Calimus sighed and looked back towards the trees. Alexander knew he wanted to run, it was written on his countenance.

Alexander unfastened his two swords from Zeus and fastened one around his waist and placed the fire sword on his back. He also grabbed a dagger and attached it to his belt while Sofia and Katrina did the same.

Calimus huffed in frustration and dismounted his horse as did Bishop Malachius and Alexander's closest guards.

There was silence between the men as they armed themselves. The entrance to the cave had been removed to the side and Alexander felt confident that there would be many Bete'szek hidden within the cave.

"This better not be a trap or your brother will hear of it," warned the Alveun.

"What's your name?" Alexander demanded.

The Alveun opened his mouth to reply, but Alexander cut him off.

"I don't really care." Alexander turned his attention to Jack, Chauncey, Fergus and Farkas who prepared to go down into the black with him.

"Are we resolved?" Alexander asked and they nodded their head. Alexander shook off his own fears and shut his eyes.

He exhaled his doubts and the warnings of evil that were laid out ahead of him. The Prince opened his eyes and stepped through the cave's entrance into the darkness.

The intruders took a moment as their eyes adjusted to the darkness. They made out torches flickering in the distance and after drawing their swords, walked towards them. They quickly came to another entrance that opened into a very well lit chamber. The chamber was very large and a large stream ran through it.

Alexander and the group made their way down the path into the heart of the chamber. They saw no signs of life, yet Alexander felt evil tugging at his heart even more.

"There's something that isn't right here," Calimus whispered nervously.

"Alexander," Malachius stated,

"I think we should return to the horses."

"You return to the horses," Alexander said strongly, "We are here and now we will see what evil plans are laid out. Turning back now would defeat our purpose."

"I remember when life was less complicated," Sofia remarked remorsefully.

Alexander whipped his head around and gave Sofia a dirty look. "You need to be back with the horses."

"You aren't my liege," she mocked. He conceded that point to her. She was going to do whatever she wanted to anyway.

"You're like a wild pony," Chauncey commented.

Sofia threw him a look of extreme annoyance.

"So you are calling a princess a horse now, are you? Very chivalrous of you."

Chauncey regretted his words immediately and stuttered an apology. Alexander placed his finger on his lips and shushed a soft command for them to cease talking.

They went fifty paces until they stood in front of an opening in the cave floor. The tip of a ladder was at the top of it and Alexander pointed at the Alveun he had chosen to take the lead.

"Robert, you and your men are going first," he ordered.

"That's not my name," the Alveun whispered. Alexander shrugged his shoulders and pointed to the hole.

Calimus' so-called protectors strapped their shields to their back and grabbed onto the wooden ladder. It creaked and groaned as if it would snap, so they descended slowly and cautiously. The ladder was the height of three tall men which offered enough height for them to comfortably move about the cavern.

There were lit torches which shined enough light to illuminate some subterranean features which fascinated the party. It was rocky, but the rocks were big enough to climb over without much effort.

They found themselves descending into another part of the cavern where strange rocks rising from the floor and descending from the ceiling made it seem like the cave had teeth.

"Have you ever seen anything like this?" Sofia asked Katrina. The young girl shook her head that she had not, and reached out to touch one. She shivered when she grasped it and explained it must have been ice.

Without warning a gust of wind ripped through the chamber, sending the party scrambling for cover behind rocks. The cave's teeth began to groan and crack under the strain of the burst. The wind stopped the men in their tracks and they struggled to stay upright. In the din, Jack heard the cracking of ice, and guessed what was coming.

"Get down!" Jack yelled. With loud cracks from all over the cavern, the ice daggers hurtled in their direction, narrowly missed their targets. The ice kept going until finally they shattered against the walls of the cave, sending a shower of ice cubes throughout the cave. When the wind finally died down, the men waited a few moments and collected themselves.

Alexander took a breath to calm himself and rose to his feet. "I think the worst of it is over," he commented, "so let's continue on."

"Wait!" Bishop Malachius said.

"We must be sanctified. This cave is full of an ancient evil. If we are not blessed by God then evil will claim us!" He reached into his pocket and produced a vial of liquid. "Holy water will protect us! Kneel quickly!"

The Alveun soldiers chuckled.

"Has fright made you take leave of your senses? Water doesn't stop a blade from slicing and cutting. All we need is our steel."

"You truly have no idea what is coming do you?" The bishop threw a look of disgust at the soldiers.

"If you called yourselves Alveuns than you would kneel and take the blessing."

"We are here to kill evil, Master Bishop. Our orders are to extinguish that flame. We won't have a difficult time of it."

Sofia bowed to her knee. "I will take the blessing, Your Grace."

Alexander's men and Katrina agreed and followed suit. The bishop poured a few drops over each of their heads and invoked a blessing for their souls. He stood in front of Alexander. "Will you kneel my son?"

Alexander exchanged glances with Calimus. He could tell that Calimus had no desire to be blessed in front of the mockery of the other men.

He still knows nothing of politics, Alexander thought. "Come, brother, we must kneel for support from the Church." These words, vaguely encoded, struck a chord within Calimus. He gave Alexander an understanding glance and joined him on bended knee. The bishop smiled approvingly and uttered the same blessing.

"God be with you. God protect you. God be your light in the darkness. Amen." The bishop returned the vial into his pocket and the men stood confident and ready.

"Evil is ahead of us," the bishop whispered as the group moved forward bravely.

Malachius was proved correct moments later for when they arrived at the heart of a large chamber another cold wind, this time bone chilling as opposed to bone killing, rushed through the chamber and made their hair stand on end.

"I've been expecting you," a voice said in the shadows.

"All of you." The men behind Alexander drew their swords quickly and prepared for an onslaught.

The Alveun soldiers took a half-moon position around the voice. Alexander's men spread out arms-length from one another and placed their shields firmly in front of them. Alexander remained calm, keeping his sword sheathed and issued his response.

"Do all of you hide in the shadows? Is there not one of you with the courage to face me as a warrior? Reveal yourself and do your worst," Alexander challenged.

A robed man stepped out from the shadows on the other side of the small river that ran through the cavern. One hand held a sorcerer's staff which glowed crystal blue and he stretched forth the other hand.

"I am disappointed," Alexander mocked.

"I was expecting Abiyram and not one of his servants."

"You'll find I am no servant," the robed man replied. "I am Nicodemus, and I have been waiting so long for this meeting between us."

"Very well," Alexander said and smiled,

"let's get on with it then." He directed his men to their places. Katrina took an arrow and fitted it into her bow. With one swift motion, she aimed it at the sorcerer.

"In the name of God," Malachius walked in front of Alexander and bellowed, "And as His servant I command you to submit to His will. Put down your tools of evil and save your soul from torment."

Their opponent closed his eyes and chanted a few quiet words. "I do not fear you or your God, Malachius. I am fear incarnate!" He chanted more words and raised his staff in the air.

"Katrina! Loose!" Alexander ordered and Katrina let her arrow fly toward the enchanter. He stopped chanting momentarily and lifted his hand towards the incoming arrow. It stopped in mid-flight and dropped harmlessly to the ground.

"Katrina, keep your arrows pointed at his heart. Men, we're going over the river." Alexander advanced on the water as Katrina let another arrow fly.

Sofia also drew her sword and advanced on the river while the bishop stood near Katrina. Her arrow again dropped harmlessly to the ground and the chants grew louder.

A sudden burst of light flew from the top of Nicodemus' staff and flew through the chamber. Alexander and his men lost their balance as the earth shook beneath them. They jumped back up on their feet quickly and made sure their bodies were intact.

They cautiously advanced their way over the river as the sorcerer backed up and placed his staff on the ground. He raised his arms and mocked the warriors, the staff staying completely still

"How many Alveuns do you need for one old man? Look, I have put my staff down. Can not one of you face me unarmed?"

His laughter filled their hearts with an uneasiness and they slowed their advance.

The sorcerer closed his eyes mumbling incoherently until he at last picked his rod up. He swung his weapon in a circle above his head and again a blast of light flew from his staff.

Alexander fell to his knees and rubbed his eyes as he tried desperately to focus his sight on the ground beneath him. He had lost sight, the flash had temporarily suspended his vision.

"Alex?" Calimus shouted.

"We should leave!"

"Stand fast!" Alexander yelled back as his eyesight began to return. "This old man's tricks are not enough to delay his judgment."

"You must submit to God's judgment!" Bishop Malachius shouted and Alexander noticed the bishop was the only one who never fell. He stood defiantly against each trick. Alexander scrambled back to his feet as a rumbling noise grew within the chamber.

"Prince Alexander, forgive me for my deceit," the priest said mockingly.

"I am not alone. You will, of course, recognize my friends."

A familiar face appeared alongside the priest. Her appearance had changed much since the last time Alexander saw her.

Her once beautiful features were now haggard and no flicker of emotion could be seen on her face.

"Hello, Alex," she said flatly. "I see you've brought me your friends."

"Is this all you can summon conjurer?" Alexander replied sarcastically.

"You bring Angelica as your protection. With my apologies love, the last place you want to be is between me and this man."

"What?!" Sofia shrieked, a look of horror creeping over her face. "Alexander, is that our maid?"

Alexander remembered that Sofia had asked where Angelica went, because she was no longer in the castle. Alexander had forgotten to tell her which, of course, would serve to agitate Sofia more.

"It's not just me," Angelica said.

Calimus shrieked loudly and Alexander turned around. His brother struggled against a hand that arose from the ground. The hand held onto him tightly and refused to let go as he struggled. The Prince freed himself and at the same moment the hand let go, a body ripped through the sand and sat up. It screeched some inaudible words while staring at Calimus with the vilest of intentions.

All the men gasped and took several steps back except Alexander, who walked over to it calmly and stopped it from screaming by severing the head from its body. The head dropped to the ground and its body slumped over lifelessly.

Alexander turned and smiled triumphantly at the sorcerer, but Nicodemus merely nodded and pointed towards the walls of the chamber behind him.

Alexander hadn't noticed, but the wall of the chamber functioned as a catacomb. In every few feet on the wall, a hole had been dug into it and hands were grabbing the sides and pulling their bodies out. When they were free of the tombs, they reached back and dragged whatever weapons they were buried with. Most had axes. None of the weapons were in good condition. Several of the axes were chipped and rusted, but sharp enough to do their damage.

The Alveun soldiers were the first to be targeted with their bloodlust. As the dead soldiers brandished their weapons, they attacked the soldiers in fury. Angelica joined the fray and one by one they began to overwhelm each soldier.

The guards along with the siblings quickly moved back into the river as other bodies began to claw their way out of the ground beneath them.

Bodies also began to rise on the other side of the stream near the enchanter and Angelica.

"What is this evil?" Calimus yelled terrified.

"I have warned you all," Alexander responded. "They have the power to raise the dead!"

"I'm sorry my son, for not believing you," Bishop Malachius said quietly. His grim expression quietly accepted that the notion of heresy no longer applied here. Whether his textbooks called it a lie, the sword in these dead soldier's hands were quite real.

The Alveun soldiers that were still on the wrong side of the river fought bravely and managed to hold off the vicious creatures for a moment. Although able to take wound after wound, the dead acted as vicious animals and kept hacking at the soldiers. Several of the soldiers screamed in agony as swords went through their bodies.

"Help us!" their captain begged Alexander. The Prince took a deep breath and motioned to his men. They came back over the stream and pushed their way forward past several of the dead who stood in their path.

Calimus joined them in an effort to prove his worth.

"Farkas! Protect Alexander and Calimus!" Jack ordered. It was too late to save the Alveun soldiers. Each one of them had succumbed to the onslaught of the madness the sorcerer had created.

They paused from hacking at the fallen men in order to encircle Alexander and his men. They waited for the last command from their master to tear Alexander apart.

The atmosphere was filled with tension. Sofia crept to her brother's side and kept her sword drawn. He made eye contact with her.

"I will protect you," he whispered.

"They will not lay a hand on you."

"Katrina?" A voice from behind the sorcerer broke the standoff. Katrina peeked from behind Malachius and her eyes widened.

"Daddy?" Her voice broke as she took another step away from Malachius. The Bishop grabbed Katrina's arm and pulled her back towards him.

"Don't Katrina. It's not your father anymore."

"Katrina, why are you with these men? They mean to harm you. Run to us, now!" Katrina tried to pull away, but Malachius held her arm tightly.

"Katrina! Listen to me!" Alexander shouted.

"That is not your father anymore!" He was closer than Katrina and realized that her father was dead. A huge chunk of flesh had been cut off his shoulder, more than likely a result of a death blow.

"Enough! Kill them!" Angelica shouted. The soldiers, who to that point had waited for a command, ran towards the small party in an attempt to overwhelm them. The remaining Alveuns found themselves locked in battle as they engaged their swords at the advancing corpses.

"The heads! Separate the heads!" Alexander commanded as he swung his sword and separated one dead man's head from his body.

"Kevin?" Jack asked in amazement. Alexander recognized the faces of their attackers and realized the worst.

"They are the villagers from Greystone," he murmured sadly.

"Katrina?" A voice yelled over the din of swords.

"Mommy?" Katrina broke free from Malachius' side and ran towards the stream. The dead ignored her as they struggled with the soldiers and allowed her to pass through. She stopped nervously when she made eye contact with the sorcerer and looked at her parents who stood next to him. Nicodemus made a sweeping gesture as if he gave her permission to pass.

"Jack! Help me!" Alexander shouted as he tried to free himself from three others that struggled to bring him down.

He punched one in the face, but it had no effect. It screeched at him and threw the prince to the ground. The other two dead men flipped Alexander over onto his back and tried to wrestle the sword from his hand.

Jack's sword swung through and beheaded the one that stood over him allowing Alexander to squirm his way out of the hold that the other two had on him. Together he and Jack swiftly decapitated the other two.

Sofia tried to make her way to Katrina but found herself face-to-face with Angelica.

"Hello Princess," Angelica said sardonically.

"Angelica? What have they done to you?" Sofia asked with earnest concern. She had always liked Angelica as someone who was close to her age and tried to take her under her wing.

"You mean what has your brother done to me?" Angelica snarled. She raised her sword and sent it crashing down. Sofia blocked it and backed away.

"Doesn't he tell you anything, Sofia? Did he tell you how he pretended to love me and made advances towards me?"

Sofia's eyes widened.

Angelica's lips curled in an empty smile.

"I see how much he tells you." She launched another vicious attack at Sofia which Sofia managed to fend off, but not without effort. She stumbled a bit, but she managed to keep her balance to avoid falling over.

"Katrina, hurry to us," Katrina's mother shouted. "Do not let them take you. They deceive you." Katrina hesitated but began to cross the stream. Her mother and father walked through the melee and held out their hands to help her across the water. Katrina reached up to take their offer of help.

Alexander ran as fast as he could to the stream and launched himself towards it with all of his power. He brought his sword up and with one clean strike he separated Katrina's father's head from its body. He landed on his feet, spun around, and in one motion took her mother's head for good measure.

"No!" Katrina screamed. The young girl froze in the stream with the water up to her knees. She started sobbing and moved towards her mother's body.

Turn and block.

Alexander listened to the armor and wheeled around in time to block Angelica's vengeful swing. She brought down her sword with all of her strength. Sofia had been rescued by Jack and Calimus and together they safely escorted her to the other side of the waters.

Alexander noticed that Angelica had more power than he did and he did everything he could to keep her sword off of him. She pressed and pressed and he felt himself buckling under the pressure.

The dead wench grew impatient and threw him backward into the water. She refrained from following him, and stood there offering her hands to Katrina.

"Katrina, you belong with us. Alexander has killed your parents just like he killed me." Katrina stopped sobbing and inexplicably reached her hands out to Angelica.

"No!" Alexander shouted. He thrashed through the water to grab Katrina and carried her across the stream. She yelled in objection and kicked at him.

"You killed my parents! You lied to me! You said you would save them. You are a murderer!" He held on to her even as her feet and hands connected with his body. He dropped to the other side of the stream and held her head next to his.

"Stop this madness," he whispered as she struggled. "Your parents were already dead." He clenched his teeth tightly. "I have saved your life."

"You're a monster," she replied sadly. He ignored her tears and carried her to Jack who finished off the last of the dead who had followed them across the stream.

"Is that it?" Alexander called out to Nicodemus. The old man had sat on a nearby rock to watch the attempted decimation of the Alveuns.

He frowned and stroked his beard.

A few moments later, he rubbed his face in frustration and removed the hood from his head. He was balding and had strands of hair that looked out of place on his head.

"Nicodemus, I am arresting you for compliance in the murder of Edward, Prince of Alveus. Will you come peaceably?"

Nicodemus laughed at Alexander's demand.

"You have lost half of your men, and there are less than ten of you here."

"And there's only you and Angelica," Calimus added.

"We've killed your army!" He exclaimed confidently.

The sorcerer mumbled more chants from his side of the stream. Bodies from undisturbed portions of dirt reached their hands above the soil. Alexander sighed and quickly counted at least fifty hands.

"Jack, pull everyone out of here and get to the horses. Calimus, Farkas, Your Grace....follow him, we don't have much time."

"Sir? What about you?" Jack wiped sweat from his face and took Katrina's hand.

"Go now!" Alexander ordered.

"Everyone needs to get out now!"

Jack and the others obeyed and ran along the path to the entrance to the chamber. Alexander sheathed his sword at his side and drew the fire sword he had fastened to his back. The sword glowed red in his hands and he felt the heat rise, but his hands did not burn.

He had been given the fire sword that, as he understood, burned through evil.
It failed to produce a spark around men and was a mere tool of death, but near this evil, it could produce a wall of fire.

"I know that sword," the old sorcerer commented. He cocked his head for a better look.

"Why not put that sword down and give it to me. If you give it to me, I will let you and your siblings live."

"I do not need anyone's protection," Alexander breathed heavily as he focused his thoughts.

Several corpses freed themselves from the soft earth and ran up the path towards the chambers entrance in an attempt to follow his men. Alexander closed his eyes and brought the sword above his head and quickly thrust it down towards the earth.

A maelstrom of fire encircled Alexander and it swept forward to the dead in front of him and burned their flesh down to their bones.

They fell harmlessly to the surface and the ones that attempted to follow Alexander's men also met their fate quickly. The fire shot forward to the sorcerer, but Nicodemus raised his staff in command of his elements. The water from the river made a wall and the fire bounced off of blandly, producing a stalemate.

Alexander grabbed his fire sword and ran towards the wall of water.

He jumped through the sheet of water, surprising the old man and the dead warriors that surrounded him.

He swung the sword at Angelica which she easily blocked but then he kicked her in the ribs and the force carried her to the ground.

He grabbed the evil man by the neck and as the wall of water fell back into the stream he pulled Nicodemus backward into the waters with him. The water collapsed upon them and sent a shower of water into the ranks of the dead. Upon hitting some of them, the water caused some of the flesh to burn. Two corpses collapsed completely as the flesh dissipated and no longer held their bones together.

Alexander pulled Nicodemus with him onto the other side of the stream and brought the sword to his throat.

"Do I kill you now, or will you be my prisoner?" He asked the sorcerer with an even tone.

"It is completely up to you."

"I would like to remind you that again, you trespass on our lands, noble prince." Nicodemus looked at him defiantly. "This is another deed that will not go unpunished."

"I do not care about your punishments nor do I care what words you use.
You and your people are responsible for the death of my brother. I will kill every last one of you if you do not give me what I want. You will hand over Duncan or you will forfeit your life. Are we understood?"

"Yes, I understand." The enemy's face was soured with contempt for his predicament.

"On your feet then." Alexander pulled the old man up to his feet and pushed him towards the path leading out of the cave.

"Alexander, my love," a voice sang out.

"Yes, my angel?" Alexander replied sarcastically.

"I will see you soon."

"I look forward to it. In the meantime, you might want to freshen up. I would recommend a bath. It would do wonders for your complexion. You have something, right here." Alexander pointed towards a blotch of skin that had been eaten away by the water.

Angelica launched her sword at Alexander and it hurtled through the air. He sidestepped it so it smashed against the wall harmlessly and dropped to the ground.

"Temper, Love," he smirked and continued to push the sorcerer to the entrance.

Alexander exited the cave with his prisoner and his appearance elicited the joy of his companions.

Jack clapped him on the back and Calimus gave him a great hug, more out of relief than love. The women were less pleased to see him. Sofia confronted him immediately.

"What was that?" she shouted.

"What?" Alexander questioned.

"I have rather enjoyed this trip for it gives me a chance to see what kind of man by brother is becoming."

"I don't understand what you are saying," Alexander said hotly. "I just captured a sorcerer and you are arguing with me?"

He pointed at Nicodemus who smiled and said, "Don't mind me, I rather enjoy this."

"Shut up!" Sofia shouted.

"Tell me about Angelica. She was our kitchen maid and you made love to her!"

"I knew it!" Calimus exclaimed.

"You knew it?" Sofia said in exasperation.

"You know nothing!" Alexander argued.

"There was never anything inappropriate that went on. I never made love to her."

"Oh, but I bet you tried, brother." Calimus grinned at the ability to dig into Alexander.

"I caught him sneaking forlorn looks at her. He had a severe case of forbidden love, and as I heard it, tried to sneak off with her. That's why she left isn't it?"

"Go to hell." Alexander got in Calimus' face. He glared hatefully at his brother and pointed a finger in his chest. "You say one more word, any word, and I will make it your last."

Sofia pushed them apart and started pounding on his chest. "What is wrong with you? You don't talk like that to your family! But I guess you don't even talk to your family do you? I am so upset with you!" Sofia started crying.

"It's not fair. What did I do to get shut out?"

"I have a feeling I am going to enjoy this journey," Nicodemus said gleefully. "I love the hatred that I am feeling right now. You have so much of it," he motioned to Alexander. "There's so much power with hatred. Use it."

Alexander regained his composure and ignored the cajoling from the sorcerer.

"We need to move now before they figure out how to follow us. Chauncey, have the dogs moved?"

"Haven't moved. They just watch and wait." The men breathed a sigh of relief because the family quarrel had passed and the awkwardness dissipated.

Alexander sighed for he figured they would make a move while he was in the cave. They did not and now their actions were even more curious. Would they wait to strike when they were unprepared to defend themselves?

"Heathen," Alexander spat the derogatory term at Nicodemus.

"I have a name," came the reply.

"It does not matter to me what your name is. What matters to me is in what direction does my enemy lie?" Alexander pointed his sword at the barbarian's neck and prepared to shove the sword through his throat.

"Duncan will seek you out. Have no fear. His anger for his sister still burns uncontrollably."

"Tell us where Duncan is so we can leave!" Calimus begged.

"I am not privy to the machinations of my master. I am merely an instrument."

"I'm the harbinger of death," Alexander whispered quietly in Nicodemus' ear. "I will prove that to you as you watch me destroy your people and your way of life. How many of your people die rest squarely on these shoulders. Remember that."

"What will we do with this heretic?" The bishop asked.

"We will bring him with us so that he may witness all that he has brought upon his people."

"Alex, maybe it is best for you to hand him over to the church. We may be able to convince him to part with his secrets." The bishop approached Nicodemus and muttered to no one in particular.

"We'll see how long this heretic keeps secrets when he stand before God."

Nicodemus laughed at the Bishop. "You and your religion, nothing but fear and politics. You have no power. I have all of the power. If not for Alexander standing between us I would bring you to your knees and you would submit to me as your master."

"You will never inhabit our lands. Your time of existence is at an end." Malachius splashed some holy water on the sorcerer who shook his head in annoyance.

"The future is already written," Nicodemus sneered, "And it has already been revealed.

We will sit in power in Middlebrooke and you will be no more. The Royal Family and the nobility will be gone, the church will be eradicated, and we will once again lord over our lands. If any of you surrender now, I will consider being merciful."

The men fell silent and looked uneasily at each other. Bishop Malachius pulled Alexander aside and talked with him.

"Alexander, I must take leave of you.

"What? Why?"

"I must return to my abbey and report what we have discovered. It is important that I return with this news as soon as possible."

"You would desert me then? You would leave me on a path to destruction? I would have thought you would like to see where all of this ends."

"Alexander, you will find a way because your destiny will continue to keep you on that path. It was foolish of us to come out here, but since we have and we know what lies ahead, I must follow my path. My prayers are with you and I will send you whatever support I can."

"What about the hellhounds?" Alexander motioned to the area where the dogs still abided.

"I worry not about them. I do not think they worry about me much. They only have contempt for me. If you move now, they will certainly follow you rather than me."

"It is agreed then." Alexander and the Bishop clasped hands and shook them.

"Godspeed my son."

Malachius mounted his horse and Alexander directed Nicodemus to mount Katrina's horse. Alexander went to Katrina who had sat on a nearby rock and said nothing.

"You will ride with me, Katrina."

"I'm not going anywhere with you." She yelled. She folded her arms defiantly and refused to look at him.

"I understand what you think you saw, Katrina."

"I saw you behead my parents! You swore to me that you would save them!"

Alexander held his hands in the air and motioned for her to stop yelling. "Katrina, I grieve for your loss, but your parents were already dead. This is what they," he pointed at the evil man, "This is what they do. They cut out your heart, bury you, and then resurrect you to fight for them. If there was any way I could have saved them, I would have done so. You must believe me."

Katrina sobbed into her hands and refused to face Alexander.

"I hate you," she said quietly.

"Fine. Then ride with Sofia or in the wagon with Keira and the gryphon. You will direct me the way to Duncan."

"I'd rather go with the bishop."

"I can't let you do that, Katrina. You are coming with us, I would prefer it if you chose it willingly."

Katrina stopped crying for a moment and wiped her eyes. She took refuge in the wagon and refused to engage with anyone.

Alexander and Jack mounted their horses and after a brief exchange with Malachius rode north and away from the cave.

Bishop Malachius whirled around and rode towards the forest and just as he had predicted, the giant black dogs picked up Alexander's trail and ignored the Bishop as he returned to Edgebrooke.

CHAPTER VI

The riders left the mountain pass quickly and traveled into the uncharted north as Katrina led them on the trail of Edward's killer. Cartographically, Alexander had often noticed that the maps showed first the borders, then the Northern Forests as the Frontier, and the beyond the Northern Forests was the Shadowlands. Because the Alveun army had few survivors from their last excursion into the Shadowlands, no one had taken the time to chart their path. The best course of action was to plot the course of the sun and follow it. The further north they went, the closer they would come to their destination. Alexander joked that they were the first to journey north willingly, with Calimus carrying on in sharp disagreement.

Katrina's path took them through the remainder of the forest and brought them to a badlands, which she described as a tiny desert which appeared to carry on for miles.

Nicodemus discouraged the riders and lied to them that the desert was an endless expanse and there was no water for miles. Katrina insisted it wasn't. They bedded down for the night and headed through the badlands the next day. Katrina proved it was a smaller distance and after a day of riding they came to a set of three small dormant volcanos that stood as monuments to the land's creation.

Katrina explained that, from the top of the volcanos, they would be able to see the beginnings of a lush woodland, a river, and a village that lay nearby. It was there that their antagonists had stopped for supplies before they moved on. Katrina had not followed them any further as her situation had become perilous and she feared discovery. The riders paused momentarily as Alexander contemplated the situation from his horse.

He beckoned Jack to follow, and with Katrina riding with him, the three made their way to the top of the tallest volcano and dismounted once they arrived at its pinnacle.

"Out there is a village," Katrina pointed out. They weren't very far from it. There were some trees but from where they stood, Alexander could make out the shapes of huts.

"Do you know how many warriors live there?" Jack asked kindly.

Katrina responded that she didn't.

"You are a brave girl," Jack encouraged.

"You have done a masterful job getting us here." Katrina gave Jack a half smile then turned to gaze over the horizon.

"I think we'll bed down here for the day," Alexander mused.

"I will figure out what to do, and whatever that comes to will be in the early hours of the dawn. We'll catch them sleeping."

"You going to kill them too?" Katrina's voice was like a dagger to him.

"If they get in my way," he responded with a matter-of-fact shrug. "Come now. Let's make camp at the base."

"I'll sleep here," she pointed to a nearby hole in the rock. It was large enough for a child to fit in.

"Suit yourself," Alexander said.

"I hope a wolf doesn't pick up your scent." He walked off with Zeus in tow and carefully made his way down the volcano.

"Farkas?" he called out to his chief scout. Farkas rode up to Alexander and listened for his orders. His matted, greasy hair and his dirty appearance made him the least favorite among Alexander's bodyguard, but no one tracked man or animal better. He resisted sleeping on beds, and instead insisted on the floor, with his preference being a straw bedding.

"Yes, My Lord?"

"Scout ahead for me. Take Devin and Keira with you. If you see any sign of life, return immediately."

Alexander whistled for Keira to follow Farkas. The two men saluted Alexander and headed to the forest. The rest of his men began to build a small campsite for the night. While they built their campsite, Nicodemus entertained them with his commentary.

"You should make sure to build a very large fire," he said excitedly. "The inhabitants of this forest are very accommodating for your needs. They will not hesitate to kill you when they find you." His even tone irritated Calimus who did his best not to show his concern.

"If this is true, you should be happy to return to them."

Alexander shot an irritated look in Nicodemus' direction but pushed his feelings outside of his mind.

The enchanter continued,

"They are my servants and they will free me. Let us not forget that the dead also hunt you."

"The dead?" Chauncey asked startled. "What's this about the dead?"

"It seems that these sorcerers have found a way to raise the dead," Jack explained. "The dead rise with no ideas of pain, no feelings, no memories and they attack without fear or care."

"They do have memories," Katrina whispered bitterly. Alexander sighed when he heard her but was glad she had decided to leave her solitude on top of the ridge.

"So how do you kill the dead?" Fergus asked.

"Separate head from the body," Jack replied.

"That ends their life."

"I don't know if I agree with that," Fergus commented.

"You don't agree with what we fought in the cave?" Jack said with annoyance.

"I know what we saw."

"Well, I'm not disagreeing with what you said, just how you said it."

"Oh, do tell brother," Chauncey said with a hint of sarcasm.

"It just appears to me, that if they are dead, they are not living. If they are not living, then they can't die because they are dead." Fergus raised his hands with a knowing look.

The other men grunted and continued their labor.

"I'm not following you and I was in the cave," Calimus said holding his head in mocked pain.

"You can't take life from the dead. That is what I am telling you," Fergus argued.

"But they're not dead anymore," Calimus shot back.

"So they're living?" Fergus queried.

"No," Jack interjected,

"They're the dead army."

"That goes to my point then," Chauncey said triumphantly, "That they cannot cease to live because they are dead, ergo to say that cutting off their heads ends their life is rubbish."

"Are you calling my words rubbish?" Jack began to redden in anger.

"I'm just explaining that it's a minor question of semantics."

"Holy hop toads Chauncey," Fergus crowed,

"What would you call it then?"

"I don't know, but you haven't killed them because they're already dead."

"They are undead," Calimus added.

"That's not a word. I don't care if you are the Prince of Alveus. You cannot go around making up words that are not real."

"I'm pretty sure he can, Chauncey," Alexander said as he grinned back at his guard.

"But sir, it takes many scholars to agree that the word does indeed have merit."

"Divine right teaches us that Princes and Kings can do whatever they want because God tells us." Alexander grinned at the guard again. Since his arrival in Alveus, Chauncey had begun, in a manner of speaking, to stalk scholars. His appetite for learning was voracious and in a very short time, had learned to read and write. This gave him a sense of superiority over some of the other men, and he delighted in arguing with them.

"Thank you, Alexander," Calimus said delightedly. "So from now on we will refer to what we have done as 'deading the undead'."

"But you cannot say that. It doesn't make any sense. No scholar would accept that phrase or those words." Chauncey's mocking had changed to a very serious expression.

"Sorry Chauncey, but Prince Calimus and I are in agreement. 'Deading the undead' it is," Alexander ruled with a wink.

Chauncey looked crestfallen and sulked as he muttered over the manipulation and violation of the semantics of their language.

Sofia rolled her eyes at them.

"It's nice to see the secrets of your guard finally being revealed." She sat on a blanket and leaned against her horse's saddle.

"The mystery of the greatest warriors in Alveus."

"What?" Jack laughed awkwardly and humbly added. "We aren't the greatest."

The men nodded their agreement and went about clearing the campsite.

"Come now, I have seen you all in action! Let's play a game. We have spent very little time getting to know each other so I am going to guess where Alexander found you, and you tell me if I am right or not!"

The men agreed tentatively if she agreed to wager some coin on how close she was to the truth. Calimus impishly tossed some coins in as well for when money was involved, he was all ears.

"Let's start with Jack," Sofia started. Jack was attending to a plate of vegetables and cured meat for Sofia and handed it to her.

"This one is simple. Handsome Jack has an air of authority and able to complete tasks with little or no supervision. He's built like a Bete'szek. I wager," she thought carefully,

"You are a blacksmith and from the area around Edgebrooke."

"Not bad," he said,

"You're correct."

"That's not all," Calimus added.

"He owned that shop I wager or co-owned it with his father or grandfather."

"Right again," Jack nodded.

"You are an open book, Jack. That's what I like about you," Sofia smiled.

"Now on to Chauncey and Fergus."

"This should be fun," Fergus commented. Chauncey rolled his eyes and went about his work laying out the weapons in an efficient manner. Each man would sleep with sword and axe by his side.

"You are twins and you are trouble. You swing swords with ease and look like your red heads have been busted a time or two in a fight. You have probably been in prison, not for anything smart, and you are miners. Am I right?"

"I have never been to prison!" Fergus insisted. "That's slander!"

"Easy now," Jack said.

"Tell the truth."

"That was Chauncey's fault! And it was only once." Fergus threw his hands in the air in mock protest, and Chauncey gave him an 'is that so' look.

Jack also gave Fergus a cold hard stare.

"Alright," Fergus whined.

"But it was his fault not mine." He looked Chauncey's way and continued.

"Chauncey was always talking me into all sorts of trouble, and we visited the sheriff on a weekly basis."

"Oh, I see," Chauncey added, shaking his head. "You're the good twin. It never mattered if we tried to be good, with our red hair, the townspeople expected us to steal their souls."

"It's an ironic twist of fate that we are fighting for them to keep their souls," Fergus mourned.

No, Alexander laughed to himself. These curly redheads are still trouble, regardless of how much they fight for me.

"Very good Sofia," Calimus gleefully rubbed his hands together and took out three gold coins.

"They'll be broke before they wished never to tangle bets with a Wolfield!"

"Now for another easy one," she grinned.

"Gerard. With your well-manicured appearance and your taste for fine linen, I guess you come from a noble family?"

Gerard frowned but nodded his head in agreement.

"Let's not forget the girls swoon over him when he is in town," Calimus added with a wink.

"Ha!" Sofia exclaimed then giggled.

"You're not an Alveun?"

"The hell I'm not!" Gerard bellowed.

"I was born in Edgebrooke. I was part of the town watch. I've never been anywhere else. Now you owe me the coins."

"Wait," Calimus interjected.

"You're on to something sister. Look at those cheekbones and that skin. He tans easier than our fair skin. You were born in Alveus?"

Gerard nodded.

"But your parents weren't? What are they?" Calimus slapped Sofia's back in enjoyment.

"You are very good at this," he remarked.

Gerard was extremely irritated. The rest of the group poked and prodded at him until he finally gave in.

"My name is Gerard Tildor, son of Santhil Tildor. My parents came here from the lands of Kimdar." Gerard bit his lip and sat down. The other men looked at each other and wrinkled their noses. They wouldn't say it publicly, but Kimdar was a far-off tribe that didn't have a very good reputation. They were thought of as a more than an inept nomadic people. It was no wonder that Gerard wanted to keep that a secret.

"It doesn't matter where your parents are from," Sofia said.

"You are an Alveun and you fight like the great warriors of old."

She managed to get a smile and a nod from Gerard and an encouragement from Alexander to stop, which she ignored.

"The other brothers, Linus and Mayer. With your sunburnt skin and your calloused hands, I wager that Linus and Mayer are farmers. Why so silent all the time?"

They shrugged.

"Comes with the job," Linus said.

"You work in the fields all day, you get used to not speaking."

Mayer agreed.

"We would make great monks," he laughed.

"Who knows," his voice trailed off.

"Maybe when the land is at peace again."

"Aye," Linus went on.

"We are farmers in a different sense now. We traded plowshares for swords and now we separate the wheat from the chaff."

"Well said, Brother Linus," Mayer affirmed.

"Spoken like a priest."

"We win again!" Calimus giggled gleefully.

"Not exactly," Linus said.

"You have it right except that we aren't brothers."

"It must be a peasantry joke," Mayer continued. "All sons of peasants look the same."

The air turned awkward as Sofia stammered her way through. Linus and Mayer teased her a bit more and told her to pay no mind. They enjoyed Sofia blushing and flirted a bit, much to Alexander's chagrin.

"This is silly," Brennan said.

"I'm a blacksmith and so is Ferris. Not much guesswork needed there. Maybe if you could figure out where Farkas comes from."

"Why don't you know where Farkas comes from?"

"He doesn't say much to any of us," Jack said.

"He definitely isn't Alveun, but he isn't Bete'szek either."

"He's a cat," Linus joked.

"He prowls around all day looking sour because someone stole his milk."

The men let out a guffaw, but Alexander scolded them for teasing the man when he was out of sight. There's no honor in that, he reminded them.

It was Sean's turn to reveal a portion of himself. He and his brother Devin were there with Alexander and Jean when they were almost sacrificed.

Their father was a spy for the Church and they grew up in a tiny house with some field work and some animal work.

They had a higher ambition than just being soldiers but weren't quite sure what they wanted to do. They had almost settled on being merchants but figured a long career in the military was what they needed.

By the time their stories were done, it was time to bed down for the night. Alexander took leave of the camp and went to the top of the volcano to catch another glimpse of the lay of the land.

The gryphon followed him and begged for a snack on the way out. Alexander took some fruit out of his pouch and tossed it to the creature.

Thank you, it communicated to him, and its beak appeared to curve in a bit of a smile.

You seem to be getting bigger. With every day, you gain another inch. Alexander placed his hands next to the gryphon. It was now his hands length, the size of a small adult dog.

Alexander felt a wind start to lift his spirit out of his soul. He closed his eyes and when he opened them, he was in the Gryphon's world. He found himself sitting on a throne in the temple.

"Why am I sitting on a throne," he asked?

"Because it was made for you," came a familiar voice.

"Brendan?" Alexander asked curiously. He scanned the room until he recognized the familiar face. The last time he saw Brendan was in a hut before it was about to collapse. He had taken off with the last adult gryphon in Alveus. The prophet walked across the room until he stood before Alexander.

"Your Highness," he said and bowed to him.

"How are you here? What is this place?" Alexander asked the questions quickly and eagerly.

"This is a meeting place for, lacking a better term, the spirit world. The gryphons use this place to communicate with each other as one. At their peak, these halls would be filled with their statues. As time went on, it became emptier and emptier." Brendan pointed to a statue. "See, we have a visitor."

"If it's for gryphons, then how are we here?" Alexander made his way to the statue and patted it on its head.

"That's not what I am here for," the gryphon warned him. "I am not a dog, don't pat me like one."

"Gryphons are very prideful," Brendan interceded. "It would be as if your dad did that to you. As to your question of how we are here: The gryphon's blood bonded with yours. You now have the key to passing back and forth between the physical world and this one."

"Do you have gryphon's blood too?" Alexander asked.

"No," Brendan laughed.

"I am a guardian of this land. I would go into more detail, but you would find the story impossible to believe."

"Try me," Alexander challenged.

"I have had a lot of unbelievable moments. I'm still alive too if you'd care to congratulate me."

"Why would I?" Brendan frowned.

"You served your purpose and your fate had been decided. Your brother's death has thrown the written accounts into chaos. Fate and destiny are scrambling for a back-up plan and one man is seeking to plunge this world into madness. The scales have been knocked out of balance. Do you understand what I am saying, Alexander?"

Alexander admitted that he did not understand. Brendan sighed and placed a hand on the Prince's shoulder as a concerned father would.

"You are brilliant," Brendan said.

"I can see why he saved you. We will just have to manage this time until we have another chance of slaying Abiyram. Our time is short Alexander, I will see you soon."

With a flash of light, the dream ended. Alexander found himself stumbling back onto a rock but steadied himself in time to avoid a catastrophic end. The gryphon looked at him curiously and stretched out its wings.

You'd better learn to fly and quick, Alexander quietly stated. *I have a feeling you're going to need to take to the skies soon.*

CHAPTER VII

Alexander had fallen into a deep sleep and for once, slept well. He was eventually awakened early by the sounds of a rustle in the camp. He opened his eyes and caught sight of a figure running from the campsite. He followed it quietly until it came to a large bush. The sound of retching could be heard coming from it.

"Sofia? What's the matter?" He rushed to Sofia as she was steadying herself to throw up the previous night's meal.

"Talk to me," he urged.

"I feel poisoned," she moaned. She threw up again. Alexander threw her arm around his neck. He picked her up gently and carried her back to the campsite. The noise had woken up the others and they rushed to his aid.

"What's wrong with her?" Katrina asked, worried for her newfound friend.

"She is sick," Alexander replied and handed her over to Jack. "Like she was poisoned." He walked over to Nicodemus who had been bound the night before. He lifted him up, grabbed his ear, and walked back to his sister.

"Tell me what you have done," he demanded and pushed the sorcerer's head closer to Sofia.

"I haven't said two words to her," the sorcerer insisted.

Alexander accused him. "But you have poisoned her. Tell me now how to fix it and I may be merciful."

The sorcerer looked Sofia over and laughed.

"She's a picture of health my lord."

She pushed everyone away from her and vomited over a rock. Alexander punched Nicodemus so hard in the face that the sorcerer crumpled to the ground in pain. Alexander lifted him up to hit him again but was restrained by Brennan. Fortunately for Nicodemus, Brennan was so large that there was no way the enraged prince could get to him again.

"Careful boy!" Nicodemus warned.

"I could take her life very easily if I wanted to, but I haven't so you should be grateful."

"If she dies, you will die," Alexander warned.

"I said she's a picture of health," the sorcerer repeated. "She will be better in a few hours."

"I'm dying," Sofia moaned. Alexander grabbed Calimus and took him aside.

"I am at a loss for what to do," Alexander pleaded. "Tell me something that makes sense brother."

"We need to go back. She should never have made this trip." Calimus didn't mean the judgment behind his words.

"I told her to stay behind!" Alexander argued.

"And my men aren't back." The scouts were overdue.

"Stop talking about me," Sofia complained. She had recovered and joined their conference.

"You two or worse than a woman." She leaned on Alexander. "You are very sweet for carrying me, brother."

"We have to take you back," Calimus insisted.

To Alexander's surprise, Sofia agreed.

"Send a few of your men with me, but stay here and finish your duty."

"Do you mean that?" Alexander searched her eyes for any sense of insincerity and was relieved to find none. "If that is what you want. I will send everyone except the men on patrol, Jack, and the twins. Katrina will also stay with me."

"Take the wagon," Calimus said,

"So you can rest."

"No," Sofia insisted.

"That will take too long. We will take some supplies and leave immediately."

Alexander frowned for he had sworn to protect Sofia from harm. Sofia mussed his hair and squeezed his face in her hands.

"Stop frowning so much unless you want wrinkles!" She teased. "I know we have had some arguments, but I want you to know that I love you more than anything. You and Calimus better come home in one piece. Understand?"

The siblings said their goodbyes and Alexander's men set about tearing down the campsite. As soon as the horses were ready, Sofia and her guardsmen left on the southern route. Alexander said a quick prayer for her safety and bade his men to prepare their horses. They needed to find their lost patrol.

Once Sofia was safely out of sight, Alexander ordered his men to mount and start their trek into the woodland. Unlike the Northern Forests, this was a beautiful open-canopied forest.

The seasons had begun a change and the trees responded in kind. The leaves were in the midst of changing colors, from a beautiful green to yellows and reds. Autumn was non-existent in Alveus, for their trees stayed green year round. For a moment, the men were distracted over the colors and they picked a few samples to hold onto and display in Middlebrooke.

Most of the leaves had fallen, and this morning the start of a biting chill was evident as a few of the men put on an extra shirt for warmth.

"I always thought coming north was a journey into certain death," Fergus remarked. He tore a leaf off a tree and examined it, before crumpling it up and letting the wind carry the pieces away.

"It is certainly prettier than the stories I heard," Jack agreed. "Everywhere I turn, I see evidence of life. I see squirrels and rabbits, deer and boars. I'm surprised we haven't moved north will this land to expand."

"The forest is beautiful, but that same beauty causes our army to become ineffective," Alexander explained. "Our army is trained to fight in open spaces, with a heavy emphasis on horses. With this thick cluster of trees, our horses aren't as effective. Combine that with the fact that this is their home, they'd know every hiding place, and would just strike at us. Our ranks would become thinner, the troops would panic. No, this would be a ruinous place."

"I'm confused," Chauncey interjected.

"So is this the Shadowlands?"

Alexander pondered this for a moment.

"I don't think so. Every lesson I have had refers to a wasteland. When you think about it, our grandparents came through this very same forest on their way north.

They would have fought through this entire forest just to die there."

Jack shuddered. The thought had caused a cold chill to run through the group. "It is overwhelming, thinking that we follow in their same footsteps. It is also frightening, knowing that most of them didn't come back to their families."

"Good thing we're not married then," Fergus joked.

The companions became solemn, increasing their vigilance along their path. Katrina continued to lead in front, checking the position of the sun every few moments to make sure they were on the right path.

The distraction of nature's beauty ceased once they came to a large flowing river. Katrina stated the village was less than one hundred yards or so away from them, so they tied their horse's reigns to trees and began searching for a place to cross. Jack placed a gag over Nicodemus' mouth for assurance that he would remain quiet and not alert anyone else in the woods. Then he tied the man's hands around a tree trunk, ensuring there would be no escape.

Alexander, Chauncey, and Jack walked along the riverbank, looking for a place shallow enough for them to cross. As they walked along,

Fergus spotted four Bete'szek warriors on the other side of the bank and whistled to the group to hide. They did so and watched as the Bete'szek walked up and down the embankment. They were both very large men, wearing fur coats to protect against the chill. To Alexander, they looked very different then when he last saw them. The war paint they usually wore was not painted on, making them look human. Katrina had led them to the right place.

The barbarian axmen stopped for a moment at the river's edge. They stopped for a moment to fill their animal skins with water, gulping greedily and then filling them up again. Their leader looked downstream and across the river. Alexander's men ducked down behind their cover, staying still to not utter a sound.

Satisfied there was no one in sight, the lead Bete'szek grunted orders to his men. They pulled themselves away from the water and continued to walk along the river.

"Whew," Alexander whispered to Jack, "It's just a patrol."

He motioned for Jack to tap the others on the shoulder and follow him.

They started to move opposite the Bete'szek when an alarm went up on the other side of the river.

"Swords," Alexander commanded.

He was confused as to whether the Bete'szek had spotted them or not, because they weren't running back into the bushes or across the river. Instead, the four warriors were backtracking to where they were first spotted.

"Katrina! Get your bow ready," Alexander ordered. Kneeling down, Katrina removed the quiver from her back and leaned it up against a rock. She took an arrow from its resting place and fitted one to her bowstring. She aimed it across the river and held very still.

Within moments, the object for the alarm appeared on the riverbank. Another two large warriors became appeared on the bank in front of the four warriors. A woman was dragged along by the hair and she struggled in vain to free herself. One of her captors gulped down a drink that drizzled down his beard and he wiped off the excess with his arm. He handed the pouch to his friend and threw the woman down on the ground. She hit the ground, turning over, and stretching out her hand in a plea to stop.

The other four warriors joined them in what appeared to be an argument over what to do with the woman.

The patrol leader pushed one of the other men who had brought the women to the riverbank.

They shouted back and forth at each other, with the men who brought her apparently winning the argument.

The patrol began walking away, leaving them to their fun.

The girl wept and begged for the men to have mercy upon her, even calling after the patrol to intervene. The bigger one laughed and unfastened his belt. His axe dropped to the ground and the woman, who realized her predicament, turned and tried running into the river. His companion caught her and pulled her beneath him. The other man finished what drink was in the gourd and laughed priggishly.

"Alexander!" Jack whispered. Jack had desperation in his eyes. Alexander realized that he wanted to intervene.

"Our concealment must be preserved," he whispered back. "There are six of them and we still need a place to cross."

"I think our best bet is right here. It's twelve feet from here to that side," Chauncey added.

"Would you have us swim across? So that we could be sitting targets? By the time we swam across, they would be gone to their villages."

"We must do something. What about Katrina?" Calimus had emerged from his hiding spot in the trees, having watched the scene on the river.

"One arrow, six men. Again, think with your head."

In the tree above him, a pair of wings flapped and a bird appeared above him. It was another raven, and it cocked its head at the Prince. The more intensely the raven stared at him, the more a mounting pressure started to build in his head. He hadn't had a headache in some time, and this was a bad time for it.

He bit his lip as hard as he could to not make a sound. The woman's cries for help affected everyone's well-being and added to the pain. Alexander struggled to think and make a decision.

Chauncey closed his eyes and muttered a prayer of protection. They all looked at their leader and their eyes begged for him to release them from their protected positions. Alexander said nothing and kept biting his lip. He grimaced a bit and sought relief by closing his eyes.

"Prince?" Jack hissed.

"What are your orders?"

Alexander grasped at his head, rubbing his temples, trying desperately to ease the pain. He was seeing stars, his vision was blurry, and he wanted to gasp in pain.

The worst of it, he wasn't able to think clearly. The pressure mounted, crippling him from making a decision.

The barbarian held on to the girl so tightly that some of her dress ripped. With a frightened yelp she kicked him between his legs. He howled in pain, and she used the confusion to again flee towards the river.

The patrol turned to watch, laughing and pointing at the man in pain. This infuriated his friend, and he went chasing the young lady. She hit the water ran as fast as she could. With each she took, her waist stayed above water. The prince struggled to form a coherent decision, but couldn't overcome his pain. It felt as though a hand squeezed his brain, and meant to crush his skull.

A horse's whinny echoed across the river and Alexander used that as an anchor to come out of his haze. Zeus' noise was timely for him, but not for his enemies. He turned his attention back to the two barbarians who had stopped in their merriment of tormenting the maiden. The original patrol began to ford the river in search of the reason for the sound. The Bete'szek weren't particularly fond of traveling by horse, so the sound of one was as close to an alarm of an ambush if there was one.

The barbarian finally grabbed the maiden's hair and pulled her back to shore.

The other man joined the four in walking across the river, giving the girl a well-timed slap as he passed by her. The five warriors cautiously waded through the water, with their gleaming axes out.

The pain in his head had subsided, and Alexander gave Jack the command to attack. Jack leaped up from his hiding place and ran into the river, followed by Chauncey and Fergus.

Alexander started late but once his body jumped into the cool water, he started feeling his strength return. The barbarians let out a cry of surprise when the guards appeared and when they spotted the armor, they realized who was coming after them. The gryphon had become their bane at Edgebrooke, so they turned to flee back across the river.

Jack fell upon the patrol leader and swung his sword at him. The axmen, sensing a blow, turned and blocked Jack's blow with his axe. The force of the hit caught the already off balance Bete'szek, and pushed him back into the river.

The axe fell back into the river, and jack made quick work of his enemy, stabbing the man in the chest with his sword.

Seeing their leader die, the barbarians ran even faster, trying to reach the riverbank.

An arrow whizzed by Alexander's head, and stuck in a barbarians back. The barbarian yelped and stumbled into the water. He struggled to regain his footing but Chauncey jumped on him and held his head under water until he stopped moving.

Alexander and Fergus ran unimpeded to the other side of the river. The three barbarians jumped out of the river, ready to run back to their village.

The fourth barbarian pushed the girl into the men's way to slow them down. He turned and followed his people into the trees to avoid Katrina's arrows.

As the barbarians reached the trees, the fighters heard a growl that made them hesitate following them. A large black dog leaped from its hiding place, onto one of the fleeing warriors. Her weight caught the man and brought him down. She tore at his arm and he howled in pain, trying to fight her off. The three remaining barbarians changed course, fearing more dogs, and ran up the riverbank. Two swordsmen appeared from the trees, cutting down the axmen with ease. The last barbarian was almost away, with no one around to stop him.

"Katrina!" Alexander shouted.

An arrow flew across the riverbank and struck the barbarian in the waist. He fell to the ground, still alive and tried to crawl away into the trees. Looking around at the barbarian faces, he realized it was the one that tried to violate the girl. Alexander whistled for Keira. Her prey, laying deadly still, was no longer a threat. He pointed her target and she went running down the shore. The barbarian was crying for help. Another arrow whizzed across the river, landing with a thud in his back. The man refused to give up, crawling out of view. Kiera found him easily, and his screams of death told Alexander the threat was over.

The men wiped their bloody swords on the barbarians' trousers, signaling their greatest insult, and sheathed their swords.

Alexander picked the maiden up from the river's mud and carried her to the embankment. Calimus and Katrina made their way across the river and they all gathered around the woman, making sure she was unharmed. The woman was traumatized, afraid of her new captors, and she laid on the ground sobbing.

Calimus voiced his displeasure to his brother.

"You would have let that happen?" Calimus challenged.

"Stop," Alexander warned. The pain had not completely subsided. If he could have spilt his own blood to ease the pain, Alexander would have done so. He angrily lashed back at Calimus, the pain pushing him on. "What if we gave ourselves away at the wrong moment? What then? Were you ready to die on that whim? Are you ever? There are times when a leader must sacrifice one for many. You would fare well to remember any lessons on leadership I may teach you." Alexander sat on a rock protruding out of the river and splashed cool water on his head and neck, seeking calmness.

The young woman had calmed a little but was still shaken over the shock of her experience. With her dress being torn, she held up a piece of her dress to cover herself. She was covered in dirt and mud and her long hair was messy and tangled. Alexander felt sympathy for her, a sign that he was starting to recover.

"Who are you?" he demanded.

When she looked at him, her eyes lit up and her tears disappeared as she recognized him.

"Prince Alexander?" She bowed respectfully and in spite of her situation.

"How do you know who I am?" He asked uncomfortably.

She looked up at him and her expression showed a bitter disappointment beneath the tears that ran down her cheeks.

"Prince Alexander, we have met before on your birthday. I am Lady Emma from the Northern Islands." She gently brushed her greasy hair away from her face and wiped the tears off her face. The tears managed to rub more of the dirt around her features, making her less recognizable.

Alexander kept his eyes fixated on her face and tried to piece together the images of his eighteenth birthday. He had been incredibly focused that night and left the castle which started the whole mess that the kingdom was in now.

He mentally moved past every character he interacted with that night and he vaguely referenced a freckle-faced young girl in his path. She initially left little impression upon him. Regardless the woman in front of him held no resemblance to her.

"You bear no resemblance to her. I fear you may be a spy, and until we know for sure, on your feet," he ordered, "Fergus, tie her up and place her with our prisoner."

Katrina protested her treatment, but Alexander had his reasons.

"We are in a foreign country, where many of our forefathers now lay sleeping, buried in the ground. My goal is not to treat people fairly and civilized. It's to make sure we return home when we are done. For all I know, she could be a witch or a sorcerer or an assassin. Which of you wants to vouch for her innocence. Will I be able to say I-told-you-so when we bury you?"

Fergus moved forward obediently and bound the woman's hands. Kiera rushed to Alexander's side and forced him to give her a great big hug.

He scratched her head and back when her exuberance got the best of her.

"Kiera, where have you been?" Alexander asked. Farkas swept his dirty black hair back across his face and eyed the girl.

"Tracking," Farkas replied with annoyance.

"We couldn't come back right away because of this lot. It was everything we could do to not be discovered. These people are everywhere. We followed these two pigs from the village because the villagers didn't seem to be concerned about this one at all."

"That's because I am a prisoner," the woman, who called herself Emma, insisted.

"I was brought here when their people raided my father's island.

They carried off most of us and I was brought here as a slave. I can lead you to the village and get you inside, but they are well armed."

Farkas laughed at the maiden's words with a sarcastic laugh.

"There's yet been born a Bete'szek that can kill any of us. I would rather have this magnificent dog at my side in a war than their best warriors." Fergus and Chauncey agreed in unison.

"I would prefer you silenced so that you are unable to alert them to our presence," Alexander explained as he placed his sword back in its scabbard.

"Please do not make me have to bind you any further. We'll go now in case these two are missed. Farkas and I will disguise ourselves and sneak into the village."

Alexander and Farkas exchanged their armor for the barbarians. These Bete'szek warriors wore patchwork leather armor, a weaker armor than the Alveun iron, which had given the Alveuns their prime advantage in war. The Bete'szek armor was good for avoiding scrapes in the underbrush, but nor for stopping spears. As Alexander finished adjusting the leather armor, Calimus approached him quietly.

"Alexander, I believe that you've made a mistake."

Alexander was shocked at Calimus' statement. Was Calimus really questioning one of my decisions, he thought.

"Which mistake would that be, brother?" Alexander furrowed his brow and glared at Calimus.

"The maiden that we have, I am sure that it is Lady Emma from the Northern Islands." Calimus eyed their prisoner carefully.

"How can you be so sure?"

"The two years that you were gone, she stayed with us. She is Sofia's closest confidante. I mean, besides you." Calimus looked extremely nervous as he waited for Alexander's response. The Prince studied the situation and Calimus' words carefully.

"How much time did you spend with her?" Alexander asked curiously.

"Not like that!" Calimus protested.

"Our sister would have made that the death of me. Obviously she grew from where you last saw her. She has certain features that make her easy to identify, washed or unwashed."

"Oh Calimus," Alexander sighed. His brother had an extreme penchant for the fairer sex, so maybe what he was saying made sense.

"Very well," Alexander whispered,

"But there are two things you will need to remember. One, she is in your care and you are responsible for her. Two, she is no longer nobility and will not be treated as such. She is not an Alveun and, therefore, has no loyalties to the Royal Family, which makes her no better than the Bete'szek out here. Am I understood?"

"Quite," Calimus said quietly.

"It appears that my brother has vouched for you, Emma." Alexander nodded at Fergus, who released her from the ropes that he had bound her with.

"You have my apologies."

"Thank you, Prince Alexander, and thank you, Prince Calimus. I was not aware that I had made such an impression upon you." She curtsied before the brothers and smiled kindly.

"Because I was drunk. Yes, thank you. I may be a drunk, but I am not blind as to your beauty and charm." Calimus smiled flirtatiously at their new companion and prepared his belongings for their continued journey.

"Prince Alexander, I owe you my life. You have my loyalty. I will support you in every way possible. I pledge my life in your service."

"You pledge your life to me?" Alexander felt irritated and a twinge of pain returned to his head. He exhaled slowly and the pain subsided.

"I will put your words to the test then. You will accompany Farkas and me inside the village. If something were to go wrong, and I believe that you are responsible…" Alexander's voice trailed off and he locked eyes with Emma and glared harshly at her.

"I understand, I will do my part, my lord." She closed her eyes and bowed her head in obedience to him.

Jack retrieved Nicodemus and the gryphon from across the river. Nicodemus stood proudly and refused to cower in shame.
His hands were bound behind him and a cloth was tied around his mouth, but he still exuded an aura of confidence.

"Do you smell what I smell, Nicodemus? My revenge is close at hand, and you will witness it firsthand." Alexander briefly removed the gag from his mouth.

"I may indeed witness your revenge, but I will also bear witness to your destruction." The sorcerer smiled gleefully as if he possessed a knowledge that only he knew about. He eyed Emma lustily. "And who is this? She would make a fine trophy for me."

"Never an interesting conversation with you," Alexander remarked and shoved the gag back into his mouth. "We will leave the horses across the river for now and travel the rest of the way on foot. Farkas and I will go into the village to find the chief's hut. Once there, at point of sword I will retrieve the information that I require. The rest of you will wait for my signal."

"What if you don't get the information?" Calimus asked.

"Then a lot of people will die tonight," Alexander retorted. The Bete'szek chieftain would talk and even if he did disclose the necessary information, Alexander would not guarantee any man, woman, or child's security in the village until he had that information.

When they arrived the outskirts of the village, Alexander observed the layout in front of him. It was larger than he thought it would be but mostly because there was no semblance of order to the village. Many hovels and huts were spread out across the terrain so Alexander assumed that the greater of the hovels would be the chieftain's hut. His men spread out around the village at various intervals so that if something went wrong, he was covered from all angles.

He bade Keira stay with Katrina and took a place alongside Emma and opposite of Farkas. He bound her hands loosely and tied a small axe to the back of her dress.

"Can you handle a weapon?" he asked sincerely.

"With the best of them My Lord."

"We're the best of them Miss," Farkas replied arrogantly. "Don't be getting ideas of where to place that axe except in them."

"You're right to fear a woman," Emma replied with a smile. "We are God's most formidable weapons against men."

"Shut it both of you," Alexander said with irritation. "Emma, you are our prisoner, so maybe if you stopped smiling."

"I'm sorry, My Lord," she replied and replaced her smile with a frown and quickly shed some tears.

"That's really good," Farkas marveled and nodded his head in approval.

Alexander grabbed Emma's arm and walked forward towards the main path that led into the village. The village itself appeared sparse with activity, but Alexander assumed that the early morning had much to do with it. Even so, the guards that were on duty paid them no heed but instead waved and nodded approvingly as Emma was dragged by.

"Up ahead," Alexander whispered and they approached the wooden steps into the hut. They checked them and ensured that no one followed them. He nodded to Farkas who cut the ropes around Emma's hands. She produced the small hand axe that was tied behind her and they quietly tiptoed up the small set of stairs. Alexander peered through the flap into the hut and caught sight of two guards who stood just inside and guarded their chieftain who was fast asleep. Alexander made a hand motion to Farkas that he would go right, and Alexander would go directly to the chieftain.

Farkas understood it immediately and agreed. Alexander made a hand motion to Emma that she would go left and Emma looked at him without understanding and shrugged her shoulders.

Alexander made the hand motion again and Emma shrugged her shoulders again and replied that she didn't understand Alexander's plan.

"You go left and overpower the guard, I go to the chieftain, and Farkas goes left," Alexander whispered in frustration.

"Why are we both going left?" Emma asked. "That seems counterproductive."

"No," Alexander hissed.

"You are going left and Farkas is going right, then I am going to take on the chieftain."

"You did not say that before," Emma said as she shook her head.

"Do not disagree with me," Alexander commanded, "I am a Prince and you do not argue with me."

"Well then," Emma said with an injured air,

"You have everything sorted then, I will leave you to it. Godspeed." Emma handed the axe to Alexander who took it from her and stood there dumbfounded. Emma turned and just as she began to leave Alexander grabbed her arm and brought her back to him.

"You will stay here as per our agreement and you will complete this with us," Alexander said assertively.

"I'm sure the guards will be out here any moment," Farkas moaned. "There goes the element of surprise."

"Fine," Emma said and she took her axe back from Alexander. "I will go left and take the guard."

Alexander and Farkas crouched down as Emma prepared to open the flap.

He nodded to her and in one motion she opened the flap and the three of them rushed inside the hut.

The guards were taken by surprise and Emma and Farkas had their charges disarmed with their hands in the air.

Alexander leapt to the bed and pointed his sword at the chieftain's throat. The commotion woke the chieftain and he instantly rose from his bed. Alexander's sword touched the chieftain's throat and the large man froze in fear. Alexander stood above him and smiled broadly.

"What do we have here?" Alexander said as he flashed a wide grin. "God couldn't have given me a better sign than this."

The large barbarian laid back down on his bed to move the sword away from his throat and his face flashed with fury. His cheeks reddened and he spat as he spoke.

"Alexander Wolfield, the bane of my people. Murderer and destroyer of nations. Give me my sword so that I may end your pathetic existence."

"You sound a little upset," Alexander retorted as he backed away and poured a pitcher's contents into a cup that stood nearby.

He drank some water and made a sound of satisfaction. "I can understand your anger. I bested you at Edgebrooke and I bested you at the altar, and here I am in your home. It's a wonder your people have allowed you to live. Perhaps they'd be so inclined to a new leader.

"We are loyal people," the chieftain said,

"And we will not be your slaves. My people will not abandon me to follow you. Kill me and get it over with."

"I had something different in mind, the scenario where you can keep your life," Alexander replied.

"I need information. Give it to me, and save your life and your people's lives. If I do not receive exactly what I am looking for, you will die, your men will die, and then everyone in this village will suffer the same fate. All because their leader's courage disappeared in the face of one question."

"What question is that?"

"Where is Duncan?"

A puzzled look crossed the chieftain's face and he wrinkled his nose in thought. "Why would you come to our village looking for him?"

"Because he had been followed. I have had men scouring the land for him and one scout finally reported back that he had been seen him coming by your village. I will not allow you to take me for a fool. Get up!"

Dragonus grunted and swung himself out of bed. Although grey-haired and older, he was a physically imposing specimen. Alexander had heard the chieftains were selected by their strength, and at any time they could be challenged for the leadership of the tribe. Failure to protect his throne would mean death for the chieftain, and vice versa for his challenger. Dragonus glared at his watchmen for their failure in protecting him.

Alexander's vision began to blur. He grunted quietly, feeling a stabbing of pain in his head. His teeth clenched and his eyes widened, trying to manage the pain mounting inside of him.

Farkas noticed Alexander's change in demeanor, as did Dragonus. The Prince's grip on his sword lessened, and the wily chief took the advantage and knocked Alexander to the floor with his fist. Alexander offered no resistance as he fell to the floor. The four guards stood still, completely confused as to what happened. The Bete'szek picked up the Prince and his sword.

"Put your weapons down," he commanded. Emma and Farkas obeyed, handing their axes to their captors. "Where are the rest of your soldiers?"

"There are none," Farkas admitted. Dragonus eyed him curiously. "No soldiers?"

"None," Farkas repeated.

The grey-haired man shook his head in disbelief.

"I would never have believed in one hundred years that anyone would have been foolish enough to come north. How arrogant your Prince is, thinking he could just walk in to my camp with a handful of men." He strode out of the flap, followed by his guards and new prisoners, dragging Alexander as he went.

"Men of Alveus!" he shouted in the direction of the trees. "Listen to the words of Dragonus, lord of the lands that you trespass on. There is no war between us, and yet your prince comes to me as a dog and a coward who seeks to do me harm in my sleep."

He picked Alexander up and held him like a child with a straw doll.

"Put down your weapons and come out now or I will kill this dog now."

An arrow flashed by the chieftain and embedded behind him into the guard closest to Emma. He fell without a sound. Emma picked up his axe, ready to fight. Dragonus grunted and held the sword against Alexander's throat.

The noise from the chieftain's hut caused panic in the village. Armed men and women appeared and they ran to their chieftain and surrounded him, readying themselves to defend him to the death. Emma was quickly overwhelmed and disarmed by the tribe and Farkas stayed motionless.

"What will it be men of Alveus? Will you favor burying another one of your princes today?"

The pain had finally subsided in Alexander's head and Dragonus' words enflamed him. He struggled against his grip, but the chieftain pressed the sword tighter against his throat.

"Wait!" a voice shouted. Calimus appeared from the trees and walked towards them. Alexander groaned and wished Calimus would have stayed put. Dragonus began to laugh once the Prince came into view.

"What is this? Do my eyes deceive me? Two Princes of Alveus? Where are the rest of your men? Come out now or I kill your Prince."

From around the village, Fergus and Chauncey stepped forward and made their way by Calimus. All were armed and all kept their swords drawn and faced the nervous barbarian encampment. Katrina walked forward with her arrow fixated on Dragonus.

"Where are your other guards, Alexander? I know there's more," Dragonus whispered.

"Where's your dog?"

"They are in Edgebrooke," Alexander confessed, partially lying to hide the gryphons' presence. Dragonus eyes opened in amazement and he twisted Alexander to face him.

"You thought to slay my village with three men, a drunk Prince, a slave, and a child? Why do you continue to insult me with your arrogance? We are not so easily taken and yet you treat me like a helpless animal. I am a great chieftain and you will know that before I kill you."

"Put a sword in my hand and I will prove you wrong," Alexander said as his eyesight slowly returned to him. Dragonus swung his sword with intent to cut off Alexander's head.

"Stay your blade!" Jack shouted. Dragonus froze as Jack walked with Nicodemus in front of him, still bound and gagged.

"You said that was all of your men," Dragonus sneered.

"I lied," Alexander responded.

"Jack! Do not do it. Take him back to Middlebrooke."

"A deal can be had," Jack yelled.

"Your sorcerer for our Prince and the other two prisoners."

Dragonus released his grip from Alexander and made his way through the throng of Bete'szek in front of him. The captives were pushed behind him and Dragonus finally reached Jack.

"Nicodemus!" Dragonus snorted.

"Here I thought your trap was brilliant and you stand before me in chains.

It seems as though we have an agreement, a prince for a sorcerer. I would advise you to flee my land before my generous nature changes."

Emma and Farkas were pushed forward and Nicodemus was pushed back to the Bete'szek where they quickly untied his hands. They allowed Alexander to walk back under his own power to where his men stood.

"Until we meet again, harbinger," Dragonus said sarcastically. "Perhaps you and I would meet in a fair fight before then." Nicodemus' hands were finally untied and he ripped the gag from his mouth.

"Imprison them!" he ordered, and pointed at Alexander.

"We had a deal!" Jack shouted.

"I agree," Dragonus said.

"An agreement was made, I will not go back on it."

"You will or you will suffer our consequences," the sorcerer demanded coolly.

"Take them."

"Drop your weapons," Dragonus ordered. There was a pause between the Bete'szek who hesitated from taking the weapons and the Alveuns who declined to drop them.

"Would you have more blood spilled?" Dragonus asked Alexander.

"Drop your weapons," Alexander said quietly.

"But sir," Jack started and Alexander cut him off.

"Farkas, Emma, and I are unarmed. There's nothing we can do." Alexander turned to Nicodemus whose face had broken into an evil grin.

"This isn't over."

"For you, it is," Nicodemus turned to address Dragonus. "There's a gryphon out there, and it's with his dog. I must find it so I will go enlist my brothers for help and find the hunters. You will hold them until our return. You may kill any that you like except Alexander. Do not dismember them. They can all serve our purpose for they are brilliant fighters."

"You will never have our allegiance," Fergus stated defiantly.

"I don't need your loyalty, I just need your bodies." The evil man smiled at Alexander and rubbed his wrists.

"The endgame is never in doubt,
just the methods." He walked off hurriedly to the north and left an awkward silence between the two enemies until Dragonus finally spoke.

"Put them in the pit," he said and walked away.

Alexander and his companions were pushed at prodded at spear point until they came to a small hole in the ground.

One by one they were each forced to jump into the hole until finally the last of them hopped in and the Bete'szek covered the pit with an animal hide. The last bit of sunlight disappeared and they were alone in the darkness.

CHAPTER VIII

"I didn't have this in mind for our journey," Calimus said irritatingly. He folded his arms in frustration and rolled his eyes. He followed his display with a pretentious snort as if he was a young school boy protesting a punishment.

"My fault," Alexander admitted. He attempted to take the frustration from Calimus in hopes that it would at least spark a conversation to distract them.

It didn't. They sat in the pit for hours without sunlight and the sounds of anything except for their breathing. Eventually, they heard the buzzing of excited villagers. Alexander wondered how much longer they had until Dragonus began to get rid of them.

"How do you feel, My Lord?" Jack's concerned tone shamed Alexander because it was now being seen as a sign of weakness.

"Better," the prince replied.

"I have had little spells but nothing I can't handle."

"As your men, we grow concerned that these headaches have been becoming more frequent and severe," Farkas interjected.

"Perhaps if you sought out a surgeon."

"There's an easier way to cure headaches, cutting off your head," Chauncey joked.

"Brilliant reasoning," Fergus said.

"At least you won't be undead."

"Undead?" Emma asked.

"What does that mean?"

"Oh no," Calimus groaned.

"Not this again."

"They take the dead and use their magic to make them their slaves," Jack explained.

"They are more effective than the living because they feel no pain. Separate their heads from their bodies or set them on fire."

The red-haired lass scrunched her face into a quizzical look. It was fairly obvious that she had a certain amount of disbelief to this tale. Analyzing Jack as the source of the information was more believable than if Chauncey or Fergus had delivered the lesson.

"I'm scared," Katrina admitted.

"What do you think they'll do to us?"

"I'll watch out for you Katrina. I promise. Nothing's going to happen to you." Alexander gave her a strong hug in a half-hearted attempt to reassure her, but in truth, he wasn't sure what would happen next.

Once Alexander finished his last word, the animal hide was pulled back and moonlight entered the pit.

"We have been down here all day," Fergus marveled.

"You did sleep through most of it," Chauncey mocked.

"I was very tired, but now I feel refreshed!" Fergus retorted.

A ladder was thrown down to the group and several Bete'szek waived their axes to instruct them to climb the ladder. Once each prisoner climbed out of the pit they were whisked off to a stone building in the middle of the village. Alexander guessed when he was brought inside that this was their meeting hall, but all the benches had been cleared off to the side as well as all the chairs. The Bete'szek surrounded the floor and when they spotted Alexander a silence fell over the village.

Dragonus sat in a throne that was decorated with animal bones. A deer skull with antlers sat above Dragonus' head and other smaller skulls decorated the outline of his throne. Alexander and Calimus were separated from the others who were forced to sit off to the side, and instead the brothers were pushed in front of the throne.

"Alexander and Calimus of the house of Wolfield. I bid you welcome and hope you will enjoy our hospitality."

"It has been terrific so far," Alexander replied, "Perhaps you would come to Middlebrooke and enjoy what my people can offer."

"Sadly, I cannot accept that," Dragonus said, with a hint of mockery.

"Will you be killing us with words or axes tonight? I'm sure my brother Calimus would agree with me when we would like to complain about our accommodations today."

"Indeed, Alex," Calimus agreed,

"I am very unhappy that I have had neither food nor drink today. I am afraid that your inhospitality is bound to be more known. You won't get many traveler's coming to your village if this is how you treat them. Is there someone else we could speak to about these conditions?"

"I do so love the Alveun arrogance and their wit," Dragonus responded. "Perhaps I should do the world a favor and cut out your tongues and send you back. The best Alveun is the one that cannot talk."

"And the best Bete'szek is one that can handle a weapon and not run in the face of their enemies." Alexander mocked.

"Remember me? The hero of Edgebrooke who cut your men down?" He shouted his response to the crowd who responded with hurling rotted vegetables and fruit at them. Alexander and Calimus bowed their heads as the spoiled fruit crashed into them.

Dragonus was infuriated and the villagers who broke their silence to scream obscenities at the brothers. The villagers poured mead on their captives and started throwing blows at the prisoners.

"Silence!" Dragonus yelled. His presence as the largest warrior helped him regain control of his people. They stopped beating the captives and made their way back to their positions.

"Prince Alexander you bring a great point to your defense…and yes, you are on trial for your life tonight…the Alveun, with his armor and professional training…his weapons and his horses have driven my people from their rightful land. But the Bete'szek is noble, we fight hand to hand, with little armor, on foot, and little regard for our enemies."

"Perhaps if you had more regard," Calimus stated but stopped when Alexander slapped his shoulder.

Alexander tried very hard to stifle his chuckle which further infuriated Dragonus.

"Tonight we will find out who is more superior. We will fight!" He exclaimed as he pointed at Alexander and Calimus.

"Very well, will it be axes or swords?" Alexander asked confidently.

"Fists," Dragonus grinned.

"My fists against yours. If you win, you keep your life."

Alexander studied the chieftain for a moment as courage departed from Calimus. Dragonus was a beast of a man and had already proved his strength earlier when he held Alexander captive.

"Calimus shall fight me first," he proclaimed and his people cheered and raised their cups to him. More vegetables were thrown at Alexander and Calimus. Calimus avoided as many as he could, but Alexander calmly bent over and picked some carrots off of the floor. After the Prince filled his hands he walked over to his companions.

"Alexander! I can't do this!" Calimus was panic stricken. Alexander munched on a couple of carrots he held in his hand and handed several to Katrina and Emma.

"Are you listening to me?"

Jack stood up and looked over Alexander.

"How do you feel? You look a little weak."

"I'll be okay. It's just a small one." In truth, Alexander thought this was one of his worst spells and the blurred vision didn't help him. He bluffed his way through his pain as much as he could.

"Calimus," he said calmly,

"Stay away from his fists and use all parts of your body as a weapon."

"That doesn't help me," Calimus moaned.

A lone drumbeat began what appeared to the Alveuns as a signal for something to begin. The beat started off very slowly at first, and with each new drum that joined in, the pace went a bit faster.

Several Bete'szek warriors were dressed in a ceremonial garb and wore masks. The masks indicated an animal, and the warriors danced around a fire in the center of the floor. An aged man sang a song in their native language. Alexander wondered if it was a happy song, because everyone in the Hall cheered at certain verses. When the song had finished, everyone refilled the cups of mead and set about dancing to a new song.

The beat was much quicker now and started a frenzy in the floor. The Bete'szek continued to chant and drink in a manner that Alexander had never seen.

It was much different here than in Alveus. Alveuns handled themselves with a certain décor. This was a primitive display of animalism. Alexander began to understand his captors a bit more.

"Come on coward!" Dragonus thundered. The music and dancing stopped at once. The chieftain walked into the center of the floor and bade Calimus advance on him. The villagers scurried to their seat and a few prodded Calimus to the center. Alexander tried to focus his eyesight on the image of Calimus but without success. The music hadn't helped his headache.

The crowd cheered as Dragonus threw a punch at Calimus that just missed him. Calimus backed away slightly but found himself too close to the hostile villagers. Several villagers had spears, so they gently poked him to encourage him back to the center of the floor. Dragonus swung again and Calimus ducked under his punch. The chief was visibly frustrated that Calimus kept bouncing away from his punches so Dragonus dropped his hands to the side and walked towards Calimus and stood in front of him. Calimus was confused by this tactic and hesitated to move.

"Punch him!" Emma yelled above the din. Calimus swung his fist at Dragonus' face, but Dragonus caught his fist and squeezed his massive hands around Calimus' fist.

The Alveuns Prince bravely punched Dragonus' stomach with his left hand repeatedly until the pain of his hand being crushed brought him to his knees. In response, with just one punch, Dragonus sent Calimus to the floor. Admirably, the Prince jumped back up quickly with a cut that had formed on his cheek.

The barbarian crowd cheered their leader on, and Dragonus stalked Calimus like a wolf hunting a wounded deer. Calimus managed to punch Dragonus' face but to little effect. Within moments, the fight was over.

Dragonus caught Calimus' face with a left-handed jab that stunned him and finished him off with a right hand that broke his nose. The prince crumpled to the floor in pain, and blood flowed freely from his wound.

Emma and Jack ran to Calimus and picked him up. Emma tore a piece of cloth from her dress and tried to slow the bleeding. They brought him back to where Alexander waited and laid him down.

Alexander knelt down next to his brother.

"What did it feel like?" he asked sympathetically.

"Like being crushed by stone," Calimus replied.

Dragonus raised his arms to the cheers of his people. He was gaining back his lost honor.

Alexander made his way to the middle of the floor, looked back at his companions and took a deep breath.

"Alexander. It's just you and me now." Dragonus circled around him slowly, came to a stop and stood directly in front of him. They regarded each other and Alexander erased any display of emotion from his face.

"Your life depends upon this," the Bete'szek whispered.

"Stop talking," Alexander whispered back and focused all of his energy on making out his opponents shape. The images had stopped blurring, and he needed to take advantage quickly.

Dragonus threw two quick punches at Alexander who dodged them both.

"You're slower than I thought," Alexander deadpanned.

Dragonus snorted and rushed towards him in an attempt to grapple with him. Alexander moved aside at the last second and managed to use his opponent's weight against him to send him sprawling to the floor. Once the chieftain fell to the ground he jumped right back up enraged.

He again swung at Alexander who again moved quickly that Dragonus' punches continued to miss.

The Prince noticed that he tired easily and took the opportunity to land punches immediately after he missed.

Several shots to the body and to the face made Dragonus breathe heavily. But the chieftain finally caught Alexander with a glancing blow to his head and Alexander teetered off balance. Dragonus wrapped his arms around his neck and choked him. Alexander gasped for air and threw sharp elbows at Dragonus' face.

The brute howled in fury and ran towards the nearest wall with the intention to smash Alexander against it. Alexander lifted his legs at the last moment and brought them up against the wall. He pushed off the wall with all of his might and Dragonus' momentum shifted backward. He stumbled backward and tripped over Katrina's leg that she had stuck under him.

Dragonus released his hold on Alexander and the Prince hit the floor hard. Dragonus fell too and together they rolled over and got back on their feet. The Bete'szek ran to Alexander and tried to grapple with him again.

Alexander punched his way out and kept Dragonus and his strength at bay.

Alexander used a flurry of punches against his enemy and bloody cuts were forming on the barbarian's face.

The prolonged engagement tired the Prince and Dragonus managed to grab his left fist when Alexander threw a half-hearted punch at his face.

Dragonus took advantage and slammed his fist into Alexander's head.

Alexander felt as though his head had hit rock and his body fell to the floor. He stopped himself with his hand, balled up his fist, and threw an uppercut into Dragonus' jaw. Dragonus responded with another punch to Alexander's head. The Prince dropped to one knee and again slammed Dragonus' face with an uppercut. The entire Hall quieted down as the two opponents punched each other with all of the hate and violence they mustered within themselves. Alexander punched Dragonus one more time and Dragonus freed his hand, staggered back, and fell to the ground.

Alexander collapsed to the floor and drops of blood and sweat gathered beneath him.

"Do you yield?" Dragonus asked through his swollen lips. He spit blood on the floor and wiped the remaining spittle from his beard.

"I yield to no one," Alexander said defiantly, blood dripping to the floor. "You will not defeat me." Alexander prayed silently that the large man would not hit him again.

"I can see that." Dragonus gathered his strength and walked over to Alexander. Alexander got up summoned his composure to return. Dragonus spread his arms and addressed the crowd.

"Everyone outside!" He bellowed his order and his people readily obeyed him.

They whisked away Alexander's companions leaving Dragonus and Alexander alone in the great hall.

"You punch very hard for someone of your size. There is much anger in your fists," said the barbarian.

"Thank you for your kind words," Alexander said mockingly. "I must agree, I have never been hit this hard before. I am glad you ended the match when you did. I do not think I could have stood against you much longer."

"And yet you did," Dragonus laughed.

"You're an interesting young man Alexander. Our spies report you with great inaccuracy. You are more than just the lucky son of the king."

"Thank you," Alexander said graciously. "Compliments from a man's enemies are always held in high regard. I sincerely mean that. What will you do with us now?" Alexander breathed slowly and tried to calm his beating heart.

"Now we talk," Dragonus said and joined Alexander sitting on the floor.

"While I give you credit, Alexander, you are strong and brilliant, but you are also arrogant and stubborn. Those two things will get you and your people killed."

"I am doing well so far," Alexander replied.

"If you continue this course of action you are going to die very soon," Dragonus offered.

"I have a plan. Or I will. Soon."

"Allow me to offer this. Tonight you will escape and move south."

Alexander's eyes widened and he looked quizzically at Dragonus.

"Why would you do that for me?"

"You and I made a deal, and Nicodemus made me lose honor by breaking it. I am a man of my word. I will let you go."

"But the sorcerers will kill you!" Alexander felt an initial tinge of concern for this warrior. He wasn't going to object any further, and he would gladly leave this camp and certain death behind.

"I am tired of them. I blame you in front of my people for what happened to my people. Half of my men were cut down in front of Edgebrooke, but you are a warrior and warriors kill each other.
 They came to my men and lied to them, they said we would be successful and we would reclaim Edgebrooke.

They promised we would no longer live like dogs and forage." Dragonus grit his teeth and spit on the floor in disgust.

"They use us like dogs and I am done with it."

"Dragonus," Alexander said confused, "Are you switching your allegiance?"

"I am not, but at the right time it is something that may possibly happen. I have lived a long time. I have no use for their ways. They murder people for power, they prevent us from doing anything more than living in squalor. I am saving your life today, Alexander, and in turn I want you to save my people when that time comes."

Alexander pondered these words for a moment and was amazed at the thought that perhaps the Bete'szek could be subjugated peacefully. That would truly make Alveus an empire.

"We have a deal," Alexander said.

"But tell me where Duncan is."

"I can tell you nothing about him," Dragonus apologized.

"Take your companions and head south to safety. I will send word to you if I can."

"I will go, and I thank you for this. I am indebted. I will be heading north, though. I will avenge my brother's death before I do anything more."

"Arrogance and stubbornness are not qualities in a Prince."

"Then they shouldn't have killed my brother, for he had neither of those traits. I am everything you see before you. I am flawed beyond belief. I realize and accept this, which is why I choose not to lead my people." It was irritating to Alexander to continue to receive this lesson.

"I want to be perfectly clear Alexander, that my people will not be led by anyone that I could best in battle. I will not go quietly and I will not submit to anyone other than yourself. Do keep that in mind. Until that time, Alveus and the Bete'szek are still enemies." Dragonus stood up and offered his outstretched hand. Alexander took his hand and Dragonus pulled him up.

They shook hands in uneasy friendship and left the meeting hall. The prince headed back towards the pit where his men were held. Several Bete'szek warriors eyed him suspiciously and ensured that he jumped back into the pit. Once Alexander was inside, they covered the hole with the animal skin.

"What happened?" Jack asked.

"We thought you would be killed."

"Not today," Alexander replied.

"Today has been a good day." He turned to Calimus who was still being looked after by Emma.

"How are you?"

"Not well, but you look worse."

"I feel worse," Alexander laughed. It was true, he thought. His face was incredibly tender to touch, but Dragonus had beat the pain out of his head.

Calimus looked fondly at Emma.

"At least I have a capable angel to attend to me. Perhaps she could use her magic on you and make you feel better."

Emma smiled kindly at Alexander and he rolled his eyes. "Thank you but I will be fine.

"There's one other thing," Jack said and motioned to Alexander that a ladder that had been tossed into the bottom of the pit.

"What does it mean?" Fergus asked.

"It means we will be escaping shortly. We will head back to get the horses and make our way north. Jack, where are Keira and the gryphon?"

"They're safe, I placed the Gryphon in a tree across the river and Keira is close by guarding her. They are on the outskirts of the village."

"I'll go and get them. Shouldn't be too hard to find my own dog." Alexander touched his face.

"How bad do I look?"

"Honestly?" Jack asked.

"You look like you got the wrong end of a beating."

"You should see the other guy," Alexander said with a bit of wry humor. He never wanted to match fists with Dragonus again.

Fergus and Chauncey positioned the ladder and held onto it as Alexander climbed and surveyed the village.

The village had fallen asleep and Dragonus had stayed true to his word. Alexander and Jack made their way to where the gryphon was hidden while the others headed back to the river towards the horses.

CHAPTER IX

Jack and Alexander had just reached the trees when Alexander began to feel light headed. Before they had set out, he was the picture of health and he was in great condition, but these spells of headaches would suddenly creep up on him and paralyze him. Jack was momentarily ahead of the prince but looked back in concern because Alexander tarried.

"My Lord, are you alright?" Jack asked.

Alexander steadied himself and sat on a nearby tree's root. He had taken several hard punches from Dragonus and experienced three awful headaches in the last day, so he waited for the pain to come.

When he caught his breath and felt some pain subside, he answered his friend.

"I think I'm alright, I just feel a little dizzy. How much farther until we get to their hiding place?"

It's not much farther," Jack pointed,

"I wonder why Nicodemus ran off for help and did not look for the gryphon himself."

"They are all cowards," Alexander spat. He followed the direction of the spittle and was bothered that it was colored dark red. He felt around his tender face and found a small stream of blood dripping from his nose and trickling down onto his lips. He wiped the blood away and held his face upward in an attempt to stop the bleeding. Jack handed him a small cloth which Alexander used to wipe away the excess blood.

"Damn that Dragonus. He has fists like iron clubs," he muttered.

"He hits like an anvil." In a way, Alexander felt over-complimentary to his opponent. This was a rare occasion, losing a fight to someone.

"What did he want from you?" Jack asked.

Alexander rested his tilted head against a large tree trunk for support.

"He offered a deal and an interesting one at that. An alliance between Alveus and the Bete'szek." Alexander scoffed quietly at the notion.

"Will you take it then? An alliance will be sure to drive the priests away and bring peace to our lands!" Jack clapped his hands together excitedly.

"I do not see why we need them. They are nothing compared to us. Ten of my men are worth two hundred of theirs." While Alexander had found a new respect for the leader, having an entire barbarian tribe who fought like fodder wasn't the most appealing scenario.

Alexander listened to the sounds of the forest and thought that he heard something of importance. Jack was about to respond, but he held up his hand to stop him from talking. There had been a noise in the forest and Alexander strained his ears to hear it.

"Jack? Did you hear that?"

"Hear what?"

"There's something out there...listen." Jack and Alexander listened intently to the sounds around them. Alexander heard it again, louder than before.

"*Prince!!!!*" It screamed.

"The gryphon!" Alexander pulled out his sword and ran in the direction of the sound.

"Prince! The gryphon is this way." Jack pointed the opposite direction that Alexander headed in. Alexander paused and listened again. The voice was in the direction he headed in, but Jack swore that the gryphon was the other way.

"Take that path," Alexander ordered,

"And come quickly to me if they are not there.

If they are there, come quicker."

"Prince, you are not wearing any armor." Jack pointed out that Alexander had left his armor with the horses the previous day.

"I have to stay by your side."

"There is no time," Alexander insisted.

"I have my sword, and that will be my protection."

Jack nodded and ran off in his direction while Alexander continued on in search of the voice.

Gryphon? He projected his thoughts as best he could. *Where are you?*

He strained for a response and tried to project his voice yelling louder. He finally received a response.

"Help me! Hurry!"

Alexander rushed in the voices direction until he came to the source. The gryphon was perched high in a tree. It was frightened and emitted small screams to the threats that threatened it from the forest floor. Alexander positioned his sword in front of him as their enemy came into view. Three large black dogs approached Alexander from behind the large tree.

Alexander recognized them as the same dogs that had followed him to the cave and were always nearby when events spiraled out of control. Their yellows eyes blazed like flickering candles and shone through the night.

Why are you here and not with Keira? Alexander thought.

I was hungry, the Gryphon replied indignantly.

Maybe you will be a meal instead of eating one, Alexander snapped back. *The next time someone tells you to stay put...do it!*

Alexander shook his head in annoyance and kept his focus on the dogs. Two of them circled back to the tree and tried to leap while snapping at the gryphon's legs. They barely missed and the gryphon screeched back at the angry mongrels. The infuriated dogs joined its companion and they encircled Alexander. He took a deep breath to calm himself and pushed the thoughts and fears out from his mind.

The dog closest to him was a hand smaller than Keira but carried much more weight. Although its fur was jet black, it also had patches of grey, which Alexander surmised was indicative of old age.

Alexander deduced he was the pack leader. He waited patiently for an attack, but the dog remained eerily still. Black smoke started drifting off its fur and enveloped the shape of the dog until it lost solid form and completely dissipated into a cloud of smoke. The dark cloud surrounded the dog's image like a shroud until it reformed into a pillar.

The dog had completely disappeared and in its place, the pillar of smoke shaped into a human body.

When the smoke disappeared, Alexander recognized the grey hair and scars immediately. He gasped and stepped back in astonishment.

"Alexander," Duncan said as he straightened out his cloak. "Rumor has it you've been looking for me."

"This is impossible," Alexander marveled. His mind instantly debated the reality of this turn of events, but he could not overturn what he had just witnessed. He quickly regained his wits and focused on the revenge that was now at hand.

"There will be no banter with you today, Duncan. I'm here to put our affairs in order," the prince said with complete malice.

"You murdered Edward and I have come to avenge his death."

"You are the reason my sister is dead!" Duncan yelled back.

"No one asked you to come to the forest or to cloud her mind with your princely charms and empty promises. A life for a life is a fair trade. Put your sword away, and leave the gryphon. Do this, and I will consider our affairs at an end."

The gryphon was clearly distressed at her situation. She paced back and forth on the tree branch, screeching at Duncan and the two remaining dogs.

The starry night lost its luminescence as storm clouds formed overhead and blocked the starlight. The air grew colder and Alexander shivered. He had never felt a cold such as this, and every breath he took produced an icy mist from his own mouth. The growls from the dogs began to produce their own icy fog.

"I loved your sister!" Alexander insisted as his eyes moistened. The memory of her broken body lying in front of him and being powerless to save her built a mountain of anger within him.

"You knew nothing of her!" Duncan yelled back.

"You knew nothing about her. You found her flaw of loneliness and you exploited it. Empty promises of an empty life. The prince and the thief? Are you just as blind as my sister? Are you as weak?"

"I'm not weak!" Alexander yelled petulantly and he raised his sword to strike at Duncan. The two dogs quickly closed the gap between them as they stood in defense of Duncan.

"I am unarmed, Alex," Duncan chided.

"Would you strike an unarmed man? Are you no better than the very person you've sworn revenge upon?"

"My brother did nothing to you!" Alexander screamed in fury.

"He was innocent!"

"It's me you should have killed if you blame me so much for your sister's death. She made her choice! You should have accepted that she hated the life you made her live. You are just as responsible for her death."

"A life for a life, Alexander," Duncan said bitterly.

"You deserve to walk through life with all of the pain of losing a loved one."

"I do not care if you're unarmed. I do not care if you have conjured this storm! I only care about putting my blade through your heart." Raindrops fell harder on Alexander, but he remained undeterred and focused on Duncan. His nemesis backed away slightly as did the dogs.

My Lord, you should think about this. Something's not right! The gryphon paced back and forth on the tree branch continuing its tiny screeches.

"Do you hear that, Alexander?" Duncan chuckled and pointed at the gryphon.

"Once we dispatch you, we will ensure the death of the last gryphon of Alveus."

"Like you said, you're unarmed, and you have a bad leg" Alexander pointed at his waist and his leg.

"Do I?" Duncan smiled with the question.

"How does one become the greatest and most feared assassin with a bad leg? Let me show you." Duncan closed his eyes and smoke swirled about his body.

His body disappeared into the smoke, his face followed suit, and the cloud reformed his body into that of a snarling dog.

Alexander yelled and charged at the dog with his sword in the air. The dog turned tail and ran as fast as it could while Alexander pursued it closely. He swung his sword at its body and just missed, clipping a patch of hair. He heard the other two dogs as they nipped at his heels, but he paid them no mind and stayed in pursuit of Duncan.

In his haste, Alexander stumbled over a tree root and lost sight of the black dog he chased. It quickly veered off its course and Alexander suspected it would make its way back to the gryphon. He turned around and swung his sword at the other two dogs that had pursued him. They respected his blade and veered away from him. The prince rushed past them and headed back towards the tree while he kept his eye out for Duncan.

Alexander passed a thick oak and turned his head as he passed it. Suddenly Duncan appeared in his path and their bodies collided.
Alexander fell to the forest floor and lost his grip on his sword.

He scrambled to get his knees and reached out to grab his sword. Duncan dove at him and together they wrestled over the position to reach it. Duncan rolled Alexander on to his back and attempted to punch him.

Alexander quickly grabbed Duncan's throat and squeezed as hard as he could. Duncan fought to release Alexander's grip, but the prince held on as best he could.

Duncan flashed a wicked grin at his opponent. Smoke shrouded the thief and in an instant he was back as a dog. The dog snarled and flashed his teeth at Alexander and began to bite at him. Alexander kept his hands around the dog's throat and tried desperately to keep the teeth from puncturing his throat.

The other two dogs appeared and began biting at Alexander's legs. He kicked his legs and squirmed as best he could and succeeded kicking the dog's faces. Alexander pushed Duncan off of him, scrambled to his knees, and went for the sword that laid inches away from him. He reached for the sword and felt immense pain. One of the dog's bites had found their mark.

Its razor sharp teeth clamped down on Alexander's leg and dragged him away from the sword. Alexander screamed in agony. Duncan materialized in front of him and picked the prince's sword off the damp earth.

Alexander tried to twist his leg, but the dog had clamped down so hard that he was unable to move.

"Looks like I am no longer unarmed," Duncan smirked. "What a pity, to be killed by the same hands as your brother while failing to avenge his death. Sad."

He knelt by Alexander grabbed his hair, lifted his head up and looked directly at his face.

"You've failed again, Alex. This next stroke will be for Angelica. Oh, and don't worry. I won't be cutting out your heart. I will behead you. This ends today."

Duncan measured the distance between the sword and Alexander. He lifted his sword up and prepared to strike.

"Edward," Alexander whispered,

"Help me!" He struggled and moved around and tried to free himself from the clenches of the dog. The dog refused to release its grip and Duncan dropped the sword and punched Alexander. The punch landed on the bruise that Dragonus had inflicted on him earlier and Alexander howled in pain. The assassin picked up the sword again.

"Your death is inevitable, Prince!"

The blade flashed above him and Alexander closed his eyes to feel the cold drops of rain splash against his face.

Each drop brought a sense of calm to his fate and he breathed slowly. An angry roar shattered his calm and he immediately felt hope rise in his heart.

"Keira!!!" he shouted

Keira ran towards Duncan at full speed with her teeth bared and murder in her eyes. The thief was shocked and he dropped the sword and dissipated into black smoke just as the wolfhound jumped at him. She cleared through the smoke and Duncan was again a snarling dog. The sword fell towards Alexander's neck, but he caught the handle and with one motion, swung the sword at the dog that held a grip on his blood soaked leg.

The dog let go of his leg as Keira struck it with her brute force. His protector sent it sprawling into a puddle. Keira leapt upon it as the third dog tried to protect its friend. Alexander regained his balance and swung his sword at any black dog that was near him. He turned his back to Duncan and limped over to help Keira who was besting the two dogs.

Duncan quickly seized the opportunity and took human form. He locked his arm around Alexander's neck and began to choke him.
Alexander delivered a sharp blow to Duncan's ribs and Duncan exhaled in pain.

They were both knocked onto the wet ground by another body that had launched its presence into both of them. Jack stood over Duncan with a sword in his hand. Duncan morphed back into a dog and Jack jumped back in surprise, unsure of how to react.

Duncan bounded away from the fray and was joined by the other two dogs as Keira chased them for a short distance.

She came back to Alexander and wagged her tail furiously. She sniffed and licked his leg wound and then sniffed his face. He buried his head into her neck and held her tightly.

"Thank you Keira! Good girl," he whispered into her ear. He was so relieved for that was too close.

"Jack? That's another one I owe you," he said. "Thank you."

Jack just shook his head and attended to his wound.

"What's the matter?" Alexander asked him. Jack carried a surly look on his face.

"Nothing, Sir," Jack responded.

"I'm sworn to protect you, but you seem to have this nasty habit of always running off and getting into trouble."

"You did protect me though, and you did an excellent job." Alexander patted him on the shoulder as a way to show thanks.

"I came here last minute to find you near death. You aren't thinking of the consequences. I am your guard. I am sworn to protect you. Let me do my duty." Jack tore off some of his tunic and wrapped it around Alexander's leg.

"Do you presume to tell me what to do?"

"No, Your Highness," Jack said respectfully.

"I am asking you to let your guard do what we were hired to do.

We are sworn to protect you and yet you do not trust us with your life." Jack finished tying the bandage around Alexander's leg and they sat quietly for a moment. Keira laid her head on Alexander's wound and whimpered softly.

"I need to chase Duncan. I won't have another chance like this," Alexander said determinedly.

"My Lord, your leg is wounded. You can't chase anyone with this wound."

As much as he hated admitting it, Jack was right. Alexander thought through any other options he might have, but he truly had none. He could give chase with his horses, but then what? The further north they went, the worse it would become, and he was in no position to do any more fighting tonight.

Alexander felt bitterly disappointed and angry with himself. Duncan had presented himself and he couldn't capitalize on this opportunity.

There was so much he had learned about his enemy, but that meant very little to him.

They heard the sound of horses nearby so Jack stood up and shouted a greeting. His companions had found them and brought their horses. Emma caught sight of Alexander's wound and slid down Zeus and instantly attended to his wound.

"Jack, that's an excellent job of dressing his wound," she said sweetly.

"I wonder if it's improved his disposition at all."

Alexander scoffed and rolled his eyes. They took his hand and helped him mount Zeus.

"It seems as if I lack a horse, and if we continue to travel north I will need one unless your highness has no further use of me and would have me wander these woods alone." Emma smiled amiably at Alexander and he felt a growing sense of irritation towards her.

"You can ride with me," Calimus said eagerly. He offered his hand to Emma, but the maiden's eyes were fixated upon Alexander.

"I ride alone," Alexander said blithely.

"I can see that," Emma replied.

"I will ride with Katrina, as her horse has the lightest load."

Calimus frowned in disappointment but said nothing in response.

"We're riding north," Alexander announced firmly to his companions.

Calimus' face showed disappointment in Alexander's decision. He looked at the ground and shook his head.

"Do you have a concern you would like me to address Calimus?" Alexander glared at Calimus and rode Zeus next to his horse so Calimus felt the fire in his eyes.

"Duncan is nearby and I will wager he headed north. It's our duty to follow him as he murdered our brother. Best resign yourself to that fact and ride on. We ride for our brother's memory."

"Edward's memory or yours, Alexander?" Calimus issued a direct challenge to Alexander's orders and folded his arms in defiance.

An uncomfortable silence fell over the group. Alexander and Calimus regarded each other for a moment with hostility.

"Calimus, you frustrate me with your complaints and your boorishness. Edward was resilient.
He would have never backed down from a fight or run from his responsibilities."

"I am not Edward!" Calimus exclaimed in frustration.

"Indeed," Alexander responded quietly.

"I am reminded of that frequently." He instructed Devin and Farkas to scout the path ahead with Keira. He wanted to be alerted the moment the dogs were found.

The group retrieved the shivering gryphon from the tree and Emma swooned over the creature. The gryphon took to her quickly, like she did with Sofia, and preferred to sit with Katrina and Emma for the ride.

Why do they hunt me? She asked Alexander.

Because when you are full grown, you will be a threat to them. Once the scouts left, Alexander nudged Zeus forward and everyone, including Calimus, fell in quietly behind him.

CHAPTER X

Alexander followed the river upstream where it veered eastward and they continued on until they came to a large waterfall. The men were at the base of a very large pair of mountains. The waterfall emptied into a giant pool and flowed into the river that they had followed. Their scouts returned at this pool and Alexander decided to refresh the horses and allow his men to rest. Because of the massive downpour, there had been no way for them to pick up Duncan's trail. At this point, their quest had reached its possible ending.

Alexander's bandages needed to be cleaned before they turned foul, and Emma insisted that he cleanse his wound before he became sick. Alexander agreed reluctantly but only because he wanted to avoid another of Jack's lectures for not allowing them to care for him.

Emma and Katrina were mesmerized by the waterfall and Emma felt that she needed refreshing and a good face wash. Katrina jumped into the water and they splashed about in the water while they had fun. Keira joined in and bounded back and forth between the shore and the water.

Alexander slid off of Zeus and limped over to a pile of river rocks that stood out of the water, and allowed him to wash his legs with ease. Emma sloshed through the water to where he sat and she moved his hands away when he tried to remove the bandages.

"I am quite capable of removing bandages," he snarled.

"You are indeed, Prince Alexander," she said pleasantly, "But I am your servant and, therefore, it is my duty to serve you and take care of you." She unwrapped the bandages and Alexander cringed in pain as she pressed down on the wound.

"You're not my servant," he said firmly.

"You're not one of my people."

"You saved my life and by the traditions of my people, I am your servant. It makes it even more important because I am no longer considered nobility." She frowned, but she continued to wash his wound with the cold water.

"I am sorry for what happened to you." Alexander tried his best to sound empathetic.

"Are you? I wonder…" Her voice trailed off.

"They fell upon our island and carried off all that survived the slaughter. It was senseless, we had no enemies. We lived off the sea." She finished washing the bandage and rewrapped it around Alexander's leg.

"And yet we never heard from the Lords of Alveus." She looked at him, expecting a response. It wouldn't come. "How does it feel?" She asked referring to his leg.

"It feels better," he said with gratitude.

"Thank you."

She smiled at him and for a moment he smiled back at her until he realized how awkward she was making it, and he quickly changed the subject.

"How come you were not married off? Or were you arranged?" Alexander took note that tradition had begun to become a historical footnote with these new noblewomen.

"Sofia should have been married by now as well, but I fear she makes her own arrangements."

Emma blushed and giggled at her own thoughts.

"My family is not like that. We were lords of that island and subject to the whims of King Gustav.
I was free to marry whomever I wanted unless the king saw fit for me to marry into his line.

I was fortunate that he did not have any eligible sons." She grinned at Alexander and he felt an immediate curiosity to know why.

"What?" he asked. "What's with the smile?"

"I always knew whom I wanted," she said boldly. She said it with such conviction that Alexander immediately understood what she meant. His first and only thoughts were of Isadora, and it became awkward for him to continue the conversation.

"I'd better see to the camp," he said.

"We should take this opportunity for some fresh meat. Thank you again for your assistance." He stood delicately and pressed down weight on his injured leg. Emma helped support him up and there was another awkward silence as their eyes met. Her blue eyes softened and he felt himself becoming lost in her eyes until he broke eye contact.

He limped away from her and turned his head for a brief moment. He caught her looking at him. She smiled and he did his best to stay cordial and he politely nodded back at her. He glanced towards Katrina, but she had folded her arms and her expressions were twisted into a defiant mixture of hatred and disgust.

Alexander sighed and joined Fergus and Chauncey at the camp. He sent them out in hopes of finding fresh meat so they could rest from living off of fruits and berries. He missed Sara, the royal cook, and felt the pangs of homesickness.

"Do you miss home?" Jack asked reflectively.

"We've been gone almost a month now."

Alexander checked his camp before answering. It was a foreign land, and you never knew what was behind each rock or tree. The girls had retreated behind the waterfall to bathe, Fergus and Chauncey sought some easy prey, and Farkas lay asleep on the soft grass. Keira slept blissfully and kicked her feet as if in a dream while the gryphon stalked mice in the grass.

"I have no answers to that question," Alexander said sadly. "There are some things I do miss. I miss my sister, I miss my mother. I miss the quietness. But being here amazes me."

Alexander pointed towards the waterfall and the soft grass near them. "This place is a paradise and we have nothing like it back home."

Jack stretched out and laid back on the grass.

"And all the while we are both the hunter and the hunted. This seems to dampen the enjoyment."

Alexander silently agreed with Jack and started to feel himself tire of the cat-and-mouse game that was being played out before him.

He wanted to strike a blow to Abiyram and that blow he wanted was Duncan's death. But where did he go? Alexander wondered.

The blast of a woman's scream pierced Alexander's thoughts and he looked at Jack.

"Katrina!" They shouted in unison.

Farkas awoke and followed Alexander and Jack to the waterfall with Keira and the gryphon close behind. After a frantic search, Alexander found a small path behind the waterfall that went behind the wall of water.

"Katrina!" he shouted.

The splash of the water was so intense that he didn't see that figure that approached him until they collided.

"Calimus?" He sputtered.

"Where have you been?"

"Sleeping!" was the irritated reply.

"There's a cave. I just passed it. I think they are in there!"

"Why didn't you go inside?" Alexander asked angrily, but Calimus made no attempt at a reply.

"Bah! That's just like you isn't it?"

Alexander pushed Calimus aside and drew his sword and stopped when he came to the cave's entrance.

"Katrina? Emma!" He shouted into the blackness but heard nothing.

"Calimus check the water!" he ordered.

"Jack and Farkas come with me. Keira, stay here."

There's evil in there, his thoughts warned him.

Alexander looked at the gryphon and nodded his head. *I know this*, he thought. S*tay here and out of trouble.*

The three men entered the cave and peered into the blackness. A light flickered ahead and they heard the sounds of a struggle and muffled voices. Behind Alexander, someone shrieked. He wheeled around and almost ran into his brother.

"What now?"

"Alexander," he said trembling,

"The walls!"

Alexander examined the wall and witnessed a grisly scene. Various bodies outlined the wall as decoration in a macabre display of sacrifice. Several bodies were headless and others had torsos completely separated from their legs. Alexander felt a natural convulsion inside of him but fought the urge. Calimus was less successful and threw up on the ground.

"Hold yourself together, Prince," Farkas snarled.

"Don't you see?" Calimus whined and pointed at the bodies. He ripped the fabric off of one torso and produced it to Alexander. "These were our men."

Calimus was right. The bodies of the Alveuns who had died fighting Nicodemus had been brought back here. They were part of some sort of sick pagan ritual, Alexander thought.

Alexander breathed deeply for panic gripped at his soul. He too wanted to run, for fear of what lay ahead of them in the cave, but Katrina and Emma were in danger so he pressed on. They approached the light and the closer they came, the brighter the cave became until they entered its chamber.

The cave was filled with crystals that reflected the light of the one lone torch that flickered on the side of the wall. The light bounced from crystal to crystal and illuminated the room.

On one side of the chamber, Emma and Katrina were pressed against the wall by an unseen force. Their arms were outstretched and their feet could not touch the ground. They struggled valiantly against the unseen magic, but their efforts were useless.

And in the middle of the room behind a large crystal that jutted out from the cavern floor stood their old enemy, Nicodemus.
He had changed his cloak to one that was pure white and the purity of the cloak used the reflective light of the crystals to project its brilliance.

He had recovered his staff and held it in his hand. He smiled evilly and even chuckled as Alexander stepped forward.

"Welcome Alexander," he said,

"To my home."

"I do not care much for your home, Nicodemus, but you have two of my people and I would have them back. Release them now." Alexander's tone was firm and he gripped his sword firmly.

"Alexander Wolfield. Prince of Alveus and the harbinger of death." Nicodemus stopped chuckling and grew very serious. "The efforts to kill you are most frustrating. You avoid death from the dead warriors, you avoid our best animagus, and you manage to talk your way out of the Bete'szek village."

"I have no idea what you are saying," Alexander said flatly.

"Do not take me for a fool," Nicodemus' voice thundered through the cavern.

"On your way into my home you have learned the fate of those who seek to fight us. When I am through with you, they will know the penalty for their disobedience. They will line my home as ornaments to their folly. I will have Dragonus and his son torn apart!"

Nicodemus shouted these words with such vile hatred and he slammed his staff on the ground. Five dead warriors broke through the soil and climbed their way out of the earth's womb.

"My dead servants," he yelled,

"Tear them limb from limb."

He motioned his staff at Farkas and a bolt of energy passed by Alexander and collided into the unsuspecting guard. Farkas flew backwards and landed onto the ground. For a moment, he was stunned, but he managed to get up and ready himself for another attack.

The dead warriors followed the bolt and attacked Alexander and his men. Alexander swung his sword so hard at the first warrior that he knocked the sword out of his hand and then swung back and cut the head from his shoulders.

"My Lord!" Katrina screamed. Nicodemus pointed his weapon in her direction. He lifted his staff and levitated Katrina to the top of the cavern. He locked eyes with Alexander and brought his staff to the ground. Katrina screamed again and hurtled towards the cavern floor. Alexander ran to catch her, but his wounded leg hampered his ability to get to her in time.

Jack rushed in, caught Katrina, and tumbled to the ground with her in his arms.

"I have her!" Jack shouted.

His armor filled his head with a voice that warned him a sword's blow was coming. Alexander wheeled around and blocked the cut that had been meant for his head.

Calimus swung his sword at the distracted soldier, cutting off the dead man's head as Farkas took on the last two dead warriors on his own.

Nicodemus swung his staff towards Jack and sent a strong wind towards him. Katrina scrambled behind a rock as debris and rocks flew in their direction. Jack scrambled towards the rocks, but the wind bumped him off balance and his head knocked against a rock. He crumbled to the ground and clutched his head in agony.

Alexander and Calimus ran at Nicodemus to improve Jack's predicament. The sorcerer swung his staff and planted it firmly in the ground. The shock that was sent out stung Alexander and Calimus and knocked them to the floor. Farkas finally dispatched both dead warriors and took his turn rushing into the fray.

The evil man turned his attention back to Jack and swung his staff towards his head. Jack ducked and the wooden rod impacted the rock above him and shot sparks and dust from the impact.

Nicodemus grunted and brought his staff to lunge it into Jack's torso. The top of the staff, the crystal, turned bright red and he brought it down into Jack.

Jack placed his left hand between the crystal and his body, grabbing the staff with his right hand.

Jack screamed in pain and writhed about on the ground as Nicodemus tried to push it to his body. Katrina sprang out of hiding and jumped on the sorcerer's back from her rock. She punched his head with her free hand and tried to bite his ear. Nicodemus howled in anger and pulled Katrina off his back. The lack of concentration changed the color of the crystal and Emma fell to the ground, released from the power that imprisoned her. Farkas swung his sword at Nicodemus, who blocked it. The prince's recovered from the shock of Nicodemus' magic. Together they tackled Nicodemus and wrestled his weapon out of his hand. Alexander sat on top of his enemy as he struggled and struck him violently. He struck him again and again as he struggled underneath him until Calimus finally pulled the prince away from him.

Nicodemus lay there bleeding profusely from the cuts Alexander inflicted and laughed sickly. Emma rushed to Jack's side who was shaking and sweating from his profuse pain.

His left hand had been burned and charred so badly that Alexander doubted he would ever have use of his hand again.

"Prince," Jack said gasping in pain.

"It's okay Jack, you're safe," Alexander said as he tried to soothe Jack.

"It burns," Jack said through clenched teeth and tears.

"Emma," Alexander stepped aside and allowed Emma to care for Jack and he turned his attention back to Nicodemus. Farkas lifted the old man into a sitting position and placed his blade next to his throat. He was still laughing regardless of his predicament.

"Truly, his highness Prince Àlexander and his men are the greatest warriors in the land." Nicodemus gaped at Alexander in amazement.

"How is it that none of the greatest powers in this land have bested you? You are immune to our magic, as if you had your own." He looked as if an amazing knowledge had been discovered.

"Flattery will get you nowhere," Alexander growled,

"Except your head on a spike. What did you do to Jack?"

"When human flesh touches the source of our powers, any number of things can happen.

Flesh melts, blood is poisoned. Anything. If he had held onto it, he would have died in a most excruciating way."

"Shall I kill him, My Lord?" Farkas lifted the blade deeper into his neck and a trickle of blood ran down Nicodemus' neck.

"Wait! Wait!" The sorcerer's tone sounded desperate, and he raised a pleading hand up in the air.

Perhaps he is afraid of death, Alexander thought. Alexander picked up the staff and examined it.

"That's not a toy, boy, even for such an accomplished warrior," he growled, but the prick of Farkas' blade quieted him down.

Alexander felt an incredible surge of power and confidence surge through his veins. Thoughts of his brother's death churned hatred and vengeance inside of him. The crystal glowed red and Alexander felt its heat begging to be used.

Revenge is yours, it whispered. *Nicodemus is a murderer and murderers must be punished. Use me as an instrument of your power, and take down every murderer. Let me help you. Use me.*

Alexander's hands shook and his body reacted to the thoughts the staff hinted at.

This is not the way Edward would want it, his conscience soothed. *It is too great an evil for you to manage. Destroy the staff or risk having it used on you and your people.*

Destroy your enemies and bring peace, the staff bargained.

Destroy the staff or face destruction, his conscience replied. The flame burned hotter and Alexander waved the staff slowly around the room and noticed the fear on the faces of his friends.

Emma mouthed words to him but he could not hear them. He inspected the staff once more and made his choice. He walked to the crystal pillar and swung the staff as hard as he could. The staff shattered in half and pieces of the staff flew through the chamber. The voices quieted in his mind and he could no longer hear the staff's whispers.

"Alexander?" Emma asked concerned,

"Are you okay?"

"I'm fine," Alexander replied and he rolled his head in a circle to loosen up his neck muscles. It felt like a hand had gripped his mind and he sought to shake the feeling. He turned to the sniveling man that sat imprisoned on the cave's floor.

"We should kill him, Sir," Farkas recommended and pointed his sword into the prisoner's neck.

"He's too powerful to bring with us."

Alexander eyed the sorcerer and said nothing as he sifted through his feelings. On one hand, Alexander thought, Nicodemus was no better than a murderous thug and to be rid of him was what was best for the land. On the other hand…there was no other way for Alexander. The bastard needed to pay for Jack's hand.

"Kill him," he said, without remorse.

"Wait!" cried Nicodemus.

"I can be of service to Your Highness!"

Alexander raised his hand and stopped Farkas from puncturing the throat. Farkas groaned but stayed his blade.

"Of what value is saving your life?"

"What if I could predict for Your Highness the whereabouts of his enemies? That benefit alone would be enough for my life."

"You're lying," Alexander replied.

"Am I?" The prisoner queried.

"Every move you have made, we have seen. We always know where you are going and where you have been.

Would you not care for that same advantage and to be able to wreak havoc on your enemies?

Allow me to demonstrate." The elder stood up and carefully placed his fingers inside a small pouch that hung from his rope belt. Farkas stayed close by and prepared to strike him in case of treachery.

"I don't trust him," Emma whispered.

"This doesn't feel right."

Alexander kept his gaze focused and the sorcerer walked to a large crystal mound in front of him. He motioned for Alexander to approach, and he made his way next to the mound.

"These are what we call runes," Nicodemus explained. "By asking the right questions of them we can discern the future....Ask me a question."

"Where is Duncan?" Alexander didn't hesitate at all.

"The runes can't answer that," was the tactful response.

"What good are they?"

"The runes can answer questions that result in a yes or no."

Alexander rolled his eyes with impatience.

"It seems I have no use for them...or you."

"Trust the runes, let them work!" Nicodemus insisted in a panicked voice.

"Please, one last question."

"Is Duncan nearby?"

The sorcerer closed his eyes and murmured a few words and then tossed the runes into the air. Alexander watched as the little bones flipped over and over and then finally gathered around the deepest part of the crystal. They looked down and saw all the pieces were identical.

"What does that mean?" Alexander asked.

"Duncan is not nearby."

"Interesting," Alexander mused and he pondered the effectiveness of runes.

"Do one for me!" Calimus shouted.

"Will I be king?"

"Of course," Tacitus smiled, and he repeated the process. Calimus watched intently as again the runes bounced around the crystal and showed a different pattern than before.

"You will be king one day," Nicodemus remarked, "And all will bow before you."

Calimus' mouth dropped in astonishment and tears formed in his eyes. Alexander was pleased to see his brother's happiness.

"Here's another one," Calimus playfully asked, "Will my brother marry Isadora?"

Nicodemus smiled kindly at Calimus and gathered up the runes into his pouch.

"Come on! I asked a question, let us see the answers."

"Prince Calimus the runes are not dice that you can play with over and over. I am sorry, but they should only be used for important, heart-felt emotions like anger or revenge and not silly games."

"What's to stop us from killing you and taking them?" Alexander asked matter-of-factly.

'If you kill me, they'll be of no use to you, I can I assure you of that," he replied flatly.

"I do not see these runes as a reason to keep you alive. But I will make an agreement with you. You are going to give me answers to all of my questions, and then I will spare your life if I believe that you are being truthful. Are we understood?"

Nicodemus took stock of the people in the cavern and took note of the anger that reflected in their faces. Satisfied he could not escape, he nodded his head in agreement to Alexander's terms.

"Now, tell me everything," Alexander whispered and he grabbed Nicodemus' arm and pushed him in front of him as he motioned to his companions to follow him.

CHAPTER XI

The party cautiously made their way through the caves entrance and avoided the corpses that hung on the walls of the cave.

"You are so sick," Emma commented,

"Who would do such a thing to people?"

"They died nobly," the sorcerer said with an injured air. "They cannot feel what happens to their body. Now of course there are such times, when punishment is needed, as with the Bete'szek."

"This isn't punishment, this is disgusting. You are a monster! Am I to understand that Katrina and I would have received the same treatment?" Emma wheeled into Nicodemus' face as if she meant to strike him.

"No, sweet girl, I had other plans." Nicodemus' lips curled in a sick smile. Emma responded in disgust and grabbed Katrina's hand and hurried in front of them.

They stayed quiet until they came to the mouth of the cave where Keira and the gryphon sat and waited. Keira barked happily when she saw the men emerge. The gryphon quickly backed away and hid behind Keira when the sorcerer came out of the tunnel. Keira snarled and bared her teeth at their enemy.

"Good dog," Alexander rubbed Keira's head to soothe her. "I might not get an opportunity to kill you, for my dog might save me the trouble."

They reached the mouth of the cave and carefully made their way to the side of the waterfall. Devin, Fergus, and Chauncey caught sight of them and ran to them immediately.

"What's happened?" Fergus called out.

"Jack's been hurt badly," Emma replied.

"Help him down and watch his hand. Do not touch it."

They waited for Jack as he tentatively made his way down the steps. His face was pale and he walked cautiously and steadied himself as best he could. Once down he stumbled into the waiting hands of Chauncey and Fergus. They carried him back to their campsite as Emma took charge of his care and sent Katrina and Calimus scouring the surrounding area to find herbs and salve for his wound.

"It's a shame about that," Nicodemus remarked to no one in particular. "Better to die than to lose a part of your body."

"Sorcerer, your sympathies are unwarranted and unneeded. I suggest you stay very still and very quiet." Alexander left him to Farkas' care and knelt by Jack's side. Jack smiled weakly and Alexander grasped his right hand firmly.

"How do you feel?" Alexander asked at the point of ridiculousness. Jack sweated profusely. His hand was charred badly.

"I will live, I think," Jack said,

"He needs to rest," Emma said with firmness.

"He won't rest if you speak to him. Please, My Lord, let him sleep."

Alexander nodded and leaned down and whispered in Jack's ear.

"This was my fault, Jack. I should have listened to you." Alexander was more sincere about those words than any other he had uttered in his life.

"No," Jack struggled to sit up and had to be restrained by Emma.

"It is my duty to protect you and not to question you. I swore to give my life for you, I have only given my hand. I still will give my life for you."

"Alex! Please!" Emma held Jack's head in her lap and stroked his dark hair and tried to calm him.

Alexander was taken aback by Emma's tone. Up to this moment, she had acted subservient and took her place as a servant. She called him Alex, and that was unacceptable, he thought quietly. But for the sake of Jack's peace of mind, he remained quiet for now.

Calimus returned with Katrina and together they joined Alexander and his three guards near Nicodemus.

"Night is falling," Alexander remarked upon the shadows that increased near him,

"It's time for you to answer my questions." The magician nodded his head and everyone gathered closer to hear them.

"Why do you seek to eliminate the gryphons?"

"The gryphons," he sighed,

"Are impervious to magic. There are a number of things that man can do in regards to the gryphon. Think of it…the blood forged with swords or armor…think of the power one would have!"

Alexander's eyes flickered in thought and wandered down to the armor that sat beside him. Nicodemus saw this and clenched his fist.

"Now answer my question," he ventured.

"How long have you known your armor is forged with gryphon's blood? I recognized in the cavern that even though you all wear the same crest, there is something different about this one. That's very interesting."

"What is interesting?" Chauncey asked.

"The question that has perplexed us…and by us I mean Abiyram… Why does Alexander not die when even the prophet has seen it and prophesied it? Even the runes tell us of your death, and yet you cheat death time and time again."

"I sincerely apologize on your befuddlement," Alexander said, mixing sarcasm and cynicism.

"I am not quite sure why my light has not been extinguished from this life, but I'm sure it's because you and your assassins are quite inept at killing me." Fergus and Chauncey laughed in unison and Alexander allowed himself a moment of mirth as well.

Nicodemus pointed at Alexander's armor.

"The answer is here. It has nothing to do with you. What would happen to you without that armor, I wonder."

Calimus snorted and rolled his eyes.

"With or without armor, he's one of the most fearsome swordsmen in the kingdom."

"I hope you truly believe that," the sorcerer said menacingly,

"Because the brotherhood will not rest until he is dead. Especially now. Your armor and your new pet. In order for the brotherhood to move forward, you must both be killed."

"Why not let the gryphon go o ff on its own if it truly is the last one?"

"The things that you and the gryphon can accomplish together, you can scarcely be able to comprehend. Do you think that when your ancestors invaded this land that horses were the reason why our armies were defeated? I can conjure the dead, why would I fear a horse? No, your ancestors were handed the secret of our only weakness."

"Why not leave us in peace? You have these lands, rule them as you would."

"When you are a demigod you do not compromise." Nicodemus' eyes blazed with hatred for Alexander.

"It seems that being a demigod has not improved your situation, Sir. Now that your staff is destroyed, how will you continue to live as before?"

"I do not plan on living as before." The old man sighed and looked towards the skies. "I have failed my brothers and my punishment is death. The fact that

I am talking to you now will almost certainly be the final spear in my fate. They will find me and kill anyone who stands in their path."

"So why do you not escape and run to other lands?"

"You haven't seen the evil and power that we are capable of doing. I stand a better chance of living with you then I would on my own. So, I cast my lot with you, and I will help you, in exchange for my life."

"Tell me about Duncan and Angelica."

"Duncan…well you have seen what he is. He's an Animagus."

"Anima-who?" Fergus asked.

"Animagus," Nicodemus corrected.

"He can shift into shapes between human and beast. Duncan and Angelica were orphaned years ago through some unfortunate tragedy that befell their parents."

"That you had nothing to do with. Is that it?" Alexander asked accusingly and his prisoner narrowed his brows.

"We had nothing to do with it! What you don't seem to understand in this series of events is this world is full of cruelty and it comes from heroes and villains. It could come from the royal family as easy as from our brotherhood."

The old man relaxed and the tenseness disappeared so he continued.

"Abiyram found them hiding and took them in. He trained them both to be his killers and unlocked the secrets of shape shifting with Duncan. Duncan was an incredible pupil and as you know became the most dangerous killer in this land. You will never see him coming."

"There are three dogs in total. Duncan and who else? Is it Patrick?"

"I do not know this Patrick except in conversations with Abiyram. He is not one of us and I do not know the identity of the other dogs. If they haven't already shifted, they must just be animals."

"What of Angelica? What is her sentence?"

"Angelica was killed at the altar and the ritual was performed. They removed her heart and buried her. Care was taken to resurrect her at the precise time, in order to take command of Abiyram's armies."

"You mean the Bete'szek?"

"No, I mean the Dead Army."

"So the undead dead have an undead Dead Army, is that it? Where the hell are we when these things happen, Chauncey?" Fergus interjected and then quieted when everyone stared at him.

"Abiyram has collected bodies from countries for years. If you look into your graveyards it's doubtful that you will find any bodies there.
Emma's people were the last ones he carried off."

"Why does he do this?"

"Imagine your soldiers going to war against their grandparents, or deceased siblings. You saw this with Katrina. Family members can be extremely effective in demoralizing an army." Nicodemus beamed proudly.

"So now, Prince Alexander, Duncan wants you dead as he holds you responsible for Angelica's death. Angelica is controlled by Abiyram and her only reason for living is to murder you. Welcome to the war that has gone on for hundreds of years."

"How can I end it?"

"Kill the brotherhood…no small feat, but you already have the tools. Your sword is very effective as well. Yes, that sword, an easy way to destroy the undead. Nice of the prophet to maintain the balance between good and evil by giving it to you."

"I am not sure I understand this sword."

"It's quite simple. It becomes more than just a sword when sorcery is near. You focus your mind on it and you can create a wall of fire that seeks out and destroys anything that is under the spell of a sorcerer."

"So I can destroy the undead with fire and water? Back in the cave, the water burned their flesh away…."

Nicodemus waved his hand and cut off Alexander's thoughts.

"When the bodies are resurrected there is a period of time where their flesh must readjust to the elements. If they had left the cave, the sun would have assisted the process and their skin would not be impacted by water, only fire."

"So where will your brothers strike next?"

"Nowhere. Abiyram has made it clear that we are to allow Alveus to crumble from within. Our sources already indicate a friction between the sons of Magnus." Nicodemus allowed himself a chuckle. "The more you struggle against your fate, the more entwined you become."

"You are murderers, all of you!" Alexander stood in disgust.

"Innocent people die and you all stand in approval…for what? Power? An extra field of grass?"

"This war is older than you and like all wars, this one needs an ending."

"Can I kill him now?" Fergas begged Alexander and drew his sword to take his life.

"No," Alexander said,

"We are better than them."

"You seem very sure of this," Nicodemus replied. "But we know better don't we?"

Alexander ignored his last comment and set his men up to keep watch through the night. They ate the deer that Fergus and Chauncey killed in the forest and settled down quietly. Jack ate sparingly and fell asleep early. Alexander was left with his thoughts and eventually settled down into a very light and very troubled sleep.

Alexander had scarcely nodded off to sleep when the visions began again. He found himself on the other side of a wall of a ruined building and he walked amongst tall grass with a sword in his hand. He took a moment and gathered his bearings and steadied himself against the cold brick wall. He had a nagging thought…there was something here…was it an answer that he sought? He focused his energies as much as he could upon this thought. There was something ahead of him and he needed it. It held an answer he desperately needed, for what he did not know, but he moved forward and peered around the corner of the wall.

He saw nothing but the brick wall and grass that moved as if something or someone had just been there. He jogged to the next corner and examined the grass and the ground for footprints. There were none, but the grass seemed pressed down as if someone indeed stood there.

I've got to hurry, Alexander thought to himself and peered around the next corner. Again, grass moved as if something had been there but when he examined it, there was nothing. He sprinted to the next corner and turned it rapidly and he ran to the next one determined to catch what stayed just out of reach. Corner by corner he turned with little regard for his own safety and felt confident that he almost caught up with this mystery. As his confidence grew, so did a sense of dread. He was not alone, he sensed, for something was following him. He turned and looked back, but nothing was there.

He assured himself that there was nothing there, but the feeling multiplied and grew stronger within him. There was a darkness coming and it threatened to consume him. No longer obsessed with what lay ahead of him, he fled and turned the corner of the building and raced along the side.

He refused to look back for fear of what followed him, but he felt the darkness draw closer.

It was the same feeling that he had in the cave when he held Nicodemus' staff, but it no longer invited him. This darkness threatened to overwhelm him and engulf him.

He ran and ran as the rain began to fall which made the path slippery beneath him. He slipped and fell numerous times but got back up and continued to run. His heart pounded faster as he felt it creep closer and closer to him. At the last moment when it threatened to overtake him, he turned to face it. He saw nothing but darkness and felt a jarring collision as it reached him.

He woke upon its impact and sat up and gasped for air. Fergus, who had stood guard over Nicodemus, reacted immediately.

"Sir, what happened? Are you alright?" His face paled with concern.

"A dream," Alexander replied as he tried to catch his breath. "Nothing to worry over."

"But you're bleeding." Fergus motioned to his nose. Alexander wiped beneath his nose and looked at the blood on his fingertips.

"I am fine," he insisted to Fergus. "I am going to the lake to wash the blood off my face. Stand guard over the prisoner."

Fergus obeyed and Alexander wandered off from the campsite until he came to a cluster of river rocks where he could conceal himself from the others. If anyone woke up he would not need to answer their concerns. The water was cool and felt wonderful against his bearded face. He looked at his reflection in the water as the ripples slowed and the water was once again peaceful.

His appearance tonight was nearly unrecognizable from the face he was used to seeing. The beard had become fuller and grown almost an inch from his chin. His blue eyes no longer sparkled with the mischief of his youth, and seemed cold and empty. There was blood on his hands and his arms and he diligently washed them and tried to remove the stain of blood from him. The blood refused to wash easily and he rubbed his hands against his arms maniacally.

I must remove this blood off of me, he thought. *I have to! Why won't it leave me?*

He scooped up mud from the lake and rubbed his arm with the mud. The blood finally dissipated and the mixture of blood and mud trickled off his arms and fell back into the lake. His mind was eased from the burden once the blood was finally removed from his skin. He took one last look at his reflection and mused upon it. He looked so different from what he knew.

"I am not alright," he whispered quietly to himself.

He caught sight of several lights flickering in the distance. For a moment, he debated whether to rouse his guard or not. He weighed how irritated Jack would be if he knew Alexander went to explore the lights, especially without his swords. But Jack was sick now, and he needed his rest.

The flapping of winds shifted his attention. A crow landed on a rock near him. Remembering his wound, Alexander backed away from the large bird. It cawed at him twice, then flapped its wings and took off in the direction of the camp.

When a soft melody came dancing across the water, Alexander's curiosity got the better of him and he made his way around the large pool of water to see who was camped near them.

CHAPTER XII

A small band of travelers had camped near the lake and busied themselves with cooking a meal over their campfire. The adults outfitted themselves strangely, for one did not find their clothes north of Alveus. They had nice clothes, colored brightly with tassels hanging off of them, and each of the women wore large golden earrings. The men wore leather boots and covered their tunics with large sheepskin vests. Alexander assumed that these were not Bete'szek, their appearance far too refined for their tastes, and their skin tone far too swarthy.

There were several wagons that looked as if they served as housing for these strangers as they moved their possessions from place to place. Little children ran about the wagons and around the small clearing where they had built a fire. It was a bit carefree, Alexander observed, after he had seen what truly lived in these woods.

There was an older white haired lady with a hunched back near the tree that Alexander had chosen to conceal himself behind. She was the only one in the camp not dressed in its finery. She pulled a small pouch off her frayed clothing and emptied its contents into her hands. She cupped her hands and whispered into them. When finished, she tossed them into the air. The old woman caught them in her hands, cupped her hands and opened them again. She smiled and addressed the tree that Alexander hid behind.

"My children," she crooned,

"We have an honored guest, Prince Alexander of the Alveuns. Make him up some delicious stew for he is tired and does not sleep well these days." Alexander sank back behind the tree further, and he wondered how she saw through his concealment.

"Come, Prince," she continued,

"I am an old lady and we are a family of poor travelers. We mean you no harm. We can help you."

Alexander left his hiding spot and into full sight of the encampment. He counted twenty-five men, women, and children. They did not appear to be heavily armed, except for hand axes.

"Prince Alexander," she said sweetly and curtsied, "Your name is a famous one, and it is on all of our lips. We welcome you to our encampment."

"Who are your people? Are you Bete'szek?" Alexander asked suspiciously.

"Even before the Bete'szek, we are. I am a Savonite, and we are the oldest inhabitants of this land," she stated. The rest of her people eyed Alexander suspiciously, but seemed to respond to her cues. They respectfully nodded and remained near their wagons.

"I have never heard of you," Alexander responded.

"And yet here we are," the larger of the men responded. His words elicited nods from the rest of the group. For all their finery, the men wore their hair long, and the women's hairstyles were completely undone.

"My name is Jezebel," the old woman explained. "We Savonites are simple traders who bring our gifts and talents from kingdom to kingdom."

"What gifts and services would those be?"

Jezebel smiled, and Alexander was put off by the crone's teeth. They were crooked and stained; he was immediately repulsed and tried his best to conceal his disdain.

"We are a very talented people. My sisters and I have amassed a great deal of knowledge over our years.

Come inside with me, and I will show you how we may be of service." She guided Alexander and led him past her people to a covered wagon. Jezebel snarled at a woman who stood nearby to bring her guest food and drink.

They entered the wagon, and Alexander was shocked at the amount of trinkets it held. It seemed larger inside the wagon than he assumed, and had enough room to stretch if he so desired.

In the center of the wagon stood a table and on that table sat a silver orb. The orb was transparent, but there was an energy that surrounded it. Jezebel bade him sit down across from her, and she produced small cards and tossed them on the table in front of him.

"What are these things?" Alexander asked curiously.

"Portents to the future," Jezebel responded helpfully. "You need to know what it is you are up against." She poured a dark liquid into a wooden bowl and set it by her right hand.

"What is that for?" Alexander eyed the bowl suspiciously. It was neither wine nor water.

"It is for cleaning hands once we're finished," she said in a tone that stood Alexander's hair on end. Jezebel sat down across from him and put her hand over the crystal orb.

"All you have known is this weak religion, Your Highness," she began,

"But you have begun to see what man can do with real power. This power is yours for the taking; the brotherhood fears you and the damage you can inflict. Watch closely to what I am going to show you."

The woman who was commanded to bring food for Alexander clumsily entered the wagon, breaking Jezebel's focus for a moment. Anger flashed in the old woman's eyes, but she recovered her composure enough for the other woman to set food and drink in front of Alexander.

Several small pieces of meat, some olives, and a few wild vegetables were organized loosely on the plate. Another goblet was placed in front of him to quench his thirst.

When the woman left, Jezebel focused her gaze upon the orb and slowly moved her hand over it. Fog swirled in the crystal ball as if she was stirring it, and it became less transparent.

"Ask me a question, Prince, what do you want?" she hissed.

"Where will Duncan be next?"

The old woman sighed with disappointed.

"You are missing what I would offer to you. My powers unlock doors to see the future."

Jezebel's face twisted as she focused her energy on the orb that glowed before her.

The other old woman that she had addressed entered silently and placed a wooden bowl with some olives and bread in front of the Prince, and a wooden cup filled with water.

"Spirits! Listen to your servant. I enlist you to answer my query. Show Alexander his true path!" The candles in the wagon dimmed, and the only light was the orb. The cloud dissipated and images began forming. The Prince held the sorcerer's staff in one hand, and a sword in another. His powers crushed every enemy that tried to do him harm. He laid waste to the countryside and had a huge army at his command.

The last vision that Alexander saw was that he wore the Alveun crown on his head, and eventually, everyone bowed to him.

"No," Alexander finally insisted. The orb returned to its normal function, and the candles flicked back to produce light. "This is not what I want." He spoke emphatically and popped an olive in his mouth.

"I am here for Duncan only, not for anything else." He spit the pit onto the floor in an attempt to invoke a reaction from his hostess.

Jezebel grumbled a bit and set her hand back over the orb. "Spirits!" she shouted.

"Where does the assassin Duncan go?"

The cloudiness separated inside the orb to reveal a deserted castle turret. Alexander studied the turret intently and analyzed it brick by brick.

"I do not know this turret, it's not an Alveun design. None of this is helpful," Alexander complained in frustration. The Alveuns were perfectionists, and they made their turrets with smooth stones. This one was jagged and while a solid construction, was not as aesthetically pleasing. "Show me who he is after," he commanded.

Jezebel broke her concentration with the orb and made eye contact with Alexander.

"I cannot tell you whom he goes after," she insisted. "The spirits show images of the future. With Duncan, it shows his destination."

"You do know, and you will tell me," Alexander commanded.

"Let me read your fate in the cards," she pleaded as she began flipping them over,

"Look, for this one, love awaits."

"I am not interested in your cards. Bring back this image," he insisted. He tapped the globe which tested the old woman's patience.

Jezebel gritted her teeth into a smile and stretched her hand out to Alexander.

"Perhaps your palm. I can read the lines on your palm and tell you how this ends. I can show you how your life will be."

"I will only ask you once more," Alexander demanded menacingly,

"Bring back that image and show me who Duncan will go after!" A tense moment existed for a moment as he glared at Jezebel.

"Very well," she said,

"Eat some food, and I will show you."

Alexander eyed the food suspiciously and assessed his situation. He tapped the table subtly, enough to release some nervous energy, but not to alert the old woman to his thoughts. There was obviously much more to this woman than met his eye. He had left his weapons at the camp and had nothing on him except the gryphon goblet that had been given to him by Bishop Malachius. He doubted he could overwhelm the camp with a goblet.

He was now very concerned that this was a trap. He closed his eyes and brought his hands down to the goblet. It was a gryphon's claw, and he touched the bony claw. He concentrated on the gryphon, and tried to reach it through his thoughts.

In an instant, he stood in the gryphon temple and in front of the tiny gryphon's statue.

"Wake up!" he shouted. He rubbed its cheeks as if trying to massage the statue to life. It took a moment, but the statue's yellow eyes flickered open, and it looked curiously at Alexander.

"My Lord, what are you doing here?" the gryphon asked.

"Listen to me, I am in a campsite near the lake. Wake Keira and Jack and hurry to my side."

"You are where?"

"Just hurry! I haven't much time. There's something about to go wrong."

Alexander felt as if he was grabbed forcefully from his thoughts and when he opened his eyes he found Jezebel eyeing him with suspicion.

"Is there something amiss?" she hissed.

He brought his hand back to the table and smiled cordially. "Nothing."

"Then we shall continue." She raised her goblet to him in a toast. It was very ordinary, probably made of pewter. "Join me in this toast, and I will reveal what you seek. To your health and prosperity and the death of your enemies."

He raised the goblet on the table to her.

"To the death of my enemies." He set the cup back down on the small table without as much as a sip.

He reached down to his belt and untied his gryphon goblet from his waist and placed it on the table. Jezebel's eyes widened at the sight of the gryphon's claw.

"Where did you get that?"

"You know what it is?"

"It's a gryphon clawed goblet," Jezebel looked equal parts curious and fearful.

"And you know what it does?"

"It tells you if you have poison in your cup." The two continued to eye each other suspiciously.

"Show me who Duncan is after," he finally commanded.

Jezebel concentrated her thoughts and began to commune with her spirits. She situated her wrinkled hand over the orb and quietly murmured her commands. The orb's cloudiness again dissipated to show the castle turret. Alexander quietly poured the contents of the cup into his gryphon goblet. The water slowly started to change color from its clear state to a blood red.

Alexander's attention shifted back briefly to the orb. A young woman appeared in view and walked towards the edge of the turret. He did not notice Jezebel's free hand had moved into the bowl of liquid that sat nearby her.

The figure in the orb turned around, and Alexander gasped as he recognized her face.

"Sofia," he said quietly.

"No. No, he will not kill my sister." His face contorted in rage and he looked questioningly at Jezebel.

"He will succeed because you will be dead, Prince."

An animal's barking came from the direction of the woods and the cry of a surprised encampment arose. Sounds of steel clashing and excited voices echoed throughout the camp. He heard Jack shouting orders to his men. Jezebel jumped out of her chair, and Alexander flipped the table back and into her. She stumbled backwards but maintained her balance.

"You are unarmed," she hissed gleefully as she brandished the left hand that she had dipped in the bowl. Her nails were an inch long and they dripped with the purple liquid. She leaped over the table and struck at Alexander with her right hand. He caught it mid-flight and did everything he could to keep Jezebel from puncturing him with her claw.

She came close. He didn't know why, but he had an overwhelming sense of foreboding if she should scratch him. He used both hands, but then she jammed her right hand into his eyes and began pushing upwards, into his eyes.

After a brief grapple, he tripped and fell backwards out of the wagon, landing on the ground with a hard thud.

The campsite had emptied of its original users, for Alexander's men had frightened them into fleeing. Undaunted with the lack of support, Jezebel leapt out of the wagon and landed on top of him.

"Do not let her scratch the Prince!" Nicodemus yelled.

Fergus jumped into the melee and pulled Jezebel off of Alexander. Chauncey grabbed her hands and together they quickly tied her hands behind her back.

"Brother?" Calimus asked.

"I am fine. No scrapes." He checked his arms and legs for any sign of a new cut, but since he had been beaten up over the last week, he just looked for any signs of fresh blood. When satisfied that he had not been cut, so he turned his attention to his pets, who tussled with each other over the wild beast that had been roasted on a spit.

"Give me a sword," he commanded. Jack handed him his blade and he stood in front of Jezebel. Chauncey held her arms still, careful that she did not break her bonds.

"I have a riddle for you, hag," Alexander said.

"A nightmare I am for most, but for others, I am a savior. My hands are cold and bleak, but it's the warm hearts I seek."

Jezebel grinned and let out a cackle.

"I do not fear death," she said boldly.

"I am not like the coward that holds your company. She spat at Nicodemus, landing on his beard

"The brotherhood will enjoy your death as much as any other. You best hope for a quick death than a prolonged painful one."

"Is that poison on your fingers? Who were you hoping to kill with it?"

The sorcerer shook his head and muttered an old proverb. "I am a tool for who in darkness dwell. I am within you, corrupting you more than a deadly spell."

"What does that mean?" Devin asked.

Nicodemus approached the witch cautiously and motioned to her hand. "Her fingernails were dipped in poison. It is injected into your blood stream through a scrape or a cut. From there the poison works its way into your heart and will expel the heart from your chest."

"Dear God!" Fergus exclaimed.

"That's blasphemy!" Chauncey corrected.

"I don't care!" Fergus responded.

"This whole frontier is blasphemy! The undead dead, magical sorcerers, this whole frontier has lost its mind! The whole lot of them can go to hell."

"And indeed they shall Fergus," Alexander said.

"Starting with this one."

"Alexander!" Emma exclaimed.

"She is unarmed, you are not going to murder her right here?"

"Is there a better place?" He thundered.

"She is too dangerous to be left alive and she is not unarmed. She swears loyalty to their necromancers and is fanatical in her devotion. Perhaps you would like to wake up to a missing heart?"

Emma agreed silently and took Katrina away quietly. When the two women were out of sight, Alexander handed the sword to Nicodemus.

"Kill her," was all Alexander said.

"Do it, Nicodemus," Jezebel sneered.

"You're a traitor to your kind and when Duncan finishes with Sofia he will deal with you. Alveus will lie in ruin with the death of you."

Alexander grabbed Jezebel by the hair and looked directly into her cold grey eyes. Her hair was oily and disgusting, he noticed several bugs darting in and out of her scalp.

"He will not lay a hand on my sister and I will kill anyone who threatens her."

"You fight against the future and fate. Edward was a victim in your quest to change events. You do not understand you cannot change fate."

Alexander made a sign of the cross and nodded to Nicodemus.

"I would invite you to watch, but your fate is decided."

Jezebel gasped as the sorcerer ran his sword through her stomach. She fell onto her knees and glared coldly at him as he pulled the sword back out. She fell on her side and her eyes closed as her breath expired.

"Thank you," Alexander said to Nicodemus,

"For proving your loyalty."

"I have sealed my own fate," he said sadly.

"We spit at fate here," Alexander replied ruefully. His thoughts were immediately consumed with Sofia's security. He did not recognize the castle towers, but he had left her at Edgebrooke in Isadora's care. They were at least a week's journey away, and they needed to hurry if he wanted to save her.

"Pack the camp men," Alexander ordered,

"We're going home."

CHAPTER XIII

Alexander counted himself fortunate that the six days he had traveled from the waterfall in the frontier to Edgebrooke passed without incidents. Neither bird nor beast distracted them from their mission. The strange encounter with the Bete'szek had created an uneasy truce within the forest. The barbarians did not hide themselves as before and contented themselves with boldly approaching and walking by them. Calimus commented that he would never have expected this within a hundred lifetimes.

By the sixth day of traveling, his men were exhausted and needed to rest. The color had again drained from Jack's face, and his wound weakened him so that he could not walk to give his horse a rest.

He wore a glove on his left hand to hide the grotesque sight and lifted it only for Emma when she inspected the wound. Alexander's wounds had also begun to heal, a scar forming on his leg wound where the dog had bit him. Calimus' face returned to its previously unbloodied countenance.

To his brother's pleasure, Emma remarked how he was starting to look more like a King and less like a pampered noble.

The gryphon grew in size and measured half of the size of Keira, and her wings had finally grown with her. She had not flown yet, and Alexander wondered that if she could fly, would she have flown away and seek out what was left of her family.

The gryphon and Keira played and hunted with each other, and together they created a formidable hunting pair. Keira's superior hunting nose and the gryphon's eyesight eliminated the ability for any quarry to stay hidden.

Jack's weakened appearance concerned Alexander, so he grudgingly camped a half day away from Edgebrooke. For Alexander, every second was crucial for he needed to reach Sofia before Duncan, but he could not afford to lose his trusted lieutenant. As they camped for the night, Alexander searched his memory for a clue as to where the turret was located, but he found himself frustrated instead.

For an easier rest, he removed his armor and stretched out lazily in the grass. The thick blades of grass created a perfect bed for him and his thoughts carried to Isadora. He had been away from her for weeks. Perhaps, he thought, I should shave before she sees me. It would do me no good for her to see me like this.

He left his bed and headed to a little pond where the animals had watered and brought his dagger out to shave. Fergus and Chauncey assisted Emma with the watering of the horses and Alexander listen in to the playful banter that had become so commonplace on their journey.

"All I am saying," Chauncey said as he removed the horse's bridle, "Is that we are the best warriors in all of Alveus."

"And I am saying that I could defeat the best warriors in Alveus," Emma countered.

"How is that?" Fergus questioned.

"We've had years of training, and we have killed real men with our weapons. You did very well being captured by men with weapons." He referred to her lands being seized and her being carried off.

Chauncey found humor within Emma's bold claim and laughed at her impertinence.

"If you are that handy with a blade, maybe you should take a practice swing with me?" Chauncey asked half seriously and offered her the handle of a sword.

"What do you think, My Lord?" Fergus called out. Alexander ignored them and continued to scrape the knife along his skin, removing the scruffy beard hair by hair.

"No response, My Lord?" Emma teased.

"Perhaps I could cross swords with you? Your men tell me you're quite the legend."

"A legend?" Chauncey said incredulously.

"He is damn near immortal!"

"That's blasphemy," Fergus reminded him.

"I do not care what blasphemy is when it comes to Prince Alexander. The man's a crafted killer. There is no one in Alveus that could cross swords with him and live. He's unbeatable."

"So why does he not care to tutor me?" Emma pouted as she watched Alexander shave.

"Who is he shaving for?"

"For his love, Lady Isadora of Edgebrooke."
Calimus emerged from the bushes proudly and announced
Alexander's interests much to his irritation. His brother's
brash entrance distracted him, and he cut his cheek. He
cheek was tinged a bit of blood, but he said nothing and
washed his face with the water.

Emma's smile turned into a frown, but she managed
to recover and smiled sweetly in the Prince's direction.

"My lord," she curtsied sweetly,

"Lady Isadora's beauty is known throughout the
Northern Isles. I congratulate you on your match. She will
bring you much happiness."

"There is no match," he said sourly. He finished his
last shaving stroke and walked past Calimus. He made sure
to bump his shoulder into his brother's arm to express his
displeasure. Calimus scoffed behind him.

"I am very sorry to hear it, My Lord, for she is a rare
and exquisite beauty," Emma continued breathlessly as she
caught up to Alexander.

"I thank you for your concern, but these are matters
that do not require your attention," he said exasperated.

"When we reach Edgebrooke you are free to take
leave of my presence. I will consider your debt paid for the
care you have given Jack.

I will also ensure that you receive a small sum of coins to help you on your travels."

"But, My Lord," she said concerned,

"The dangers that I have seen are great. How will I protect myself from this evil? Perhaps if you were to teach me your legendary sword skills?"

"Swords are not toys," he chided.

"You do not pick up a sword and consider yourself a swordsman.
Go and find a peaceful apprenticeship. The death of another does not give you solace nor should you seek out the means to do it."

"And yet what are you chasing? Why have you been on this journey?"

"Do not question me. I am a Prince!" Alexander snarled at Emma and for a moment the entire camp quieted and watched for her reaction.

"Yes Emma, do not question the great Prince," an amused Calimus interjected.

"Alexander must never be questioned, did you not know this law?"

"Perhaps my brother should remember where he was six months ago and who pulled him out of the bottle."
Alexander turned his disgust to Calimus and his upper lip curled. His temper was flaring.

He did not care to be put on the spot.

"Quite right, brother," Calimus replied.

"I forget that I must always be eternally grateful to you for saving my life. I shall erect a statue in your honor and send you monthly gifts in remembrance of your kindness."

"I do not need any of that, but what I would like is for you to act as a leader and not undermine me."

"I apologize, Sirs," Emma said quickly.

"I am at fault for bringing this discord. Perhaps Prince Alexander would consider a wager."

"I have no need for wagers." Alexander turned and walked back to his bed of grass.

"Trust me, you will enjoy this." Emma stood over him boldly. "Duel with me. If you defeat me, I will leave your camp now, take your advice and perhaps enter a nunnery. But if I defeat you, I will join your bodyguard."

Farkus, Fergus, and Chauncey howled with laughter at her bold wager. Jack and Devin grinned and offered their encouragement. Calimus sighed and rolled his eyes while Nicodemus broke his meditation to watch what would happen next.

"Emma challenges the Defender of Edgebrooke then?" Fergus howled.

"The same man that saved her twice and defeated dark sorcerers and their dead army?"

"Not just the Dead Army," Chauncey chimed in, "But the undead Dead Army as well!"

Alexander smiled condescendingly at Emma and closed his eyes.

"Or we can forget the next few breaths of time, and you can take your horse and just ride off," he said uncaringly.

"Prince Alexander, I am challenging you to a duel," she said in frustration.

"And I am ignoring it," he continued in mock civility. "Play warrior far away from here. I have nothing to prove."

"Emma," Calimus interjected but she shook off his words.

"No! I will not be treated like a servant girl. He insults me with his disdain and mocks me under his breath. I am of noble blood and whether or not I have land it does not make me any less of a person. Get up!" She kicked at his leg in frustration.

Alexander stood up immediately, straightened himself, and looked directly in her eyes. They remained frozen in their spots, staring at each other and refusing to back down.

"You are wasting your time," Katrina added her thoughts. "The Prince will not risk his reputation of being such a skilled master with the blade."

Alexander broke his glance with Emma and surveyed the faces of his companions. Each man's expression, although having mocked Emma's challenge, now waited for his reaction.

"Fergus, toss her a sword," Alexander ordered and he picked up his sword and waited. Fergus tossed the sword at Emma's feet and Emma bent down to retrieve it. She grunted at first for it was heavy and had difficulty picking it up.

Alexander squinted in disbelief and watched Emma struggle with the weight of the sword.

"Maybe I should come back later?"

Emma grunted in annoyance and squatted down to get a firm grip on the handle.

"The wager is the same? Yes?" She asked.

"If I win you leave. If you win, you join my bodyguard," he said as he rolled his eyes.

"I'm sure we will all remember to bid you a fond farewell." Alexander waited another moment and was clearly unsatisfied with Emma's attempts to pick up the sword.

"Allow me to put an end to your embarrassment," he huffed and walked towards her. His strategy simply outlined was to point his sword at her, so the fight would be over before it began.

"A woman that seeks to be an equal to men that have no equals," he muttered irritatingly. His men snickered as he stood over Emma with his sword pointed at her. He made eye contact with several men and grinned.

When he turned his attention back to Emma, he flinched as a sword flew up towards his head. Startled, he moved backwards and his heel caught hold of a root. He lost his balance and Emma seized the initiative. As soon as his body fell to the ground, Emma stood above him with her sword pointed at his neck. Alexander's men stopped their snickering, and their mouths dropped in astonishment. Katrina giggled and clapped her hands in approval.

"You cheated," Alexander said with disgust.

"No fight is fair, is it brother?" Calimus asked with amusement.

"Touché," Alexander responded. Emma backed away from him and beamed with pride. Alexander did not share her joy and plotted his next move. He thrust his sword towards Emma who successfully parried it to the side.

"Alex!" Calimus shouted.

"Stop this now! She won your wager!"

Alexander swung his sword again, but Emma ducked out of the path of the swing and backed away.

"She has shown nothing," Alexander responded, "Except that she can lift a sword in amazement to her enemies."

"I'm full of amazing," Emma countered saucily and immediately went on the attack. Her sword cut through the air and Alexander stepped to the side to avoid it, but Emma quickly swung her sword to his other side. Alexander's sword flashed, and he caused her sword to glance off of his blade.

She momentarily lost balance, and he grabbed her throat with his left hand and their blades pushed against each other.

Alexander was the stronger one, and he began to push Emma backward and closed his fingers tighter. She responded to the tightening and punched him in the face with her left hand. Alexander laughed and squeezed even harder, so she punched him harder. Alexander yelped after getting hit again, so he wrestled the sword out of her right hand and spun her around to choke her.

She had her back towards him, and he brought her closer to control her movement. She brought her arm up and threw a sharp elbow into his stomach and before he reacted she threw another one up towards his throat. Alexander gasped for breath and his grip on Emma lessened.

Emma pulled a dagger from her dress' belt and brought the dagger to Alexander's throat as Alexander brought his sword to hers. They stood there for a moment catching their breath which Alexander felt increasingly difficult as Emma's elbow had hit him in two parts of his body. He gasped for a few seconds until he could breathe again.

"My Lord," Jack suggested diplomatically,

"Perhaps there is room enough for Emma to join us."

"Are you a jester now too? A woman in my personal guard? They cannot endure hardships like men and I will not have my men distracted in battle."

"You decry my being a woman as a weakness, and yet here I stand with a blade pressed against the throat of a Prince of Alveus. I did not need magic to accomplish this." Emma glared at him in defiance and shook her blade in the air.

"Your skills are notable," Alexander granted and lowered his sword, "But you must understand Emma, I cannot have my men looking out for you. You would be their death."

"I swear my loyalty and my life to you Prince Alexander," she said as she bowed to him on one knee. "My sword is yours and I will fight for you and forfeit my life if I do not fulfill all of my obligations to you."

The men fell silent while Alexander tried to make up his mind about Emma. He was concerned that he had given his word, and now the worst possible scenario had happened.

"My Lord?" Jack quietly reminded him.

"Rise, servant of Alveus," Alexander relented.

"You are welcome in your Lord's presence." He shook his head in disappointment.

"I had better not regret this moment."

"Yes, My Lord," she whispered with devotion.

Jack and the men surrounded Emma and welcomed her into the guard with a loud cheer.

"Where did you learn to fight like that?" Fergus asked in awe.

"I spent months visiting his sister, the Princess Sofia, in Middlebrooke. When we weren't talking about Prince Youssef, she was instructing me on everything she knew about combat."

"She's excellent in combat," Chauncey said in reverence and Fergus nodded in agreement.

"She killed a chicken, I believe, at twenty paces with one arrow," Fergus said.

"No," Chauncey argued,

"It was thirty paces and she was in an elevated position."

"What does that even mean?" Farkas asked.

"Well, Farkas," Chauncey began with an arrogant air, "She was in an elevated position like thus," he moved his hand up, "And the chicken was here. As you can see the degree of difficulty is such that killing a chicken from a platform makes it as hard as killing an ant by dropping a stone on it."

"I think you make these stories up." Farkas sat and picked a rock up and sharpened his blade.

"I do not!" Chauncey protested.

"I have taken the time to study the scholarly parchments.

You cannot expect to win every battle with a sword."

"I can," Farkas grinned evilly.

"Oh, can you? Can you defeat the Prince? Or by reasoning, if Emma defeated the Prince could you then defeat Emma?"

Farkas shook his head and returned to sharpening his sword. He would not take the bait.

"I wonder if you threw a rock at a chicken, would that be enough to kill it?" Chauncey mused to Fergus who had closed his eyes.

"I stopped listening at chicken," Fergus said playfully and threw a mound of dirt at his brother.

Alexander washed the sweat off his face as he wanted himself to be at his finest when he saw Isadora. Emma was not done with teasing him, so she joined his side.

"There's no need to freshen up on my account, My Lord," she joked.

"I'm not," Alexander responded so flatly an awkward air came between the two of them.

"I hope you forgive my impertinence in joining you," she finally said.

"I do not understand why you have decided to take up arms. Go and be a wife and a mother or if you feel that is beneath you then go and learn a trade."

"I am afraid I have made an oath to serve you."

"I can release you from that oath, here and now if you will swear to me anew that you will pursue a different path."

"Your servant finds your compassion touching."

Alexander waved her words off with a disregarded motion of his hands.

"There is no compassion inside of me. I have a path that I must follow, and I do not want the people around me to suffer more for what I bring than they already do now."

"Your oath to me is not a testament to your courage, it is in deference to your life. I apologize Emma, but with your oath you will receive no compassion or heartfelt sympathy from me should I have to say words over your body. This was your choice." Alexander dipped his dagger in the water and sheathed it back into his belt.

"Regardless of whether you believe me to be competent or not," she stated slowly,

"I swear that I will not disappoint you."

You already have," Alexander sighed and went back to his bed in the grass. He caught a glimpse of Emma and thought he heard her quietly sobbing. He cared little that he hurt her feelings, but he hoped that her loyalty would be of use in the coming weeks.

CHAPTER XIV

After a week of traveling on horseback and foot, they finally arrived back in Alveun territory at the gates of Edgebrooke. The climate change was enough that it no longer felt like the onset of winter. They were back in the Alveun sunshine and thankful for it.

Nicodemus had become increasingly unhappy since the encounter with the witch. He moped and feuded with Alexander at every turn. He never expressly said that he wanted to leave the group, for there was fear in eyes, but he hated his captors at the same time.

Alexander and Calimus discussed potential protection scenarios for Sofia. The fact that Calimus went with them, established credibility to every astonishing event they had witnessed.

By mid-morning, Alexander was relieved to see the walls of Edgebrooke and the banners that came into view. Alexander dispatched Devin with Kiera and the gryphon, sending them south of the city to avoid the questions and suspicions. He would join them as they would eventually leave the town.

The banners fluttered gaily in the breeze and the townsfolk were going about their daily business with only a minor nod at the travelers. The few that recognized Alexander bowed and waved at him as they were still overjoyed to be alive and not slaves to the Bete'szek.

News of their arrival reached the Baron's palace quickly, for when Alexander arrived at the palace the Baron and Isadora stood on the steps and waited to greet him. Alexander's heart sank a little at the sight of the Baron, regardless of the Baron's support in front of the council, he still held much disdain for him. If not for Isadora, he sighed, this world could burn forever. The Baron approached first with his minions to his side. It seemed as if the Baron took his personal security seriously as a result of his current political state. He was flanked by ten well-armed men with shaved heads and dark skin.

Alexander recognized them as the swarthy foreigners from beyond the sea, which shared the same continent with the Atreides.

They were notoriously ferocious fighters and hired themselves out to the highest bidder and since the Baron had somehow accumulated a vast treasury, he was now the highest bidder for their services. The guards carried a curved sword, instead of the Alveun broadsword, a spear, and a shield. They eyed Alexander's party warily but relaxed as the Baron welcomed them.

"Alexander and Calimus! Princes of Alveus!" The Baron rubbed his hands happily and seemed to be genuinely relieved to see them.

"You have returned from the frontier and it does my heart good to see that you have favored me with your company. Please make yourself comfortable within my humble palace."

Alexander and his men dismounted and they set about taking care of their horses which gave the princes an opportunity to catch up on events they had missed.

"Baron, I thank you for your hospitality again," Calimus said with an impressive air of diplomacy.

"Of course," the baron replied.

"May I say that Prince Calimus has returned to us with an aura of confidence and looks extremely healthy? Your skin has lost its paleness, and you walk tall among us."

Calimus smiled with the compliment and tried to stand even straighter. Alexander thought that if the Baron had noticed the change, perhaps this would be enough for the other council members to fall in line.

"Is there anything new in relation to Mattias?" Alexander was curious to what his brother was doing in their absence.

"Your father has put him in charge of the internal security of the kingdom in an order to placate him. We have had several council meetings where he presses continuously to be named king regent. He bullies Lords Carter and Fitzwilliam and he seems to be incredibly frustrated with Bishop Malachius and the Church's reluctance to give him the popular support of the people."

"He's not king regent then, so that works in our favor, isn't that right, Alex?" Calimus offered his thought tentatively, as he was still not confident in talking about political matters.

Alexander nodded the point to Calimus.

"What does internal security mean, Baron?"

"It means a lot, I'm afraid," The Baron whispered.

"That means that he is formulating a network of spies across the kingdom. Why do you think I went outside of Alveus for my own security? He's building more palisades and is reconstructing the town of Greystone. That is a good thing because the interruption of commerce has been hurting my fair city, and whatever hurts this city will ultimately spell doom for the country."

"More palisades? That is an interesting development."
Alexander muttered as he stroked his chin in thought. "Where is he placing them?"

"Here and there, around the frontier. He is building several of them in the forest and preparing to reinforce with heavy garrisons."

"My Lord is always focused on the future," a soft voice cooed behind him. Alexander turned and caught sight of Isadora. Her long black hair was braided and pulled away from her soft face. Her desire for Alexander was unmistakable and so was his for her.

"Not always," Alexander said. He felt drawn towards her and wanted to take her in his arms and taste her lips once again.

The passion that had left him for battle quickly returned, each and every thought and memory was of her.

"My Lord, the horses have been cared for. What are your orders?" Emma stood close by and waited for his response.

Isadora's face flashed jealousy at the beautiful young woman who addressed the Prince.

"And who is this?" she said sweetly.

"I did not remember a woman besides young Katrina with you when you left our walls."

"Oh yes," Alexander said absently,

"May I introduce you to Emma from the Northern Islands. Emma has taken Jean's place within my guard."

"Fascinating," Isadora said with an air of disapproval. "And where did we find such a pretty girl amongst the frontiers of our kingdom?"

"My brother saved her life from the savages and Emma swore an oath to protect him. It's all very interesting," Calimus interjected. There was a hint of bitterness in his tone.

"Is my sister well? I would like to see her immediately." Alexander asked and deferred the subject elsewhere.

"We are unsure of her health," the Baron avoided answering the question directly.

"Where is she? We would like to see her, she is the reason that we've come back ahead of schedule."

"She is not here," Baron Brutus answered uncomfortably.

"Where is she? Give me an answer to the question I am asking," Alexander demanded in frustration.

"Sofia was returned to Middlebrooke and their physicians. She remained sick for a week after you left and we worried for her health.

We sent word to your mother, and the Queen requested that Sofia return home." Isadora reached forward and touched his shoulder in sympathy.

"I am sure she is fine."

Calimus and Isadora exchanged words that Alexander did not hear. His vision blurred and his hearing began to go as a sharp pain gripped his head and it felt as if something had grabbed his left eye and threatening to burst it from his face.

He grimaced and knelt down and clutched his face in agony. Everyone rushed to his side and Alexander was quickly carried inside and placed upon a long wooden table to rest. The pain intensified and Alexander rolled onto his side and brought his knees to his chest and clutched his head.

He was propped up into a sitting position by Calimus and felt the taste of wine brought to his lips.

He swallowed the cups contents unwillingly and laid back down on the table. In a very short time, the pain disappeared completely and he opened his eyes to faces of concern.

"The pain is gone," Alexander said in amazement. "What did I drink?"

"The wine that you drank is our private stock," Isadora purred.

"My headaches have never disappeared that quickly," he responded in wonder.

"If you would like, I can prepare some for you to take with you."

"That may be best,"

Calimus and Emma held concerned looks for his health, but his smile removed the worried looks. He felt an aura of calm wash over him and he hopped off of the table and then remembered why they had returned to Edgebrooke.

"Sofia is in Middlebrooke?"

"Yes," the Baron admitted.

"She returned to the capital a week after you crossed into the frontier."

"I beg your forgiveness if I am slow to understand," Alexander said slowly,

"But that is a favorable sign, is it not? She was sick but was well enough to travel back to Middlebrooke."

"Not entirely," Isadora added,

"She was not well when she left. She felt it better to be treated by the royal physician. Your sister suspected with the continual episodes of sickness that perhaps she had been poisoned."

"Poisoned?!" Calimus gasped.

"It has to be the assassin's guild. Alex, we must return to Middlebrooke at once!"

Alexander agreed with his brother and remembered the images he had seen in the crystal ball. Perhaps Duncan had started to poison his sister and wanted to finish her off in her weakened state. He ordered Jack and Emma to run to the men and have their horses fed and watered.

They would need their supplies provisioned so that they could leave as soon as the horses were refreshed. Isadora produced a few bottles of her elixir and wrapped them in a cloth for Alexander.

As she handed them over to him, they briefly shared a moment as their hands touched. Neither of them stood on ceremony and they disregarded the presence of her father and his brother. They locked in a long embrace and the heat between them grew. The heat between them grew, and they unwillingly separated to regain their composure.

Calimus raised his eyebrows and gave his younger brother an approving smile while the Baron bit his lip and said nothing. When their embrace ended the Baron escorted the three of them towards the door where Alexander caught sight of a huge portrait. He eyed it with a growing sense of disgust.

"Do you like it Alexander?" The Baron asked.

"I found an excellent painter and commissioned him for my portrait. It is one of the most beautiful sights in the kingdom."

The painting amused Alexander especially that the weight of the Baron's body had been reduced into a healthier frame.

"Vibrant colors!" Calimus said in agreement.

"A portrait worthy of hanging in the Royal Hall."

Alexander rolled his eyes behind the Baron's back and shook his head. The Baron would always put his corpulent desires above all others.

"It's very flattering," Alexander finally expressed, with little emotion. "But we need to be on our way." He led the others into the courtyard and noticed that the wind had begun to blow harder. Jack hurried up the steps with concern in his face.

"Prince! Look north, we may have a problem."

The blue skies they had traveled under were rapidly disappearing. Dark storm clouds had formed over the forest and were headed their way. A strong wind blew south and within minutes the clouds had settled over Edgebrooke. The horses neighed nervously and tried to escape from their handlers.

"What do they want?" Alexander shouted to Nicodemus over the din of the horses.

"I don't know," he responded.

"It could be you or me or perhaps they think your sister is here."

The clang of a bell caught their attention and it repeated itself every few seconds.

"What does that mean?" Calimus asked.

"That's our bell of alarm if there is a problem at the gates! Something has happened!"
Isadora's voice was full of worry and she pointed in the direction of the city's entrance.

"Let's hurry to the gate then," Alexander said. "Grab your weapons and we will head to the gate. Chauncey and Devin will stay back with the gryphon and the Baron." Chauncey protested in vain and threw his helmet on the ground. Fergus clapped his brother's shoulder in farewell and followed Alexander in the direction of the alarm.

Katrina grabbed her bow and Emma grabbed her sword. Together the group headed off to quickly halt whatever problem had arrived. When they arrived at the gate they found the garrison's militia fighting for their lives.

A dozen dead soldiers were hacking their way through the militia without mercy. From Alexander's vantage point, the garrison was ill-equipped to deal with the tenacious blood-thirst of the attackers. Alexander pulled one bloodied soldier aside for information on what had happened.

"What happened? How did they reach the gate?" Alexander asked quickly.

"I don't know! They just appeared and fell on us. We can't kill them! There's no stopping them!" The man struggled from Alexander's grip and ran past his men to hide in the city.

"The heads! Strike off the heads!" Alexander shouted to the militia. The dead warriors cleared themselves a path through the militia, who now fought only for the preservation of their own life and not the safety of their city.

The dead charged up the path towards Alexander and their focus of attention shifted on Nicodemus. Instead of trying to engage Alexander and his men, they blocked the slices and ran towards the sorcerer.

He ran away from them when he realized they had come for him.

"No!" Alexander shouted.

"Stay here!" It was too late as Nicodemus fled in haste.

"Split into groups and catch up with them," he ordered.

"We have to get them before they get our prisoner. Emma, Katrina, and Fergus follow me.

Jack and Farkas will follow Isadora. Close that gate!"

The city soldiers ran and swung the iron-gate shut. Once closed they attended to the cries of their wounded.

Alexander followed the dead's footprints down the path that he last saw them going down. Their trail was easily spotted other than footprints. Slashed bodies of men, women, and children lined the streets. They had been unfortunate to be outside of their homes, not being properly warned of the dangers inside Edgebrooke, and it had cost them their life.

"Listen!" Emma put her fingers to her lips and they stayed very still. They heard the pounding of iron against wood and they quickly worked to assess where the sounds came from.

"This way," Emma said confidently, and led them through several half-timbered homes until they came to the source of the banging. The door to the house was shut and angry banging continued inside.

"Nicodemus?" Alexander shouted.

"Up here!" The sorcerer had been trapped on the roof and had done his best to keep the dead from reaching the rooftop. The banging inside stopped and the door flew open and out came the dead. They came so quickly that one knocked Alexander off of his feet before Alexander had time to respond.

Fergus jumped to Alexander's defense and blocked the axe that the crazed fiend tried to send plunging into Alexander's chest.

Alexander quickly rolled out from under it and got back on his feet to fight his enemy. Two of the dead men focused their attention on Emma and she became hard pressed to keep them from injuring her. Eight of the lifeless fiends surrounded Alexander and Fergus, who stood back to back so they could see all of their enemies.

The four closest to Alexander charged him with axes raised and Alexander knew he could not block all four of their axes. He blocked the axes overhead from cleaving his skull, but the last axe was headed directly to his heart.

Just then, Nicodemus jumped from the top of the house and buried a sword into the warriors' neck. The slice severed the lifeline of the warrior while the axe dropped harmlessly to the ground. Katrina fired an arrow directly into the throat of the one of the three warriors that attacked the Prince. The arrow cut cleanly through the throat, came out the front, with its blade pointing directly at Alexander.

The warrior fell lifelessly to the ground and Alexander seized the opportunity by kicking one warrior back and grabbed the arm of another.

With one strike he decapitated the warriors head whose arm he held, and then removed the other warriors head as it came back to fight him.

Alexander shifted over to assist Emma who was dodging several lethal cuts. She showed complete mastery of the sword, but lacked the instinct to finish them off. Alexander attributed that to a lack of battle experience. Her face was a mixture of confidence in her abilities, and a fear of their predicament.

As Alexander moved to assist her, two other warriors jumped out of hiding in the house behind the guards.

One sliced at Fergus' back and cut him badly. Fergus howled in pain and dropped to the ground.

He recovered his balance in time to deflect an incoming blow and then stood up to plunge his sword into the warriors' neck.

Two ambushers continued through the melee and grabbed Katrina to whisk her away. The other two warriors that had engaged Emma left their stations and followed their comrades carrying Katrina in the direction of the city gates. Fortunately, the trio of Isadora, Farkas, and Jack arrived in time to finish off the three that were left. Farkas sent a dagger flying into the skull of one, dropping him immediately.

Isadora clashed swords with one, and gracefully spun around, slicing the head off of her foes head. Jack matched swords with his adversary, who seemed to have a better idea of what to do with his weapon. After the second clash of his sword, Jack kicked the dead man backwards against the wall and followed up by plunging his sword into the man's belly, sticking him into the wall. The man struggled at be free, and slashed his sword wildly.

Farkas tossed his sword to Jack, who caught it with his right hand, and sliced the head off, quieting down his foe.

Alexander ordered them to tend to Fergus and immediately ran off in pursuit of Katrina's captors without waiting for anyone to follow him.

He caught sight of the four of them as they closed in on militia at the gate.

"Stop them!" Alexander screamed as loudly as he could. "Do not let them escape!" The militia looked up in confusion and fear as they watched the dead run towards them. Several of them fled, but the few that were left blocked the door and stood in front of it with their spears and shields readied for combat.

The warriors didn't slow down but instead of rushing towards the door, they made their way to the same tower that Alexander had used to defend Edgebrooke from the Bete'szek.

The stairs ran up next to the gate and looked out into the open field. The dead soldiers ran up the stairs and Alexander followed in hot pursuit.

"Prince Alexander! Help me!" Katrina shouted. Her cries pushed Alexander past his breaking point. He was exhausted, every bone in his body felt sapped of energy from the earlier headache but he had to press on and save Katrina.

He exited the tower and came to a stop. The four dead warriors stood still on the wall looking down to the grass below.

"Put your swords down and give me Katrina,"

Alexander ordered as he cautiously walked towards them. They looked at him with expressionless faces and back to the ground beneath them. A moment of silence passed and they backed away from the edge of the wall while Alexander breathed a sigh of relief.

"Now just put her down." The words had barely left his lips when one hurled his sword directly at Alexander and then all four ran to the edge of the wall and jumped. Alexander dove to the side to avoid being struck by the blade.

 It bounced harmlessly off the wall and rattled as it came to rest on the ground.

He ran to where they had stood and watched three of them running in the direction of the forest while the fourth one crawled on its stomach. Alexander made his mind up quickly and he prepared to jump off of the wall in pursuit.

"Alexander!" A soft hand grabbed his arm and broke him of his concentration. Emma gripped it hard and refused to let it go. "You can't jump, use the gate!"

"You use the gate," Alexander snarled,

"I have to save her." He shook her hand off his arm and jumped from the top of the wall.

He fell towards the ground with his stomach leading the way, but he found himself able to manipulate his body in the air and adjusted his body to land on his feet.

He landed on the soft earth feet first, and tumbled a bit, but he was extremely happy that his body was unharmed from the jump.

Emma yelled from above the wall for the gate to be opened. Alexander ignored the calamity behind him and set off in pursuit of the enemy. He meant to first deal with the warrior that crawled towards the forest but was momentarily distracted when he saw Katrina had wiggled free and trying to run back to him.

This distraction caused him to miss the outstretched hand of the crawling warrior.
The warrior grabbed his leg and Alexander fell face first into the dirt and turned over to the contorted face of the enemy warrior.

Bones stuck out of the warrior's legs and the face had been smashed, as if it had fallen face first onto a rock. Alexander kicked at the warrior but it kept creeping up his leg in an attempt to get closer. Alexander swung his free leg over the warriors head and maneuvered his way into a kneeling position on top of the warrior where he plunged the sword into it.

It released Alexander immediately and he jumped up and continued his pursuit of the other warriors. They had just caught up with the fleeing Katrina and had again captured her.

One dead soldier swung her back onto his shoulder and ran towards the forest.

Alexander closed in quickly when raindrops began to pelt him. The unexpected precipitation quickened and turned the grassy field into a shallow marsh. It slowed him down, but it did the same to the enemy in front of him. The one that carried Katrina slipped in a patch of mud and crashed to the ground. Katrina seized its dropped sword and quickly freed herself by cutting off its head.

Alexander shouted a word of encouragement and continued to make his way to Katrina. The rain had thickened and he did not see a figure rise from its hiding position in the grass. His armor sent a message warning him about the blow being imminent, but he didn't process the danger that had come unexpectedly. The figure swung a huge club that impacted into his chest. The blow sent him flying back in pain. The club had collided with him so violently that the wind was knocked out of him and as he gasped for air, he coughed up blood at the same time. With the force of the blow, the rain lessened in severity so Alexander could make out his would be killer.

"Alexander, it's good to see you again. I am enjoying this new image of you looking up to me."

"Angelica..." he wheezed. He grasped at his armor as he tried to loosen it in a vain attempt to catch his breath.

"I love your devotion to Katrina, it's very touching. I can always count on you to be near her and to risk yourself for foolishness. You should be very happy Katrina, he hasn't always been this devoted." She delivered a sharp kick into his face. Alexander's body was in agony and he continued to cough up blood. Angelica knelt down next to Alexander and her cold wet hands rubbed the hair from Alexander's forehead. He cringed as she touched him and crawled away from her desperately.

"It does me a world of good to watch you suffer, but even misery has to end."

She picked up his sword with two hands and pointed the tip at his neck. Katrina shouted in fury and swung her sword, but Angelica blocked it easily and pushed her down.

The dead girl gasped in surprise and found a sword had been pushed through her stomach. She looked behind her and found Emma holding the sword. Alexander's men were roaring across the field and they were bringing the rest of the garrison from Edgebrooke to save their prince. Emma pulled her sword out but Angelica spun and punched her with such force she fell back onto the ground.

"You seem very interested in this. Too interested." Angelica tried to move her sword quickly to strike at

Emma where she lay but Alexander got up and wrapped his arm around Angelica's
throat and grabbed her sword with his free hand. They wrestled a moment until Angelica threw her elbow into Alexander's face. The pain was so great that he lost his grip and dropped down to one knee. Tears of pain rolled down Alexander's cheeks and he struggled to get back up.

His men were close so she tossed the sword down in disgust, and left Alexander with little regard for the carnage she had left behind.

"Katrina?" He propped himself and placed his hand on her shoulder. "I will not let anything happen to you, you have my promise."

Katrina sobbed and threw her little arms around him. He grimaced in pain and in a surprised reaction, he responded by hugging her and stroking her hair.

"I promised. I always keep my promises." He kept his eyes on Angelica as she disappeared into the forest and noticed the black dogs had returned at the entrance to the forest. They were very still, except their black fur that moved with the wind. Alexander released his embrace of Katrina and stood up. His jaw tightened and the ever present hatred energized his body and his mind forgot the pain that was searing through his body.

"I know your secret!" He yelled loudly at the dogs. "I will kill you before you can bring harm to another person! You're a coward Duncan. You have no stomach for a worthy opponent. Stay in your shadows! I don't fear you!"

As if a response to his fury, the rain hardened and pounded Alexander's face angrily until the numbness of his face ignored it. He stretched his arms out as if he embraced its cold sting; he felt so alive with each drop.

When the dogs disappeared from view, his anger departed from him, and his body quickly remembered the near devastation of his torso. He doubled over in pain and grimaced. Emma took his arm and tugged on him. Blood trickled from her lip but the rain was washing it down her face. She motioned Alexander to return to the town. He scowled and silently agreed.

He took Katrina's hand and they joined the rest of the bodyguard that had joined them outside of the walls. At last, the rain subsided so the sun could poke its head through the clouds and warm them up.

"Tell me," Alexander asked. "Are we prepared for our journey back to Middlebrooke?"

"Aye," Fergus said, "Calimus has overseen the preparation. The horses should be ready and provisioned."

"What do the brothers have to say now about the dead? Is there any further question about what they are?" Farkas asked with a sarcastic air.

"No," Chauncey responded,

"I think we have a good idea of what is going on."

"No doubt," Fergus agreed.

"I am thinking the sea presents an excellent opportunity for such adventurers as we."

"Agreed brother," Chauncey said as he looked behind him nervously,

"Becoming a ship's captain and exploring new lands would be safer than what we have disturbed here."

"Come now," Alexander interjected,

"What's more evil? The evil that you know, or the evil that you don't know? Be satisfied that we know what we are up against."

"Mark my words Prince," Nicodemus gravely said,

"There's more evil and death to come."

"And when it is finally my turn, I hope you say something nice when they place my body on the pyre," Alexander stated with a wry smile. The prisoner did not return the smile and stayed quiet until the came upon Calimus and the horses.

"You are very quiet conjurer, could it be the disappointment that your master's assassins held a different target than the one you suspected?"

"Prince Alexander, you are perceptive. I hope your perceptiveness continues to carry you through a long and productive life."

"Why Nicodemus, that's the kindest thing I have heard you say." The men laughed with Alexander while the sorcerer mounted his horse with an embittered look on his face. Alexander paid little attention as Isadora and the Baron approached them with the Baron's guards behind them.

"Alexander saves the day again!" The Baron smiled and clapped him on the back.

"What would we do without the mighty Prince?"

Alexander winced at the contact and involuntarily wheezed. "We were fortunate today Baron," he replied modestly. "We must all remember that our fortunes are whims as far and they go only as far as the angels will go with us."

"Well that's encouraging," Emma said sarcastically from her mount. "Nothing like words that motivate us to battle."

Alexander turned to address Emma's impertinence, but Isadora intervened to turn his attention back to her. She brought her hand to his smooth face and he instantly moved his eyes back to meet hers.

She smiled and he felt captivated by it. He smiled back and they spent a moment in silence.

"I have provisioned your horse Zeus with wine for your headaches."

"That is very kind of you." He found nothing more to say and he allowed her hand to guide his face closer to hers and he readily accepted the kiss she held for him. His thoughts and his anger cleared from his mind and he thought of nothing more than the desire to be with her.

"Maybe I should have a conversation with your father," the Baron said, which interrupted the moment and feelings that Alexander enjoyed. Isadora broke away from the kiss and her face reddened a bit.

"I am sorry," the Baron continued,

"I meant that in a good way, that perhaps we should discuss the future of the sons of the Royal Family."

"Indeed," Alexander murmured. He felt light headed but gathered his thoughts to be able to mount Zeus, and though he was successful he managed to catch Emma rolling her eyes and Calimus' frown.

He ignored their expressions and leaned down from Zeus for one last kiss with Isadora.

Contorting from the pain in his gut, but genuinely happy with the kiss, he saluted the Baron and led his company outside the walls of Edgebrooke. When they caught up to the other men outside the walls he stopped the company and spoke with Nicodemus.

"Consult the runes," he demanded. Nicodemus obeyed and produced the runes. The rest of the company stayed quiet and their horses shifted nervously.

"Am I on the right path?" Nicodemus tossed the runes in the air and they fell back into his hand.

"Yes."

"Is Duncan following us?"

"Yes."

"Good. As long as he's near, I can keep my eye on him." Alexander rode back to the front of the group and found himself traveling alongside Calimus who still regarded him with a disapproving glance.

"A Prince will express his thoughts in a constructive fashion," Alexander said with an air of superiority.

"Someone used to tell me that I needed to act more like a Prince and less like a commoner."

"Go on."

"Nothing. Perhaps it's just jealousy on my part." Calimus stared off into the distance.

"But I'd give anything for a woman whose devotion to me was so great; she would shed her own blood for my safety."

"I agree Calimus. And I would risk my life to save her. I would never hesitate."

"We do not discuss the same thing," Calimus shook his head. "But I would not show as much affection with a woman who I was not betrothed to."

"Really?" Alexander said in surprise. "Calimus! You have improved your disposition. You sound almost kingly! My work is almost complete. Bishop Malachius will be proud of us both!" Alexander slapped Calimus on the back in approval and winced when Calimus jabbed his ribs in return.

The group continued their way to Middlebrooke and Alexander was quite relieved to have Sofia in front of him and Duncan behind him. He sensed that his opportunity for revenge drew near and it made him feel quite content with the day's events.

CHAPTER XV

There was a different feeling in the air within the castle of Edgebrooke. Alexander and Calimus both felt it the moment they walked through the gates with their men. Alexander had often mocked the men who stood guard over the gates, as they had passed by easily many times before, but this time was different. For starters, the gate soldiers demanded that they dismount, open their pouches, and uncover their supply wagon. Alexander would have none of it. "How dare you order me to turn out my pockets," he bellowed. "Do you not recognize me as your Prince? Do you not recognize him?" He pointed at Calimus who tapped his foot impatiently.

"I do recognize you, Your Lordship," the guard fidgeted.

"I do apologize to both of you.

But these are King's orders. Everyone who comes to this city is to be searched and any militant or suspicious properties are to be seized."

"That doesn't apply to the King's sons!" Calimus protested.

A stalemate existed between the men. Alexander refused to budge, and the gatekeepers refused to allow passage. Soldiers began filing out of the gatehouse, alerted that a commotion was occurring. The guards were armed with swords and shields, and looked more like regular army than garrison soldiers. Their armor was dented and scratched, signs of having either been in battle or constant bouts of practicing.

One of the guards, emboldened by reinforcements, climbed into the wagon only to jump back in shock when a small creature hissed and nearly bit him.

"They've got snakes in this wagon!" he shouted.

"Why would you bring snakes, My Lord?" The commander eyed the wagon cautiously and snapped his fingers. Twenty men surrounded the wagon in an instant, spears pointed at it. Alexander was confident his group could best them, but how would that play out from there? Would he have to fight the entire garrison to make it to the palace?

He sighed in annoyance and decided diplomacy was his best directive. He addressed the commander in hopes the gate guards were inexperienced enough to be bullied.

"It is not a snake," he said flatly.

"It's a gryphon."

"A what?" The guard and his men mumbled about in confusion.

"He said a gryphon," chimed in another guard.

The men huddled around the wagon to see for themselves. Alexander understood how they felt. Three years ago, he wouldn't have believed it either. The gryphon served as a beacon of hope and inspiration a long time ago, and maybe it could again, he thought.

"That settles it," the head guard said.

"We will be impounding this creature."

"What did you say to me?" Alexander dismounted his horse, grabbed the commander's arm, and pressed tightly. "You will not be impounding anything of mine, let alone this gryphon."

"Orders Your Highness," the guard whined.

"It's the King's orders!" The other guards that had held back, stepped forward to Alexander's men to make their presence felt. They looked ready to impose their will upon the party.

Nicodemus spoke up to alleviate the issue.

"Now, now, children of Alveus. Must it always be swords with you?"

"Who's this one?" The guard shrugged off Alexander's grip and brought his sword out.

"I'm just a mere magician," he lied.

"I do all manner of tricks and conjuring. Shall I do an example for you? Does one of you have a coin?"

The abnormality of his request sent a ripple of humor through the group. It was enough to defuse the tension and distract from the gryphon. Nicodemus coaxed them out of their suspicions with a congenial smile.

Finally, a young guard produced a coin and flipped it to Nicodemus. He caught it easily and held it up for all to see. He clasped his hands together, coin in between them, and spoke a few words. He blew into his hands and slowly moved his hand sideways. The coin remained suspended in mid-air and didn't move.

The guards murmured in disbelief as Nicodemus turned his hands around the coin till he had only one hand placed underneath it. The coin stayed suspended as it had before until Nicodemus clenched it within his right hand. He blew into his fist again and opened his hand up. The coin had disappeared.

The guards applauded in amazement and started shouting their own theories of how this happened.

The majority insisted that a string had somehow been tied to the coin.

Nicodemus smiled and shook his head that there had been no string. He opened his left hand and showed them the coin again.

The magician coolly shut his fist, blew into his hand and re-opened it. In the coin's place was a very fine gold powder, as if he had crushed the coin. The guards applauded and laughed incredulously while they continued to shout various theories of how he did that.
They remarked he must have superior strength to be able to crush a coin.

Nicodemus invited them closer to have a look at the powder, as he promised them how a lesson in how to do their very own magic trick. The guards moved in eagerly, and Nicodemus flashed a wicked grin. He tossed the powder in the air over the guards and when he brought his hand back down, the coin was there.

Again, the guards applauded and insisted he tell them how he did it. What the guards didn't see, but Alexander did, was that the powder that Nicodemus had tossed into the air had settled amongst them, mostly settling in the hair.

Within a minute, each one of them dropped to the ground unconscious without so much of a word. Alexander was furious and he grabbed Nicodemus by the shoulder.

"What have you done?

Did you kill these men?"

Nicodemus feigned injury at the Prince's rough treatment.

"Of course not, Prince. They are only sleeping. Although to the condition of their sleep I cannot guarantee."

"What does that mean?" Calimus asked.

"It means that their dreams are not their own. The brothers own their dreams now."

Nicodemus shrugged his shoulders.

"Would you rather have let them take your pet?"

Alexander made a slight admission to himself that he forgot that underneath his new ally, was nothing but evil. Regardless of how events played out, there could never be a moment where he could turn his back.

"Very well," Alexander said.

"Let us move to the abbey quickly so that we can hide the gryphon. It is apparent that even my own people cannot be trusted to leave the gryphon alone. They would put it in a petting garden if they had the opportunity."

The group quickly made their way through the streets of the city to the abbey. When the guards awoke, there would be a furious outcry in his direction. Haste was their best asset. It wasn't long before they were at the abbey. There were less people on the streets that day, a curiosity that wasn't lost upon the men.

Once they were at the church steps, Alexander picked up the gryphon from the wagon, like a pet dog, and carried it inside the church. He entered the clerk's office and found Bishop Malachius in a conference with a few of his friars. The Bishop's eyes lit up when he saw Alexander.

"Alexander, my son!" he exclaimed.

"You have returned!"

He gave Alexander a fatherly hug and a pat on the back.

"We have much to catch up about your journey. And how is our little one? She is getting very big." He tickled the gryphon underneath its beak and moved the finger out of reach when it went to bite him. The priest chuckled.

"Not again, little friend."

"Agreed," Alexander said.

"She is gaining weight every day and I think soon her wings will be strong enough to fly.

Might she stay here with you? I need to get to the citadel as quickly as possible. There is a threat upon Sofia's life."

"A threat?" the Bishop queried.

"How do you know this?"

"About a week ago, I discovered Duncan's new target was Sofia. He won't get to her this time. She is still guarded by those I left her with, and there isn't a man alive that can slay them so easily. I will say, however, that this incident at the gate with the guardsmen is most distressing. I will have a few things to say to my father about that."

Bishop Malachius sighed.

"It's not your father, Alexander. A lot has happened in the time that you have been gone. I fear that many things are about to change for the worse."

Alexander nodded in understanding.

"Mattias," he muttered.

"I will deal with him when I see him."

"That's not all," the Bishop said in great reluctance. He was unable to discuss further with the bellowing that commanded their attention.

"Prince Alexander?" he called with much authority.

"Who addresses me?" Alexander responded. He and the Bishop walked back into the chapel.

The sun had moved just enough to play tricks with his eyes.

The friars had yet to light the torches, and they declined to leave the Bishop's office until it was safe.

The man moved from the shadows and closer towards the altar where they stood. With each step, Alexander's eyes widened just a bit more.

The physical prowess of the man was breathtaking. He was easily the tallest man that Alexander had ever laid eyes on.

As a comparison, the Prince thought of Dragonus.

This man was four inches taller and several pounds heavier. His footsteps were heavy, as if he broke stones as he stepped.

"What are you," Alexander asked in awe.

"I am Philo," he stared at the gryphon suspiciously but without a true glimmer of caring.

"Some call me 'The Marauder'.

Maybe you have heard of me?" Alexander shook his head, but a feeling of dread began to creep over him.

"Are you here to try and kill me?"

"I make it a rule never to talk to people if I need to kill them," he said. He sat in a pew and lifted his legs onto a resting position on the bench in front of him.

He was an extremely chiseled specimen, and with his height, looked as if carrying stones of granite or marble would be inconsequential to him. His powerful shoulders bulged from his armor, and his hands were so large they could crush a melon.

"Well, I've never heard of you. So what do you want with me?" Alexander motioned the Bishop to leave the room and take the gryphon with him.

Malachius quietly ushered himself from the abbey and into the courtyard where Brother Peter met him where together they hurried into the church's living quarters.

"Your brother is less than happy about your entrance to the city," Philo remarked.

"Ah, I see," Alexander said.

"You work for my brother.

I should have guessed." Alexander caught sight of Keira creeping in behind the intruder.

She crept below the benches and tread softly through the church to protect her master.

It didn't stay secret for long. Philo took a deep breath through his nostril and grinned.

"That's a good dog you have. I haven't smelled a war dog since my youth." He turned his head around and motioned to Keira. "There's a good dog, looking out for its master."

He turned to Alexander.

"Since your brother sent me, I know all about you. I know your men and your tricks. Since you do not know me, I will at least give you a professional warning. I have killed over a thousand men in my lifetime. There is very little you or anyone else can do to sneak up on me."

"Then what do you want with me?"

"You are under arrest Prince Alexander, by order of the King." The Marauder swung his large boots to the floor and stood up, his size again casting an intimidating shadow across the floor.

"You're relying. I have done nothing to be arrested for."

"Indeed?" Philo countered.

"Treason and sedition are the charges. I am ordered to take your party at once to the dungeon. You will be taken to the council for a hearing on these charges."

"And if I refuse?" Alexander placed his hand on his sword's hilt.

The bald man grinned and placed his hand on his sword.

"Nothing would please me more."

"First, I kill your pretty dog. If you resist when I am done, I will then kill you. Then when I am finished wiping your blood from my sword, I will walk outside and execute each one of your party, starting with that sorcerer who invaded the minds of our guardsmen and drove them to the brink of madness."

"You seem very confident," Alexander challenged.

"One thousand men," Philo repeated,

"With weapons in their hands. You draw that sword, you will hang on my wall as a trophy."

There was a moment, that Alexander knew the brute spoke the truth. "You give me your word that no harm shall befall any of us if I surrender to you?" Philo shrugged. "I am only a messenger. Your fate is up to the council."

"So I am to believe that you are a soulless killer? You have been hired by my brother to protect him from me?" Alexander dropped the sword around his waist to the ground and kicked it to Philo. In an act of defiance, he left the fire-sword on his back.

Philo drew his sword. "The other one too, Prince Alexander, and call your dog to your side."

Alexander obeyed as he was commanded, Kiera reluctantly headed to his side.
She growled at the Marauder, ready to protect her master. Philo mentioned for him to move forward and he was ushered out of the abbey onto the city's streets. His companions had already been rounded up and had their hands bound in front of them.

Calimus was noticeably absent and Alexander wondered how that happened. Another large man chained Kiera to the back of the wagon, and she lowered her tail and head in sympathy to her master's plight.

They were all seated in the back of the wagon and escorted into the Middlebrooke citadel. From there, as promised, his men along with Emma and Katrina were taken away to the dungeon.

Philo forced him to remove his armor, then two of his men whisked away the armor and swords into the Great Hall. Keira was dragged to the kennels by a few other men and that left Philo with Alexander.

"Where are my other guards? The ones who protect Sofia?" Alexander asked.

"They are in the dungeon waiting for you." Philo suppressed a small chuckle.

"Did you know I have actually been looking forward to meeting you?
 That battle against the Bete'szek where you held off an entire horde is truly a legendary story. The continent is singing your praises. It's truly a pity that your palace intrigue does not match your fighting abilities."

"What do you mean?" Alexander asked.

"It means if you are ever looking for work, I'd think you'd do very well as a mercenary captain, but as a Prince you leave a lot to be desired."

"So the killer is giving me tips on leadership and how to behave as a prince?"
Alexander scoffed.

"Please don't lecture me. I doubt you've had any schooling and I am pretty sure the reason why you sell your sword is because an illiterate giant can do precious little else."

"I'll remember those words," the Marauder said. He grabbed Alexander by the hair. He bent the Prince's head back until he winced in pain.

"If you get found guilty, someone gets to chop your head off. Maybe that someone will be me. Maybe as I lift the sword, I don't swing it so hard. Do you know what happens if the sword isn't swung hard enough? You don't die. You sit there with your neck half hanging, but your spine is still intact. You can still breathe. But instead of breathing you'll be screaming.
So let me know young Prince, what more insults you have for me, because I will make your last moments your very worst moments."

He released his grip on Alexander's hair and shoved him forward. "Move," he commanded.

Alexander complied and walked up the steps into the Great Hall. Something had gone very wrong, he thought. I'll just bide my time and see what Mattias has awaiting me. As soon as Sofia hears about this, she'll be enraged enough to set all of this straight.

CHAPTER XVI

The only thing more worrisome than Philo behind him, was the realization that there were more like him. Once Alexander stood in the Great Hall, he found five other huge men stationed near the exits. He wasn't quite sure if they were meant to keep him from running, or to keep others from entering.

The Marauders differed very little from each other. They were all big and bald, with the slight difference being a beard that varied in length and style from man to man. They were armed with axe and shield and wore a heavier armor than the Alveuns did. It was easy to assume their strength for their shields and armor matched their dimensions.

The Great Halls benches had been moved into a half-moon shape, with a lone chair sitting in the middle of them.

Philo pushed Alexander forward and ordered him to sit in the empty chair.

The Prince complied reluctantly, and as soon as he sat down, several men entered the Great Hall.

Mattias was at the forefront, dressed in robes instead of armor, and Philo pulled Alexander back to his feet to show his respects.

"Make up your mind," Alexander gritted through his teeth. He glared at Philo but let it go with just the look.

Mattias wearing dress robes was an odd look for a man who was always in uniform. He looked as if he tried to emulate Manfred, the House Steward, wearing an ugly overcoat of dark brown. It looked as if beavers had been strung together lazily to make a coat.

The Lords Carter and Fitzwilliam were there, dressed down to not overshadow Mattias, but definitely with a better sense of Alveun fashion. They took their places and waited for Mattias to sit.

Lord Burrows also came in, supported by Elsie, and several other nobles from the east and west borders were also gathered.

Alexander wasn't familiar with them, and they made no attempt at a greeting.

Lord Burrows was frowning, obviously irritated with the proceedings. Elsie mimicked her father's expression, and as no one paid her any mind, gave a look of pure hatred to Mattias.

General Valmont was firmly positioned behind Mattias' chair as if he were a bird perched on his shoulder. When Mattias finally sat, in the King's seat of judgment, all the other attendants except Elsie and General Valmont followed his lead.

"Lords of Alveus," Mattias began,

"We are here under great importance as Prince Alexander has been charged with treason and sedition. He is attempting to undermine and destroy the Alveun way of life."

Alexander stood up to object, but Philo pushed him back into his seat.

"You will follow this tribunal's protocol," Mattias insisted, wagging his finger at Alexander.

"Surely you all jest," Alexander scoffed,

"That the man who saved the kingdom three months ago should be accused of trying to destroy it."

"You will answer the charge!" Mattias thundered. He waved his hand at an older man that sat near Lord Carter. He wore a funny black hat that hung ton one side, with dark purple robes.

His beard was long and white, not very well managed, and Alexander imagined a flock of birds nesting inside.

There were scrolls laid out in front of this man, and he rummaged through them. Once he located the one he desired, he stood to make his point.

"Prince Alexander," he began. "With all due respect, I am High Judge Osfrith and I am here to give advice on legal matters. Your brother is quite right, you must follow protocol to the letter or you will be found guilty. To offer unwarranted dissenting opinions is a waste of the court's time as it attempts to establish the truth."

"The truth," Alexander argued,

"Is that Sofia's life is in danger." The Lords murmured amongst each other until Mattias hushed them.

"We will get to those charges in another moment," he stated flatly. He adjusted his eye patch ever so slightly and continued to read the scrolls in front of him.

"What charges?" Alexander argued.

"Did you not hear me when I said Sofia's life is in danger?

Our sister's life is in danger, Mattias! Must I spell that out for you? Ask Calimus, he will defend me."

"Ask Calimus," Mattias chuckled.

"Once in the city he disappeared. I am sure he is at a local inn recuperating from your plots." He folded his arms with a smug look on his face.

"What plots?" Alexander groaned with exasperation.

"Give me your ridiculous charges so that I may go on my way." Lord Carter took Osfrith's place as the man standing to give the charges, and cleared his voice before he read.

"The charges you stand accused of are the following: You do maliciously and knowingly consort with a sorcerer to the point where it jeopardizes our nation. You brought the sorcerer into the city where he did injure over twenty Alveun guards."

"He is my prisoner!" Alexander objected.

"Did you know these charges before I came into the city? Were you ready to go for trial once I crossed the city threshold?"

Lord Carter continued, undeterred.

"The charges extend to assuming that since you have a sorcerer in your midst, the chances of you being in league with them and taking part of the murder of our beloved Crown Prince Edward has been one of great debate."

"I object," stated old Lord Burrows.

"Am I to assume that you Lords, and even you Mattias, believe that Alexander is capable of murdering a family member in cold blood? They were inseparable. Wherever Edward went, Alexander was three steps behind him."

"Thank you for your words as always, Lord Burrows. They are good enough to help us remember that the truth will always guide us,"
Mattias said with such a silky cunningness that Alexander thought his brother to be a snake ready to strike.

"As with truth, there must be proof, especially when a man's life hangs in the balance."
He made a gesture towards one of the large men guarding the entrance.

"Bring in the Bishop."

Bishop Malachius was led in and seated in the chair closest to Alexander. He had a grim look on his face.

Judge Osfrith walked around the table and in front of Alexander. He bowed once to Mattias and began the questioning of the man that Alexander once called Father.

"Bishop Malachius, upon your journey into the frontier, you stated that you came upon a cave, is that right?" Osfrith took the scroll from Lord Carter and read over it just to be sure.

"Yes," the Bishop replied.

"I am reading your testimony. There was a sorcerer and a swordfight ensued.
Several Alveun soldiers were killed, isn't that right?"

"Yes they were."

"By whom you claim to be, let me see, the undead?"

"Yes."

Mattias jumped out of his chair and pointed his finger at the Bishop.
"That's a lie though isn't it? Alexander knew I assigned those men to watch him. He had them killed with help from the sorcerer, didn't he?"

"No!" the Bishop insisted.

"They were killed in a fair combat, and not by Alexander's hands."

"And yet that sorcerer is in this castle injuring my men, and assisting Alexander with running around my country with impunity? Tell us where you have gone. Tell us who you have consorted with!" He shouted the last words that echoed around the chamber.

"How fitting that Alexander should always be involved when an Alveun lies fallen." He sat back in his chair and again folded his arms with as much malice as his body gave him.

Alexander began to feel the pressure building up inside of him and decided that talking was a risk worth taking.

"That man is my prisoner," he insisted.

"He led me north beyond the borders to Duncan, where I almost had him. We have chased Duncan back here, where he seeks to kill one of us again." He paused and caught his breath.

"Putting me on trial and threatening to dispose of me does nothing but shorten your own lifespans. All of you!"

Mattias clapped his hands and shook his head. "Bravo, brother. That was so impassioned, I might have believed in some chamber of my heart that Alexander the Hero has come to save Sofia. We did hear that, My Lords?"

The Alveun Lords rapped their knuckles to show that they understood and were in alignment with his point.

"Where is Sofia now? Will someone bring her forward?" No one spoke, so Mattias said it louder. "Someone bring her forward!"

"Your Highness," Philo mentioned,

"Sofia is not in this city anymore."

"Oh that's right," Mattias feigned mock confusion. "Judge Osfrith, please continue with the next charges."

The old judge bowed stiffly, and brought the scroll close to his face. "We bring forth the charge that Alexander did in fact knowingly destabilize this nation by not reporting the love affair between Princess Sofia and Prince Youssef of the Western Isles."

"I had nothing to do with this," Alexander protested.

My God, he pleaded silently, what is going on?

"But you knew about this!" Mattias yelled.

"Yes I knew!" Alexander shouted.

"So she fell in love and corresponded with the man. So what?"

"Her choice was not hers to make. She is a Princess to the Crown and subject to whatever designs the King has for her." The Lords nodded in approval.

"So I am on trial for treason because my sister flexes her independence like she has for the last twenty-one years? How can I defend myself against that charge? Shall I read all love letters and poetry that leave Middlebrooke? At least I will never have to read yours, because it's beyond you to write."

"Enough," Mattias commanded.

"Osfrith, continue." Osfrith bowed compliantly and continued reading.

"During this time of destabilization and potential war from outside forces, you did knowingly allow this affair to continue.
As such, the child born of this illegitimate union could cause a pretender to the throne to arise. As such, a reason for a revolt that our enemies could exploit and overthrow the ruling dynasty." Alexander shrugged his shoulders.

"Then tell her to stop," he insisted.

"Put her in the dungeon for a week. I have no time for silly love fantasies. Where is she now?"

Mattias pointed at the Bishop and wagged his finger intently. "Tell my idiot brother where she is!"

Alexander made eye contact with the Bishop, but the Bishop broke it off quickly.

"She's been sent to the monastery."

"Well," he considered thoughtfully.

"That may be the safest place for her. Duncan would have to go through Jean-Paul and the rest of the clerics to get to her. Let me go and get her."

"I am sorry, Alexander," the Bishop said.

"She is banished there."

"What?" Alexander's mind twisted and turned with everything that he had been accused of the last hour.

"Why would you banish my sister?"

"Because," the old man said,

"That's what happens when you sin against the Church. Your sister is-"

"Stop!" Alexander commanded.

"Not another word. Sofia would never do that. Not in three hundred lifetimes. You have to be wrong. She was poisoned when I last saw her. There is no child."

"Lie to yourself all you want, brother. The truth is a far greater responsibility laying at your feet than you realized.

It's up to this tribunal to find out how much."

Manfred's voice interrupted the proceedings, for he suddenly announced King Magnus and Queen Caroline were making their appearance. Caroline entered the room ahead of the King, a rarity for her. Her steely gaze and frown let the council know she was extremely unhappy.

"I am curious to know why one of my sons assumes a chair that is not his," Queen Caroline commented with a profoundly annoyed tone.

"We are in the midst of a tribunal. It is where I should sit, as the head of the tribunal."
Mattias shoved the chair backwards a bit and it groaned under its weight.

"Do not talk to your mother like that," King Magnus wagged his finger in Mattias' face.

"You are not king, and even when you are king, if you are disrespectful I will come back from the dead and beat you senseless."

King Magnus chuckled lightheartedly.

"Did you hear what I said, my love?" He put a warm arm around his wife.

"All this talk of people rising from the dead, maybe I will too after I am gone."

"My love, when you are at rest, you will not want to come back."

"To beat these two senseless? Oh yes, I absolutely would. Look at all my profound disappointments." He sighed heavily and sank into his chair. He gently pushed Mattias away from his chair and shook his finger disapprovingly.

"When this one was eight years old, he'd climb onto the throne and pretend to be king. Should have drowned him like any other king would have. Such presumption."

"I find regret in hearing you say that, father." For a moment Alexander thought he read genuine hurt on Mattias' face.

"I am down a son and a daughter. I am left with three imperfect candidates and thanks to that one," he motioned to Alexander,

"I get to lose sleep every night. Is it a sorcerer? Is it the dead? Is it another kingdom who has some illegitimate claim to my throne?"

"My King, these are your children," Queen Caroline soothed and she rubbed the shoulders of the king.

"Children, yes," he responded thoughtfully.

"If I could take it all back. Every blood stain, every horror.
Someone bring me back Edward. Bring me back my son."

"I miss him too," his wife said mournfully.

"But look, Alexander is a son worthy of your attention. Would you keep him on trial with these charges?"

"Osfrith!" Magnus bellowed.

"Read me the charges."

The Judge read them quickly, and the king shook his head in disgust.

"Who do I feel more contempt for? The son who accuses a brother of killing his hero, or the son who can't seem to make a good decision. This tribunal is dissolved."

Mattias threw his hands in frustration.

"Father, these charges have merit and validity. How can you throw these out?"

"Because I am King!" Magnus explained.

"And my word is law. Alexander did not conspire to murder his brother."

"Thank you, Father!" Alexander stood up and looked relieved. He shared a smile with his mother and turned to say something sarcastic to Philo.

"However," the King thundered.

"Consorting with sorcerers, and this error in judgment letting Sofia consort with this foreigner. These will be punished. Put him in the dungeon. I will make the final determination for his fate."

"Magnus!" Caroline shrieked.

"How can you do this to our son?" Her stoic appearance melted into horror over the king's words.

"Our son has broken the laws. He has gone his own way, and like his sister, there will be a punishment for his sins." "He is our boy!" she hissed.

"And I am his King!"

He surveyed the room and made a promise.

"I am still breathing. I am the Great King. Nothing happens without my permission. I am the law. If any of you forget this, so help you because I will cut off your heads myself, blood relative or not. Am I understood?

The council, quieted and nervous, bowed their heads in silence. The King shuffled away with Manfred's assistance, leaving the council in disarray.

Lords Carter and Fitzwilliam left immediately, declining to exchange any words with anyone there. Mattias gestured to Philo to escort Alexander out of the Hall. Philo went to shove the Prince forward, but Queen Caroline held up a hand, commanding him to stop.

"You heard His Majesty," Mattias warned, "he is to go to the dungeon."

"Never get between a mother and her cub," she cautioned back. "I will have a word with my son, and neither you nor this brute will stand in my way."

Philo bowed his head in respect and backed away. He knew his place, and wasn't about to interfere with Her Majesty.

Caroline and Alexander walked to the corner of the hall, out of earshot of Mattias.

"How could I have been so blind," Alexander said remorsefully.

"She is stubborn and has mind of her own," Caroline explained. "She has always been a wild horse, bucking all those who try to control her."

"I sent her back. I should have come back with her. What was I thinking?" Alexander grunted in frustration. "She's going to die."

She snapped at him. "Don't say that! Jean-Paul has her secure and tucked away."

"Until when?" He challenged.

"Until her child is born? What will her future be then? You let the Bishop carry her off for her transgressions without a second thought to her future."

"She is with child!" Her eyes widened in disbelief.

"Your grandchild."

"She transgressed."

Alexander sighed in exasperation.

"I will go after her."

"To where?"

"Where she can raise her child."

"Alexander!" Mattias had his hands on his hips, patience fully tested. He directed Philo back to Alexander's side. The large man approached politely, wary of Caroline's temper, and directed the captive to follow him outside.

It had gotten dark now, and being a guest in the dungeon was the least of Alexander's worries. As he was led down the stairs, he memorized every detail, hoping it would help him escape.

CHAPTER XVII

"This is starting to become a pattern with us," Fergus remarked mournfully.

"Aye," Chauncey agreed. "We have saved a city, captured a sorcerer, defeated undead soldiers, and protected countless lives. And still, we always seem to end up in the dungeons."

"I don't mind giving my life for this kingdom, but the least they could do is treat us better,"

Farkas interjected. The rest of Alexander's men agreed with grunts of approval. In their situation, they at least found comfort in knowing they were together again. The men that Alexander had dispatched to guard Sofia were behind bars too.

"At least you have seen the sun," Simon groused.

"We haven't seen the sun in weeks now. We have been here waiting for you all to come back."

"Haven't had a decent meal in days," Brennan added. "I think I'm losing weight. I didn't have a lot of weight to begin with!"

The men laughed with Brennan. Alexander noticed that his guard was becoming fractured. Their morale and spirits were dampened from their time underground. *I can't blame them,* he thought. *I would be irritated being kept underground for days on end, with nothing more to eat than the morsels that fell from the King's table.*

Alexander straightened himself up and leaned on cell's bars. "Men, I warned you when you signed up. There would be precious little room for error, and we would have enemies at every turn."

"We know that, My Lord," Jack responded.

"These last few months have been harder than most of us imagined."

"What did we expect?" Alexander challenged.

"We are in the midst of trying to remove the Crown from Mattias' succession. Can you think of a time in history when blood was not shed over a dispute to the Crown? I think we have done very well that a civil war hasn't broken out yet."

"So then Mattias executes us, and then that's it?" Linus asked.

"No war and no us?"

"That won't happen," Alexander said stoically. "As long as my mother stands next to my father, she will influence him. And I don't see my father executing me anytime soon. We just have to wait this out."

The words seemed to have little impact on the spirits of the men. The disappointment of their situation just dampened them into a melancholy state.

Alexander turned to his cell mates for comfort. Nicodemus, hands and legs bound, laid on a small patch of dirty hay.

Jack sat upright, back against the hard dirt wall. There was a sound of light scratching against the wall in the next cell. Alexander dismissed it as a rat or other animal trying to scratch its way out of the underground dungeon.

"How is the hand?" Alexander asked sympathetically. The color had returned to Jack's body and even with only flickering torches around, he could tell Jack was in better health.

"I'll never use it again," Jack said ruefully. He had begun hiding his hand in a sling with an overcoat to avoid the whispers from the others.

"I am sorry," Alexander said.

"It's my fault."

"No!" Jack insisted. "It's this dog's fault." He kicked Nicodemus' leg which irritated the sorcerer quickly.

"You touched the orb," he hissed.

"What brilliant mind is yours to touch the orb?"

"If I hadn't touched the orb, the staff would have burned through my stomach," Jack countered.

"Then you should count yourself fortunate that you only lost your hand," Nicodemus argued.

"Why haven't you used your powers to help us escape?" Jack asked.

"And go where, young Jack?" Nicodemus answered.

"Let's say we pick the lock. Next we get past the guards and the jailor. Then we make it up the stairs and get out into the open. We don't have enough weapons. Most of you would get cut down as soon as an alarm is sounded. I would make it as far as the gate. One man versus a city, especially with the Marauders here? No thank you. I am perfectly content to stay here and wait."

"Why are you worried about them?" Alexander asked.

"Because they're big," the sorcerer replied sarcastically.

"Linus!" Alexander called out.

"Yes, My Lord?"

"Tell me how it happened since you came here." Alexander listened to his guard shuffle to the bars to be heard.

"We followed your orders and took Sofia back to Edgebrooke. She was still showing signs of sickness and so we put her in the charge of Lady Isadora."

"Wait," Alexander said in surprise.

"Isadora knew?"

"I assume so, My Lord," Linus answered.

"Stupid of any of us not to realize." Linus suddenly realized who else was inferred and stammered an apology.

"You are fine," Alexander assured him.

"I was too blind on the task at hand to realize. Please continue."

"Lady Isadora sent us back here with a note for the Bishop and one for the Physician. When we realized what was going on, it was too late."

"What do you mean?" Alexander asked.

"The Marauders showed up in Middlebrooke before we got here. At first, we assumed they were just mercenaries that Mattias employed for consultation.

Once word got out that Sofia was pregnant, all hell broke loose. The Bishop demanded she be sent to the monastery and started railing against your family from the abbey steps.

Darn near started a riot with his impassioned pleas of accountability for the royals."

"First Isadora, and then Bishop Malachius?" Alexander was exasperated.

"Is there no one I can still trust within this city?"

"We are still here," Emma's voice reminded him.

"Emma?" Alexander asked.

"Is Katrina with you?"

"Yes," she assured him.

"Can she speak for herself," Alexander asked with a groan.

"She's a little busy at the moment," Emma answered.

Alexander shook his head and sighed. She had continued to find ways to be grating to his nerves. Very well then, if she was going to continue to be a thorn, than he would ignore her.

Still, the scraping sound was coming from their cell. No matter. If they are digging their way out it will take forever.

"What else happened?" Alexander asked.

"The choices were to banish Sofia or risk a city-wide riot," Linus explained.

"The King made the order.

When we tried to protect her, we were arrested on the spot. As it turns out,

the Maruaders are working directly for Mattias as dung gatherers. They will clean whatever mess needs cleaning."

"And they are impervious to magic. Very important in this day and age." That voice signaled Mattias had joined the conversation. He had entered the dungeon to continue his repartee with his imprisoned brother.

"What do you want?" Alexander demanded.

"The Crown," Mattias said succinctly.

"I have come to ask you a favor, brother to brother."

"What is it?" Alexander snarled.

"Go away," Mattias answered.

"Far away. You can take Calimus or leave him, I don't care.

Or drop this nonsense and give me your support. And we will hang that one." He pointed through the bars at Nicodemus.

"I can still touch you from here,"

Nicodemus threatened. He held up his hands as if he wanted to do some malice to Mattias. The brother jumped back nervously and Nicodemus chuckled.

"You can hide, but we will still come for you. Look! I am right here, close enough to touch you."

Mattias' nose twitched and he turned to the jailor.

"If that man even so much as moves, execute him."

"Why not kill me now?" Nicodemus grinned.

"Maybe I will have Philo come and get you," Mattias hissed. "Alexander, think about my offer. You support me, and I will see all of you except the sorcerer freed."

"Father will never let you go through with this," Alexander said confidently.

"Have you not noticed Father isn't well these days," Mattias commented.

"One moment he thinks you're Edward, and the next moment he is the Great King. We are looking at the end very soon, Alex. Choose your decision carefully."

With that last statement, he wheeled around and walked up the stairs and out of the dungeon. The jailor picked up a bucket of food and some plates and went about dispersing it between the cells.

"You that been here for the week know the drill. You say present, then you get your food."

He went to the first cell and knocked on the door.

"Here," Linus, Simon, and Ferris said in unison. In return the jailor slid food underneath the slit in the door.

He went to the next one and banged on the door. Brennan, Devin, and Sean also acknowledged their presence. Once the food was shoved through, Brennan let his complaint known.

"Please sir, could I have some more?"

"More?" The jailor asked incredulously.

"More you say? Each prisoner gets rationed food. No more, no less. You're lucky you're a royal guard. Instead of duck and potatoes, you should be getting bread and dirty water.

Be thanking the king for what you have!"

Brennan groaned while the jailor moved on. He banged on the brothers door, and they both acknowledged the jailor, as did Farkas.

Alexander, Jack, and Nicodemus followed suit and they busied themselves munching on some finely prepared duck.

"I'd almost forgotten how phenomenal Sara cooks," Alexander boasted. The jailor brought the girls food to the cell and rapped on the door. The result was silence. Again the jailor banged on the door and demanded they answer. He was very frustrated and banged on Alexander's door.

"Prince Alexander, please order these women to comply with me," he said in a very respectful tone.

Alexander rolled his eyes. There really was no making the women do anything.

"Answer him and get some food," he ordered. There was no response.

"Emma! Katrina! Answer him!"
There was still no response. Alexander shrugged his shoulders and went back to eating his potatoes.

The jailor scoffed at the women.

"I suppose this is a trick to get me to open the doors so that you can attack me and release everyone.

Well, it won't work. I've heard about how our Prince likes to spring people out of the dungeon. No offense, My Lord."

"None taken," Alexander said. His dinner was finished and oddly enough, so was the scraping.

A few hours later, Alexander was stretching his arms in an attempt to force himself to yawn. It was late and it was uncomfortable. He yearned for a bed. How long had it been since he slept on one?

He dusted up what straw he could find into a makeshift pillow and laid his head on it. It poked and prodded his face and aggravated his nose to the need of sneezing.

He was miserable and now his arm was throbbing. He felt around his sleeve where the pain came from, and his fingers found a cut that seeped some fluid. It didn't smell like blood and he couldn't remember how he cut himself.

He checked on the sorcerer and Jack, but they were both fast asleep. He grimaced as he tightened his fist. The pain was searing, where could he have cut himself?

He heard the jailor coming down the stairs. Perhaps he could get some water and clean his wound, he thought.

The voices were hushed and angry and immediately Alexander feared that they were about to be murdered. He placed his hand over Jack's mouth who immediately woke and tried to struggle.

When he saw it was Alexander he stopped when Alexander shushed him.

The sorcerer was the next one to wake and, as he was bound, had no choice but to stay very still.

Alexander and Jack took places on either side of the door and listened as a key turned slowly in the lock. The door swung open and a figure walked in. Alexander tackled the figure and brought them down quickly.

"Get your hands away from my chest!" the voice scolded. "Unless we're engaged, you are never to touch those!"

"Emma!" Alexander asked incredulously. He sprang up, embarrassed and held his hands in the air.

"What? How?"

"This is an odd turn,"

Jack agreed. Katrina and Emma held the very angry jailor at knifepoint, with Bishop Malachius' assistance.

"How did this happen?" Alexander was completely confused. The Bishop led the jailor to the other cells and forced him to open one by one. The men were excited and clapped each other on the back in hushed tones.

"I remember as a young girl reading about the secret passages under Alveus. And we found one!" She grinned delightedly and Alexander couldn't help but return her smile.

"We have a stone wall in our cell, so I knew that behind one of those stones was our way out."

"So that was the scratching I heard? Very impressive," Alexander concluded. His men agreed. "So will we go up that way?"

"No," the Bishop interjected.

"We are going up the stairs. Everyone but the sorcerer. He stays."

Nicodemus laughed and showed Malachius his irons.

"As if you could make me stay." The irons unshackled themselves and fell beside him.

"I'll make short work of the guards above us."

"You will not," the Bishop stated.

"They are asleep. Their food and drink were sprinkled with sleep powder. They will not wake up for another hour. In the meantime, Alexander, you need to get as far away as possible. Go to your mother's people. They will protect you."

"No," Alexander said firmly.

"I'm going to find Calimus and then rescue my sister."

"Your sister is in the hands of God now." The Bishop made a sign of the cross and pressed Alexander's loyalties.

"The hell she is," Alexander defiantly stated.

"She sinned against her vows," Malachius argued.

"She is my sister," Alexander said, gritting his teeth.

"You and God don't get to make that decision." The hair on his arms stood on end and he felt a chill run down his spine. "No one will take my sister away. Not you and not Duncan. If this is where we part ways, then so be it."

Malachius was aghast.

"Alexander, listen to yourself. Is this from the influence of this unholy man?" The guards shifted their feet nervously. The conflict between church and liege was not what they had signed up for.

"I ride for the loyalty to my sister," Alexander promised. "I have lost my brother, who I love dearly. I will not lose another sibling."

Malachius shook his head. "You will follow the course that you have already decided on, although I fear it will lead to our downfall. And I don't mean you or me, I mean our county and the people that live within its borders."

"So how will running behind my mother help me?"

Malachius offered no solution to his question and Alexander affirmed his decision to go after his sister.

"Very well, here is the plan." His men gathered around and listened intently.

"We need weapons and horses. Katrina, Simon, Brennan, and Fergus will get the horses. Chauncey, Farkas, and Linus, and Ferris will gather our weapons. Bishop, we will need Keira and the Gryphon with us. Mayer will go with you and assist you. The rest of you will come with me. We must find Calimus, and I suppose he's either in a brothel or a tavern." He pointed at Emma.

"Emma, you will need to check the brothels."

"Why me?"

"Because you're a woman, and you won't be distracted." There was some silent agreement between the men and they nodded their heads.

"There aren't any brothels in Middlebrooke," the bishop insisted.

"Yeah there are," the jailor muttered.

He was quickly ushered into a cell and they locked the door behind him. He sighed and sat on the damp floor.

"Once we have gathered weapons and horses, half of you will head to Brookhaven and command my ship.

You will then take it around the western side of Alveus and make camp on the beach. The rest of us will ride to the monastery, take possession of Sofia and then climb over the mountain.

From there, I will acquiesce to Bishop Malachius' wishes and set sail for the east.

By my reckoning, we have two hours before the garrison notices we are missing. They will most likely give chase to the monastery, but they will not be expecting us to have a boat waiting on the other side of the mountains."

All the men nodded that it was a good plan. A lot could go wrong, but if they snuck out of the castle without an alarm being sounded, they would be one step ahead, not just of Mattias, but the whole Alveun military that would be sure to mobilize.

One by one, they ascended the stairs of the dungeon, poking their heads out to ensure safety and then set about executing Alexander's plan.

CHAPTER XVIII

Jack, Sean, Devin, and Alexander made their way through the city streets with quiet haste. They didn't bother to wait for their weapons; every moment was crucial for them to leave Middlebrooke without capture.

The citadel appeared to have fallen asleep as if a spell had been cast over it. Once the men exited the castle gate, and into the stronghold's town, they turned in the direction of the city's quiet indiscretions. The Church had made being a person of ill refinement's work to be difficult.

There were regular examples of the stocks or banishment here or there, but they always managed to spring up and stay one step ahead.

This was in dark contrast to Edgebrooke, where sin was encouraged and shady characters outnumbered monks three-to-one.

To speed their efforts, Alexander asked the men to define which establishments they thought Calimus was more apt to be found in. They settled on three distinctly named taverns.

There were The Dirty Prince, The Rotten Swine, and the worst of the lot, The Devils Brew. They checked into the first two and made their way through the elements.

Amazingly, the occupants cared little for the Prince's presence once they realized he wasn't there to provide a cleaning service. A few of them respectfully clanked their steins in his direction and then went about their merriment.

They were a few yards away from The Devils Brew when they heard the sound of a man screaming. Worried that it was Calimus, they quickened their pace. From a well-gardened villa beside them, a man dove through the door. The men stiffened themselves for a fight, but the man fell harmlessly at their feet, clutching his midsection in pain.

Out the broken door walked Emma, enraged like a bull. She stepped over the man and stood half an arms-length from Alexander.

"Any luck?" Alexander started to ask.

His face was caught midsentence by a well-timed slap by Emma's right hand.

"What?" Alexander shrieked. He reeled back in shock but Emma wouldn't let him get away.

"Emma, check the brothels?" She mimicked Alexander's voice angrily. "You sent a woman to check the brothels?"

"I thought it safer than sending the men," Alexander replied weakly.

"But you sent me instead? Have you been to a brothel?" Her face turned crimson red and matched the intensity of her hair.

"Well, no."

"Do you know what brothels are for? You do realize what women and men do in brothels?"

Alexander hadn't really ever thought about it, but now he definitely did. He shook his head meekly in understanding.

"And as a woman, you know what they expect from me?" Alexander shrugged his shoulders and that cost him another slap from Emma.

This time from her left hand.

"Stop slapping me!" He ordered.

"I should slap you the number of times my posterior has been grabbed tonight. I signed up to be a warrior, not to be some plaything fondled by dirty men. If you ever-!" And she stopped there. I swear, Alexander, you don't know much about women do you?"

Alexander had nothing to say in response. His men hadn't moved and they were still in the street with the man still groaning on the ground.

"Perhaps we should move on, My Lord?" Jack offered.

"Yes, I think so," Alexander replied.

"Emma you're welcome to stay here if you'd like." He made a feeble attempt at making amends.

"With this pig?" She knelt down beside the yowling man.

"Come here again, and I'll cut off the dangly between your legs."

The four men gave her a wide berth as they made their way into the tavern. Thankfully, Alexander breathed a sigh of relief, she was unarmed.

The tavern was quite busy for being well after midnight. Hay was on the floor to sop up the puddles of ale, and large casks lined the walls. Men sang their drunken tales of bravery to the barmaids who ran about keeping each stein filled.

A crowd had gathered, both men and women, around a solitary man telling wild tales of amazement. Alexander recognized him and pressed in for a closer listen.

"All these tales are true good people!" Calimus exclaimed. "All the stories that we thought our parents were telling us to scare us are true!" He took another stein from the wench beside him and stood on a bench so everyone would hear him.

"People of Alveus, the time to be afraid has come. Dark forces are at work outside of these walls."

"Come off it!" A man laughed.

"There are dark forces at work here too!" Several people joined in laughing at the man's joke and agreed with him.

"I mean really dark!" Calimus insisted.

"How many of you enjoy your ale?"

The occupants cried a loud huzzah and clinked their cups together.

"That's what I mean!" Calimus argued.

"Dark forces want to enslave us. They aim to take away our food. Our drink! And our women! Who enjoys the pleasure from a few doors down, eh?"

Again the crowd roared. Alexander was amazed at the spectacle. They hung on every one of Calimus' words, even if they were completely sloshed.

"I have spent the last three months fighting these forces and I have seen the horrors that wait us. You need an heir that will fight to protect you. We need our armies to smash through their lines. And you need a leader that knows these enemies and will defeat them. It is I, Calimus Wolfield, who is destined to lead this kingdom."

Alexander's mouth opened in shock. He traded glances with Jack.

"What is he doing?" Jack asked. His question was answered quickly.

"People of Middlebrooke, we need a revolution. We need to take Mattias off the chair that he lusts after, and we need to do it now!"

"I hate that pig," a random man at the bar shouted. "He's always talking about war. He wants our sons to fight and conquer. Why should we give them to him?"

"He doesn't care about us!" A woman shouted.

"That's because he's a eunuch!" Another man mocked.

"Eunuch indeed!" Calimus railed.

"Who here has the nobility and care to lead you!"

"Calimus!" the tavern cried out in unison.

"Our revolution starts today!" His last words sent the tavern into an uproar. Several young men excitedly ran from the tavern.

No doubt to excite their neighbors and families, Alexander thought. He sighed. This would not be easy.

He stepped over a bench and made his way through the crowd to his brother's side. His men and Emma followed closely. Calimus was overjoyed at the sight of his brother and gave him a huge hug.

"How did you escape!" he gasped.

"Never mind, you're here! I'm starting a revolution with these good people."

"So I heard," Alexander said politely.

"But it's time to go." Calimus resisted immediately.

"Go? Go where?" Alexander felt his patience level diminishing. "Sofia's in trouble, we have to go to her now."

"Ha!" Calimus snorted. "She was sent to a nunnery. A bit ironic, considering. I have yet to hear that I have a child, and then Sofia happens!"

The words pricked Alexander, and he did his best to grit his teeth and not lose his temper. "You've had your fun, now let's go."

He grabbed Calimus' arm and began to lead him outside.

A couple of fellows in the bar noticed this and stopped them from going any further.

"And where do you think you're going?" One asked.

"I am Prince Alexander Wolfield, and I am taking my brother on a journey that he is required for."

"Well hold on," another said.

"We just decided Calimus was going to be King."

"We are in the middle of a revolution," Calimus interjected. His breath caught Alexander by surprise, and he stumbled backwards at the strength of the stench.

"Shut up," Alexander muttered,

"And in God's name stop breathing on me."

"That's no way to speak to the King, even if you are his brother. What do we do, Your Highness?" More drunks appeared at Calimus' side, inspired to do his bidding.

Calimus seized on the opportunity and grinned at Alexander. "Throw them out!" he commanded.

He grabbed Emma's hand and a stein.

"But you can stay," he grinned. Despite Alexander's protests, all of the men in the room banded together and picked him and his men off of the ground.

With a great heave and fanfare, they were tossed from the tavern and into the street.

"Maybe we could leave him?" Devin offered, but Alexander was in no mood to give up.

"In there," he muttered as he stood up,

"It's an entire group of drunken morons. Should we leave Calimus here?

They will no doubt be slaughtered senselessly as they fling their poo at the city's gates. Calimus will be beheaded and be *very* dead because he is actually starting a rebellion as we sit here."

"Where's Emma?" Jack wondered.

"Now we really have to go back in," Alexander muttered, although it was more for Calimus' safety than hers. "What's the plan?

We are unarmed." Devin surveyed the street for any help that could be offered, but there was none.

"We have our fists," Alexander answered.

"There's four of us, and an entire bar full of drunks. My money is on us. Just punch anything that moves and hit them hard, fast, and repeatedly."

Devin and Sean nodded their agreement. Although the youngest, they tended to be the best fighters in close distance.

While neither of them carried the force of a punch from Brennan, their wiry and muscular frames were excellent for grappling.

The men nodded in agreement and stood in front of the door. With a nod, Sean opened the door and walked through. There was a smack and a thud as a townsman stumbled out of the door.

Devin followed suit and another man flew out of the door. Alexander heard an alarm raised inside of the bar as the tavern's occupants understood they were under attack. He winked at Jack and together they entered the pub.

Devin and Sean were already being set upon by a group of men, but Alexander's delay in getting in the bar was a great piece of strategy on his part. He and Jack went by, pulling people off the boys and punching them as hard as they could.

Blood began to flow in concert with the sounds of noses cracking and cuts opening up on faces. Calimus panicked and started shouting for everyone to get involved against the counter revolutionaries. Bar wenches threw steins at everyone, as they were breaking their source of income.

Alexander made his way jumping over benches and sending drunken men reeling backward from the weights of his punches.

He felt his wound throb but a source of energy surged through his veins.

The anger helped him ignore the pain of punches when they landed on him.

He willingly began taking punches to get a devastating uppercut in.

Jack started to tire. His withered left hand could only block punches, and a one handed puncher could only deal so much damage without getting more in return.

Devin instinctively left to help Alexander's lieutenant and together they gained an upper hand in the tavern.

Calimus grabbed Emma's hand and looked as if he would join the rest of the townsmen fleeing through the back door. She resisted and he attempted to swing her body over his shoulder. This failed and she crashed a goblet against his skull. He fell to the ground unconscious and Emma sat on top of him as the men finished off the rest of the tavern.

As Sean sent the last man flying out the entrance of the tavern, the men glanced around at the damage they had caused. There wasn't a bench or table that wasn't broken or upended. There was ale spewing from casks and blood and beer everywhere.

Alexander caught sight of Calimus and Emma and shook his head.

"Thank you for joining your rescuers," he said grimly.

"Was that what this was? I wish I been told that. I was having a glass of ale with your brother." She took the last remaining cup of ale anywhere and took a swig. She coughed heavily and grimaced.

"Oh! That is thick ale. Horrible!"

"Come," Alexander ordered.

"Bring Calimus. It won't be long till all manner of town watch will be here." Jack had propped himself against a wall and was breathing heavily.

"How are you, my friend?" Alexander asked with concern.

"Seems like you caught the worst of it this time."
Jack shrugged it off.

"This is usually your face. I wear it with pride, My Lord."

With Devin and Sean carrying Calimus, they moved swiftly toward the gate. Alexander was relieved to see that everyone had accomplished their mission. The gates guards were again unconscious, and Alexander assumed it was Nicodemus' dirty work.

Simon handed Alexander his armor, and the Prince brought it over his head and fastened it.

Being unarmed and without his swords was one thing, being without his armor was completely different.

He tended to feel alone. He wondered if maybe he depended too much on the armor. Was he anything without it?

"Nicodemus," he called out.

"Come and bring your runes."

"Alexander?" Bishop Malachius asked.

"Do not consult with these? They lie to you."

"Do you have answers to what's ahead?"

"I've already told you." His voice was soothing and calm, but not what Alexander wanted.

"You tell me nothing," Alexander argued. "Nicodemus, is my sister safe."

The sorcerer tossed the runes in the air and they came falling down into his palm. He opened his hand for Alexander to see.

"Yes."

"Is she in danger?"

Nicodemus repeated the process.

"Yes."

"Will she die?"

"The runes will not tell you this," Nicodemus said with a suspicious assurance.

"Is Duncan near her?"

Nicodemus flipped the runes again.

"Yes."

Bishop Malachius scoffed at them.

"That was very helpful. Your sister is safe in the monastery, but Duncan seeks to kill her. We already know that. These are cheap tricks for the weak minded."

Alexander ignored the Bishop's words and set about finalizing the plan.

"We divide our group in half. The same ones that guarded Sofia will get my ship out of Brookehaven."

"My Lord?" Jack asked. He still seemed taxed from the brawl. "I beg you leave. Allow me to travel to the boat."

"What? Why would you leave my side?" Alexander was shocked at this.

"It's not you, My Lord." Jack held up his hand. "This wound taxes my strength. I would only weaken your cause. Let me be your eyes and ears on the ship."

Alexander felt his heart prick for a moment. Beyond being his trusted lieutenant, Jack was a great friend. He nodded agreement with Jack's request and modified his strategy.

"Devin, Sean, you're with me. Chauncey, Fergus, you too. Emma, Katrina, with me. Nicodemus, you're not leaving my sight.

Linus, you're with my detail. The rest of you, hightail it to Brookhaven. We can't be hung out to dry on the beach." Alexander and his men got to fastening their armor and arming themselves. The sun's first light could be spotted on the horizon.

"I will do my best to delay them when they start hunting for you," Bishop Malachius promised. He uttered a blessing over the group and sprinkled water on each of their heads. He noticeably skipped Nicodemus.

It won't be much longer, Alexander thought.

Do you know where we're headed? The gryphon asked him.

We haven't spoken in awhile, Alexander grinned. *You haven't been listening. Again, do you know what you're doing?*

No, Alexander admitted, *but eventually we will find out.*

Once they were mounted, they hurried their way through the gates. Alexander and his riders turned east and onto the road to the monastery. He figured a three-hour head start, nothing more. They couldn't stop moving at any time except to feed and water the horses.

CHAPTER XIX

The journey to the monastery would take, at most, two days. The terrain in front of them would be easy on the horses and potentially move them faster. The countryside was mostly flat, with a few rolling hills here and there. The southwest was considered the breadbasket for the kingdom and farms and orchards dotted the landscape, as did a few livestock farms.

Alexander felt extremely fortunate that they were headed west because, in their haste, they hadn't packed much in supplies. There would be more than enough from the orchards and fields to keep them fed.

They eschewed bringing the wagon, because speed mattered, and kept the horses at a brisk pace, but not a gallop. There was a king's highway that went westward, but it wasn't more than a dirt path.

Their horse's quick pace wasn't enough to labor Keira and the gryphon, and they were able to keep up. At times, the gryphon would tire of walking and set about to try flying. The men shouted encouragements to her, but she could get no more than a few feet off the ground, in a strong headwind, and then coast for a few seconds before having to land.

Keira was an adult war dog now and her head came to Alexander's chest. If she stood on her hind legs, she could place her front paws on Alexander's shoulders. In contrast, the gryphon was as tall as a young Keira, and her wingspan had grown larger than an eagles.

Regardless of how large the gryphon had become, Keira still played the role of mother to her young charge. She did her best at teaching the young gryphon how to hunt and stalk her quarry. The young gryphon was appreciative and would always allow Keira the best of her kill as a sign of respect.

Alexander was relieved the beasts had bonded so well. Between them, they were an extremely formidable pair. Once the gryphon could hold flights for more than a few moments, she could attack her enemies in the air while Keira would hit them from the ground. The Prince hoped that eventually they would be able to enjoy each other's company in a less aggressive atmosphere.

Alexander mused upon the dichotomy of his situation. He always wanted to travel, and that is all he seemed to do in the last six months. He was tiring of it and readjusted his desire to travel into a more peaceful venture. Maybe there was an uncharted island that he could sail to that was far away from here. He assumed he could get his wish if the Alveuns caught up with them. Banishment was not looking as an unpleasant solution for him, although his men would certainly suffer leaving their homeland.

Regardless of the reality of their situation, the group was in good spirits. Riding under the warm sunshine would have a positive effect on anyone who had been locked in a dank dungeon. Simon was incredibly happy for, as a former farmer, he yearned for sunshine.

The only one unhappy was Calimus, who laid across his horse, still unconscious from the previous night's activities. His stirring coincided with a feeling of dread that swept over the party.

The clanging of bells in unison, ever so faint, came from the direction of Middlebrooke. The alarm was sounded and now the chase was on.

"Why am I tied to a horse and riding face down," Calimus moaned.
He tried his best to steady himself to ride it but managed to slide off onto the ground.

Alexander and the rest of the group kept going, and when Calimus realized no one was stopping, he hurried himself back to his horse.

"Wait!" he shouted. Alexander wheeled his horse Zeus around and went to meet his brother. He ordered the others to continue and not worry about him.

"You need to hurry," Alexander said flatly, no hint or trace of emotion in his voice.

"Where are we going? How did you get out of the dungeon?" Calimus' mind was a sieve for recent events when he had been drinking.

"Don't worry about how I am here. We are on our way to the monastery to rescue Sofia from her chains. From there, I am not completely sure," Alexander sighed.

"I suppose putting her on my ship and sailing far away would be the best choice."

"That's the extent of your plan?" Calimus grimaced as he remounted his horse.

"Smash into a monastery, battle a bunch of grumpy clerics, hop over a mountain range, and then sail off to an undetermined location?" Alexander nodded.

"That is the long and short of it. Yes."

"That is the worst plan you have ever had. Have you noticed most of your plans are just smashing and grabbing?"

The Prince's turned their horses towards the rest of the group and quickened their mounts pace.

"Then what's your plan, oh great one? I fished you out of being stupid in a tavern last night. Do you remember trying to start a rebellion last night? Or were you too drunk to realize you were deliberately disobeying me?" Calimus grinned slightly at the thought of his escapade. Some merriment twinkled in his eyes and he chuckled a bit.

"So being drunk is funny to you now?" Alexander asked very accusingly.

"I was preparing to rescue my dimwitted brother and his men from the dungeons." Calimus mockingly bowed his head to Alexander, who scrunched up his face in confusion.

"You got a tavern full of people drunk and were going to incite a mob to overrun the palace?" Alexander repeated slowly as if the idea was completely inane to him.

"Absolutely!" Calimus spoke with a great deal of confidence that surprised Alexander further.

"The people *hate* Mattias. After buying them rivers of ale, they *loved* me. So by getting everyone drunk and in an uproar, they would storm the gates in a riot. In the confusion, I, your fantastic and noble brother, would come to release you.

Then perhaps we could overthrow Mattias while we were there, and save ourselves the trouble of all of this nonsense you put me through."

Alexander clasped his hand to his head in exasperation. "So let me understand this better. Your job was to get the city drunk on ale, throw them against trained swordsmen, and dance your way into the dungeon?"

"Let's not forget be crowned King." Calimus winked at his brother surreptitiously.

"Amazing," Alexander said in disbelief. Calimus' grin broke into a smile.

"That is the worst plan I have ever heard." Calimus' smile dissipated. "Getting a city drunk," Alexander repeated, "and throwing them against well-trained swordsmen? Unbelievable."

Alexander rode to the lead of the procession. He couldn't stand to hear any more of his brother's nonsense.

Emma had overheard the men and decided to join in the fun. "I thought it was a brilliant plan, in theory, Calimus. Alexander can't deviate from a smash and grab. That's the only tactic he knows." She winked at Calimus and that irritated Alexander to no end.

As the group moved through the fields and orchards, they grabbed as many fruits and vegetables as their sacks could carry.

To buy silence, Alexander made sure that money was paid to each one of the farmers. The group fed and watered their horses and allowed them breaks, but Alexander had a feeling of dread creeping over him that there wasn't much time left. He left Sean behind as scout to measure how much time they had left.

When Sean met them at nightfall, he had dire news. The Alveuns were coming upon them quickly, and the Marauders were leading the way. Nicodemus lectured Alexander that if he had his staff with him, he could conjure a storm that would slow them down. As it was, the best that he could do was completely blot out the moonlight.

It turned out to be extremely helpful. With a heavy cloud cover, the moonlight was kept in check, and a darkness settled over the land. If not for the fire in front of them, the group would be blind. This meant the Alveuns were jammed waiting too. They could light torches and come after them, but then they would be sitting targets for Alexander's superb archer, Katrina. Her reputation as a deadly archer had reached the castle guard.

Alexander wondered if Katrina's demeanor had improved at all since their time in the north.

She was reaching her teens now, and rarely said a word to anyone.

She just followed them. Probably because she had nowhere else to go. He picked a spot to sit near her, just to get in a few words.

"Is your bow nearby?" he asked, trying to get her guard lowered enough to talk.

"Yes, My Lord," she said and she showed him that her bow was on the other side of her body, as well as the arrows. "If anyone comes carrying a torch, I'll extinguish them and the torch."

"I have never seen anyone handle a bow so well, except for my sister. You two are amazing archers." He hoped the flattery helped his cause, but she rolled her eyes and pulled a blanket over her clothes. Alexander noticed that she had begun to outgrow the clothes that she had been given. Why hadn't he noticed that?

"I haven't been a very good Lord to you," he admitted, hoping for a response. She said nothing, so he went on.

"I forget how much has been taken away from you."

"Its fine," she said and turned her body away from him. "You lost family, I lost family. We are at war."

Alexander nodded.

"It's not your war if you don't want it to be," he said. He meant it to be an olive branch, but it wasn't received well.

"Oh good," Katrina said sarcastically.

"I can leave and go home at any moment. I don't have any parents, so maybe I can be an orphan. I have a bow and arrow, so I can hire myself out as a hunter." She kicked her blankets off and faced Alexander angrily.

"I am an outcast. What do I have except this war? Now you feel it's time to release me?

Can you pay me a decent wage then so I might purchase rags that fit me?"

"If you needed something, you could have told me," Alexander pleaded.

"Your sister gave me this, months ago. Look, Lady Emma is wearing the same clothes from when we rescued her. The least you could do is treat me as one of you. Like I matter."

The words hurt Alexander, for in his heart he knew she was right.

"Everything from your lips is an order. Do this, do that," she continued.

"You are the Prince, so you have that right. But you took my parents away from me, you owe me the respect of caring about me." She wiped away the tears from her eyes, grabbed her blanket, and moved to the other side of the fire.

"Sir?" Sean was still awake and he whispered over the crackling of the fire.

"Yes, Sean?"

"I wouldn't take what she says too hard."

"Why is that?" Alexander was curious.

"We all joined you on a matter of principle. You have saved everyone's life here, and if you haven't noticed we are all outcasts. Who wanted any of us? Who would have given us this chance? I don't care if you order us into hell, I'll follow you past the gates. That's what we signed up for."

Alexander appreciated that vote of courage from Sean. "Thank you, Sean. That means a lot. Out of everyone here, though, she never asked to be part of it. It was forced on her."

Sean nodded and turned over. Alexander felt a sense of loss within himself. Without Sofia or Jack, he had no one to talk his feelings through. It was just him, barking orders at his men and taking it for granted.

What if they weren't loyal, he thought. *What if they betray me? What if?*

Voices stirred inside of him. He had heard these voices before when he had destroyed Nicodemus' staff.

They were dark voices in the deep recesses of his mind. *You are alone*, they told him. *You don't need them for they hold you back.*

Silently, he grit his teeth and pushed the voices from his head. After a minute or two, he felt better, and the voices subsided. He caught Nicodemus' glance and the evil old man flashed him a knowing smile. *How much does he know?* Alexander wondered as he went to sleep.

CHAPTER XX

The group woke early at Alexander's behest. They broke their camp as efficiently as possible and headed east towards the mountains.

Torch lights flickered in the distance. The Marauders were also up and giving chase.

Alexander kept an even pace, as much he wanted to break into a gallop, Keira and the gryphon could not maintain that pace for long. He bit his tongue and urged his team on, refusing to give ground.

The stress was on all the riders. They glanced nervously over their shoulders and were thankful when the cloud cover dissipated.

A least they could see their enemies and finally know what they were up against.

Sean acted as their rear guard and waited as long as he could to catch a glimpse of their pursuers. He caught up with Alexander at the base of the mountain range. His report included forty riders closing in. Thirty-nine of them wore Alveun uniforms, the fortieth was unquestionably Philo.

Their pursuers were holding back and Alexander understood why they weren't hurried with their approach. They assumed once Alexander was in the monastery he was pinned. They didn't expect him to go over the mountains, and if they did, probably didn't expect his ship to be there.

Or Jack was caught. And then it really didn't matter where they fled.

Alexander kept churning the thoughts inside of his head. He also hadn't taken into consideration that Monsignor Jean-Paul wouldn't be likely to just hand Sofia over. Still, everything had worked out so far. The clerics in the monastery were extremely vigilant today, for instead of wearing their traditional church robes they were dressed in armor.

They hadn't seen the clerics since Edgebrooke, but he knew when something was amiss. There were many men on the walls, overlooking the path down the mountain at their pursuers.

"Stop there, Lord of Alveus." Alexander recognized the guard as one of the clerics he fought with at Edgebrooke.

"It is good to see you, my friend," Alexander stuck his hand out in an attempt at friendship. He was surprised that the cleric took it and shook it warmly.

"It is good to see you, My Lord," the cleric saluted. "I am Brother Mark of the Protective Order."

"It is good to know you," Alexander affirmed.

"Why is everyone dressed for battle today? More drills?" Alexander alluded to the constant drilling this order seemed to put themselves through. Suspicious as it was, they were hardy fighters in the battle against the northern tribes.

"There have been some events. Come inside quickly and the Monsignor will fill you in." The companions hurried inside the monastery and the doors shut behind them.

"Alexander," a familiar voice boomed.

"Monsignor!" Alexander smiled and clasped the hands of his swords mentor. He had begun to age, being just a few years younger than the King. Jean-Paul was still an imposing swordsman and worked his talents regularly. This was one of the reasons why the clerics were among the most skilled in the land.

"I know why you're here." Jean-Paul rubbed his hands together and blew into them. The first flurries of a snowfall were fluttering to the ground.

"How?" Alexander asked in amazement. He threw a blanket over his shoulders and chafed against the sudden temperature drop.

"Carrier pigeon, of course. How else do you think we get news being as isolated as we are?"

This struck Alexander as being funny. He had never noticed the birds fluttering in and out when he trained here, and yet Jean-Paul always knew what was transpiring outside the walls.

"That's good then if you will allow me to take command of my sister's safety from here." Alexander barked out several commands to his group.

"Sean, take a position on the wall. Let me know when the soldiers are making the climb. Everyone else except for Calimus, out the back way.
Begin the climb up the mountain. We will have to leave the horses here because it's too steep so grab what you need."

They hastened to obey. Each person grabbed their blanket, a sack of food and tied their horse's reigns.

Emma took charge of Keira and the gryphon and they all hurried towards the back of the monastery and began their ascent. Though it was initially steep, it was manageable. Alexander worried briefly that the snowfall would hinder their progress, and in his sister's condition, could make for a slow jaunt.

The Prince turned his attention back to the Monsignor. "Is Sofia up the road in the nunnery?" The nunnery had been built as a hideaway for noble's daughters who couldn't contain themselves, but gradually came to accept all classes. Since sin was a problem in certain cities, the nunnery had been expanded and isolated from the rest of the world.

The Monsignor swallowed hard and gave Alexander some unexpected news.

"I'm sorry Prince. She isn't here." Alexander stiffened up.

"Did Bishop Malachius not tell you I was here to take her? Why do you profess lies to me?"

Jean-Paul took offense and his clerical training came to the surface. "Do not accuse me of lying, young Prince. There's no man alive who would leave alive with that sort of filth on his lips. Your sister is not here."

"Where is she then?" Alexander demanded.

"Look around Alexander. Do you see that we are on full watch? We have been raided, not once, but twice."

"Raided by whom? I've heard nothing of this."
Sean called out in alarm,

"Riders on the path! They are coming this way." He jumped down from the wall and scurried to Alexander's side.

"She was kidnapped from the nunnery one week ago. I sent twenty men over the range to bring her back. I haven't heard back from them."

"Who took her?" Alexander asked. He was beyond feeling furious, now he was afraid for his sister's life.

"That coward Youssef," the Monsignor spat.

"Then two nights ago, we had another raid. They ransacked the nunnery, killing the men who watched over them, and several of the nuns as well. We had to move the nuns into the monastery for better protection." He paused and considered the information that Sean had given Alexander.

"Now who is following you?"

"Mattias has sent men to bring me back for treason," Alexander admitted.

"Then you should probably take some fur coats for your men and get going.

I will delay them as much as possible." Monsignor Jean-Paul placed his hand on Alexander's shoulder and frowned.

"I apologize to you that I did not keep your sister safe. I owe you a debt for this."

"Don't go dying for me here," Alexander joked.

"That was not close to what I meant," the Monsignor responded sternly.

"I will stay here," Calimus interjected

. "You will not," Alexander ordered.

"Sean, get the furs. Calimus, get moving before I make you move."

"Think about this, Alexander. I know what your plan is."

Calimus pointed up the steep climb.

"Once you are over that mountain, you are headed to the isles. These men are going to report back to Mattias and he is going to come after you with the Alveun Navy. Who is going to intercede for you with the father? Besides our mother, only me. You need me by his ear."

Alexander hated to admit it, but his brother was right. He embraced Calimus farewell and jogged towards the gate with Sean in tow. They started ascending up the mountain in pursuit of their comrades.

The snow was falling a bit more now, and Alexander stopped to catch his breath at a small clearing. He took a look back at the monastery.

He could make out that the Alveuns were in the abbey deciding whether to give chase or not. He kept backing up the mountain, step by step, to give himself additional steps that might give him an advantage.

The Alveun soldiers mounted their horses and rode out of the monastery. Calimus was with them, and Alexander chuckled to himself that they took their horses as well.

"That was a little much," he remarked to Sean. Sean grinned back.

"I guess we're committed now." Sean's smile disappeared when he recognized a figure headed up the mountain. "Look," he pointed.

"Philo," Alexander muttered in disgust.

"Time to run!" Sean and the Prince took off running up the hill. They followed the footprints of his men that were already ahead of them. They had a solid head start, and Alexander hoped they were traveling at a rapid pace. If they were not, then Philo would catch them all up.

They hadn't gone very far when they started to get winded.

The altitude was thin and Sean wheezed constantly from losing his breath. To make matters worse, they were still carrying some coats for the others. If they didn't reach them soon, they could freeze or become ill from exposure.

They had come upon a crevice where Alexander stumbled over a rock. His utterance of pain elicited a warm cry from an unexpected source. "Prince!" Chauncey shouted gladly.

"Are we happy to see you!" Alexander tossed him the furs.

"Put these on," he ordered.

"We have to keep moving. We are being followed."

Everyone quickly went about putting their furs around them and shifting their weapons when Alexander heard that voice he had been dreading.

"Prince!" Philo's voice echoed through the wilderness. "Prince!!! I am getting very tired of chasing you. So why don't you come back and allow me to take you back to Edgebrooke."

"Go!" Alexander whispered. They were very close to the summit, once there they would be able to fly down the mountain at full speed.

"I can't," Sean wheezed.

"Go without me, I will catch up."

"Sean we were trained for this," Chauncey encouraged.

"It's just a bit more to the peak."

"I cannot breathe," he gasped.

"I need a minute. Just go, I will be alright when he gets here."

"No," Alexander said firmly.

"I will stay with you, and Nicodemus will stay here as well. Everyone else, you have rested. You should make it to the summit by nightfall. Besides, it's starting to snow and you have to find shelter before it gets dark. We will join you when we can."

There was a groan of dissatisfaction for they wanted to stay with their companions. The weather and the fast closing Marauder persuaded the group to drop their objections.

"I wonder what it is you think that I can do," Nicodemus muttered.

"At the appropriate time, use some magic," Alexander responded.

"Philo is in a special class of people. Much like you, he is impervious to magic."

"How does that happen?" Alexander asked. "Gryphon's blood?"

"No," Nicodemus smiled.

"He is not as blessed as you are. He is a descendant of a race of giants. He and his brothers are the last ones."

"Prince!" Philo was at it again.

"Your brother agreed that I can take you dead or alive. If you make me walk to the summit to take you, I will choose which condition you return in."

"I'm here!" Alexander yelled back. He closed his eyes and listened to the armor that he wore. He envisioned his opponent, the strength and skill that presented a challenge. The armor melded with his mind to formulate any special tactic that might give him an advantage. When nothing presented itself, he figured he would have to improvise.

The two men drew their swords in response to Philo's challenge. Sean finally caught his breath and only looked winded now. They crept down the mountain in an attempt to meet their foe. Alexander felt it first. He crept along the trees, quietly concealing himself behind the trunks and then listening for movement.

His armor warned him the strike was coming. He couldn't see it, but he ducked.

Philo's sword crashed above him into the tree trunk. The tree shuddered under the power as if a woodcutter had made several attempts at taking the tree down.

Alexander scrambled around the tree and backed away. Philo's hulking figure appeared as the tree fell to the ground.

"I will give you the credit you deserve," he lauded.

"Prince Alexander never backs down from a fight. Not the right decision today, but I respect it."

Philo brought his sword down to slice through Alexander's neck and into his chest. Alexander blocked the swing, but the force of the blow knocked him down to his knees. He swung his sword up and down trying to gain an advantage on Philo. His opponent held the high ground though and easily deflected his blows.

Alexander scurried to his left in an attempt to flank him, but Philo continued to block him.

"And where are you going?" Philo said with amusement.

"Flanking me?"

He struck towards Alexander, and again in a quick motion. The armor communicated with the Prince's reflexes and he blocked his opponent's attempts. The armor was in perfect sync with his body, but it couldn't account for the sheer force behind the blows. Each blow forced him to stagger back.

Suddenly, Sean appeared to the Marauder's side and launched a vicious number of blows.

Philo was caught by surprise but managed to deflect each of the thrusts. Alexander seized the opportunity and scrambled back to the high ground. Meanwhile, Sean felt the force of Philo's blows and stumbled backwards over the fallen tree. Philo raised his sword for the kill when he was struck in the side by a large rock. He fell and rolled a bit, and Nicodemus laughed at his plight.

"What's wrong, Marauder? Did you lose your footing?"

"So I get to kill three of you today," Philo said, regaining his balance. "I hate sorcerers." He put his sword tip into the earth and took off his cloak. He stood very still with his hands at his side.

Nicodemus conjured another rock to fly directly towards Philo. Philo picked up his sword and started sprinting towards the sorcerer. Nicodemus sent a second rock and then a third hurtling towards Philo. The mercenary swung his sword effortlessly and the rocks shattered at the impact from the blade. Alexander and Sean ran from their respective sides to stop Philo from reaching Nicodemus. The Marauder reached inside his belt and flung a dagger at Sean.

His hands were so quick that Sean didn't realize what happened. He fell to the ground in pain with the dagger buried in his left shoulder.

Alexander brought his sword up and spun around. He aimed for Philo's waist. Philo blocked it and sent Alexander spinning onto the earth.

This slowed Philo's momentum and brought his attention back to Alexander. Their swords clashed in such fury that Alexander's broadsword shattered into bits. The momentum from Philo's blade carried through, narrowly missing Alexander's neck.

Sean pulled the blade out of his own shoulder with a cry of pain and tried to protect his Prince. His strength was sapped from the loss of blood, and Philo blocked his blow easily and punched him to the forest floor.

Nicodemus brought his hands up and a tree root grabbed Philo's sword hand. Philo struggled for a moment before he crushed the root into little bits.

Alexander drew the flaming sword from the scabbard resting on his back. He only used it when evil was about, but this was it for his protection. Philo grinned and went to smash this last sword. He yowled in pain and turned ever so slightly. An arrow protruded from his back and Katrina pulled back her bowstring, ready to let another one fly.

Alexander seized the moment and sliced his sword into Philo's hip. The man fell hard towards the earth and met it with a crash.

The Prince jumped up to get away, but Philo grabbed his leg and pulled him down. Another arrow flew into the Marauder's chest and he growled in anger.

Alexander summoned all of his strength and kicked him in the face, breaking his nose. The force caught Philo off balance and sent him tumbling down the mountain. Katrina and Alexander moved over to Sean who bled profusely. Katrina tore off a small piece of her dress and fashioned a makeshift bandage to block the wound.

The young girl molded an old remedy of spit and moss to put inside the wound, in hopes of stopping any infection. They helped Sean to his feet and, after making sure their enemy was nowhere to be seen, started back up the mountain.

CHAPTER XXI

Alexander was relieved to rejoin his companions at the summit. Chauncey and Fergus quickly fashioned a stretcher for Sean from tree branches and a blanket. His wound was deep but if they got him to a physician in time, he would live without complication. The brothers volunteered to carry him over the next few miles until they arrive at the ocean.

A small valley ran through between the mountains that created a pass that was easier to navigate through. This brought relief to their tired feet and since there appeared to be another hour or two of daylight left, Alexander decided making camp in the pass would be easier on Sean. As they descended, Devin caught sight of a few huts below them. There were three huts and a livestock farm with a few gardens dotted around them.

Their spirits lifted even more at the thought of spending the night out of the snowfall. Carefully walking through a snowbank, Fergus tripped over something buried in the snow. Chauncey berated him for dropping the stretcher, but Fergus waved his arms frantically that it wasn't his fault. To settle the argument, Fergus dug through the snow to find the source of his embarrassment.

He felt something metal and reached down through the snow and grabbed hold of it.

"Here it is," Fergus said.

"Now you can take back what you said. A silver bowl? Odd distance from the hut to find a silver bowl."

"Odd place to find a silver bowl," Devin corrected as he examined it.

"A silver bowl near thatch huts?" He tossed the bowl to Chauncey for inspection.

"A bowl?" Chauncey crowed as he turned it over. "It's a helmet you twits. God help Alveus if this is what we have to look forward to as leaders."

"A helmet?" Alexander said intrigued.

"Let me see that." He took the helmet from Chauncey and studied it a bit.

"This is a cleric's helmet," he gasped.

"Maybe a patrol?" Linus offered.

Realization crept over Alexander's face.

"The Monsignor said that twenty men went in search of my sister and none come back."

Keira dug frantically in the exact spot where Fergus had found the helmet.

"Start digging where you are," Alexander ordered.

Each of them ignored their frostbitten fingers and tore away at the snow. Emma came across something immediately and her shriek had everyone join her side.

Buried in the snow, was the body of a dead cleric. Alexander and Chauncey moved more snow away from his body and examined it. Fergus and Devin found bodies as well and together they arrived at a determination.

"These aren't sword wounds," Chauncey commented. "These are animal wounds. Punctures to the skin. Teeth gashes. Maybe they came across some bears?"

"What is that?" Alexander mused and brought the dead man closer to him. There were burn marks on the back of his head as if someone had set his hair on fire.

"This doesn't make any sense," Devin said. "Was it the men who kidnapped Sofia?"

"No," Alexander considered.

"These men came after her. But there was someone else tracking Sofia too. Duncan." He glanced at the hut and noticed smoke swirling from the chimney.

"Swords out," he ordered.

They took off towards the huts to take a look around. Alexander peered inside the window and saw there was one person inside the hut. None of them could get a good look at him to tell his identity. Devin knocked on the door while they took cover behind the walls and away from the windows. There was scuffling inside, but the door remained closed.

Frustrated, Alexander went to kick the door down. Unsuccessful in his attempts at banging down the door, Chauncey and Fergus join in bashing the sword hilts against the door.

"Sir!" Linus had panic in his voice.

"Not now, Linus. Help us open this door."

"How confident are you those men weren't killed by bears?"

"Extremely, why do you ask?" Alexander turned to chastise Linus and nearly lost his nerve as three large bears ambled across the field of snow.
The men became disoriented and were confused as to what to do next.

Katrina knew. The bears were much too close to where she and Emma were hidden taking care of Sean. One bear picked up her scent and walked in their direction. From her hiding place she placed an arrow and held back the string.

There was the sweet sound of flight followed by the thud as it hit the bear's shoulder. While a remarkable shot, the bear was not impressed. It roared angrily and picked up its pace towards their hiding place. Katrina and Emma sensed the danger and tried to pick up Sean's stretcher. When they found it too heavy to carry, Emma encouraged Sean to his feet and together they struggled to get to higher ground.

The gryphon also scurried away. She was not as fast on land, thanks to her front bird legs. She did her best to gain speed by flapping her wings.

The three bears saw them as an easy meal making its way across the field and they picked up pursuit. Alexander and his men watched their companions lose ground to these beasts even though they ran as fast as they could.

Instinctively, the men left their attempts at breaking into the house and sprinted towards the bears. Keira was ahead of all of them, desperate to protect her gryphon. They shouted and cursed and threw any rocks that they could pick up.

Nicodemus stayed at the hut unsure of what magic could do against such a beast.

Finally, the bears came to an awareness that they were being chased by adversaries wanting to do them harm.

They ceased their pursuit of their meal and turned to face the guards. They stood on their hind legs and bellowed a challenge.

The men halted and backed off carefully step-by-step.

"Anyone know how to fight a bear?" Fergus queried in amusement.

"Skirmish formation!" Alexander ordered. The men separated into a loose fighting force. There were at least two of them per bear. By being on either side of the bears, the bears would not be able to go very far to one side without being stabbed on the other.

Keira rushed in between the bears gnashing at them and drawing their attention away from the men. The soldiers shouted at the top of their lungs and waved their swords in a frenzy. Each of the men slashed and swung their weapons at the beasts in an effort to confuse them.

Eventually, each bear was riled to the point of a frenzy.

A bear would chase a man for a ways, but his partner slashed at the animal to open up a wound.

The bears slowed their attack and it became clear that they had enough of being outnumbered. Alexander hadn't finished yet. The voices that he associated with the armor were gone.

Anger and adrenaline surged through his veins as its replacement. He felt the power inside of him and he sought to finish the bears off. He yelled orders to his men to close ranks and they did.

And then a bear did the oddest thing. It stood on its hind legs, but instead of unleashing a terrifying growl, it uttered a mournful and plaintive howl. It sounded just like a cub that howled for its mother.

In response, the door to the hut swing open and a figure appeared next to Nicodemus. The sorcerer gasped in surprise as the figure punched him in the nose and knocked him down. The man placed his hood over his head and walked towards the men and beasts. Alexander's heart slowed and the rage subsided in him. The man walked with a staff that bore striking similarities to Nicodemus' staff, but its crystal shined bright blue. The bears stood in their spots respectfully, whining like cubs.
The man walked up to the grizzlies and inspected their wounds.

"Stupid soldiers and their swords," he muttered. "What do they know about you? That's a good bear."

He placed his hand on the worst of the wounds and as soon as he touched them, the wound disappeared with no sign of a scar.

He repeated the process to each bear and with the last one he scratched its hair affectionately. He whispered into its ear and the bear shook its head like it was tickled. It nodded in agreement and ambled to the slopes, with the other bears following.

The men exchanged glances and readied themselves for whatever irrational challenge was next. The old man stuck his staff in the snow and pulled the cloak off his head. "What are you doing here?" he demanded.

"Brendan?" Alexander asked in amazement.

"How did you get here? I haven't seen you since the stone hut."

"A lot of good that did for me," he responded angrily.

"You still found me." He sighed and picked up his staff. "Tell everyone to come inside and get out of this cold. You can use my fire."

They trudged back to the hut and Alexander made sure he gave Keira some extra attention. *Phenomenal,* he thought. *I'm lucky to have her.*

"Luck has nothing to do with it," Brendan winked. "Everyone inside!"

The group hurried inside and quickly laid themselves out near the fire in an attempt to get dry.

"Stew is on, help yourselves!" Brendan stopped Alexander from walking inside. "Look at her!" he gasped while he looked at the gryphon.

"You are gorgeous," he smiled. For a moment he closed his eyes and Alexander had the strangest feeling that Brendan was connecting to the gryphon, just like he was able to do.

When Brendan open his eyes, he had a frown on his face. He ushered the gryphon inside and closed the door behind it.

"I had a very interesting talk with her," he began. "By the way, what's her name?"

"I don't know," Alexander stammered.

"I haven't named her yet."

"You don't name a gryphon, boy! They come pre-named. You mean to tell me that all this time you've been walking around with her and you never asked? You weren't the least bit curious?"

Alexander shuffled his feet and bit his tongue.

"I've been busy," was his excuse.

"Arydia. Her name is Arydia." The prophet shook his head. "Now would you like to tell me what you're doing with a dark wizard in your party? Especially one who is adept at killing creatures like Arydia?"

"He's on my side," Alexander dismissed the prophet with a wave of his hand.

"A dark wizard isn't on anyone's side, lad," Brendan whispered. "Once he has what he wants, he'll be on his way. There's no denying the evil in that man."

"He's being hunted by Abiyram," Alexander protested.

"He has enough of a reason to help us, and I'm using him to get close,"

Alexander said the last words proudly.

"That's right, I am using him. Putting him and Abiyram together is going to help me achieve my ends."

"Is that what the voices tell you?" Brendan pushed his arm gently. He made contact where Alexander's mysterious wound was.

"I have no idea what you're saying. You know I can connect with gryphons. I can hear them." Alexander didn't like where this conversation was headed.

"Arydia says she has been trying to talk to you, but there are other voices drowning her out. She feels that you have been poisoned."

"That's ridiculous," Alexander scoffed.

"I'm a little beat up by I can assure you no poison has passed my lips."

"Not even a hidden wound?" Brendan asked and then he grabbed Alexander's wounded arm and pressed down hard against the flesh.

Alexander saw a flash of white before his eyes and the voices returned. *Who is this man?* It was desperate to know. He felt the adrenaline and rage build up inside him.

Brendan massaged his arm to the point of agony.

"Stop it," Alexander begged as he fell to his knees.

"What did you hear?" Brendan demanded.

"Nothing," Alexander insisted.

"You jabbed fingers into a wound. I'm in pain!" Alexander sat up and clutched his arm. The voices hadn't left, though. They were telling him how to deal with Brendan.   A crow landed on the roof of the hut. Its song sounded like it chuckled at the situation.

Brendan nodded at the crow and seemed to make a connection. He walked to the door nonchalantly. He called Katrina to join them for a moment on the steps and to bring the gryphon with her.

He patted the gryphon and asked Katrina to escort Arydia to what was a tomato garden during the springtime. Katrina did so and Brendan offered a hand to Alexander to pull him up off the ground.

"Katrina," Brendan asked,

"how much do you trust Prince Alexander?"

"Enough," she said.

"Come closer, I need you to witness something because I believe only a teenager would be brave enough to defy a Prince's orders, and I can sense that defiance in you." Katrina left Arydia sitting in the garden and joined Alexander's side.

"What do you need?"

In an instant, Brendan sprang upon Alexander's wounded arm and clutched it. Again, as Alexander felt the rage inside him build, he felt the power growing inside of him. He wrestled against the grip Brendan held on his arm. His vision blurred and faces started melting off. He finally eluded Brendan's grasp and roared in relief.

"Do you see him for what he is, Katrina?"

"What's happening to him?"

"He's infected. His blood has been working at keeping it at bay, but I fear he succumbs to it now." The crow caws became measured and grew louder. Several other large birds joined him on the roof.

"Even now, Abiyram watches us."

Kill them all, the voice told Alexander. He drew out his sword and slashed at the images. He kept swinging even when the voice sounded like a young girl screaming.

Brendan's face came into focus for him, and Alexander knew what he had to do.

He ran at him and prepared to slice him in two. A tree root grabbed his sword hand and swung it down.

With a deft stroke from his left hand, he cut it down. He again went to swing his sword at Brendan. This time a branch wrapped around his throat.

A cry arose from the hut. The guard heard the commotion of the birds and peeked curiously outside. When they saw that Alexander was in danger, they grabbed their weapons and headed for the door. With a wave of his hand, Brendan sealed the door shut.

Alexander spun around and sliced the branch in half. He tore it away from his throat and kept slashing. Finally, Brendan sent a root that wrapped around his legs. The Prince fell and another root grabbed his throat again. It constricted his throat so completely he was forced to drop his sword. His fingers ripped against the bark and he clawed desperately to remove it.

Brendan hovered over him.

"There's an infection in you, Alexander. I have to get it out or you are going to die."

"You will die!" Alexander hissed.

Alexander moved as best he could and lashed his hands out at the prophet. Another root grabbed his right hand, and Brendan grabbed his left.

He motioned for Arydia to come to them immediately, and he produced a small dagger from his calfskin boots.He moved the clothing that blocked the entrance to the wound and made a slit against it. Alexander gasped in pain and struggled against the forces that held him down.

"My apologies, Arydia. I only do this to save him." He dug a small cut into her back and squeezed her drops of blood into Alexander's wound. To him, it felt like acid had been dropped into his whole body. His body was on fire now, and he screamed for it to stop. The flames were burning him alive, and eventually the pain became so great he couldn't stand it anymore.

He felt as if his heart would explode out of his chest and just as it seemed to burst out, he lost consciousness.

CHAPTER XXII

Alexander awoke in the midst of a calm ocean, with a small wave lapping next to his body. He felt the water's presence, but it left no sign of dampness on him. The young prince realized that he was no longer on that mountain and assumed that this was it for him.

He spotted Brendan not far from where he sat. He sat on a small dune that overlooked the ocean. Beside him was Arydia, his Gryphon.

Alexander's feet sank in the deep sand as he made his way over to them. Not far off was the Gryphon Temple, and he wondered how it was that Arydia had been able to leave. Up until this point, they had always been statues, but here she was as flesh-and-bone. Except they weren't. None of them were.

Brendan barely acknowledged Alexander as he finished a conversation with the gryphon.

"Hello?" Alexander shouted once he got close.

"Can you hear me?"

"Good God, Alexander," Brendan remarked as he covered his ears. "Don't shout. I can hear you."

"Oh," the Prince replied. After a moment of silence he asked, "Am I dead? Is this heaven?"

"Not quite," the prophet said, gauging the wind.

"But we haven't much time.

Have a seat." Alexander obediently sat on the dune and looked off to the horizon.
He saw black sails of a dozen ships headed towards the beach. A million questions ran through his head.

"Brendan, why are their ships out there?

I thought this was where gryphons gathered together as one?"

"It's not just that," Brendan explained.

"It's not even simple enough to explain.

""Try me," he pleaded.

"Trying to figure this all out hurts my head."
Brendan chuckled. "That is why this land is not for mortal men. Think of this land like the Alveus River. The Alveus flows within your country bringing goods from Edgebrooke.

It's refined in Middlebrooke and taken to Brookhaven where it's distributed all over the world. This place is much like that."

Alexander had a blank stare on his face. It was difficult to understand the analogy.

"This place is like a river," Brendan continued.

"It connects a stream of consciousness with certain creatures and spirits. It is here that they can commune with each other and it doesn't matter where they are physically because their thoughts are connected."

"How come I've never heard of this?" Alexander quizzed him. "Because the Church would assign it as evil. It defies their explanations and logic. It also has a sense of power that goes along with it. There are secrets hidden here that many men would die to find."

Brendan motioned his hand in the direction of the ships. Arydia nodded and took off in full flight towards them. "She can fly!" Alexander gasped.

"Will you look at her?!"

"She can fly here," Brendan warned.

"This is The Reach. It is not heaven or hell. Just a place between them, where men aren't welcome."

"Then how are we here?" Alexander asked.

"The blood that flows in your veins is now half gryphon. That gives you an ability that very few others have."

"Do you have their blood in your veins?"

Brendan laughed freely at Alexander's question but stopped when he noticed Alexander's furrowed brow.

"I am sorry. I am not mocking you. I am a Guardian of this land." He waved his hand towards the land behind them. "I have been here for over one thousand years, charged with protecting The Reach and Alveus too."

"Why?"

"Because Alveus is a special land. It holds the secrets of life and death. I am charged with keeping the balance between good and evil. Should evil win out, darkness will cover this land. I'm not meaning Alveus as a kingdom, but the entire earth will fall. These sorcerers will stop at nothing."

"Why don't you just kill them then? If you're over a thousand years old then surely you can stop everything now." Brendan shook his head no.

"My duty is clearly written. I can only support you in your battles. I cannot fight them for you." Arydia flew back and landed in front of the men. "What did you see Arydia?"

"The hunters are on the ships, but the mist prevents them from finding their bearings."

"What mist?" Alexander asked curiously.

"There a mist that shrouds this land from those who seek it. Should the mist ever lift, that would become a problem." Brendan tested the air again. "Our time here is running out."

"What happened to me? If I am not dead then that means I can go back to my body, yes?" Alexander felt a lump in his throat. "You were infected with a poison," Brendan explained.

"Because of the gryphon's blood that was already in your body, it fought the infection as much as possible, which is why the wound never healed. There was too much poison and your body became overwhelmed."

"But I was never cut with anything," Alexander insisted. "I would know if I was cut by anyone!"

"Oh, but you were. You were scratched by a crow that Abiyram had sent," Brendan corrected him.

"Your body never allowed the wound to heal as that was its way of pushing the poison out. The poison sits inside of you and attaches to your anger and rage.

There is so much darkness inside of you over Edward's death that it was easy for the poison to latch onto you. It amplified your thoughts and emotions.

When I pressed your wound, I made it attack me."

"It felt as if my heart would explode," Alexander remembered. He placed his head in his hand and rubbed it thoughtfully. "Am I undead now? Is that what happened?"

"No," Brendan insisted. "Arydia sacrificed her blood into you as well to defeat the infection. You should be okay with a side effect or two."

"We found some men near the cabin that had been killed recently. Did you kill them?"

"No." Brendan was resolute in his answer.

"Then how?" Alexander asked.

"I was coming back to the hut from my visit east when I saw it," the old man explained.

"They were set upon both by Abiyram and a pack of dogs. They were vicious in their kill." Brendan wiped his eyes. "It's difficult to watch brave men be slaughtered like sheep. Their screams and pleadings…" Brendan wept openly for them.

"Did you know them?" Alexander offered.

"Only for what I saw. Their souls were pure. There was no fault in them. They were looking to rescue your sister, and instead they were ambushed in the cruelest of the ways. I hid myself from Abiyram, and when they had passed, I recruited those bears to be my protectors."

"But you're a guardian!" Alexander said in surprise.

"You could have stopped them!"

"I have rules that govern what I do." Brendan stood up and tested the wind again by tossing sand in the air. The wind was becoming more forceful.

"My life ends the moment I actively interfere in the struggle."

He was gone in the blink of an eye, leaving Arydia and Alexander on the beach alone.

"Thank you," he said.

"You saved my life."

"If you die, then I die. We are linked together by blood, Alexander, now more than ever. Do be careful," she pleaded.

With that, Alexander's body was pulled out of The Reach. He shot through the clouds and as he was being pulled up took note of the mist that surrounded the island. The black sails were circling around it, looking for a way in.

Alexander was making his way back to his body when he started thinking even more about what had just happened to him. He felt calmer and the rage that had controlled him so vigorously had subsided.

His spirit settled down and he became aware of voices talking around him.

He recognized them as his men, with concerned tones, and whispers of the madness they had seen. He had truly been mad.

His intent was to kill anyone in his path. He wondered if that was how Angelica was, focused on her rage and bent on killing the object of her hatred. He was thankful that they were shut in the hut.

Everyone except for Katrina that is. His spirit grew anxious and he tried desperately to wake himself up. What happened to Katrina? He fought the blurriness once more and forced himself to open his eyes. He looked around the room at his wide-eyed men and demanded to know, "Where is Katrina?

"His men pointed meekly to the door and he scrambled outside. He braced himself against the doorframe and braced himself for the worst. Katrina sat quietly, looking up at the night sky.

He breathed a huge sigh of relief and sat next to her. She stifled a scream, for he surprised her. She was about to say something, but he held up his hand asking her not to say a word.

Alexander placed his arm around her and gave her a hug. He brought her ear closer to his lips to give a whisper.

"I am sorry," he said quietly.

He released her from his grasp and for a second they stayed quiet. A tear ran down her face and he gave her another little hug. "And thank you," he added quickly. He left her sitting outside and went back into the hut. His men hadn't moved from when he walked outside. They were staring at him, Alexander thought he noticed fear in a few eyes. "Am I mad?" he quietly asked Brendan.

Brendan chuckled.

"Do you feel mad?"

"You know what I mean," Alexander said impatiently. "Am I crazy?"

"I told you, there would be some side effects," Brendan elaborated.

"We are always one step away from madness. It's the burden we bear."

Alexander walked bravely into the center of the hut to address his men. He knew their doubts, and they had every right to fear him after what they had witnessed.

"I understand," Alexander began,

"What you are thinking. Is the Prince mad? Has he taken leave of his senses?"

Some of the men glanced at each other, and Alexander knew he was on the right path.

"We have fought against the darkness since we came together in that tavern which seems like a lifetime ago. We have mourned personal losses of family and buried our friends. There will be more funerals and there will be many more times where our lives hang in the balance. I wish I could explain what happened to me, just know that our friend Brendan caught it in time and healed me."

"He healed me too," Sean chimed in ecstatically. He pulled up his shirt to reveal that his wound had been healed without as much as a scar. Alexander grinned.

"Don't let the doubts and fears nag at you. There are countless enemies out there that are waiting for us to be weak. They all fear us. Every attack they have tried has failed. Tomorrow we are going down the mountain to meet Jack on the coast. We're going to sail to the Isles and rescue Sofia."

"What about the sorcerer," Fergus asked with concern.

"We are no use against the sorcerer."

"We have one of our own," Alexander said nodding at Nicodemus.

"I will keep an eye on you," Brendan promised. That seemed to cheer up the men, and they smiled and nodded their heads confidently.

"Prince Alexander, if that's the case then we will need to rise early," Chauncey chimed in.

"We'd best get sleep so we can look and fight our best!"

The spirits of the men lifted as they laughed and joked about each other's looks. They were used to being on campaigns by now, and they were all turning into haggard barbarians instead of the handsome clean cut sons of Alveus that the world knew. They bedded down for the night and pushed the thoughts and doubts from their mind, and replaced it with a sense of growing optimism.

CHAPTER XXIII

The party set off the next morning as if the forest was on fire. Brendan had promised them that the bears would go before them, clearing a path of anyone that wanted to harm them. Confident and fearless of the possibility of being ambushed, they kept up their quick pace through the rest of the range.

They had one more peak to cross, and it was easily ascended. Sean's journey was made easier, his shortness of breath and wound healed by Brendan's touch.

Alexander felt light-headed as he ran alongside his men. He felt freer than he had been in months from his fears and his stresses. They were still there at the forefront of his mind, but now he found himself able to dwell on solving them.

They reached the peak within a few hours and stopped to take a breather and view the layout before them.

They cheered loudly when they saw Alexander's ship, the Resolute, moored on the sands.

They were encouraged to be ahead of Mattias and the Alveuns. There were no sails for miles in any direction. Off to the horizon were the Western Isles and nothing but calm waters between them.

The Western Isles were made up of several islands, some larger than others, and the geographical anomaly of them created channels between each island that made it difficult for invaders.

Should the attacker seek to assault the main castle where the royal family lived, they would have to navigate a series of forts, and in essence sail through a killing zone of catapults and archers. The only other choice was to assault the islands one at a time. That would take time, and with the unpredictability of the winds and waves combined with the lack of natural harbors on the western shore of Alveus, it would make for a short campaign. It wasn't long before they were at the beach. Keira picked up Jack's scent and raced at full speed to greet her master's friend.

Jack waved hello once he realized how close in proximity Alexander and the guard were to him.

The sailors broke camp and loaded all the gear on the ship in preparation for an immediate departure.

The group stopped to catch their breath but managed to greet each other and salute each other's bravery in completing their tasks.

"Did you run into trouble?" Alexander asked Jack, wanting to know how much time they had before the Alveuns would be at their back.

"None at all, surprisingly," Jack said, grinning. "Once the alarm was raised, the horsemen chased after you. We didn't see a soul. Once we got to Brookehaven, Baron Idris was more than accommodating in making sure we had the ship fully provisioned. How about you? Where's the Princess?"

"Gone," Alexander said, shaking his head.

"That scum Youssef got to the monastery first. Speaking of, have you seen anyone else come this way?"

"No, My Lord," Jack said thoughtfully. "Not a soul. We saw some bears, but they took off once they saw us." Alexander smiled. Brendan had kept his promise.

"Where is Prince Calimus?" Jack asked inquisitively.

"He stayed behind. He means to influence the King as best he can. He thinks he can actually get a word in over Mattias."

"Best of luck to him," Jack smiled.

"He's working very hard at being a prince."

"Yes, he is," Alexander agreed.

"Listen up! We are leaving now. Let's put the ship in the water and strike out for the Isles."

"What's the plan for the rescue, My Lord?" Fergus asked.

Alexander pondered for a long moment. He really only had one plan, and it was usually the same plan.

"Run up a white flag of truce," he ordered.

"We will sail right into the city. Once I gain an audience with Youssef, we will free Sofia, and then we run back to the ship and sail away."

The men shrugged their shoulders nonchalantly. It wasn't the best plan that Alexander came up with, but he expressed that he was open to other ideas. As no other plans came forward, they settled on his.

With the ship freed from its mooring on the beach, the men hopped on board and took their places at the oars. Alexander's ship was originally intended to be a galley, but he had shortened the length and added a triangular sail. Speed and maneuverability on a sea where large galleys crashed into each other was a precious commodity.

While it was certain death if a galley collided with them, it would take superior seamanship and a serious error on the helmsman's part for that to be a possibility.

Once they were able to turn the ship in the direction of the island, they unfurled the sail. The men stopped their work for a moment and allowed themselves to be mesmerized by the motion of the sea.

Katrina and Emma took a place at the bow and giggled as they spotted a school of dolphins swim by.

The beasts cared little for the quick voyage. Keira curled into a large ball behind Alexander and the gryphon sought refuge with her. Alexander kept the helm straight and veered to take the channels on.

They were nearly into the first channel when Chauncey alerted the men on board that their worst fear was realized.

"My Lord!" Chauncey shouted as he pointed behind Alexander. "I see a sail!"

An exhaustive groan rose up from the ship's crew. It was too far away for an exact telling of whose ships they were, but Alexander knew that the Alveun navy was in pursuit.

"Can you guess what they are thinking?" Jack asked.

"They are coming to take Sofia. If Prince Youssef says no, then it's going to be a very interesting battle."

"Why will it be interesting?" Linus asked.

"Because," Alexander answered,

"We'll be in the middle of it."

The men affixed their armor and their weapons as they glided through the channel. The Isles-men respected the white flag they flew, and the soldiers in the forts let the ship pass without interference.

Once they were through the channels Alexander guided the ship through the waterways that they had visited only, in his mind, a few months ago. When he turned his head back around for one last view of the Alveun Navy, he noted that they had begun to close the gap. The men in the forts had also noticed the ships that were coming towards their islands, and an alarm was passed.

The Resolute made its resting place along a dock, and the men set about tying the ship to keep it from drifting. Alexander's internal questions about how he would get to Youssef were answered when members of the Palace Guard arrived at the dock.

The Palace Guard wore armor, but while Alveuns considered it the ultimate privilege to display their armor, the Guard was prohibited from showing their armor in any non-combative situations. They wore long brown robes to cover their armor and were armed with spear and shield, with a curved sword hanging at their side.

The Captain addressed Alexander once the lines had been secured.

"Good day to you, Prince of Alveus," he said icily. "My Master bids that you should join him in his banquet hall so that he may have a word with you."

Alexander smiled and winked at a few men.

"Yes, please, my men and I would like to speak with him as soon as possible."

"I am sorry, it will not be possible. Your men are under arrest and will be placed in the dungeons for safekeeping."

"I'm not going," Linus objected.

"I am done with dungeons."

"Me too," Ferris said. He picked up a large battle axe and waved it menacingly.

"I would like to see one of you step into this boat and make me." Alexander's guards nodded in agreement and they drew their weapons.

"My master assumed you would say this," the captain said with indifference.

He waved his hand to another group of men that hid behind some barrels. Fifteen archers appeared and drew their arrows and pointed them at each of the men.

"I would hope that you would not resist, or we would be forced to kill you where you stand. This way we would not need to step in the boat."

"Very well," Alexander agreed.

"Put down your weapons." The men groaned, then untied their weapons and threw them onto the deck of the boat.

"We spend more time in dungeons than we do fighting," Linus groused.

"I hope they have some better food than the last one," Brennan added, trying to make light of the situation.

"You too, My Lord," the Captain pointed to Alexander. "Your sword stays here."

Alexander groaned.

"Can you at least stow the weapons in your armory? I can't have this stolen. And what will become of my pets?"

The Captain seemed to take insult with the question.

"We are not thieves, but very well, in the armory they go. As for your pets, tie them up. If you are detained long, then other arrangements will be made."

Emma tied Keira and the gryphon to the boat. Alexander traded thoughts with Arydia. She would gnaw through the bonds at the call of her master and be by his side at a moment's notice if he called.

Alexander's guard was led off to the dungeon while the Prince was taken towards Youssef's halls.

Their pace to the hall quickened and to Alexander's observations, so did the rest of the town. It was like a controlled panic. Streets were emptied and merchants hid their goods and their livestock. Once inside the meeting hall, they were redirected to the top of the castle wall.

Prince Youssef was there waiting for them. He was dressed in full armor, minus the cloak, and gazed across the sea towards the navy approaching his shores. "Your Highness," the captain spoke.

"We have brought you, Prince Alexander."

"Thank you, Captain. You have done well." Youssef turned his grim face on Alexander. He hadn't changed in the months since Alexander last saw him, although there was now a dead seriousness about him. Same dark hair and swarthy complexion, Alexander mused, but he seemed more confident than he had been at the twin's eighteenth birthday party.

Youssef's father had died earlier that year, and he was the only heir to the throne. The Isles were not great enough to be a kingdom, and as a nation of traders, generally kept out of the way of other nations. Youssef had dangerously circumvented his nation's isolationism.

"Alexander," Youssef began,

"I am going to dispense with any formalities. Is that acceptable to you?"

"Of course," Alexander nodded.

"I really hadn't planned on pretending to like you anyway."

Youssef chuckled respectfully. "You are here as a representative to negotiate for your kingdom, as I am for mine. I am requesting that you tell your father that I have claimed Sofia as my bride as I am the father of her child. Any further action by him will be treated as a hostile incursion upon my people and we will open fire upon your ships."

"I am here to request the return of my sister," Alexander remarked. He found it interesting that Youssef assumed he was the diplomat.

"What you did was shameful, the behavior of a cowardly man. Could you not have worked out something in place with my father so that you could have had a proper wedding? If you are expecting me to sail back without my sister, you will have to understand that we will rain down ruin upon your people."

Alexander went to the edge and pointed to the horizon.

"At this moment there are thirty ships, fully armed with men and firepower, ready to launch vicious attacks upon your forts.

They will be gone in a matter of minutes. Then the fleet will sail back to Brookhaven. Is it because they are tired Youssef?

No, it is because they need more weapons. Then they will sail through the channel, firing their ballistae and catapults at your walls."

"Your army doesn't frighten us," Youssef said bravely.

"I am glad to hear it. Mattias doesn't sleep at night if his sword isn't covered with blood. I imagine this will be the cure for his ailment; an entire people, defying him and willing to make their stand." Alexander stood very close to Youssef and whispered for effect.

"Are you so very stupid that you would risk your entire kingdom, and have your subjects pay for your sins?"

"Have you ever been in love?" Youssef asked meekly.

"Come on," Alexander pleaded. "Wake up! You don't get to steal a woman away from her family and expect them to turn hind leg. If your men weren't here, I would kill you with my bare hands."

"Alexander, even if I wanted to, I couldn't." Youssef made an empty gesture with his hands.

"Two people make decisions. That's what love does, it binds you together." He motioned to the Captain to run an errand for him. He returned shortly with a fair-haired maiden.

"Sister!" Alexander cried out. He ran to her side and grabbed her with a crushing embrace. She pushed him away quickly.

"Alex!" She scolded.

"Watch the baby!" She pointed down to her belly where a sizeable bump was. He gazed at it speechless, and couldn't bring himself to say a word.

"Will you give us a moment, please?" Sofia asked gently. Youssef nodded his head in agreement and allowed Sofia and Alexander an opportunity to speak on their own. They walked in silence to the other side of the wall, away from the prying eyes.

"Why are you here?" she demanded to know.

"It appears I am negotiating your release," he said.

"Release from what? I am where I want to be."

"Have you gone mad?" Alexander shouted.

"You have a child! There was no wedding. There was a kidnapping. Do you know what you have brought on me? I've been accused of treason, of undermining the kingdom, and for being complicit in this!"

"Complicit in what?" Sofia folded her arms and impatiently waited for Alexander to finish his rant.

"They all think that I had a hand in this."

"That is the most ridiculous thing I have ever heard," Sofia said.

"We made choices. Mattias was never going to allow the treaty between us. This was my way out. I just happened to be with child."

Alexander groaned in frustration.

"All this time, you blamed me, as if I held back secrets. You wouldn't trust me to carry these for you. But then you left me! You left me and I took the fall for you. If I leave without you, I might as well sail to the furthest corners of the earth because I am a dead man within those borders."

"Then leave!" Sofia threw up her hands and sat on a wooden bench near the wall.

"Get away from them. You can stay here with us. This is a nation of merchants and traders, hasn't that been your dream?"

"There is a world of evil out there," Alexander said. He knelt down and clasped his hands around Sofia's. "How can I walk away knowing what I know? I can't do this alone. I can't fight this battle without you."

Sofia didn't respond, instead she fussed with Alexander's tussled hair.

"Would it make any difference to you if I told you your life was in danger?" Alexander slumped his shoulders in defeat.

Sofia gave him a coy smile.

"From Mattias? I don't fear Mattias. I am fortunate to have a Prince who will gladly take Mattias' challenge."

"No," Alexander sighed.

"Not Mattias. I chased Duncan here to the Western Isles. He's coming to kill you."

"What?" Sofia's face lost all color and she turned pale as a ghost. "Why would he be coming here?"

"Because he knows that if he gets to you, then I have nothing left to keep me going."

"He'll never get through my guard," she insisted.

"There's nowhere to hide," Alexander warned.

"You cannot stay here. You have to come with me."

"My baby," she said, with an increasingly panicked tone. "I have to tell Youssef." She left her seat and started to make her way across the wall.

"Wait!" Alexander commanded. There was something coming to the island.

"Look out there." Some tiny boats were headed to the shore of the island. The boats were the size of a small trading vessel. They had full sail out and were heading directly towards the beach.

"Are they Alveun?" Sofia asked.

"Not unless they completely sailed around the island," Alexander answered.

"Something's not right." There were other men on the wall too, and they regarded the ships with curiosity as well. The ships were being blown by the wind, and no one was on the deck to steer it. The guards shrugged their shoulders and scratched their heads in confusion. Occasionally, a sentry would lift a spyglass and examine the boat for any signs of life.

Confident that there was no life aboard, they went about their business and sent runners to the back gate to reinforce the garrison, just in case the Alveuns had treachery in mind. Eventually, the boats came to be stranded on the beach. The small waves pushed them ever so slightly up the sand until the wind finally died.

A few men from the garrison went out for the inspection of the boats. The twins watched intently as the ship was examined. First, the bow was inspected for damage, then a few hopped on board the deck, to investigate this oddity.

There was a small hatch that led to a level below the decks. This is where the cargo would have been held. The soldiers cautiously lifted the door and peeked inside.

They were instantly repulsed at the sight and lowered their weapons.

They reported to their runners and they went running back to the gate.

Alexander called down to one and asked him what they found. Nothing but dead bodies was the reply.

Suddenly it dawned on Alexander what was happening. "Get behind the walls!" He screamed while waving frantically. "Get off the ship!"

He closed his eyes and sent his message into the Reach.

Arydia, they are here.

CHAPTER XXIV

The soldiers investigating the boats had lost concern over the danger they initially felt while they looked for any sign of life. But, as Alexander feared, the dead began pouring out of the ships hold.

They hacked at the men on the boat, jumped onto the beach, and quickly overwhelmed the other soldiers who stood nearby. Among the initial onslaught, a dog escaped from the hold and helped bring down the Isles-men with little struggle.

The guards at the gate were horrified but had the sense to close the gates immediately, trapping several of the soldiers outside of the walls. The sounds of their cries alerted Youssef, who quickly made his way around the castle walls.

"They're here," Alexander whispered to sister grimly.

"Sofia, I need you to be calm, and I need you to get Youssef to believe and trust me. Can you do that for me?"

Sofia nodded her head yes and Alexander met Youssef at the northern tip of the turret.

"Where are you going?" Youssef demanded. His men pushed Alexander back with the tips of their swords.

"You need to free my men, and give us our weapons. You have until they get through the gate or over that wall. By then, it will be too late."

"Why? Is this Alveun treachery?"

"Much worse," Alexander explained.

"Get all of your people indoors. They are coming for Sofia, so take her to a place where they can't get to her." Youssef glanced at Sofia and in their unspoken language, she nodded, which Youssef took to mean that Alexander was telling her the truth.

"I will take her deep into the fortress. They can't get through my guard there," Youssef promised.

"Take Yakob with you. He will get you your weapons and free your men."

"I will come back," Alexander promised.

"But you better not let anything happen to my sister."

"You are talking about the mother of my child," Youssef swore.

"Go now!"

Alexander and Yakob ran down the stairs and towards the dungeon. The streets howled with rage and the panicked screams of people running for their lives. The controlled panic that had been there earlier was gone. People were pushing and trampling one another to get to safety.

Suddenly, a rock crashed through a market stall. Another one crashed into the town square.

"What's going on?" Yakob yelled.

"The ships are firing at us!" Alexander yelled back. It was impossible to hear over the screaming and wailing. The two men ran into the dungeon where Yakob shouted a few orders to the jailor and within moments the entire dungeon emptied except for Alexander and his guards.

"Listen to me carefully," Alexander explained.

"We have the navy to the front, and Duncan behind us. At any time we are going to have a bunch of corpses running around the streets, slaughtering as they go. I need you to get to the gates and stop them. Work in teams of three." Jack nodded his head.

"Groups of three, yes sir. No one loses their group! Any questions?"

Yakob directed them to the armory where they each grabbed their weapons and an extra one just in case. Alexander worked furiously to find his sword, but it wasn't there.

Frustrated, he asked Yakob, but the man had no idea. Time was running out so the Prince grabbed a regular sword and told Katrina to follow him. Once outside, they found themselves in the midst of a furious street battle. Rubble was falling to the ground from the bombardment, and the dead had broken through the back gate. Keira came running up to them and narrowly missed being squashed by a chunk of debris that fell from a tower.

The Prince's men ran out into the street and immediately engaged the dead soldiers that had been running through the streets unchecked, slaughtering whatever moved. Alexander grabbed Nicodemus by the arm and pulled him towards the banquet hall. Katrina covered them by firing arrows at any dead soldier that ventured too close. Keira stayed close to Arydia and together they joined Alexander while they sought shelter in the hall.

Alexander directed his group to the passageway leading into the great tower. They ran up the stairway unimpeded until they reached the top.

There was a large wooden square that had been closed above him. Alexander pushed it open and found himself surrounded by eight Isles-men with arrows pointing at him.

In the din of the yelling, they pulled everyone up through the doorway and quickly closed it behind them. They forced the latch through and took up spots around the perimeter of the tower.

Alexander caught his breath and took in the view. This tower was the largest on the island. It offered a full view in every direction. He could see Alveus from where he stood. When he turned his face to the south, he saw the Alveun ships who continued to fire upon the fortress. Giant rocks were flung from the ships catapults, crashing into the stone buildings. They weren't firing back at the fleet, Alexander wondered if they had been deserted.

"What is the situation in the streets?" Youssef asked. He stood solidly by Sofia, who had just enough time to grab her longbow and a quiver of arrows

"There are many people dying," Alexander said ruefully. "We need more men."

"Look," Youssef pointed to the small channels between the islands. His men from the other fortresses hadn't deserted them.

It was an orderly retreat to save their capital.

"We will wait here until the reinforcements arrive."

Alexander agreed with Youssef's assessment. He and Arydia stood near the wall and looked directly down. The tower stood on the edge of a cliff, and straight down was the ocean and quite a few rocks that waves crashed onto. He glanced at the stones that made up the tower. They weren't smoothed at all.

For years, Alveuns had smoothed down the stones on the inside of the castle to prevent unwanted scrapes and bruises. There was no such attention to detail here.

Where have I seen this before? Alexander thought. *Have I been here before?* His eyes widened as he realized where he had seen this image before.

"Sofia!" he commanded.

"You need to get away from this tower now!"

"No," Youssef said firmly.

"We are staying right here."

"Why?" Sofia questioned.

"I have seen this place before," Alexander insisted.

"They are coming here, you are not safe."

"There's only one way up or down," Youssef scoffed.

"You don't understand," Alexander insisted. He grabbed Youssef by the arm and pulled him closer. Youssef's men immediately drew their swords and surrounded Alexander. Alexander let go of his arm, but Youssef was extremely unhappy.

"Let's not forget that you are my guest, and an uninvited one," he snarled.

"Touch me again, and I will send you over to the rocks, regardless of who you are."

"My love," Sofia cooed, "Alex knows what he is saying. He has a good deal of experience with these people. Perhaps we should listen to him." There was a moment of silence as Youssef searched Alexander's face for a sign of doubt.

"Very well," he ordered his men,

"We move."

Youssef's men got into a position to hurry down the stairs and one of them men knelt down to remove the latch. Keira's hair stood on end and she began barking ferociously. Her lips curled upwards and her teeth glimmered in the sunlight.

"It's too late," Nicodemus said.

"Never," Alexander insisted. The latch was turned and the door opened.

Down the stair case they went. The echoes of crackling steel sent shivers down their spines.

Youssef hurried into the inner hall of his citadel. Like Edgebrooke, there was a myriad of rooms behind the throne. The Prince assured Alexander they were not trapped in any one direction. Multiple rooms held multiple escape rooms.

A plan was quickly formulated for Alexander to draw the attention of the sorcerer. He, Nicodemus, and a few Isles-guards would head back to the tower. They wagered they would think he was leading them from Sofia.

The eight men ran through the hall and back to the tower. They were spotted by a dismembered corpse. It had lost its left arm and was wondering around aimlessly crushing tables with a huge mace.

They thought better of engaging it, and rushed up the stairs. The dead soldier kept howling in an attempt to warn its fellow fighters. For a moment, the ground trembled underneath them and they lost their footing.

Alexander peered through a slit in the tower.

"That was no catapult!" Again, Nicodemus had the information for him.

"It's Abiyram. He's going to destroy this citadel one stone at a time."

The men reached the top of the tower and shut the door behind them. They waited nervously, licking their lips and what would come through the door. Then came the pounding. At first, it was like a knock. Then it grew in frequency and power. The door held, and eventually it grew quiet. Alexander checked the walls of the tower, just to be safe.

There was a scraping, and without warning the door blew off its hinges and went hurtling into the sky. Youssef's men surrounded the gap in the floor, in a loose formation, and drew their bowstrings tightly. A staff appeared from the hole and a burst of light shot forth from it.

Everyone fell backwards and shielded their eyes. The soldiers who were closest received the worst of it. They clutched their eyes and dropped their bows. They grasped for their swords and waved them about wildly. As quickly as the light had blinded them, it disappeared. Alexander grasped his sword and the armor took over his senses.

He sensed a sword coming towards his skull, so he threw his up to block it.
Steel crashed against steel and he knew that the battle had been joined. He sensed the danger with the cries and crashing of steel around him.

"Nicodemus?!" He yelled. There was no response and he realized he was in danger. He swung his sword to his side and connected with skin. There was a slicing cut followed by the thud of a body falling to the floor. His was grabbed from behind and he heard Nicodemus' voice a split second before he was about to send his sword into the sorcerer's belly. In moments his vision was restored, and Nicodemus dissipated into thin air.

He quickly surveyed the scene. Most of the eyesight of the group had recovered. The four Isles-men who had been closest to the tower's entry were dead. The remaining four fought valiantly against a few dead soldiers, with Duncan entering the fray. Duncan finished off three of Youssef's guards rather quickly. With blinding speed, he ripped through their attempts at subduing him and left them each with a mortal wound.

He uttered a command for the dead soldiers to stop fighting for a moment and they backed away from Alexander and Nicodemus. There were only three men left.

"She isn't here," Duncan groused with irritation.

The staff made its appearance again, above the doorway. The white haired sorcerer, Abiyram, made his way slowly from the stairwell.

He surveyed who was left on the tower and politely saluted Alexander. He wore a blue robe this time, and his once impeccable look was now dirty and disheveled.

"Do you know how hard it's been keeping up with you?" He chided Alexander.

"But I do have to thank her."

"Don't talk to her," Alexander demanded.

"You don't ever talk to her."

"I just want to say, thank you," Abiyram grinned. "Look around! Are you still so naïve as to what this is?" He pointed to the ships offshore.

"The fleet of Alveus! Complete with Prince Calimus and Mattias, and your father King Magnus. In this castle, I have Sofia and Alexander and another heir to the throne of Alveus. Killing Prince Youssef, although not in the original plan, will be a welcome addition."

"I will eradicate every heir to Alveus today, and only your sister could have made that happen!" Abiyram rubbed his hands together gleefully.

"Find Sofia and bring her here," he ordered.

Alexander shook his head in disgust. Had he fallen into another trap? Was that possible?
Alexander peered over to the ocean and rocks below him.

"Jump!" Abiyram mocked.

"Please?" The dead soldiers stood ready to attack, but Abiyram had different ideas. He called them off and waved his staff in a circle above his head. Alexander placed himself directly in front of the soldiers and waited for the onslaught. The atmosphere began to change. Strom clouds rolled in from the north and the once calm sea started to get choppy. In a flash of realization, Alexander assumed that Abiyram's plan was to sink the ships and drown his family.

From out of nowhere, Nicodemus appeared. Abiyram glared at him.

"There you are," he growled. He raised his staff to Nicodemus. "How much have you told him?"

"Not everything," Nicodemus said.

"Just enough to keep him at bay."

Abiyram considered the answer for a moment.

"Find the girl," he growled impatiently.

Alexander sighed heavily. He should have seen this coming.

Nicodemus passively shrugged at Alexander.

"Do you really think," Abiyram continued,

"That a sorcerer would bow to you? You will bow to us before this day is over."

He lowered his staff down and aimed it at the men. A bolt of lightning shot forward at the lone guard.

The bolt hit him so hard that the man flew off the tower to his death, screaming in horror. He aimed at Alexander who braced for impact. The bolt shot forward but bounced harmlessly off of him. It careened and struck the wall, leaving a hole and debris in its place. Abiyram shot two more bursts at Alexander with the same frustrating result.

Abiyram grumbled and turned around. He stretched his arm forward and acted as if he was lifting an object. The swords of Youssef's fallen men rose from the ground and levitated towards them. The swords inched closer and closer until Abiyram pushed his hand forward quickly.

Alexander took a breath and focused on what was coming to him. The armor fused to his reflexes and sent him into a whirlwind of motion. He blocked each sword that flew at him and ended with a flourish, bowing in mockery at his opponent.

"I hope you planned on something better," he chided.

Abiyram sent debris hurtling in his direction, fired bolts of energy and in the same motion, directed debris to crash into Alexander.

The Prince was knocked off balance and his sword fell out of reach. Alexander rolled over and moaned from the pain coursing through his veins.

The sorcerer's attention shifted back to the weather in his attempt to destroy the Alveun navy.

The sailors had sensed the danger that was to befall them and were turning their ships around. They continued to fire rapidly on the tower, with their shots hitting the mark and causing the tower to shake. Nicodemus returned, dragging Sofia by the hair. Youssef was also dragged along by dead soldiers. The last person through the tower floor was Duncan, and he had a broad smile.

"Master," he said. "I have a gift." He brandished the fire sword. "Nicodemus hid the sword from Alexander's sight."

"At last," Abiyram crowed.

"Give it to me." His eyes widened as he brandished the sword. It glowed with fire and the sorcerer's body shook as he tried to handle it. He couldn't stand it any longer and flipped it back to Duncan.

"Never mind," he groused.

"I will deal with it later. And now, no one shall be even remotely as powerful as I am."

Ignoring his injuries, Alexander leaped to his feet and grabbed two extra swords that lay next to him. He tossed two to his sister and her beau and grabbed another for himself.

Youssef bravely challenged Duncan, but the master assassin sent the young man sprawling with cuts to his arm and leg.

Sofia dove to his defense and defended her wounded love. She waved her sword furiously at Duncan, and waited for anyone to challenge her over her lover's life.

Duncan scoffed and transformed himself into the dog. He snarled at the couple and crouched down, looking for a weakness. He nipped at Sofia and tugged on her dress while staying out of reach of her sword. Nicodemus turned his back on them and directed a family of crows to attack Alexander. The crows flapped about him, pecking and trying to rip into his flesh. He rolled along the floor, covering his head as he went until he came to a shield, laying up against some bricks. He placed it above his body and ran back to cover Sofia. He handed the sword to her for protection and kept waving off the birds.

As suddenly as they had been aggravated into attacking, they stopped.

The necromancer uttered a gasp of surprise as the sword sank into his back.

He stumbled forward and reached behind his back. He pawed at the sword as if he meant to take it out. Duncan stood behind him, changed back into his human body, the betrayer of Nicodemus.

The assassin caught Abiyram's attention, distracting him from his work.

Abiyram pounced on the opportunity and grabbed a set of iron fingernails from his pouch.

He placed them on his fingertips and grabbed Nicodemus' throat. Nicodemus struggled for a moment but the wound was severe and blood flowed freely.

Abiyram turned the old sorcerer over and stabbed his heart with the iron fingers. The wounded sorcerer struggled and gasped against the pain. The drops of blood left Nicodemus' body, running up along the iron fingernails, into Abiyram's body. The dying sorcerer aged horribly until there was nothing left but skin and bones.

Duncan turned his attention back to Sofia, striking the shield she hid behind, sending her sprawling backwards. She dropped the shield, and tried her best to slash at Duncan. He deflected her slash, grabbing her arm, and twisted it behind her. The pain caught her by surprise and she dropped the sword.

The last dead soldier had its gaze fixed on Alexander.

It had a long sharp metal weapon, not a sword and not a spear, just a very heavy piece of metal. It swung down heavily and Alexander moved in time to watch it crash amongst the stones.

Bits and pieces were shattered from the stone, and Alexander moved away from the wild swings.

The Prince did his best to avoid the strokes, the density of the weapon would have shattered his sword.

Alexander countered with a slash at his opponent's belly, which had no effect on the dead soldier. The soldier, sensing the kill, swung at Alexander's head. Alexander ducked, the soldier over swung, and Alexander used to his momentum to push him away.

The fire-sword flashed red, as Duncan prepared to terminate the pregnant princesses' life. Thoughts of Edward swirled inside Alexander's head. A general panic consumed him, as he realized fate was about to repeat itself. He sprinted towards the assassin, ignoring the blasts of energy being shot at him from Abiyram's staff. Explosions followed him, sending debris and smoke into the air.

Duncan hesitated, realizing that Alexander was bearing down on him. His indecision of turning to face Alexander or killing Sofia cost him the initiative.

Alexander grabbed Duncan's sword hand and grappled him towards the wall, forcing him to let go of Sofia. The Princess, being let go, did what she could to help Youssef stand to his feet.

Abiyram waved his staff around, sending loose debris at the two lovers. Sofia picked up the shield, and together she and the Western Prince stumbled to the tower exit.

Duncan pushed Alexander off of him and lunged his sword towards the Prince's torso.

The sword flashed by, just missing Alexander, who grabbed the assassins arm, and shoved it down and that same time he brought his knee up. Duncan winced in pain, and grabbed Alexander's face with his left hand. He pressed his hand hard into Alexander's nose, trying to shove him away. Alexander's head bent backwards as he refused to let go off Duncan's sword hand.

From the sea, an Alveun ship catapult fired at the tower. Abiyram was distracted by five Isles soldiers running onto the tower to protect their Prince. Another ship fired a second stone, following the same trajectory as the first. The first rock struck its target, sending a shockwave through the tower.

Alexander stumbled back a step, but tried to regain his footing as Duncan bore down on him.

He kneed Duncan in the chest repeatedly. The assassin exhaled and grunted in pain, spitting blood as he went. Duncan went to gouge Alexander's eyes.

His fingernails were sharp like razors, a product of him being an animagus. The nails dug into Alexander's cheeks, and he howled in fear, understanding what Duncan was trying to do. Alexander brought his right hand up to stop Duncan from reaching his eyes, and released Duncan's sword hand, bringing his elbow into Duncan's face.

The blow made the men separate, both desperate to find a weakness in the other. Abiyram began discharging more bolts at the soldiers, driving them back, and sending them diving for safety. The floor of the tower was losing its foundation, a gaping hole had been opened up. One unlucky soldier fell through the hole to the steps below.

The last undead soldier moved to engage the guards, but just then, the second stone collided into the tower, collapsing the floor underneath its feet. The stones fell towards the city, taking the dead man with them.

Duncan laid the sword against a remaining piece of the battlement and put his fists up. Alexander mimicked him and charged him, Duncan threw an overhand punch that connected with the Prince's face.

Undeterred, he threw an uppercut that caught Duncan's chin. The assassin staggered back and Alexander pressed his advantage, throwing another punch into his chest.

Duncan responded with an elbow that caught Alexander by surprise and sent him to the ground. His foe picked up the sword by its hilt, ready to end the fight. The Prince grabbed one of the axes next to him and met Duncan's swing in midflight. The clash was so strong, sparks flew.

Duncan backed off a bit, breathing heavily.

"You're tired," Alexander observed,

"let me finish this."

"You can finish by dying."

Again, their weapons clashed. Alexander swung the axe above his head and brought it down on Duncan's sword. Alexander mustered as much strength he had left, bearing down on his foe. He pressed hard, Duncan backed towards the wall. He backed up as much as he could, with Alexander coming within a hair of his face. The men grunted, Duncan gripping the sword with both hands, and on both sides. Blood trickled from his hand as the sword cut into his flesh.

Another stone was on its way to the tower, but this time Abiyram had paid attention.

He reached out his staff at the rock, and took control of its trajectory. He moved the rock above the tower and sent it hurtling to the other side, meaning to send it the ocean.

The stone's path was imperfect, and it crashed right next to the two men. Alexander lost his footing, and began to slide off the tower.

"Help!" Duncan shouted, thinking Abiyram would save him. The four remaining soldiers stood between the sorcerer and his minion, and Abiyram began fighting with them, in an effort to get to him.

Alexander dropped the axe, and it fell to the water below, shattering on a rock protruding from the water. Duncan fought to loosen Alexander's grip on his arm, but the prince would not let go. The assassin lifted up his fire-sword, and pointed it down at Alexander's shoulder. The Prince let go with one of his hands and swung to the side as Duncan tried stabbing him. The sword missed and Alexander wrapped his arm around Duncan's neck, hanging on for dear life. Duncan began sliding forward off the edge, gasping for air, but struggling to hang on.

One more explosion rocked the tower, and the two foes fell off the tower, headed toward the water and rocks below.

Ignoring their fate, they struggled against the other, trading punches as they fell through the air. Duncan panicked, changing back and forth from a dog to a human. When a dog he snarled and snapped at Alexander, who let a few moments before they were to hit the water.

They continued to fall eye-to-eye, both weary with fighting, and resigned to what was next. In a split second, Duncan was gone, his body crashed upon a rock. One moment later, Alexander crashed into the ocean, his momentum finally slowed by the water. A wave crashed over him, against the rock that Duncan's body lay on. The Prince struggled against the weight of the water and the waves, but his armor weighed heavy and he began to sink.

He pushed against the current and grabbed a piece of the rock that Duncan had fallen on. He heaved himself up for a desperate breath, but then a waved crashed into him, sending his head below water again. He opened his eyes underwater and a glowing light caught his attention. It was the fire sword; it was still glowing as it was sinking to the ocean floor.

Alexander let the current take him to it and made a quick grasp of it. He made it back to the rock, and tried pulling himself onto it.

Above the water for a moment, he gasped for air struggling to stay above the waves. He grabbed onto the edges of the rock and pulled himself against the flow of the water.

He was close to being able to pull himself up, but his body had reached its physical limits.

With one last push, he heaved his body above the water's surface and tried to regain a hold to pull himself up.

The water rose with him, and he held his breath while he held on. He was just about out of breath when he felt a claw grab his hand. He grabbed the claw with his other hand and it pulled him out of the water.

"Arydia!" He shouted joyously. Arydia's wings beat hard as she struggled to pull him out of the sea. She made sharp movements, as several rocks fell to the sides of them. Abiyram was attempting to finish them off using stones from the tower to crush and obliterate.

Arydia flew up the tower as her wings gained strength. She weaved in and out of the falling rocks until they hovered above the tower. The sorcerer pointed his staff at Alexander, and he felt a hand squeeze his neck, cutting off his air. There was no one left to fight the conjurer.

The Isles soldiers lay dead around him, Abiyram had won handily. He walked towards the edge of the tower, each step tightened the grip around Alexander's throat. Arydia sensed this, and began moving backwards, trying to escape Abiyram's range.

Behind Abiyram, a head appeared above the tower's entrance.

Princess Sofia had come to aid Alexander, and when she saw his predicament, she made a crucial decision. She grabbed a sword and meant to slice his back. Abiyram sensed it coming. He turned round and blocked her sword with end of his staff, and then struck her face with the other end. She crumpled to the ground unconscious, her face bleeding. Arydia made haste back to the tower, with Alexander gripping on to her legs, ready to save his sister.

Fear gripped Alexander, as the sorcerer grabbed her by the throat.

"Faster!" he shouted, but Arydia's wings were tiring. Carrying the added weight of a soldier was too much.

She strained and groaned under the weight, but she kept going.

Abiyram lifted Sofia off the ground and touched her stomach. The pain was so intense that she returned to consciousness, screaming in pain, clutching her torso.

Alexander let go of Arydia as soon as he was over the battlement and took off running to Abiyram. The evil man dropped Sofia and covered his face as Alexander threw several punches. He picked up his staff and swung it round to Alexander.

He lunged the crystal at the armor in an attempt to cripple the Prince, as had happened with Jack, but the armor held fast and repelled the energy. Blasts of energy flew to all sides, striking rock and sending more debris into the air.

Alexander brought out his fire sword and crashed the sword down on the staff. For a moment, the sword and staff held fast, each one of the men unable to gain the upper hand on the other.

"All is lost for you," Alexander muttered.

"Your army is dead, Duncan lies on the ocean rocks below. You have failed."

Abiyram displayed the blood red iron fingers that were still on his hand.

"Do you see this?" he asked. "All of Nicodemus' powers are mine." He placed his staff to the side and let it go. It continued to stand as if he held it.

Alexander swung his sword at the sorcerer. With a raise of Abiyram's hand, the Prince was frozen in place, sword suspended in mid-air.

Abiyram picked him up by the neck and walked him over to the wall closest to the ocean.

"I have had enough of you, and now with this combined power, I can finally get rid of you." Abiyram forced Alexander to drop the sword and lifted his arms outstretched towards the ocean.

"Watch as I destroy your nation!" Abiyram smiled satisfactorily and raised his arms up in the air. The sea obeyed his command and the water rose up alongside the Alveun ships, as walls of water, frozen in place.

The galleys had made their turns and the rowers were beating their drums at a rapid pace. The rising of the water tipped the ships slightly and they regressed backward towards the shore. The higher that Alexander was lifted off the ground, the higher the wall of water became. The Prince hovered twelve feet in the air, suspended and unable to move. A figure appeared behind Abiyram. "Put him down," he warned.

"Brendan?" Abiyram questioned.

"You can't interfere here!"

"You have tipped the scales," Brendan seethed.

"You are done here."

Brendan aimed his own staff at Abiyram and a root shot forward to nab the evil man's feet.

"Shall we see whose powers are greater?" Abiyram's staff emanated a light that lifted up some debris around Brendan. Brendan scoffed and struck the surface. The debris fell harmlessly to the ground. Without warning, Abiyram dissipated and Alexander fell to the ground. He reappeared next to the stairwell and grabbed his staff.

The sorcerer disappeared into the tower as he ran down the stairs. Brendan took off after him and Alexander weakly pulled himself over to Sofia. She was shivering and turning blue.

"Help me," she cried as she clutched her stomach. Explosions rocked the tower below, as Brendan and Abiyram fought each other.

Blood collected underneath Sofia's legs. Alexander stifled a frantic scream.

"Help me!" Sofia pleaded, but Alexander didn't know what to do. Youssef came back to the tower, having been unable to locate where she had gone. He was followed by Alexander's guard, looking for their commander.

"Sofia!" Emma ran to her side and immediately placed her head on her legs. She noticed the blood and gasped. "Alexander! She is going to lose the baby!"

"What do I do?" Alexander shouted back in panic.

Sofia cried out in horror when she looked down at what was happening.

Alexander threw up his hands and walked towards to the wall. Youssef shouted for someone to find the physician and bring them immediately.

Then Alexander had an idea.

Arydia, I need you! He screamed into the Reach.

Arydia responded and flew to where he was.

I need some of your blood, he pleaded.

That isn't how this works, she answered. *It's only for you.*

She could die, her child could die. Please, he begged.

The gryphon relented and made her way to Sofia. She allowed Alexander to prick her paw and press it against Sofia's shoulder, where she had a scrape.

After a few moments, the crying stopped. Sofia had passed out so they all sat, holding their collective breaths.

Emma bent down and placed her ear next to her mouth. Youssef felt her neck and found a slight pulse. He breathed a sigh of relief.

"We should move her to a comfortable place," Emma suggested.

Youssef lifted her cautiously and followed Alexander and his guards downstairs.

When they came to a room with a bed, he laid Sofia down on it.

The physician came in quickly and ordered everyone from the room. He and his assistants set about seeing what they could do for her.

CHAPTER XXV

The mood outside the room was grim. Youssef and Alexander sifted through the reports their men were giving and tried to make sense if the worst was over.

Jack reported that the dead had been eliminated and the boats burned. There had been heavy losses to the garrison, fortunately the men from the other smaller keeps had retreated back to the capital.

Yakob reported that the Alveuns naval barrage had decimated their defenses. Even though the men had turned the tide of the battle, the ships had picked off each defense, keep by keep.

When Abiyram had threatened to sink the fleet, the Alveuns had moved in full retreat.

Once the water returned to normal, landings had been taking place on the outer islands.

They had surrounded Youssef and his people. Magnus' main force moved closer towards the citadel's shore, and Yakob had the gates to the canals closed. Abiyram and Brendan had disappeared. Their battle raged through the rooms of the citadel. There were holes in the walls. Tables and chairs were kindling. The once proud palace was now in shambles, with no room in the battlements, and heavy damage to their towers. Youssef ordered their army to man what was left of the defenses.

"Will you assist us?" Youssef asked. He looked genuinely worried. His arrogance was gone and he held no false pretense about their situation.

"I'm only here for Sofia," Alexander answered.

"However, if you surrender her, I am sure all of my people will leave."

"Never," the Prince exclaimed in shock.

"She is the love of my life. I will die first rather than give her up."

"A lot of people are going to die first," Farkas added.

"He's right," Alexander added. He wiped the filth off of his sword so it was pristine again.

"How many people are you going to send to their deaths just so you can have her?"

"I could ask your family the same question," Youssef murmured.

A courier ran in breathlessly and gave them the news they knew was coming. The King wanted to parley. Youssef agreed, sending the courier to Magnus offering to meet them outside of the city walls.

Alexander decided to follow Youssef. He fell in line behind him, joined by his guard, and together they made their way by boat to the mouth of the canal. The guard took their places on the wall above them while the iron-gate was lifted. The boat navigated slowly out of the canal and the two Princes hopped ashore at a small tree where Alexander's brothers and father waited for them.

Mattias scoffed upon seeing Alexander.

"Exactly as I said, Your Majesty. Alexander has fallen in league with the Isles-men. What more proof do we need as he follows this heathen?"

"I came here to bring Sofia home," Alexander responded. "Which will not be happening," Youssef insisted. He placed his hand on his swords hilt and rattled it a bit for effect.

"We will have a thousand men landed on this shore," Mattias expounded with gritted teeth.

"We have seized control of all the land surrounding your capital. Within a week we can have enough siege weapons to batter what's left of this pitiful fortress."

"Enough of your words," Magnus interrupted. "Prince Youssef, you have brought shame to our kingdoms with your behavior. Your father, God rest his soul, was a good man. He would have your head on a spike for this. Give me back my daughter or I will make sure your townspeople are unable to grieve over your body because there will be no trace of it. I will take it back to Alveus and hang it out on a stake and let the ravens finish you."

"I am not afraid of you," Youssef said bravely. "Your teeth are sharp, but you will lose a few when you try to clamp down on me."

"This is pointless," Alexander said.

"What good does any of this do?"

"Why are you saying anything? You're obviously a traitor to us," Mattias said accusingly.

"I came here to rescue Sofia. She sits up there now, lying in bed, near death. We just prattle on arguing over who's going to take her." Alexander was glad that for a moment the face of his father and brothers softened.

"Yes, she was wounded. And if she survives, do you really think we can take her home?"

"Why can't we?" Magnus demanded.

"I am the Great King of Alveus and she is my daughter."

"And that is why," Alexander said with an understanding wave to Youssef.

"Her heart is here, she'd give her life to stay. Do you really think you can keep Sofia Wolfield in a cage? She'd spend every moment of every day seeking the way out."

Calimus chuckled.

"Seems to be a family trait."

Magnus bit his lip. Sofia was his only daughter, and Alexander hoped that he held a soft spot for her.

"I want to see my daughter," Magnus said softly.

"There will be no more attacks this day, please, take me to her."

Youssef relented and they entered the small boat that Alexander had traveled in. They made their way back into the city and towards the main citadel. The inhabitants of the Western Isles stopped scurrying about and eyed the Alveuns suspiciously. They gathered along the riverbank and exchanged hateful glances with the brothers.

When they docked, Magnus was the first one off of the barge. His magnificent cloak, resplendent and decorated, was tossed back into the barge so that he could move unencumbered. Youssef led the way and the brothers fell in line behind them. They made their way to the room where Sofia had been taken.

Nightfall was coming and Youssef escorted them up the stairs by torchlight. The hall was heavily guarded, many of Youssef's men using it as a command post and armory.

Tables had been brought in to be used as makeshift beds for the wounded. Women went back and forth between the men with bandages and water to clean the wounds. The floor ran wet with a mixture of blood and water, and Alexander could tell by their determined faces that these people would not let Sofia go, whether it was a selfish whim by a careless prince or not. Going up the stairs didn't change the expressions on anyone's faces.

There were holes in the stone walls, and debris covering the stairs. Alexander took a deep breath and muttered a silent prayer of mercy for his sister.

A somber atmosphere befell the hallway leading to Sofia's room. Alexander's heart sank when he knew that even his men wouldn't make eye contact with him.

More than a few of his men wiped tears away from their eyes and struggled to keep their faces hardened. Katrina walked away from the room and pushed her way past the princes and hurried down the stairs. Keira and Arydia laid on the floor with their heads between their paws and the great dog let out a plaintive whine. The physician exited the room and was the object of every man's eyes. He wiped his face and addressed his liege with as much courage he could muster.

"I'm sorry, My Liege," he said.

"I did everything I could. It was too late." Youssef patted his shoulder as if to say he knew that he did his best.

They stood at the doorway and held their breath for what their mind told them was on the other side.

They glanced inside. A few women removed a blood-stained sheet from the bed whilst another covered Sofia with a blanket.

Emma sat next to her in a wooden chair, holding her hand and stroking it. There were tears in her eyes as she moved the hair from her eyes.

"Look, my friend," she said softly.

"It's your Prince." Sofia weakly lifted her hand in his direction. Youssef rushed inside the room and knelt down to receive it.

"My love!" He exclaimed. "Thank God, he has seen fit to keep you with me."

Alexander breathed a sigh of relief, as did his brothers and his father, but their joy was short-lived.

"Our baby," Sofia stammered.

"They took our baby." The realization of what happened sent an icy stab through each man's heart. Youssef sat on the bed and tightly embraced her body.

They wept together and it gathered such momentum that a loud wail went up. It started with Youssef and then to Yakob, who stood outside the door. Yakob began banging his sword against the stone wall, and in a moment each man in the stairwell picked up on it. A cry went up from everyone in the castle, which carried to the ones who stood outside. The ones outside knelt down and began banging what they had in their hands against the ground. Overcome with emotion, King Magnus and Alexander's brothers entered the room to support her. Magnus at once sat on the other side of the bed. With a simple touch she realized he was there.

"Father!" She cried. She threw her arms around him and sobbed in his arms. He held her close and stroked her hair as he had when she was young.

Magnus took her by the shoulders and pulled her apart from him. He took her hand and then Youssef's hand, and clasped them together with his hand over theirs. The venerable King gently kissed her forehead and left the room. He passed by Alexander and didn't say a word. Alexander moved from the door and slumped down behind the wall and seated next to Jack. His friend nodded at him kindly, but Alexander would have none of it.

"I failed her, Jack," he whispered. He put his face in his hands and grabbed his hair. He pulled on it, wanting to rip every hair from his scalp. The continued mourning of the Isles-men were not helping him.

"You did save her," he insisted.

"She's alive because of what you did up there."

"I was too late," the Prince repeated.

"First Edward and now Sofia."

"It could have been all of you," Jack said.

"Prince! You saved this kingdom."

"But it still wasn't enough!" Alexander hissed.

"Alexander, Sofia would like to see you." Youssef offered him his hand. Alexander sighed and stood face to face with Youssef. He didn't want to face her.

"No," he said flatly. He walked past the men in the stairwell and down the steps to the courtyard.

He ignored Youssef calls pleading him to come back. Alexander made his way through the halls of the castle and made his way to the shores. The agony born from the cries of the Youssef's people grated on his already frayed nerves. He glared at the townspeople, feeling anger and hate replacing the grief that was eating at him.

He shouted at several of the people to shut their mouths.

Each rhythmic pounding of their swords upon the walls only served to annoy him further.

Alexander found himself at the shore, staring up to his father's galley. It was the largest warship in the fleet, resplendent with brilliantly colored banners and armored with a two ballistas and a catapult.

His anger subsided a bit and he remembered how badly he had wanted to take a ship and sail to the world's end. He had never listened to himself, and always stopped short of leaving because he felt that he needed to stay. The war hadn't ended, but by the count of the dead bodies, the stalemate had come at too great a cost.

He sensed Jack's presence behind him.

"What is it?" Alexander growled.

"It's Princess Sofia, My Lord. She keeps asking for you."

"I can't do it, Jack," he admitted.

"I can't see her."

"It would mean a lot to her," Jack offered. He took a moment to dip his hand in the ocean water and splash it onto his face. He wiped the dirt and grime off and waited another moment for Alexander's response.

"How are you?" Alexander asked, hoping to change the subject.

"The men?

Katrina?"

"They fought well," Jack said proudly.

"Would it not be for them, this entire city would have been killed. They came after us with such a vengeance." Jack paused, conflicted with the images inside his mind.

"They came through that gate and they killed everything in their path. Men, women, children. It was clear they were here to eliminate everyone."

"They were here to kill every Wolfield," Alexander answered. "It was a clever trap indeed. They knew my family would come.

We would all be here. Every soldier, every ship, and every prince. Alveus would be an easy conquest had they succeeded."

Jack nodded his agreement.

"Your men would never let that happen. They threw themselves into the heat of the moment and beat back every assault. Brennan was a monster for us today. He crushed skulls as if he was pounding fence posts into the ground."

"Did we lose anyone?"

"No," Jack grinned.

"They still haven't figured out a way to kill us. Even my one handed self, was brilliant."

"You are a great man, Jack," Alexander said honestly.

"Someday they will write a song about you and your exploits."

"Ha!" Jack laughed.

"You are the Prince! It is because of you that we are alive."

Alexander grimaced.

"No. When this war is settled and when all of it is said and done, no one will sing for me. There will be arguments and passionate debate over my role." Jack scrunched his face in puzzlement.

"I don't understand, sir. You defeated the Bete'szek at Edgebrooke, you beat back Abiyram here and saved a nation. We might as well state that you stopped a war. How are you not a hero?"

"How much of this is my own selfish fault?" Alexander picked up a beautiful seashell from the beach and examined it.

"I feel like everything I have done is the cause of everything that is happening now. What if I never went after Duncan? What if I would have stayed home? What if I had just stayed out of that damn forest?"

"What if you would have stayed away from it?" Jack asked.

"There were already plans in place."

"But I am clearly the fool that keeps springing these traps," Alexander said.

"If I would have never left, I would have saved Sofia."

"My Lord," Jack said emphatically.

"You cannot bear this burden. This is not yours to bear."

"Isn't it?" Alexander asked.

"Edward died in my arms. Sofia's child dies and I am an arms-length away." Alexander hung his head in shame.

The pain drove deep into his heart.

"I keep failing the people that I love. This burden I bear, I am afraid that it is too heavy."

Jack's face grew beet red.

"I lost my hand," he whispered,

"And I do not regret it or a single moment of following your command. When you say these things, it minimizes all of our sacrifices. We believe in you, but we need you to believe in yourself."

Alexander's brothers and father approached them from the city. Their faces were ashen and they walked silently towards the galley.

"Father," Alexander said dutifully. He nodded to King Magnus and held his breath for the worst.

"It is time for us to hold council," Magnus replied. He motioned for the soldiers surrounding them to disperse and take up defensive positions so they might be alone for a moment. Jack followed suit, and together the family walked down the beach and towards the rocks.

"I am asking your advice instead of that of my Generals," Magnus stated.

"This is a family matter now, and I would hear what you as brothers would want for Sofia."

"Would you allow us a moment to confer?" Mattias asked. Alexander was taken by surprise as he thought Mattias would take advantage of the kingdom's weakness and take it all for himself.

Magnus agreed and the brothers formed a circle to talk about their circumstances.

"Well?" Mattias asked. Seeing neither Calimus nor Alexander offering a suggestion, he took the lead.

"There is an opportunity here, to annex these people.

They have withdrawn from their hill forts, and many people lie dead within the city."

"Of course you do," Alexander scoffed.

"There is Mattias, ever seeking conquest."

"Thank you for actually being here," Mattias retorted. "If you had stayed in Middlebrooke, you may have been part of the planning process of the invasion. Since you can't be bothered to be of any use to this kingdom, God knows why father wants your advice, why don't you try to be worthwhile."

"I saved your lives," Alexander hissed.

"And I am not sure why I did."

"Stop!" Calimus interjected.

"Fighting get us nowhere. We should each be allowed to say our thoughts and come up with something for Father. He is depending on us to make a decision together."

Alexander waved his words off and Mattias took the opportunity to continue.

"This fleet was commissioned to take these islands. Would we just walk away from that?

We are Sofia's brothers, and we cannot lose sight of our responsibility to make an example of them."

"Haven't they been punished enough already?" Alexander interceded on the Islands behalf.

"Sofia is in love with Youssef. We take this kingdom, and what does it give us? Where does Sofia go?"

"There is truth in that," Calimus agreed.

"Sofia will hate us, and she has suffered enough. We should just let it go. Allow them to marry and go back to our lands in peace."

"Are you sure?" Mattias asked.

"By subjugating this kingdom, one of us would be elevated to over this kingdom. Calimus, this would suit you and your ambition. Alexander, they have many merchant houses here. This would bring so much to Alveus."

Alexander shrugged his shoulders.

"I think Sofia should stay. I never want to come back here again. But…what do I know? I seem to be wrong most of the time."

Mattias and Calimus traded puzzled glances. Mattias rubbed his brow furiously in annoyance.

"You sound like a depressed bard," Mattias said irritatingly.

"Woe is me. No one likes me. I make bad decisions. We may have our differences Alexander, but for the love of God, shut up if you are going to self-pity."

Alexander shook his finger in Mattias' face.

"You shut up!" he insisted.

"Just listen to me for once then. If you have any love for Sofia, forget your ambition for a moment, and do the right thing."

"Agreed," Mattias said, much to Alexander's shock. The brothers rejoined Magnus and Mattias relayed their decision. Sofia would marry Youssef, and they would leave the kingdom as it was, but signing a treaty that required tribute to be paid once they were recovered from the attack.

Magnus agreed and commended his sons on reaching the right decision. He sent a runner to Youssef to relay the decision they had reached, and asked him to agree to their terms.

Alexander noticed that Arydia had perched herself on the rocks below the wall where he had fallen. She was watching something on the rock. He made his way to her, climbing carefully over the rocks, making sure he didn't fall back into the ocean. His attention was drawn to a body that laid still. Convinced that it was Duncan, he made his way through the jagged rocks to get a better look.

The seas were at their calmest, but occasionally a wave crashed on the rocks sending salt water into eyes and mouth. Arydia stood alertly and never took her gaze off of the body. When Alexander made it to the surface of the rock, he confirmed it was Duncan's body. He made no effort to move, but to be safe, Alexander drew his sword and poked Duncan's body.

Alexander gasped when Duncan's eyes opened and he coughed up a spittle of blood. Alexander shook his head in disbelief.

"How are you still alive?" Alexander asked in disgust.

"You didn't kill me," Duncan said wryly.

"This is a fitting end then, to die at the hands of your enemies," Alexander stated. He poked Duncan's neck gently.

"Are you going to stand and fight?"

"My back is broken," Duncan said despondently.

"So I guess you are going to win this day. No matter, my master will triumph in the end."

"You won't be around to see it," Alexander warned.

"He's already shown me," Duncan said, with great pain in his voice.

"Soon you will fall to his plots. It's already inside of you fighting you for control."

Alexander smirked at his bitter enemy.

"Oh, I know all about the poison. It's been dealt with."

Duncan choked back a laugh and shook his head no.

"Poison never leaves you, Alexander.

One day it will take control and you will have no way of stopping it. Then you'll have this insatiable desire to kill everyone around you. When that moment comes, Abiyram will be standing by your side. You can't resist him."

"You're wrong," Alexander argued.

"He'll never win. Look at your body. It's broken and battered." He placed his sword's blade on Duncan's neck.

"You will pay for your crimes in the hereafter."

"Make it clean," Duncan asked. He moved his chin up slightly.

"This is for my family," Alexander stated. He brought his sword up, and with a clean swing, cut Duncan's head from his body. The head rolled down into the ocean and Alexander kicked the rest of his body into the surf. He washed the blood off of his sword and slid it back into the scabbard resting on his back. He motioned for Arydia to follow him back to the boats to rejoin his family.

With the terms for peace staggering, Youssef declined to present himself to the Alveuns. Instead, he sent Yakob to inform them that he agreed to their forced treaty.

CHAPTER XXVI

Alexander commended Youssef's actions as a leader who was taking the best deal he could get. Before Abiyram' s attack that destroyed half of the city, it may have been possible to at least have forced a stalemate, but with the might of the Alveun army intact and the Westerners losses, the citadel would have been captured in a few short days. Youssef had requested a week before the wedding be held, to allow Sofia to recover emotionally and physically. Magnus agreed and prepared

to send a ship back to bring Queen Caroline. Alexander, bitter and frustrated, did everything he could to avoid being near his sister. He ignored numerous requests from envoys and Emma, who stayed close to Sofia as a handmaiden, to visit her in her grief.

Alexander volunteered to pick up his mother and departed with the Alveun vessels that were dispatched from their main force. When Alexander's dull voyage came to a brief stop in Brookehaven, his mother waited there expectantly, as did Sofia's handmaidens. When Sofia had been sent to the nunnery, her handmaidens stayed near the castle. Queen Caroline was gracious to keep them on and gave them additional jobs around the castle. They were extremely grateful, for if they had been turned out, their prospects of a happy life dimmed considerably. Queen Caroline was emotional and teary-eyed during the excursion back to the Isles. She planted her seat to wherever Alexander was while he piloted the Resolute and made her thoughts well-known to him.

"This breaks my heart," she said, for the tenth time that day.

"I know, mother," Alexander said quietly. He feigned a task that might give her the hint that he was not interested in discussing it again.

"Edward, and now Sofia," she continued mournfully. "Nothing hurts worse in this world then having your children taken away from you." She noticed Alexander's lack of response but continued.

"I know you can hear me."

"Yes, Mother," he replied.

"Have you nothing to say?"

"You point out my failures very well," he growled.

"I said nothing about you failing, although if you would have listened to my counsel," she chastised.

"I am tired of listening to counsel. I am tired of politics and fighting and looking over my shoulder every day."

"Do not talk to me in that tone!" She insisted.

"Sorry, Mother," he said indifferently. She again noticed his indifferent tone and shook her head in disapproval.

"So how about we talk about something happy for a change. What about your relationship with Isadora," she said, boldly changing the subject.

"What?" he stammered.

"I-I don't have a relationship with Isadora." Queen Caroline rolled her eyes.

"The Baron keeps suggesting a marriage between you two."

Alexander's face grew horrified.

"Marriage? It's a bit soon to be speaking of marriage isn't it?"

"You are nearing twenty and two years of age. Between your brothers and yourself, you are the closest one to giving me grandchildren."

"Mum!" he protested.

"No! No, no, no! Mattias is oldest, let him be carted off. And I am sure if we dug deep, we might find some of Calimus' progeny!"

"Heaven forbid!" she shrieked.

"A bastard as heir to the throne? I would not sit idly by and let that happen."

"Well, I assure you, there is no relationship with Isadora. She is pretty. Very pretty. Like the most exquisite stained glass in the most adorned cathedral. But I don't see myself in Alveus much longer."

"Stop running from your destiny, Alexander."

"I have no destiny, Mother. All these conversations of destiny amount to nothing. How many more horrors must I endure?" Alexander looked to his men working diligently on the ship, except for one. Chauncey seemed to have picked up with an earlier conversation with Lauren, Sofia's chief lady-in-waiting.

He was extremely talkative, and Lauren kept sweeping her long blonde curly locks behind her ears. She giggled every few minutes as Chauncey made a grand gesture with his arms.

"Those two are very much in love," his mother cooed.

"Chauncey? Love?" Alexander grimaced.

"I thought it was Fergus?" Fergus was casting an annoyed look in his brother's direction, but also took the initiative to tease his brother's grand gestures.

"Did you plan on living life without it?" The Queen tussled his hair playfully, but Alexander would have none of it. He tossed love back and forth in his mind.

"No," he admitted.

"I don't think I ever have. Always too busy fighting and chasing our enemies. All I am now is the sword of the kingdom, designed to slay our enemies."

Caroline sighed and put an arm around her son.

"All I want from you is to be the king that I know you can be. Take a wife, have a family, and rule in peace. Is that too much to ask?"

"In this kingdom, it certainly is. Excuse me, Mother, I need to see to our approach through the canals." Alexander took the helm again and guided the ship through the narrow passageways. It was on the seas where he felt the most peace.

There was nothing but the movement of the swells, and the cooling sea breeze. He could shut out the world from the helm of his boat, and not take another moment caring where the world went.

Alexander flawlessly guided his ship through the iron-gate until the ship finally came to a rest at the docks.

The mood of the city had changed, from mournful to hopeful, as colorful banners had been hung throughout the city.

The stench of the dead had been masked by flower petals that had been sprinkled everywhere.

The bodies had been taken away, leaving only the debris of the walls and buildings. His father and brothers waited near the docks, to greet the Queen. When Magnus took Caroline in a genuine embrace, Alexander ruminated at how in love they still were after all these years.

The handmaidens disembarked and were escorted to Sofia's chambers by Alexander's guard, leaving Alexander alone with Arydia and Keira.

He stayed on the boat, wanting to waste as much time as possible before Emma inevitably appeared. Now that the handmaidens were there, she was released from Sofia's side to do as she pleased. When she did arrive at the deck, Emma had replaced her armor and tunic for a fine dress. The marriage ceremony was set for later in the day, and she was quite prepared.

"My Lord," she curtsied,

"how was your travel?"

"It was fine," he replied succinctly.

"Permission to come aboard?" she teased.

He shrugged his shoulders apathetically, and she lifted up her dress train and stepped aboard. It caught for a moment on a nail, and Alexander had to stoop down to free it from tearing. As he lifted it up slightly, he caught sight of her legs. They were svelte and well proportioned, and as Alexander had little experience to compare with, they pleased him.

"That's a nice dress," he teased.

"I keep forgetting you're a woman." He patted the dress into place and straightened out the wrinkles for her.

She bit her lip and winced at his comment.

"Thank you, My Lord," she said stoically.

Alexander realized how that sounded and apologized profusely.

"That wasn't quite what I meant."

"I will need to work on your perception of me then," she stated.

"Perhaps we can start with you escorting me to your sister's wedding." She mussed with her hair and tied it in a loose bun behind her head. She moved the dress ever so slightly off the top of her shoulder and slid it down, in an effort to show her shoulders. Again, as the prince felt about her legs, suddenly Emma had shoulders, and they were nice too.

"I won't be there," Alexander said, shaking his head and moving his eyes off her shoulders.

"There's no need for me to be at the wedding. What is done is done."

"She is very hurt," Sofia pleaded.

"She is hurt because you refuse to see her." Alexander didn't respond.

"Your sister, your twin, wants you to be there. Think of all the pain she has gone through. Are you going to put her through more?"

"She isn't the only one who hurts," he whispered, pondering Emma's words.

Church bells rang out through the city calling those invited to hurry to the chapel. The wedding was soon to begin. Alexander hopped over the side onto the dock offered his hand to Emma.

"Take me to her," he commanded gently. She took his hand and he helped her over the side of the boat. This time, the dress didn't catch, and together they walked towards the abbey.

It was a smaller abbey than the one in Middlebrooke, but what it lacked in size it made up for in ornaments. It was the only building in the city that was untouched, a miracle to some and luck to others.

The stained glass windows reflected the sunlight and hues of blue and red covered the cobblestones that led to the front door.

The chapel was large enough to seat two hundred people, and it had a small building behind it, where the monks lived and tended to their gardens.

Sofia and her handmaidens were busy in a small rectory, preparing her dress and hair for the ceremony. When Alexander walked through the door, she gasped and stopped the preparation her handmaidens were focused on.

She walked over to her twin with tears in her eyes and gave him the biggest hug she had ever given. He responded in kind and they stood together in their embrace for several moments until he finally spoke.

"I'm sorry, Sofia," he whispered gently.

"You can't blame yourself," she said kindly.

"You saved us all. I would never hold you responsible."

Alexander took a deep breath and steadied his emotions, pushing back the frustration and anger that he felt. He bit his lip and said nothing more. He nodded at Sofia in understanding and curled one side of his mouth in a poor attempt at a smile.

The beautiful princess took Emma's hand and embraced her, thanking her for bringing her brother back.

"Doesn't she look gorgeous, Alex?" she commented slyly. "I like what you have done pulling your dress off the shoulders. So lovely!"

"It helped him remember that I am a woman," Emma commented dryly. She rolled her eyes in humor and the girls shared a laugh.

Sofia drew Alexander near and whispered in his ear, "I could arrange a double wedding."

Alexander made a strange noise, that was supposed to be an objection but sounded more like a drunken man stirring from his sleep.

The women in attendance giggled at Alexander's sudden awkwardness. Emma looked at him quizzingly, trying to understand whatever Sofia had told him.

He recovered his composure and grabbed Emma's hand. They made their leave of Sofia and walked back to the entrance of the abbey.

They were escorted to the front bench with his family, and they waited for the moment to begin.

The abbey was packed, with both nobility and commoner, as they came to see their Prince be married. This was an important day for them, the death of many of their families stung, but with their Prince's new beginning, they could have one too.

Youssef was the only son of the king; however, he had several sisters, each one dark haired and a tanned complexion.

Several of Alexander's men could not keep their eyes off of them, and neither could Calimus, raising their eyebrows at each other as signs of approval.

After a few moments, Youssef and several high-ranking officials arrived at the altar and waited for Sofia's arrival. A small band of musicians played a happy tune with their flutes and lyres and sang one of their Western Isles ballads.

When the song had finished, the side door opened and in walked Sofia and her maidens.

Her dress was as blue as the clear sky, and in her hair was a crown made of orange blossoms. Her face was covered with a veil, but nothing could hide the light in her eyes.

It was evident as she passed by, that she was smiling ear to ear. The pain of a week ago was steadily giving away to the euphoria of being joined in marriage to the man she loved. Alexander felt as if he was the only one in the abbey that did not partake in the excitement. How could he? His heart felt empty and sad. Until he was eighteen, they had been extremely close. She was the one person he could trust and always talk to; she could reason with him and help him think about things differently.

In a way, his sister was his heart, for he could always count on her from an emotional point of view. He was loathed to always think about others, but she gave him that ability.

Here she was, his twin, being given away by his father in marriage. The priest read verses from the Holy Text and delivered a homily about love and virtues. Alexander took note of the faces and expressions of the people around him, to ease his burden of being the only selfish person in the abbey.

Mattias sat serious and stone-faced. He's always so serious, Alexander thought. If Mattias ever laughed it would probably break him. Doubtless, he probably wished this was his coronation. Alexander looked at his other family members. Calimus seemed happy and approving of the marriage.

Calimus' eyes made their ways to one of Youssef's sisters. The grin grew wider. Alexander sighed. It was obvious Calimus was still being Calimus. Queen Caroline kept wiping her eyes, as did Emma. Were they tears of joy? Were they sorrow? His father, King Magnus, was doing his best to hide his disappointment. At times, there was a faraway look on his face and a small frown curled into his lips.

Queen Caroline would give his robes a sharp poke and he'd do his best to contrive a real smile. At least I'm not the only one that's upset, Alexander felt.

Western weddings were notoriously long, even longer than Bishop Malachius' homilies. After two hours, when Alexander felt he could stand no more, the wedding ended and Sofia's veil was lifted. The two lovers embraced and sealed their marriage vows with a kiss.

The Isles-men cheered loudly while the Alveuns politely clapped and produced a few half-hearted cheers of their own.

The nobility was escorted to Youssef's Hall were they made themselves at home among the many benches and tables littered with the very best in food.

Many of the Alveuns ate and drank graciously, not to overdo it, and not to be identified as rude and ungracious to the hosts. Magnus and Youssef sat at the same table with Sofia and Caroline in between them. Many lords came to the table pledging their allegiance and bringing wedding gifts forward. Mattias smirked and remarked to Alexander, that they should prepare some chests for transporting most of these gifts as the tribute still needed to be paid.

Alexander gave Mattias a disproving look and picked at his roast chicken.

There were musicians there, and they played many songs that encouraged the guests to dance.

Many of the lords and ladies took their turn, and Emma was very persistent at getting Alexander to dance. He resisted her efforts, but her reminder that he owed her a dance from his eighteenth birthday party won the dance for her. He reluctantly agreed and Emma took his hand and brought him to the dance floor.

At first, they clasped hands with others who danced around the singer. They took turns clapping and dancing in circles as they kept time to the music.

At various intervals the circling stopped and Emma and Alexander would have a quick reel with one another. Hands on one another's shoulders with one hand behind their backs, they danced a rapid pace until the music slowed again. Alexander found himself thoroughly entertained for a few moments and was able to let himself laugh and have a very good time with Emma.

They danced until at one point they bumped into Chauncey, who was quite keen with Lauren on his arm. Alexander gave him a knowing wink and his guard blushed immediately. He quickly whisked Lauren back into a dance and away from his lord. When it was time to bid good night, the hall emptied slowly.

The Alveuns were treated to the guest houses in the Royal Apartments, and Alexander said his blessings to Sofia.

They made their last embrace and Alexander felt empty again, knowing he might not see his sister again for some years. He gave her a tender kiss on the cheek and teased her on what a princess she had become. When it was time to say good night to Prince Youssef, he was far less political. The Prince grasped his hand and thanked him for his efforts.

"Thank you, Alexander," he said.

"For everything. My people owe you a great debt." Alexander shook his head and took Youssef aside.

"I didn't do it for you," he answered.

"I did it for my sister. You and I still have a score to settle." Youssef was taken aback and opened his mouth to protest.

"If you ever look twice at Alveus, or think about pressing a claim to the throne..." he slowed down his words for impact.

"Or if anything should happen to Sofia, I will come back." Youssef flashed a wicked grin.

"Very well, Prince Alexander. Perhaps it is you that will have to call on me one day, and you'll know what it is to show gratitude."

"Not from you," Alexander warned.

"Never from you." He wheeled away from the Prince and made his way back to his apartment.

CHAPTER XXVII

Several months later Alexander ate alone in the Great Hall of Middlebrooke. He dined on a small portion of lamb and turnips, waiting for his father to come meet him.

Between mouthfuls, he examined the tapestries on the wall. There had been ten, but a new one of Edward had been hung in the hall.

The ninth tapestry was of his grandfather. His grandfather was the spitting image of his father. They were both broad shouldered and massively built men. Mattias and Edward took after them in stature, with Alexander being the shortest by two or three inches. His grandfather had a gryphon emblem on his armor, just like the one Alexander wore.

As Alexander curiously surveyed each tapestry, each king, except his father, wore the same armor. He remembered that Bishop Malachius had once told him the armor he wore was worn by many of the kings, for it was an ancient armor. When his father finally came to meet him, he was nearly done with his lunch. Since their visit to the Western Isles, the lucidity his father had regained had begun to fade again. There were times that he called out for Edward, and once dressed for battle and had the entire garrison mobilized, thinking they were at war. The whispers, kept to the castle, were beginning to spread through the kingdom; the king had lost his mind. He sat down next to Alexander and picked a lone turnip off of Alexander's plate.

"I called a meeting of the council," he said.

"I know," Alexander replied. He had seen several lords coming in and out of the castle all day.

"When Edward died," Magnus said,

"What did he say?"

"I don't remember," Alexander said.

"That night is a blur to me. I see fragments of it in my nightmares."

"Your mother insists I name you as Regent," he said bluntly. "For which I have serious misgivings."

"I see," Alexander responded. "So you have come to tell me how much of a disappointment I am."

"I have never said that," the King insisted.

Alexander gave him a curious look.

"You tell me all the time how unlike my brothers I am. How displeased you are with me for the work that I do. Would you like to know something?"

"What?"

"Edward's killer is dead." He let the words sink into his father's head for a moment.

"I killed him. None of your other sons could have accomplished this, but I did."

"How much have you actually done that is not a result of this armor telling you?" his father accused.

"Yes, I know about the armor, I have smelt it on you since you returned. This was your grandfather's armor. By right it is mine, and the Regent's by proxy. I could give a word and have it taken from you." Alexander sensed the antagonism in his father's words and felt the hostility rising within him.

"Then do it. Would you like me to take it off for you?"

"I wouldn't do anything with that accursed armor except melt it and scatter its ashes across the ocean.

Your grandfather swore invincibility with that armor. But all it brought was his death."

"How did he die?" Alexander demanded to know.

"He died because that armor made him believe he was invincible. He took foolish risks with this kingdom and took us to a place of death. You think that you have seen death?" Magnus let out a sickly laugh.

"When you see people turning on each other because they can't get the voices out from their minds, and then are finished off in the evilest of ways, then you will know what this armor truly brings."

"Well put father," Alexander responded.

"If there is anything else that shames you about me, please let me know. In the meantime, consider Calimus as your heir. If you truly believe that this kingdom is in need of peace and stability between gentry, peasantry, army, and church, then give it to him.

The moment you give it to Mattias, we are at war."

Magnus sat back for a moment and sighed.

"The end is coming for me, but not soon enough. Come with me, the council is soon to meet."

Alexander obeyed Magnus and they walked to the council chambers.

Everyone was there and anxious to know why they were called together. Lord Burrows and his daughter Elsie sat with Baron Brutus and the other town nobles. Lords Fitzwilliam and Carter and the merchant guild heads were there.

Mattias, Calimus, and Caroline sat together in a display of unity within the family. When King Magnus entered the room the entire chamber stood to their feet. When they seated, Alexander found a corner and leaned against the wall, waiting to hear what news his father would bring.

King Magnus stayed standing and addressed the council.

"Friends, the time has come to address a few matters that are left unanswered. First, I am exonerating my son Alexander from all charges of treason and sedition." This was indeed great news for Alexander and he made eye contact with Mattias.

Mattias rolled his good eye and folded his arms.

"The Crown recognizes that he saved us and has shown extreme bravery, although it might seem as great foolishness and recklessness at the same time. He also avenged the death of our nation's beloved son, Edward. I am hereby appointing him to Commander of our Horsemen."

The council exchanged puzzled looks with one another and even exchanged a few comments under their breath. Alexander raised an eyebrow in confusion and tried to make sense of what his father was doing.

A king's son was automatically given a generalship in the army. It was more of a ceremonial post, Mattias and Edward had taken their roles quite seriously and had become respected commanders. Alexander had been trained in tactics but had not wanted to join the military at all. The fact that his father had just moved him into a post was confusing and concerning.

"Calimus," the King continued,

"Will be given Treasury and Stewardships in the hopes that he may continue to grow into a better prince."

Again the room expressed curious looks on their faces. The King was in effect, maneuvering his children into posts of power and circumventing any possible revolutions or treason that might be bubbling underneath the surface.

"Last but not least," the King banged on the table to get the full attention of the audience.

"Mattias will be appointed Regent of Alveus. I am abdicating the throne and retiring.

My current state of health being what it is, I reserve the right to be reinstated should a state of emergency exist." The entire room broke out into an argument. Papers were tossed about and men who had previously backed a particular candidate for the throne yelled at others. Bishop Malachius stayed silent and folded his hands. Mattias had a look of surprise on his face that eventually worked its way into a full-fledged smile.

"Enough," Manfred came out from the shadows and banged a gavel on the tables.

"The King has made a decision."

"Agreed," Mattias said coolly.

"The decision that we have wanted has been made.

If I need resignations brought before me, then let me know. I will happily accept those that do not accept their King's wishes."

The room fell silent and the men weighed the consequences of acting out of frustration versus losing their status and power.

Bishop Malachius summed it up when he stood and said very quietly, "God save the Regent."

The council echoed those words, and Magnus motioned for Alexander to follow him from the room. Alexander obeyed dutifully and voiced his opinions once they were back in the Great Hall.

"Do you have any idea what you have done?" Alexander cried out.

"Do you have something to say that would sway my mind?" the King bellowed.

"You are far too selfish and reckless to lead a kingdom."

"Not me!" Alexander shouted.

"Never me! Calimus should lead us."

"Calimus should never lead us," the King said softly. "You have done well with him, but a drunkard? We would be sacked in a fortnight with him in command."

"But I am with him," Alexander insisted.

"As long as I am with him, he would not fall."

"You are too reckless," the King repeated.

"Everything you have done is because you believe it to be right. That's noble and admirable, but there is no ambition in your eyes.

A king must be ambitious, for the sake of his kingdom.

A king cannot go on wild chases and put himself at risk for his own gain.

I would never give you a kingdom, but I can give you a command. I have granted you the ability to prove that you are more than just a storm beating upon the rocks."

"You have no idea who I am," Alexander argued. "You have no idea! The moment Mattias is Regent, a war begins. We will be at war with the world. That is everything I have fought to stop from happening."

"We see the world differently," Magnus offered.

"I hope that with responsibility, Calimus becomes a great man. I hope with a command, you understand how to lead more than just your guard."

"I won't stay."

"Then I will revoke your pardon." Magnus studied his son carefully.

"I know what Edward told you. He talked about you often should he fall. But he was wrong about you, as was I."

The young Prince stormed out of the citadel, pushing over barrels and throwing any loose objects he could find. He launched any trinket he could find with as much malice and anger as he could muster.

The commotion caught Chauncey and Jack's attention and they were quickly by his side. Alexander told them what his father had disclosed, and they felt the pain of losing a battle they couldn't fight with swords and axes. The men asked what they should do for Alexander.

Chauncey offered up arresting Mattias, but a coup would be put down quickly and violently due to the confusion.

"How much do you love her?" Alexander asked Chauncey. "Who?"

"You know whom I speak of. Lauren. How much do you love her?"

"She makes my heart sing, My Lord," Chauncey smiled. "But I'm afraid all I have are her letters since she is in the Isles with your sister."

"Go and marry her," Alexander insisted.

The men exchanged shocked looks.

"I have sworn an oath," Chauncey insisted.

"I am releasing you," Alexander replied.

"Go and marry her.

Or go and bring her back. Marry her in any case. You are an educated man. I need you out of my guard, and I need you elsewhere."

"Like a spy?" Chauncey queried.

"Yes," Alexander said. "This is not a fight we can win with swords and axes. Jack, I'm sorry, I am releasing you from your oath as well."

"I can't do that," Jack insisted.

"I won't leave your side. You need loyal men."

"I still have them," Alexander said kindly.

"You have given much in your service to me, but if you want to help me more, go and work for Calimus. He will need you more than me, and he will need someone to look after his figures."

The two guards looked despondent. They both grimaced the thought of leaving Alexander's employ.

"I feel nothing but shame," Chauncey remarked, and Jack nodded his agreement.

"I love you both as friends," Alexander insisted.

"You are my best men, and I need you to serve me in different ways. War is coming to Alveus, and we are about to be the aggressor."

Alexander's men took the news very hard. The band was two men short now. They each reflected upon the last few years, and they held a farewell at a tavern to say goodbye.

Calimus eagerly accepted Alexander's offering of Jack being in his employ. Chauncey sailed for the Isles in an attempt to win Lauren's heart completely , and the rest of the men did their best to send their friends off in the best possible manner.

A week later Mattias came to see Alexander in his room. Keira was none too happy to see him, and neither was Arydia.

Both of them made their displeasure known, but Mattias ignored them.

"What brings you here?" Alexander asked.

"I come bearing an olive branch," Mattias replied.

He was not wearing any armor, or any weapons and he opened his arms out wide. "I want to bury the sword between us. Father made his decision, and I need my brothers to unite with me and not against me."

"You mean unite for war," Alexander said sarcastically. "The council has made it clear that there is to be no war, without provocation. So unless we are attacked first, we won't be going to war."

"You don't sound too broken up about it," Alexander said curiously.

"It happens," Mattias smiled.

"Needless to say I am impressed at what you have accomplished. You defended two cities, saved a kingdom, and went further north than anyone else in the last twenty years and lived to tell about it. I would be honored to have you by my side."

Alexander scrunched his face in confusion.

"You are happy to work with me, now?"

"What is there to fight about now?" Mattias asked. He stretched his hand forward in friendship.

"You were someone Edward relied upon for advice.

Do that for me too."

Alexander thought about it for a moment. He didn't trust Mattias for a moment, but he supposed this might be the best way to have him.

On his good side as opposed to his bad side. He grabbed his brother's hand and shook it.

"Good," Mattias said.

"I am building apartments nearby for Calimus and yourself. No more dingy castle rooms for either of you. Who knows, maybe you'll need to start a family soon."

"Have you been talking to Mother?" Alexander asked.

"Maybe," Mattias chuckled, and he walked out. Alexander leaned back on his bed and gently stroked Keira's head. She whimpered gently and licked his hand as if she made a pacifying gesture to him.

"I know Keira," he said soothingly.

"Now we are trapped." The castle atmosphere was quiet and pensive as if every soul shared Alexander's apprehension of his father's announcement.

He gave himself a moment to think back to Calimus' subtle insurrection in the tavern. It wouldn't be long before those seeds of thought made their way elsewhere.

I could dwell on this all day, Alexander mused. He thought about going on a walk about the grounds and he started to remove his armor.

He thought twice about it and refastened the straps.

"Better safe than sorry," he mumbled to himself.

He scratched Keira's head and grabbed a small biscuit that lay on a chair near his bed. Sofia probably left it there, he thought.

Keira followed him as he made his way outside of the city. When Jack noticed his Lord was making his way through the city streets, he ensured Alexander's entire watch fell into place behind him. Alexander walked down the busy main streets and took a way through the market. He glanced at the merchant stalls and stopped to peruse a few trinkets. He couldn't help but feel a certain charge of animosity in the square. The townsfolk made their curtsies and bows in his direction, but they seemed forced and dutiful. Alexander stopped to look at some trinkets being sold by an older man. He looked to be a woodcutter, with a large build, scraggly beard, and rough hands.

He had several wood carvings around his stall, which looked to have taken ages to whittle each one. Alexander found himself drawn to a beautiful necklace that lay upon a tree stump carving of a goblin.

It was a leather necklace that was attached to a carved piece of wood. Carved into the wood was a beautiful image of an oak tree. The tree consumed most of the wood and at the center of the tree was a beautiful aquamarine gem.

"How much," he asked the woodcutter. The woodcutter quickly appraised the buyer and the necklace and offered his price.

"Three gold coins?" He asked hesitantly.

Alexander picked up the necklace and appraised it while turning it through his fingers.

"Five," he agreed, much to the man's surprise. He handed the coins to the man and left him feeling much elated at his purchase. He knelt down next to Keira and placed her head in his hands.

"Where's Katrina?

"Find Katrina!" The dog wagged her tail and sniffed the ground around them. Alexander and his men followed the great wolfhound out of the market and towards the gate. Keira stopped briefly and barked at her master as if to tell him she had picked up the scent.

Her pace quickened into a trot and she continued to follow Katrina's scent to the river. She sat there at the city docks with her feet wading in the water.

She was observing the barge's being loaded and unloaded and was flicking flower petals into the river.

Keira sidled up next to her and buried her nose into Katrina's cheek, effectively producing a surprised yelp and then a giggle from the young girl. The smile quickly faded when she realized Alexander stood behind her.

"Mind if I sit here?" Alexander pointed to a spot next to her.

She shrugged her shoulders, so he pulled off his boots and sat down next to her. He dipped his feet in the river and grimaced at how cold it was. He quickly brought his feet out and rubbed them.

"How can you keep yours in?"

"My dad would take me to the river near Edgebrooke. Didn't matter how the river was, I love the water."

"I love it too," Alexander remarked,

"but it's too cold for me today. What are you doing out here by yourself?"

"Thinking."

"About?"

"My dad." The forced words created an air of awkwardness between the two.

"I am so sorry," he offered.

"Doesn't matter," she said.

"You did it to save me. Emma talks to me a lot about these things. I just need to find out where I am going now."

"Going?" Alexander scoffed.

"You're not thinking about leaving are you? Where do you plan on going?"

"I don't fancy being a servant girl in the castle, My Lord," she remarked politely.

"I suppose you would rather have fancy clothes and an engagement to a young knight? Maybe you'd like a duel fought in your honor?" He teased her, but let up when he saw the scowl in her face.

"You don't understand anything about me," she moaned.

"I was quite contented before they took everyone I loved. I might be a poor peasant girl, but I can handle myself in a fight. Maybe I can hire out as a guard for these merchants and guard their boats?"

"Maybe," Alexander agreed.

Katrina brushed the tears from her face.

"Have I served you well?" Alexander cocked his head back in confusion.

"I honestly haven't thought about it, but yes, you have saved my life many times. I do owe you a large debt."

"Then perhaps you could pay me a small wage? Not much, but enough to help me get started? I could find a place to live, and get a job quick." There was a hint of desperation in her voice. Alexander pondered her predicament. An orphan girl, in a big city, was bound to be headed for trouble. The moment she walked away, she would disappear forever.

"No," he said emphatically.

"I would never let that happen."

Katrina looked as if her heart broke, and Alexander had immense pity for her.

"Hold out your hand," he commanded. She obeyed but kept her head squarely facing the water. He took the necklace and dropped it into her hand. She rubbed her thumb over it and in confusion glanced at her open hand. Her mouth gaped slightly.

"What is this?"

"This is my offer to you," the Prince said kindly.

"You and I have lost so much in this life, but there is so much that I can give you. I am offering for you to be my ward."

"Ward?" Her eyes narrowed and she searched her thoughts for what that could mean.

"I don't want to be your valet!"

Alexander chuckled at her and her face reddened.

"I am offering to adopt you as my daughter." He took her hand and closed her fingers over the necklace. "This is my gift to cement our arrangement."

"Your daughter?" She was dumbfounded and had a hard time grasping Alexander's offer.

"I'm not a child anymore."

"You aren't an adult either," he explained slowly. "You have saved my life so many times, and I owe you for all those times you have been there.

So I will give you my life in return, and all of the benefits that come with it. I will guard and guide you with my life. Oh, and I'm getting you a dress, and it will be one that fits."

Katrina squealed with joy and wrapped her arms around Alexander. Tears flowed down her cheeks but they were happy ones, and she gave Alexander a kiss on his cheek.

"Thank you!" She exclaimed. "You and my men will be starting school in the monastery once I talk to Bishop Malachius. I will have all of you able to read and write.

This won't be the life that you will live for much longer. I promise you that." She hugged him again and he gently picked her up in his arms.

He caught sight of Emma standing near Jack and she gave him an approving nod and smile. He returned the nod and placed her back on the dock. He put his boots back on and placed the necklace around her neck. Katrina beamed and fiddled with the necklace. Once it was on, she paused and remembered something that she had to do. She picked up a small bag on the dock and handed it to Alexander.

"What's this?" He asked. "A man asked me to give this to you. He was on a barge headed to Edgebrooke."

"Odd," Alexander replied.

"He said that this won't be forgotten." Katrina skipped happily to Emma and showed off her new necklace. Alexander opened the small sack and peeked inside. His face turned ash grey as he pulled out a white lily. Alexander scanned the riverbanks and his eyes fell upon a barge. He swore he saw Abiyram staring back at him.

Christopher (Topher) Huntingford comes from a background of stuffy middle management. Because those jobs offer very little in terms of adventure and exploration, and space travel has yet to discover warp cores, he devotes his spare time to writing. He continues on with his passions of medieval literature and fatherhood. Christopher still lives in the beach country and hides out in fancy food eateries.

Books by Christopher Huntingford

~ Harbinger Chronicles~

Book One~ The Harbinger

*The Kingdom Of Alveus is on the verge of renaissance as it has
positioned itself as the dominant economic power of its age.
A war was waged that eradicated the remnants of the lands former
inhabitants, with the spoils of victory bringing great
wealth to the kingdom.
All is not well, as the friction has built between the King's sons and
factions are quietly forming around the countryside. Alexander
Wolfild, the youngest son of the great King, will find himself tested
between duty and disdain as he discovers the ancient people, believed
to be extinct, are far more powerful than anyone has imagined.*

Book Two~ Retribution

It has been six months since the battle of Edgebrooke,
and Alexander Wolfield struggles to sleep.
When word comes to him regarding the murderer Duncan's
whereabouts, he launches a manhunt into the uncharted.
He learns that he is not the only one bent on revenge, and he races
against time to save another family member.
Alexander comes to realize that the quest for retribution is much
larger than his fight with Duncan.

Book Three~ Accession

Coming Soon

*The attainment or acquisition of a position
of rank or power, typically that of monarch or president.*